Imagining Mars

imagining
MARS

A LITERARY HISTORY

Robert Crossley

WESLEYAN UNIVERSITY PRESS ● Middletown, Connecticut

Wesleyan University Press
Middletown CT 06459
www.wesleyan.edu/wespress
2011 © Robert Crossley
Manufactured in the
United States of America

Wesleyan University Press is a member of the Green Press
Initiative. The paper used in this book meets their minimum
requirement for recycled paper.

Library of Congress Cataloging-in-Publication Data
Crossley, Robert.
Imagining Mars: a literary history / Robert Crossley.
    p. cm.
Includes bibliographical references and index.
ISBN 978-0-8195-6927-1 (cloth: alk. paper)
1. Mars (Planet)—In literature. 2. Science fiction—History
and criticism. 3. Mars (Planet) I. Title.
PN3433.6.C76   2010
809'.93329923—dc22   2009052182

5 4 3 2 1

To Andy & Corinne Crossley

contents

ILLUSTRATIONS

Color plates follow page 170.

preface

Of what value is the history of an error? That was the question that first prompted me to undertake the research that led to the writing of *Imagining Mars*. A century ago, Percival Lowell, convinced of the reality of the Martian "canals" that he thought he had seen from his observatory at Flagstaff, was keeping up a relentless campaign—in books, lectures, popular articles, and widely reproduced maps—on behalf of his notion of a Mars populated by a heroic race staving off extinction through the monumental engineering feat of a global irrigation system. Although challenged and discredited by most scientists, Lowell was the principal figure in the so-called "Mars mania" at the turn of the twentieth century and he had a strong popular following that persisted long after his death in 1916. Lowell never accepted that the work he produced was itself a dexterous if somewhat willful blending of science and fiction, but his eloquently articulated and beautifully illustrated figments took hold on the public imagination in spite of the scorn of astronomers and generated a flood of literary fantasies that lasted well into the 1960s. Even in the aftermath of the mechanical exploration of Mars by NASA's evocatively named *Mariners*, *Vikings*, and *Pathfinders*, which shredded the last vestiges of Lowell's theories, writers have continued to pay homage to Lowell by naming Martian cities and spaceships after him and by crediting him with awakening their imaginations. As the scientific exploration of Mars has accelerated since the first flyby photographic missions of the 1960s and as public interest in that exploration has grown, the time seems to have come for a history of the literary images and narratives of Mars.

In exploring the literary history of Mars—and particularly that history from 1877 to the present—I have had three aims: (1) to chart the ways in which the literary and scientific perspectives on the planet have intersected and diverged; (2) to explore how specific literary texts have used and abused, ignored and deployed science in order to create usable myths and parables; and (3) to find in the record of fiction about Mars glosses on modern cultural history. The very large body of imaginative writing on the subject of Mars contains genuine masterpieces, a fascinating array of partly successful experiments, a substantial number of mediocre and uninspired works, and some truly abominable examples of bad writing. For the sake of constructing a comprehensive literary history of Mars, the good, the bad, and the ugly all play important roles, but I have not hesitated to offer candid evaluations of the artistry of the books that I discuss since, for me, literary history and literary criticism work in tandem. While I have wanted to be comprehensive, I have found it necessary to be selective. I have focused largely on novels about Mars (and on one epic poem) but have dealt with only a few of the many short stories on the subject. And I have taken the idea of *literary* history fairly strictly; while I make occasional passing references to science-fiction films, I have not tried to cover the various cinematic treatments of Mars or film, television, and comic-book adaptations of novels about Mars.

This book begins with a meditative chapter on the human meanings of Mars. Ranging over histories and cultures and considering Mars in the ancient, early modern, and contemporary eras, this chapter asks how, why, and to what effect Mars has been invested with human significance. It explores relationships among the Marses seen with the naked eye, through the telescopic lens, and with the mind's eye as well as the various Marses that have been perceived—or created—by scientists, writers, and visual artists; it examines the nature of storytelling and the generation of myths old and new about Mars; and it surveys some of the uses to which Mars has been put as a mirror of terrestrial concerns. Chapter 1 also first lays out in broad terms an overarching concern of the entire book: how the literary and scientific imaginations collaborate with each other and exist in tension with each other.

One of my preoccupations throughout this book, stimulated by that initial question about Lowell's mistake and its impact, has been to probe the relationship between literature and science in the representation of Mars. At times, the literary mind has been energized by scientific investigation, and at other times has seemed quietly or fiercely resistant. New information about Mars has been sometimes welcomed and sometimes spurned by writers. Some writers have been left literally speechless, or at least blocked, by the latest Martian news from observatories and laboratories; others have responded with an outpouring of inventive, scientifically informed fiction. Literary Mars is now old enough that it can be said to have a life of its own independent of scientific research, but it also appears that when writers have tried to rely on that imaginative independence and ignored or defied new astronomical knowledge, the work they produce emerges dull and damaged without the fertilization of science. I have wanted to find out how this difficult, paradoxical relationship between the literary mind and the scientific mind plays itself out on the subject of Mars over the past century and a half.

As I pursued my research, I discovered that there is much more to the literary history of Mars than Lowell's great mistake. For one thing, the sheer number and variety of fictions about Mars far exceeded my anticipations. Before Lowell came on to the scene in the middle of the 1890s, a rich history already had developed of speculation and mythmaking about Mars, a history that, in the era of the telescope, produced apparent sightings of Martian vegetation, seas, lakes, and clouds. The modern collaboration of literature and astronomy can be said to begin with a specific event, itself of mythic implication, that opens chapter 2: the meeting between the young John Milton and the old Galileo, the latter under house arrest by the Inquisition. For nearly two and a half centuries after that suggestive encounter of two gigantic minds of seventeenth-century Europe, astronomical investigation fed literary speculation, although Mars was less prominent in the earliest speculations than the nearby Moon or the telescopically more dramatic planets—giant Jupiter and ringed Saturn. But by the mid-nineteenth century, when fantasies of lunar life no longer could be entertained seriously, attention shifted to Mars, the planet that the English astronomer William Herschel had said in 1784 was most like our own. The indisputable turning point came in 1877, when the American Asaph Hall first located and named the two tiny moons of Mars and when Giovanni Schiaparelli in Milan observed thin, streaky markings on the Martian surface and called them *canali*, a term fatefully translated into English not as the neutral "channels" but as "canals."

The third chapter explores the first literary products of those momentous scientific reports on Mars that began in 1877. As astronomers turned their telescopes towards Mars, journalists began paying attention. News reports created a public appetite for information—some of it actually misinformation—about Mars, and fiction writers were quick to find imaginative possibilities in this new sensation. A group of half a dozen British and American romances, mostly forgotten now, laid a foundation for the great body of melancholy fables, cautionary tales, satirical commentaries, travelogues, political parables, and adventure stories that over the following century came to constitute the "Matter of Mars" in literature.

Chapter 4 takes up the case of Lowell and tries to account for both his extraordinary success in persuading a large public to buy into his vision of Mars and the frustration of professional astronomers unable, by reasoned argument and the marshaling of evidence, to dislodge Lowell's hold on the collective imagination. The history of Mars in literature is unimaginable without the intervention of this enterprising, self-assured, difficult, and endlessly intriguing amateur astronomer who insinuated himself and his illusions into the mass media and the literary *zeitgeist*.

The later chapters of *Imagining Mars* never entirely leave Schiaparelli and Lowell and their legacies behind, but examine the effort of writers to develop new literary myths about Mars that draw on the nineteenth century's insights and errors while trying, with varying degrees of diligence, to be cognizant of changing and more nuanced scientific understandings of the planet. These chapters proceed in roughly chronological order from the late nineteenth century to the beginning of the twenty-first, but the organization has been dictated partly by large thematic concerns as well as by chronology.

Chapter 5 surveys the ways in which early imaginative writing about Mars, from the 1880s through the early 1900s, merged with and gave a new lease on the utopian tradition. In works motivated by feminist, Christian, and socialist reformers as well as by anti-war one-worlders and a Bolshevik revolutionary, Mars became a useful didactic model. Images of a culturally advanced Mars reflect possibilities for social reform and progress, and the benevolent figure of the "Man from Mars" instructs and guides his terrestrial cousins struggling to improve themselves and their world.

Chapter 6 turns to the first major literary figure to take up the subject of Mars: H. G. Wells. His determination (utopianist though he was) to use Mars not for reassuring utopian fantasies but as a scourge to human complacency resulted in 1898 in a path-breaking novel of interplanetary invasion. *The War of the Worlds*, the first literary masterpiece in the tradition of Martian fiction, upends the sentimental icon of the man from Mars and replaces him with monstrous would-be conquerors who give British imperialists a taste of their own medicine. In a decade brimming with illusions about the planet Mars, Wells aimed for a disturbing but intellectually healthy exercise in disillusionment.

Chapter 7 studies a group of works with relatively little literary merit that reveal a connection between twin popular fascinations with the mystery of Mars and with telepathy, reincarnation, and other psychic phenomena. Centered largely on mediums who wrote accounts of their travels to Mars, this chapter also has as a key figure the French astronomer Camille Flammarion, who wrote populist treatments of astronomy as well as propagandistic fiction about Mars focused on the paranormal.

From the inward-looking spiritualist fantasies about the Mars of the psychics, we move in chapter 8 to the adventure stories that treat Mars as a frontier territory modeled on the American West and imperialist Africa, as a man's world that stirs up a recrudescence of the ancient myths of the planet as the god of war and aggression. Here we find a number of fictions that celebrate masculinist power—the most well-known of which is Edgar Rice Burroughs' *A Princess of Mars* (1912)—as well as the beginnings of a line of boys' books centered on trips to Mars.

Chapter 9 concentrates on the years between World Wars I and II—a period that began with a craze for attempting to signal Mars with radio beams and ended with Orson Welles's notorious, panic-inducing radio broadcast of his 1938 adaptation of H. G. Wells's *The War of the Worlds*. In these two decades, some of the conventions of Martian fiction begin to become codified, and writers, including Olaf Stapledon, John Wyndham, and C. S. Lewis, become increasingly self-conscious about their participation in a tradition of Martian fiction.

After the Second World War, in the era dominated both by heady anticipation of real journeys by real people through outer space and by Cold War fears of global annihilation, we find, in chapter 10, an extravagant array of fictions that embody both of those dominant cultural moods. Arthur C. Clarke's *The Sands of Mars* (1951) is a tentative early effort to imagine in realistic terms what the actual exploration of Mars might entail and Rex Gordon's *No Man Friday* (1956) more grimly adapts the Robinson Crusoe story to a struggle for survival by a lone Martian explorer. But the central work in this chapter—employing Mars both as a subject of rocket-ship romance and as a critical vantage point for assessing mid-century American commercialism and arrogance, racial segregation, censorship, and anxieties about atomic war—is Ray Bradbury's *The Martian Chronicles* (1950).

Chapter 11 studies what happened to imagined Mars as scientific understanding of the planet began to accelerate with the launch of the first satellites and space probes. Much of Martian fiction turned retrograde, falling back on the familiar motifs of an obsolescent tradition, sometimes inventively and often nostalgically, or turning against the romanticism of the past with visions of a colonized Mars that is bleak and ugly both topographically and morally. The most remarkable work of this period, largely unread, is *The Earth Is Near* (1971) by Ludek Pesek.

A major turning point in the literary history of Mars took place in the 1970s, with the photographs taken by the orbiting *Mariner 9* that first revealed the huge volcanoes and canyons of the planet, and with the experiments undertaken by the twin *Viking* missions of 1976. Chapter 12 traces the remaking of Mars in the literary imagination in response to these new scientific revelations, in particular the exploration of the technical and ethical problems associated with the terraforming of Mars for human habitation in the early fiction of Kim Stanley Robinson and in the epic poem *Genesis* (1988) of Frederick Turner. A renaissance of interest in Mars as a locale for fiction occurred in the 1980s and 1990s, as writers got past the disappointments of the revelation of a lifeless Mars and saw the possibilities for making venturesome fiction out of the rich and varied and still mysterious landscape that was being disclosed by scientific investigation.

Chapter 13 discusses the increasing importance that novelists attach to imagining and representing fully and accurately the experience of actually being on Mars. Ten representative novels from the beginning of the 1990s to the turn of the new century show a consistent commitment to incorporating the most up-to-date scientific knowledge into imagined Mars, a self-conscious and sometimes humorous embrace of elements of the now-obsolete literary history of Mars in their new fictions, and a wide range of skill in achieving an artfulness to match their scientific and imaginative ambitions.

The high point of Martian fiction at the end of the twentieth century is Kim Stanley Robinson's trio, Red Mars (1993), Green Mars (1994), and Blue Mars (1996), which form the centerpiece of chapter 14. Looking at Robinson's books in the context of other novels that develop the concept of "areoformation"—the cultural transformation of human beings to fit Mars, as contrasted with the physical alteration of the planet to fit human beings—this chapter analyzes the nature and methods of Robinson's accomplishment in what many people regard as the defining contemporary literary representation of Mars.

In a brief afterword, "Mars under Construction" points to a possible new direction for post-Robinson fictionmaking about Mars in a short story by Ian McDonald.

If there is one premise that underlies the whole sweep of literary history that I have tried to capture in Imagining Mars, it is that the way people imagine other worlds is an index of how they think about themselves, their immediate world, their institutions and conventions, their rituals and habits. Mars, in other words, is a site for both critical exposure and imaginative construction. As Robinson observes at the opening of Red Mars, the literary history of Mars is a history of our own minds because "we are all the consciousness that Mars has ever had." The Mars that has for so long attracted human attention is the product both of evolving scientific understandings of the planet and of the stories that have been told about it. Tracing the history of those stories from the invention of the telescope to the current moment of remote-control exploration by NASA reveals the extent to which human beings have created Mars in their own image even as scientists have labored to discover and authenticate the truths about the planet. The Mars of the literary imagination is the complex product of an interplay between fact and fancy, between evidence and desire, between knowing with the head and knowing with the heart.

Acknowledgments

A project like this one, extending over many years, incurs debts of gratitude that can never be repaid adequately. I begin my litany of thanks with deep appreciation to the National Endowment for the Humanities, which provided the gift of a fellowship in 2000 that enabled me to undertake the first stage of research and writing, and to the University of Massachusetts Boston, which granted a sabbatical leave in 2007 that allowed me to bring the manuscript to completion. Along the route between those two milestones, I have benefited from the advice, encouragement, specialist knowledge, and practical assistance of a great many people, some of them professional friends of long standing, others who were strangers to me before the start of this project, and still other remarkably patient and generous members of institutional staffs. I hope I can remember them all.

Two colleagues in English studies on whose wisdom and support I have relied for decades have continued to be indispensable in my investigations of the literature of Mars: John Huntington of the University of Illinois Chicago and Patrick McCarthy of the University of Miami. Professor of Astronomy Richard French, director of Wellesley College's Whitin Observatory, gave me free rein in using the abundant resources, especially hard-to-come-by nineteenth-century materials, of the observatory's library. Antoinette Beiser, librarian at the Lowell Observatory in Flagstaff, guided me through the rich holdings of the Percival Lowell archive and later answered my long-distance calls for materials and references. At the Wolbach Library of the Harvard Smithsonian Observatory, Donna Coletti and Will Graves have been unfailingly helpful, not least of all in providing access to the incredible beauties of E. L. Trouvelot's drawings of Mars; their advocacy made possible the first publication in this book of a page from Trouvelot's invaluable 1873 sketchbook. Others who have provided information, suggestions, and thoughtful criticism during the long gestation of *Imagining Mars* include David Strauss at Kalamazoo College; David Seed at the University of Liverpool; the late W. Warren Wagar at the University of Binghamton; Richard Reublin at the Parlor Songs

Association; Andy Sawyer, curator of special collections at the University of Liverpool Library; Melvin Schuetz at the Chesley Bonestell Archives; the novelists Kim Stanley Robinson and William K. Hartmann; staffs at the Library of Congress, the Ray Bradbury Archive in the Rare Books Collection of Bowling Green State University Library, the Popular Culture Library at Bowling Green State University, the H. G. Wells Archive at the University of Illinois Urbana-Champaign, the New York Public Library, and the Boston Public Library. To the last of these I remain eternally grateful that, unlike many other research libraries, it has never pulped its newspaper collections and so made it possible to reproduce the glowing colors of a 1906 spread on Percival Lowell that do not survive on microfilm.

For permission to use previously published material, usually in different or abbreviated form, I am grateful to the editors of *The Massachusetts Review*, *Philological Quarterly*, and *Science Fiction Studies*. Although I eventually came to reconceive the aims and methods of contemporary fiction about Mars, I am grateful to Alan Sandison and Robert Dingell for an opportunity to stretch my wings on "The New Martian Novel" in their 2000 collection, *Histories of the Future*. Melissa Conway and George Slusser's organization of the 2008 J. Lloyd Eaton Conference on "Chronicling Mars" at the University of California Riverside gave me a final and magnificent tutorial on my subject just as I was revising my manuscript. And I thank UMass Boston undergraduate students in 2002 and 2008 in the Honors Program course "Imagining Mars"; I will always cherish the opportunity I had both to try out my ideas on them and to apply new ideas learned from them.

My colleagues at the University of Massachusetts Boston—among them Neal Bruss, Linda Dittmar, Betsy Klimasmith, Scott Maisano, Cheryl Nixon, Thomas O'Grady, Robert Johnson, Pratima Prasad, Kenneth Rothwell, and Leonard von Morzé—always had their eye out for the relevant journal article, the wayward bit of data, the odd artifact, the altered perspective that might enhance my research. For encouragement and support for my work, from the moment I was interviewed for my position nearly forty years ago to the present, I have an unrepayable debt to Shaun O'Connell, who wrote a splendid and more Earth-bound literary history entitled *Imagining Boston*. My department chair, Judith Goleman, has been a staunch backer of and fervent cheerleader for research that may have appeared to some as marginal to the work of literary scholarship. I can't imagine a better group of colleagues on this planet.

The editors, external readers, and production staff at Wesleyan University Press and the University Press of New England have supported me with both the enthusiasm and the shrewd criticism that every author craves.

I thank the celebrated English space artist David Hardy for providing the book's cover illustration. With its iconic figure of Wells's Martian invader standing in the shadow of the great arc of scientific images of Mars—from Christiaan Huygens' seventeenth-century drawing through the canaled Mars of Schiaparelli and Lowell to a pre–space age telescopic photo to the extraterrestrial camera images of *Mariner 4* and *Viking*—Hardy's painting visualizes the historical sweep and the literary–scientific interplay that I have aspired to depict in words.

Although the subject of Mars lies in a place remote from her passions for medieval literature and contemporary visual arts, my wife, Monica McAlpine, has been a terrific coach and motivator at times when I lost confidence. She brought her keen eye for detail and her even keener scholarly instincts to readings of my drafts, and supported me, as she always has, with her indispensable love.

Finally, I must recall the day when Monica unearthed from the detritus of our attic a colored drawing on butcher paper of spaceships, heavenly bodies, and squiggly lines suggesting a path through outer space, all fearlessly labeled "Jerny to Mars by Andy Crossley." At the time of its composition—around 1980—I had no idea that my four-year-old's exercise in child art would be predictive of my own "jerny." But it gives me the greatest joy, all these years later, to dedicate this book to my wonderful son and equally wonderful and essential daughter-in-law, Andy and Corinne Crossley.

Brighton, Massachusetts
February 2009

imagining Mars

THE MEANING OF MARS

O brown star burning in the east,
elliptic orbits bring you close;
as close as this no eye has seen
since sixty thousand years ago.

    JOHN UPDIKE

... we are still those animals who survived the Ice Age,
and looked up at the night sky in wonder, and told stories.
And Mars has never ceased to be what it was to us from
our very beginning—a great sign, a great symbol, a
great power.

    KIM STANLEY ROBINSON

Myn herte is Marcien

    GEOFFREY CHAUCER

• Leaving my house in Boston late on August 28, 2003, the semi-cloudy night of the closest transit of Earth and Mars in sixty millennia, I drove to the Whitin Observatory to look at Mars through Wellesley College's superb old Clark refracting telescope, the gold standard for late-Victorian viewing of the night sky. I was conscious of how antiquarian, how quixotic my little expedition must seem in the age of Hubble, when space-based lenses can offer images far crisper and clearer and more richly detailed than terrestrial instruments, and all one need do is turn on the television or boot up the computer to enjoy a wealth of such images, without the distortions of atmosphere or the backache that comes from long sessions at the telescope. I found myself thinking that a hundred years earlier, at the height of the prestige of big-science observatories and of public euphoria over the "canals" of Mars, a place like the Wellesley College Observatory would have been swamped with spectators. And so when I arrived that night, I was stunned to find that others—many others—besides me had forsaken the websites for a more old-fashioned view of Mars. Hundreds of people had gotten to Wellesley ahead of me and were patiently and quietly waiting in line for their turn at the telescope. As the queue snaked into the darkness outside the building, an occasional cheer went up from the crowd whenever Mars—surprisingly lemon-colored rather than red—emerged from an encroaching bank of clouds. It was close to midnight before I finally had my chance to gawk at the quivering image of the planet next door. After a mere thirty seconds pressed to the Clark eyepiece, I yielded to the person behind me, but I had had a taste of the enduring public fascination with Mars. I was glad to have been part of that expectant crowd, glad to have my anticipated solitary experience turn into an unexpectedly communal one.

Why has that eye-catching coal of light in the sky assumed so prominent a place in cultural mythologies and the literary imagination? What has it meant to people? How have its meanings changed over time? To what extent have scientific study and artistic invention collaborated in fashioning meanings for Mars? And what do stories about Mars, specifically those written since the invention of the telescope, have to tell us about ourselves as well as about the distant planet they attempt to portray?

Kim Stanley Robinson opens his great sequence of Martian novels of the 1990s with a suggestion that Mars has had a continuous hold on our species from the dawn of pre-civilized human curiosity. Because of its color, its ready visibility in the unpolluted atmosphere of pre-industrial centuries, its distinctive and puzzling movements in the sky, Mars was bound to attract the speculative eye. Early cultures identified the lights in the sky as deities. The red-hued star—not yet understood to be a world—the ancient Greeks called Ares and the Romans Mars. The Japanese named it Kasei and the Babylonians Nergal. "Its name in all ancient languages signifies *inflamed*," wrote the splashy nineteenth-century astronomer and scientific popularizer Camille Flammarion.[1] When Mars is in opposition—an event that Chaldean astronomers accurately measured as once every 780 days—a straight line can be drawn from it through the Earth to the Sun. Oppositions bring Mars and Earth in their solar orbits relatively close together—close enough that Mars shines steadily and especially vividly among the twinkling stars. A Babylonian text suggests that when Mars is in opposition, people need to be wary: "When Nergal is dim, it is lucky, when bright, unlucky."[2] All those cultures, struck by the brilliant color of fire and blood, associated that inflammation with strife and discord and used the name to designate their god of battles. In the *Iliad*, Ares is a "bloodthirsty marauder" (Book V, line 38) who smacks his "muscled thighs" in rage (XV.116) and swoops over fields of soldiers "like a dark whirlwind" (XX.55).[3] As the red star seemed to wander through the sky, backwards and forwards reversing field, so Homer's Ares went unpredictably back and forth, sometimes supporting the Greeks and sometimes the Trojans, personifying the wild fluctuations and indiscriminate carnage of war. Zeus finds Ares appalling: "You're the most loathsome god on Olympus. / You actually like fighting and war" (V.949–50). The so-called "Homeric Hymns" to Ares, mythographic rhapsodies probably composed in the fifth century B.C.E., contain lines that seem to depict Mars's colorful, erratic course through the heavens:

> Ares turns his fiery bright cycle
> among the Seven-signed tracks
> of the aether, where flaming chargers
> bear him forever
> over the third orbit![4]

As sign, symbol, and power Mars has an impressive pedigree in the history of our imaginations. In a long invocation to Mars at the opening of the *Troy Book*, John Lydgate's fifteenth-century account of the destruction of the ancient city, the god is addressed conventionally as the sovereign and patron of chivalry who "hast of manhood the magnificence." But the poet seems to have one eye on the symbolic tradition and one also on the luminous object in the heavens:

> O myghty Mars, that wyth thy sterne lyght
> In armys has the power & the myyt,
> And named art from est til occident
> The myghty lorde, the god armypotent,
> That, wyth schynyng of thy stremes rede,
> By influence dost the brydel lede
> Of chevalry, as sovereyn and patrown.[5]

In the Middle Ages, however, Mars was invoked more often as an astrological predictor of temperament than as an astronomical phenomenon. When the Wife of Bath proclaims that her "herte is Marcien," she makes it clear that she doesn't buy the notion that men are from Mars and women from Venus; Chaucer's often-married and seldom-intimidated storyteller is confident of her affiliation with both lust and battle. During the English Renaissance, on the eve of the invention of the telescope, the planet began to figure in poetry and on stage as more than just a representation of the classical god of war or a marker of choleric personality. Shakespeare's *Henry VI, Part I* was first performed about a dozen years before Kepler calculated the elliptical orbit of Mars and solved the ancient puzzle of its apparent reversal of direction in the night sky. In the play, the Dauphin of France, using the mysterious retrograde motions of Mars as a metaphor for the shifting fortunes of the French and English armies, observes the state of the astronomical question in the early 1590s: "Mars his true moving, even as in the heavens / So in the earth, to this day is not known" (Act I, scene ii, lines 1–2). And in All's Well That Ends Well, Helena teases the cowardly soldier Parolles, who has boasted of his birth under the astrological sign of Mars, that the event must have occurred when the planet's movement was retrograde: "You go so much backward when you fight" (I.i.200).

Of course, it is possible to exaggerate the fascination of Mars for early human observers. The Moon, after all, is so much closer, so much more distinct to the naked eye, so much more immediately imaginable as a world. More than half a century ago, in a great achievement of reading and research, Marjorie Hope Nicolson wrote a history of our lunar fascinations and fantasies, Voyages to the Moon (1948). From the "old Moon" of classical myth to the "new Moon" of the age of Galileo, from flights to the Moon powered by wild swans to the rocketship journeys of Jules Verne and Buck Rogers, Nicolson mapped two millennia of Moon stories and the conveyances that romancers concocted to put men on the Moon. In bringing her literary history up to her own present, Nicolson chose to end her book with a discussion of C. S. Lewis's 1938 Out of the Silent Planet—an interplanetary romance not about the Moon, but about Mars. "Perhaps the cosmic voyage will perish in our own time under the weight of its increasing technology," she considered at her conclusion. "Perhaps it will take on new vitality and beauty, as it has in one of Mr. Lewis' novels. Certainly it has proved a theme, as I warned you, that the world has not willingly let die, whether in poetry and fantasy, in satire or seriousness, in the pulps or in the comics."[6] Voyages to the Moon is the definitive history of Moon fantasies. Since its publication in 1948, valuable books have been written about Mars and its place in cultural history—books by thoughtful and often learned writers such as Patrick Moore, Mark Washburn, Eric Burgess, John Noble Wilford, Jay Barbree and Martin Caidin, Michael Hanlon, and Oliver Morton. The most ambitious and learned study of the relationships between literary and scientific understandings of Mars is Robert Markley's Dying Planet (2005), which pursues the various ways in which Mars has been used to adumbrate the fate of the Earth.[7] But the history of imagined Mars does not yet have its Nicolson. The range of Martian literature has not been fully grasped. This book is an effort towards a comprehensive literary history of Mars in the English-speaking world, with some attention to the most famous works in other languages.

Over the course of many centuries, and especially in the four centuries since

Galileo began using his optic glass, scientists inadvertently have contributed to the romance of Mars as, by trial and often seductive error, they slowly unveiled its mysteries. At various moments in that history, astronomers incorrectly invested Mars with oceans and lakes, canals and cities, a breathable atmosphere, vast forests, and balmy temperatures. The stripping away of error and the building of a truer picture of Mars has been a great achievement of twentieth-century planetary science, as terrestrial observation was augmented with the coming of space flight by photographic flybys and mechanical surveys and experiments on the Martian surface. Throughout the early years of the space age, imaginative writers have responded vigorously to the state of the scientific question about Mars, although the literary mind sometimes has taken decades to catch up to and apply the latest revisions in scientific understanding.

Astronomer and perceptual psychologist William Sheehan identifies three distinct stages in the history of planetary study: the era of naked-eye observation, which lasted until the early seventeenth century; the era of the terrestrial telescope, which began in 1609 with the employment of the first rudimentary tubes and lenses; and the space era, in which cameras and telescopes operating outside the envelope of Earth's atmosphere could send back more precise and detailed images than were possible even with large, high-powered, Earth-bound instruments.[8] The history of ideas about Mars is a fairly simple one for the first of those three eras; the myth-making imagination worked variations on the meaning of redness: passion, courage, anger, manliness, war. In the second era, the images of Mars became far richer, more complex, more nuanced, more contradictory, and more exciting; and, we now know, they were also full of wishful thinking and erroneous supposition. Observing Mars in the second era, as one historian of science put it, was "a matter of fathoming riddles."[9] In the seventeenth and eighteenth centuries, the best telescopes operating under the most ideal conditions could produce images no better defined than naked-eye glimpses of our own moon. Even as telescopes dramatically improved in the nineteenth and twentieth centuries, Mars refused to disclose itself fully and unambiguously to the observing eye. Mars in the mind's eye began to assume a definiteness, a density of texture and detail, that had only the slenderest foundation in astronomical fact. Blurry telescopic images left a great deal to the imagination, and literary depictions of Mars filled in the lacunae with visions of tragedy and romance, of once and future splendors on an old planet, its inhabitants variously conceived as wise, frail, ruthless, or beneficent.

For many readers, this second era, which lasted more than halfway into the twentieth century, was a golden age of fiction about Mars, but that fiction was more fantastic than scientific. In the past six decades, at the outset of the third era in which space-based telescopes and extraterrestrial vehicles carrying cameras and scientific instruments have largely displaced Earth-bound telescopes, we have begun to see a new Mars, at once less charming and more scientifically verifiable than the Mars that intrigued and frustrated astronomers who could see just enough of the planet's features to be tantalized. Paradoxically, the red planet as we now know it is both an ancient and a virgin world, titanic in the scale of its mountains and chasms but barren of living beings or artifacts. The new Mars, initially so forbidding and so empty that it seemed to leave writers nothing to imagine, has now begun to generate a fresh literary fascination with the planet, a fascination both romantic and scientific. A new respect has arisen for the ecology of Mars as a wilderness planet, and a technically conscious interest in the prospects, methods, risks, and ethical dilemmas of metamorphosing that wilderness into a future human habitat is available to the imagination. But the romance is also evident in the evocative primary-colors titles of Robinson's master works that suggest a planet coming alive over the course of near-future history: Red Mars, Green Mars, Blue Mars.

Much of the recent literature of Mars, though prophetic in intent, is not fictional in form. An engineer baldly announces his commitment to the feasibility and necessity of exploration and colonization in his title: The Case for Mars: The Plan to Settle the Red Planet and Why We Must. Another book, The Mars One Crew Manual, despite an irritating marketing strategy ("Congratulations! You have been selected as one of eleven crew members . . ."), is no put-on but an exhaustive inventory of the equipment, schedules, activities, and supports, complete with detailed diagrams, that will be required for a staffed mission to Mars. The Greening of Mars, offering a stage-by-stage preview of the process and the results of terraforming Mars, has inspired both those planning twenty-first-century voyages to Mars and those who have imagined such trips in fiction. An astronomer's account of the Martian meteorite found in Antarctica in 1996 opens up the implications for discovering evidence of past or present organic life on Mars. A self-educated and self-important scientist's outlandish writings about the gigantic, carved "face" he claims to see in photographic images of the Martian surface have been the toast of radio talk shows. For those with a taste for the technical and the encyclopedic, a fifteen-hundred-page volume titled, simply, Mars, and assembled in 1992 by a team of four scientific editors and 114 collaborating authors with six gigantic maps furnished by the U.S. Geological Survey, represents the definitive twentieth-century synthesis of the extraordinarily productive second and third eras of investigation.[10]

But these books have a long way to go to achieve the impact of the deeply engaged, mulishly wrongheaded, and yet profoundly influential books on Mars published by amateur astronomer Percival Lowell between 1895 and 1908. His arguments for a Martian civilization, built around a global canal system intended to rescue a dying planet, were so attractive and so powerfully presented that many astronomical as well as literary careers can be traced back to the reading of Lowell's books or to the many newspaper accounts of his work. The first popular American science-fiction novel about Mars, Edgar Rice Burroughs' A Princess of Mars (1912), is inconceivable without Lowell's theories and Lowell's maps, often reproduced in newspapers. To guide the terrestrial hero's journey, Burroughs' princess at one point carves into the marble floor a map that would have been very familiar to readers of the time: "It was crisscrossed in every direction with long straight lines, sometimes running parallel and sometimes converging toward some great circle. The lines, she said, were waterways; the circles, cities."[11] The parallel lines, the converging lines, and the circles are plain to see, in full color, on the cover of a 1908 issue of Cosmopolitan or in the Boston Sunday Herald Magazine for November 18, 1906, along with a photograph of Lowell and a long feature on the certainty of life on Mars (see color plates 3 and 5). Once taken by many lay readers as authoritative accounts of the scientific status of the planet, Lowell's three major books on the subject, Mars, Mars and Its Canals, and Mars as the Abode of Life, now read like fine science fiction, gloriously visionary and elegantly composed, though quite mistaken. Lowell is the bridge between the science and the literature of Mars. Because Mars is not only a natural phenomenon but a sign, a symbol, and a power, the work of poets and fiction-makers—and of repudiated and superseded scientists and even of cranks and charlatans—is also essential to our understanding of the meaning of Mars. If it is a sign and symbol, what has it symbolized? And if it was apprehended as a power, to what end?

What Mars means to us is only partly addressed by the work of astronomers, geologists, cartographers, biochemists, and aerospace engineers. Lucretius wrote about the falling off of wonder as human beings grew familiar with the heavenly bodies in the sky—"So has satiety blunted the appetite of our eyes."[12] It takes a poet, a storyteller, an artist to keep the edge on romance. Mars is part of our cultural history, a repository of human desire, a reflection of our aspirations, confusions, and anxieties. That surely is what the author of the most popular work of fiction yet written about Mars meant when he said that his book should not be read as an exercise in prediction or as an anticipation of actual human flights to Mars. Ray Bradbury insisted, "Mars is a mirror, not a crystal." That is to say, The Martian Chronicles—still the most widely read narrative set on Mars—is not a book about the future but about the then-present of

1950, not so much about the *actual* Mars but about the then-actual United States. The narrator of H. G. Wells's 1898 fantasy of invasion, *The War of the Worlds*, comments at the end of his story on the shaking-up of complacency occasioned by contact—in fact or in fiction—with our neighboring planet. The failed Martian invasion actually succeeds in chastening human pride. And the American poet Frederick Turner, writing about his remarkable ten-thousand-line *Genesis*—so far the only epic poem about Mars—suggests that the literary imagination is intrinsic to the scientific project of one day making Mars habitable for human beings: "the unwritten poem is the barren planet, and the composition of the poem is its cultivation by living organisms."[13]

What Mars has meant to us is also a product of how it has been visualized. Just as preliterate people were drawn to the steady red glow of the wandering star, people in the post-industrial era—often unable to observe Mars in the sky because of light pollution as well as the popular loss of knowledge about the heavens—have been affected by how mapmakers, painters, filmmakers, and fantasists have represented the planet. The colors of Mars have become more varied for us ever since nineteenth-century amateur astronomers such as Nathaniel Green began painting maps of Mars with delicate yellows and greens and browns. In Cambridge, Massachusetts, the French emigré Étienne Lêopold Trouvelot, befriended by the Harvard naturalist Louis Agassiz, began observing Mars at the Harvard Observatory and made pastel sketches and engravings of Mars that turn the red planet into a bewitching phantasmagoria of varied hues. Like other observers of the period, Trouvelot found in the blurred telescopic images evidence for what wasn't there at all:

> Mars has many points of resemblance to the Earth. It has an atmosphere constituted very nearly like ours; it has fogs, clouds, rains, snows, and winds. It has water, or at least some liquids resembling it; it has rivers, lakes, seas and oceans. It also has islands, peninsulas, continents, mountains and valleys.[14]

However misinformed his telescopic deductions may be, Trouvelot's images, preserved in his unpublished sketchbook as well as in the gorgeous plates of his *Astronomical Drawings*, are the forerunners of a twentieth-century line of astronomical, and specifically Martian, illustration (see color plate 1).

Pictures have had a major impact on how writers began to imagine Mars. Certainly a large factor in the public fascination with Percival Lowell's theories about Mars was the proliferation of newspaper reproductions of his many maps, based on his observations from his observatory at Flagstaff, as well as the cunningly crafted wooden globes he produced over the course of two decades, each with the canals named and carefully painted in. By the end of the twentieth century, maps of Mars had become more and more professionalized, the product not of a single observer's sketches but of teams of researchers drawing on thousands of images sent back to Earth from cameras orbiting Mars. Astrogeologists from the United States Geological Survey have produced a series of maps of astonishing complexity, detail, and beauty. These are not just maps of interest to a scientific coterie; they fire the imaginations of people with limited cartographic knowledge. As Oliver Morton has shrewdly observed in *Mapping Mars*, "The point of geological mapping is to tell a story—to turn landscape into history."[15]

Even unscientific visualizations have had an important role in engaging the public imagination with Mars. The expressionistic sets and costumes of the 1924 Russian silent film *Aelita, Queen of Mars* (1924) and even the clunky, recycled Hollywood sets and toy spaceships used for the Depression-era matinee movie serial *Flash Gordon's Trip to Mars* (1938) encouraged viewers to think about Mars as a place that belongs to the human future. Advertisements for 1964's *Robinson Crusoe on Mars* boldly declared, "This film is scientifically authentic . . . It is only one step ahead of present reality!"[16] The choice of California's Death Valley for shooting the Martian scenes is inspired and the film skillfully deploys Defoe's Crusoe story of survival by wits as a way of engendering a romance about the wilderness of Mars, but scientifically speaking it is far from authentic, with its depiction of the astronaut and his alien "Man Friday" steaming oxygen out of rocks, dining on sausage-like vegetation found in a pool of water, and enjoying temperatures warm enough to go bare-chested. For many viewers of *Total Recall*, the 1990 Arnold Schwarzenegger vehicle, the climactic scenes of the explosive greening and watering of Mars and the shattering of its domed city as a breathable atmosphere pours in may have been their first encounter with the concept of the "terraforming" of Mars. But as Robert Markley, among others, has pointed out, the film's premises are based on "miraculous technology" and "a physics-defying process."[17]

But flawed artistry has its role to play in the literary history of Mars just as much as flawed science does. The complementary central premises of this book are that to understand Mars is to understand ourselves and that to understand Mars requires the perspectives of imaginative artists as well as of scientists, both on the occasions when they have been correct and insightful and when they have been as wrong and wrongheaded as can be. That the interests, if not the methods, of scientists and of artists in understanding Mars have much in common has not always been obvious, and the star-gazing poet and the star-studying astronomer sometimes have been at loggerheads. Walt Whitman's poem is perhaps the archetypal literary assertion of the lyrical imagination's hostility to scientific exposition:

When I heard the learn'd astronomer,
When the proofs, the figures, were ranged in columns before me,
When I was shown the charts and diagrams, to add, divide, and measure
them,
When I sitting heard the astronomer where he lectured with much
applause in the lecture-room,
How soon unaccountable I became tired and sick,
Till rising and gliding out I wander'd off by myself,
In the mystical moist night-air, and from time to time,
Look'd up in perfect silence at the stars.[18]

Robert Frost felt no such disjunction between poetry and astronomy. In "The Star-Splitter," his narrator pokes fun at Brad McLaughlin, a failed farmer from Littleton, New Hampshire, who burns his house down for insurance money that he then spends to purchase a brass telescope. The disappointed narrator can see through the telescope's lens only kaleidoscopically split images of red and green planets, and for him the telescope offers less than meets the naked eye. But the poem triumphs over the naysaying of the prosaic narrator and celebrates Brad's "life-long curiosity / About our place among the infinities." Frost's poem has become a favorite of planetaria and astronomical societies for Brad McLaughlin's iconic declaration of the nobleness of his visionary ambition:

The best thing that we're put here for's to see;
The strongest thing that's given us to see with's
A telescope. Someone in every town
Seems to me owes it to the town to keep one.
In Littleton it may as well be me.[19]

A perceptive historian of nineteenth-century astronomy, Agnes Clerke, observed more than a hundred years ago that a "new astronomy" came into play about the middle of the nineteenth century, and that this phase of astronomical research was "more popular, both in its needs and in its nature, than formerly."[20] What Clerke recognized in her dual use of the term "popular" was, first, that progress in astronomical research had begun to depend to a much greater degree on public interest and support rather than on the patronage of monarchs and nobles. The excitement of planetary study was generated not by announcements from the Astronomer Royal but in news reports about discoveries and magazine articles by populist amateur astronomers. Second, astronomy had become a more popular subject because discoveries and conjectures made in the era of more sophisticated telescopes could be better grasped by the layperson, who did not need to follow the mathematical proofs on which so many of the crucial advances of seventeenth- and eighteenth-century astronomy relied in the absence of good viewing instruments.

The year 1877 is the beginning point for the modern cultural history of Mars, and the date is not arbitrary. The popular romance with and romance of Mars is largely inconceivable before that year when Asaph Hall in Washington became the first person to locate the two moons of Mars and when Giovanni Schiaparelli in Milan saw—or thought he saw—streaky lines on the Martian surface and called them *canali*. Before long, as the science journalist John Ritchie pointed out in 1890, the tide of yellow journalism had sucked in the subject of Mars as hungrily as it absorbed Washington politics.[21] Five years later, Mary Proctor, daughter of one of the most influential authors of astronomical works for the general reader in the nineteenth century, reported her astonishment at the turnout when she agreed to give a free one-hour talk on astronomical marvels at a grammar school in a tenement district, under the auspices of the New York City Board of Education. "It was positively the roughest crowd it has ever been my pleasure to lecture to, and when I mounted the platform, and looked at the scene before me, I was almost overwhelmed. Nearly eight hundred people, mostly men, had crowded into the hall, and standing room was at a premium."[22]

By the beginning of the twentieth century, the public infatuation with Mars had come into full bloom. The frequent news stories about efforts to send messages and signals to Mars (and to receive and decode any signals being sent by Martians to us) got picked up and played with by the worlds of advertising and popular culture. A magazine ad for Pears' Soap titled "The First Message from Mars" depicts a Martian projecting a beam of light from his planet to Earth containing the words "send us up some Pears' Soap." Popular composer Raymond Taylor wrote a march and two-step titled "A Signal from Mars"; the sheet music, issued in 1901, had a colorful cover with two Martian astronomers, one looking through a telescope focused on North and South America, the other pointing a beacon emitting a broad lightbeam (see color plate 2). A *New York Times* feature article in 1909, surveying the state of the scientific question on the habitability of Mars, opens: "Save the problem of immortality and of life beyond the grave, there is, perhaps, no more fascinating one than that which conjectures life on Mars and the possibility of establishing communication with that great planet."[23]

The First Message from Mars

Several names are associated routinely with the outbreak of what often has been diagnosed as "Mars mania" in the 1890s: Camille Flammarion, Percival Lowell, and H. G. Wells. Each published a landmark book in that decade. In the English-speaking world, few had actually read the most important of Flammarion's untranslated French studies, the massively documented five hundred-page *La Planète Mars* (1892). Percival Lowell's name was anathema to most astronomers but it became a household word among the nonscientific public, a large portion of which, thanks to yellow-press enterprise, knew the sensational outline of his theory of Martian life even if they hadn't actually seen his first book, *Mars* (1895). Only Wells's *The War of the Worlds*, never out of print since its publication in 1898, can claim to have had a direct popular impact. But those who had never read a word by Flammarion, Lowell, or Wells in the year 1900 nevertheless were swept up in the headlong rush of reporting on Mars that glutted magazines and newspapers. Garrett Serviss, who as journalist, editor, and romancer did as much as any American writer between the 1880s and 1920s to stimulate popular curiosity about the planets, observed that at the end of the nineteenth century, the published charts and drawings of Mars were so numerous as to "form a more complete map of the entire surface of Mars than anybody had of the earth in the time of Columbus."[24] An unsigned note in a 1907 issue of *Popular Astronomy* assessed the public fascination with the planet: "The literature about Mars in the current magazines is, some of it fanciful, some funny, some very mysterious, and some of it so wrestling with fact and theory as to show a thirst for more knowledge for a basis from which to learn what the real truth is about many of these things which are yet imperfectly and incompletely seen."[25]

The thirst for knowledge, however, had some alarming consequences for serious astronomers, who were appalled by the public's eager acceptance of all kinds of fantasies about an inhabited Mars and whose curiosity about the planet had less to do with science than with theater. "For one reason and another," a frustrated astronomer from the Lick Observatory in California wrote in a mass-circulation magazine, "the general reader has come to the conclusion that human life may exist, and probably does exist, on this planet as well as on our own earth. Hence the extraordinary attention that has been paid to quite extravagant and baseless publications regarding it."[26] One of the fundamental and perversely captivating features of the literary history of Mars is the steadfast resistance of ordinary readers to scientists' urgings of caution and reserve. The subject of Mars created an avalanche of speculation, romance, and whimsy that for many years could not be halted by scientific criticism.

Just before the outbreak of World War I, a young man with a self-declared "poetico-astronomical turn of mind" wrote to his fiancée of his meditations on the inhabitants of Mars and how they might be contending with their cooling planet: "I am always vainly speculating as to the life that may be on Mars and elsewhere, and in other systems. It is vain, but it is a pleasant holiday from this earth sometimes. If there is intelligence in other worlds how different must it be from ours, not merely greater or less, but utterly different and incomprehensible."[27] The author later gave up his ambitions to be a poet and became perhaps the century's most gifted fabricator of otherworldly lifeforms. In his fiction, Olaf Stapledon repeatedly celebrated cosmic diversity and the inexpressibility of nature's infinitely fecund invention. And, as we shall see, in his first work of fiction, *Last and First Men* (1930), he included one of the most original twentieth-century literary conceptions of Martians.

Poets and fiction writers with names better known than Stapledon's also have struck very different notes from Whitman's belletristic disdain for the scientific enterprise and the romance of astronomical discovery. In the prologue to *Peter Bell*, Wordsworth imagines sailing through the clouds in a spaceboat observing, among other sights, "the red-haired race of Mars, / Covered from top to toe with scars" (lines 38–39). Verses in Tennyson's "In Memoriam" commemorate the telescopic era and the discovery in 1846 of Neptune and its moon Triton: "When Science reaches forth her arms / To feel from world to world, and charms / Her secret from the latest moon" (21.18–20). Far from opposing the artist to the astronomer, in his later "Locksley Hall Sixty Years After" (1886), Tennyson articulates a theme that would become common in fiction about Mars. Imagining how the Earth would look from the vantage point of an observer on Venus or Mars, the voice in Tennyson's poem supposes that our planet would be revalued and our values recast in the view from afar:

> Hesper—Venus—were we native to that splendor or in Mars,
> We should see the globe we groan in, fairest of the evening stars.

> Could we dream of wars and carnage, craft and madness, lust and spite,
> Roaring London, raving Paris, in that point of peaceful light?

> Might we not in glancing heavenward on a star so silver-fair,
> Yearn, and clasp the hands and murmur, "Would to God that we were
>   there"?

In the twentieth century, poets have continued to look to Mars as a reflecting pool in which we can discern images of terrestrial concerns. Craig Raine's often-anthologized 1978 poem "A Martian Sends a Postcard Home" was the impetus for a short-lived "Martian School" of contemporary poetry characterized by alienating, shocking, sometimes comical uses of disruptive imagery and similes, in effect not unlike the "cognitive estrangement" that contemporary literary theorists see as central to the aesthetic of science fiction. In one set of couplets, Raine's Martian tries to describe for his home audience the strange behavior of an old-fashioned, finger-dialing telephone:

In homes, a haunted apparatus sleeps,
that snores when you pick it up.

If the ghost cries, they carry it
to their lips and soothe it to sleep

with sounds. And yet they wake it up
deliberately, by tickling with a finger.

In the title poem of his 2004 collection *The Canals of Mars*, Patrick McGuinness still finds poetic life in Lowell's theory of a "protracted tragedy" on our neighboring planet that may predict our own global collapse. McGuinness imagines what runs through Lowell's mind as he sits at his telescope in Flagstaff:

It could be us, but not yet . . .
from his observatory he spies
the Martian tribes following canals
across the thirsty Martian
earth to their extinction.[28]

And Kim Stanley Robinson, in words more plainspoken than lyrical, recapitulates the Tennysonian dual perspective in his poem, "A Report on the First Recorded Case of Areophagy":

I have never been able to explain
Myself but can only note that in the
Attempt to imagine Mars I came to see
Earth more clearly than ever before
This beautiful world now alive
With the drama of an everyday sunset[29]

The boldest of all such verse imaginings is Turner's *Genesis*. In the preface to his epic account of the political, philosophical, historical, and personal dimensions of the scientific project of terraforming Mars, Turner writes of the challenge of dealing with "the matter of Mars"—a phrase chosen, we must assume, deliberately to echo the terms used in literary history to encompass the many versions of the story of the Greek and Trojan war ("the matter of Troy") and the various strands of the Arthurian legend ("the matter of Britain").[30] For Turner, who also has written a prose romance about Mars and a futuristic epic poem set in the former United States, the Martian materials stand in the same mythic relationship to contemporary society as ancient myths and legends did to the psychological, ethical, and spiritual needs of earlier peoples.

Mars is not only a locale, a symbol, a mythos, it is also a tabula rasa. It is a place with a past but without a history. The past can be studied by geologists, chemists, paleobiologists; imaginative writers can provide the planet with an invented history and a projected future—and both have been done repeatedly. Lacking a history, which requires consciousness and interpretation, Mars is an empty page on which writers can sketch a critique of things as they have been and are in our own world, a vacant stage on which alternative modes of human organization and conduct can be enacted. Mars, especially in the modern era when the dependable old literary locales of uncharted islands, hidden valleys, and isolated Arcadias have lost their slender credibility, has become a preferred site for satire and for utopia. Some of the most intriguing fiction about Mars has been undertaken by writers who attempted to frame their stories of an imagined Mars within the boundaries of the best available scientific information and informed speculation about the actual planet.

But uninformed Martian fiction, and even fiction produced by authors willfully ignorant or deliberately dismissive of scientific data, also can be deeply interesting as a revelation of our cultural history, as it is imported into, reflected within, interpreted by its Martian fictional parallel. As Robinson writes at the opening of his convention-shattering Red Mars, "we are all the consciousness that Mars has ever had"—and therefore all stories about Martians are inevitably fables about ourselves.[31] It was with that understanding in the early 1990s that artist Jon Lomberg undertook a project for the Planetary Society to make a compact disc containing a representative historical sampling of verbal and visual images of Mars to be launched on a 1996 Russian Mars probe. The disc would provide a record for the future settlers on Mars of how their ancestors imagined the planet. The project made the probably unwarranted assumption that, by the time terrestrial adventurers settle on Mars and recover the disc, the equipment for playing compact discs will not have been superseded by later technological innovations. The Russian spacecraft crashed into the Andes— but duplicate copies of the Planetary Society's CD Visions of Mars survive as a compendium of significant moments in the literary history of Mars. In 2007, the Planetary Society made a second try, sending an updated silica-glass DVD of Visions of Mars aboard NASA's Phoenix Mars Lander, which arrived in the north polar region in May 2008.

If humanity establishes a permanent presence on Mars in the coming decades and centuries, the earlier literature about the planet will constitute that new civilization's mythology. Already, the mythic dimension of Mars in the human imagination is apparent. Here is an instance. A great many fictions about Mars imagine the moment when the first human beings set foot on the planet. The convention feels almost like a requirement, although the scene itself is often hokey because the astronauts of fiction have as much trouble as the American astronauts who landed on the Moon coming up with words to match the occasion. Some novelists confront the problem by consciously stressing the artificiality of ceremonial rhetoric, or by giving the astronauts a scripted statement that they are required to recite while fully aware of its banality, or by having the astronauts toss away the script in favor of deliberately demotic and anti-theatrical language. A delightful instance is in a novel not set on Mars at all, Kim Stanley Robinson's California utopia of the mid-twenty-first century, Pacific Edge. A minor episode in that novel is centered on a party to celebrate the televised first landing on Mars. At the critical moment, the party-goers turn off the sound of their television so that they can enjoy the imagery of the event without the inevitably bombastic pronouncements of either the astronauts or the television commentators. But they can't resist speculating what the astronauts might say as they watch them suiting up for their first walk on Mars:

> "If they say something stupid like on the moon, I'll throw up."
> "How about, 'Well, here we are.'"
> "Home at last."
> "The Martians have landed."
> "Take me to your leader."[32]

Pacific Edge was published five years before the first of Robinson's three Mars novels appeared, and so there is a delicious anticipation in this passage of the line that Robinson eventually gives his first man on Mars: "Well, here we are."[33] This throw-away line, this plainspoken announcement of the obvious, is a good reminder that forced eloquence can not create mythic power.

Earned eloquence, of course, is something else. C. S. Lewis, writing near the end of the era in which it was still possible to imagine a Mars with native inhabitants, took the Lowellian myth of a canaled Mars on a last turn around the dance floor of fiction. Lewis's protagonist, who has spent nearly all his time on Mars in deep valleys that the natives call "handramits," never sees the big Martian picture until he is aboard the spaceship that will carry him back to Earth. The success of the return journey, made possible by the spiritual ruler of Mars known as the Oyarsa, is far from certain. As the vessel draws away and the protagonist gains perspective, the Mars of early twentieth-century textbooks—that is the Mars based on the maps of Schiaparelli and Lowell—begins to come into view, and the protagonist's reflections, touched by the possibility of his own death, turn to the nature of myth:

Each minute more *handramits* came into view—long straight lines, some parallel, some intersecting, some building triangles. The landscape became increasingly geometrical. The waste between the purple lines appeared perfectly flat. . . . He reflected that he would have very little to show for his amazing voyage if he survived it: a smattering of the language, a few landscapes, some half-understood physics—but where were the statistics, the history, the broad survey of extra-terrestrial conditions, which such a traveller ought to bring back? Those *handramits*, for example. Seen from the height which the spaceship had now attained, in all their unmistakable geometry, they put to shame his original impression that they were natural valleys. They were gigantic feats of engineering, about which he had learned nothing; feats accomplished, if all were true, before human history began . . . before animal history began. Or was that only mythology? He knew it would seem like mythology when he got back to Earth (if he ever got back), but the presence of Oyarsa was still too fresh a memory to allow him any real doubts. It even occurred to him that the distinction between history and mythology might be itself meaningless outside the Earth.[34]

In the era since writers gave up the cherished fantasy that Mars would be gridded with geometrical waterways and broad swaths of vegetation growing along either side of them, another convention of mythmaking has emerged and, in the most skilled hands, it has generated the kind of eloquence, even almost the kind of poetry, that is missing from the scripts of technocrats. There was a difficult period between 1965—when *Mariner* 4 sent back the first, few close-up photographs ever taken of Mars and disclosed what many people thought a ghastly and dreary landscape of featureless craters—and late 1971, which saw the arrival of *Mariner* 9 into Martian orbit. After a month-long dust storm finally cleared, the *Mariner* 9 camera started recording pictures of an astonishingly varied world with its gargantuan volcanoes poking up through the atmosphere, meandering river channels, and the 3,000-mile-long canyon system, named in honor of the spacecraft that revealed it, Valles Marineris. As Arthur C. Clarke recalled, those first years after *Mariner* 4 seemed to spell the end of romance: "Mars was a cosmic fossil like the Moon—no, not even a fossil, because it could never have known life. The depressing image of a cratered, desiccated wilderness was about as far removed from the Lowell-Burroughs fantasy as it was possible to get."[35] But *Mariner* 9 and successive mechanical expeditions into the twenty-first century that have photographed and mapped the planet have replaced Lowellian figments with new realities. And writers have learned to perceive a new romance in these new realities. It is

Mars the Beautiful that is now on display in fiction, and the standard of beauty being invoked is a far cry from C. S. Lewis's "bright, pale world—a water-colour world out of a child's paint-box."[36] Consider the response of Ben Bova's Native American astronaut, who stands transfixed by the Martian landscape, at once like and unlike that of the American Southwest:

> Magnificent desolation. An astronaut had said that about the moon, de-cades ago. Jamie thought it more appropriate for Mars. The world he saw was magnificent, beautiful in a strange, clean, untouched way. Proud and austere, its desert harsh and totally empty, its cliffs stark and bare, Mars was barren yet splendidly beautiful in its own uncompromised severity.[37]

Mars has many meanings. Once upon a time, it meant a dying world that served as a grim and cautionary text for our own terrestrial destiny. It often has served as the canvas on which writers could depict their wildest fantasies, their darkest fears, their otherwise most unspeakable critiques, their spiritual aspi-rations. For some, Mars still represents a reconstituted frontier for a world in which all the frontiers have now vanished. For others, Mars is a laboratory and a playground of the mind, where speculation about alternative realities and alternative futures is sanctioned and where imagination is granted a license to explore ways in which we may save our own endangered planet. All writers—and readers—for whom Mars represents a lateral strategy for diagnosing and treating Earth's problems, all those who see in Mars a sphere for exercising social and scientific creativity, all those who are struck by the wild beauty of the place as seen and as imagined, may find themselves echoing the words of the Wife of Bath, although in a quite different mood: Myn herte is Marcien.

Dreamworlds of
The Telescope

2

At the close of the nineteenth century, in his great compendium of the first three hundred years of telescopic observations of Mars, Camille Flammarion called attention to Galileo's hesitant declaration of victory in his 1610 effort to get a clear view of the planet. Galileo had been busily fabricating telescopes, improving their magnification, and experimenting with what his instruments could do ever since he heard in the previous year about the new Dutch invention and immediately grasped its principles and its potential. His letter to his student Benedetto Castelli, says Flammarion, contains our earliest recorded observation of Mars in the age of the telescope: "Je n'ose pas assurer que je puisse observer les phases de Mars; cependant, si je ne me trompe, je crois déjà voir qu'il n'est pas parfaitement rond." [I dare not say for sure that I could observe the phases of Mars; however, if I am not mistaken, I believe I have already perceived that it is not perfectly round.][1] With his primitive tube and lenses, Galileo was better equipped to study the topography of the Moon than the distant red world that bewitched the unaided eye, but the history of the study of Mars in the era of Earth-based telescopes—with all the uncertainties and doubtful details that would be part of that history for four centuries—was underway.

The telescope not only opened a new chapter in scientific investigation, it also liberated the artistic imagination, as Karl Guthke has argued in his history of extraterrestrial literature; fictional voyages through space in the post-Copernican universe could be justified as philosophical searches for truth.[2] Among the first Europeans, and certainly among the first literary figures, to put his eye to the lens of that new technological wonder, the telescope, was the young John Milton. One of the rare, perfect symmetries of history is the meeting that took place in 1638 between the aspiring English poet and the aged Galileo, under house arrest for heresy by the Inquisition for publishing a dialogue that voiced Copernicus's then fifty-year-old position on a Sun-centered universe. Here were two of the boldest minds of the seventeenth century, one a scientist with literary gifts at the end of a shattered career and the other an artist drawn to scientific investigation on the brink of a celebrity that also would come crashing down to near-disaster. In just over twenty years, Milton would suffer a disgrace similar to Galileo's when his name appeared on the death list of the restored Royalists whom he had publicly and repeatedly denounced during the English Revolutionary period of 1642 to 1660.

Milton told the story of his encounter in Tuscany in a single, frustratingly unadorned sentence in his great prose pamphlet on the freedom to publish, *Areopagitica*: "There it was that I found and visited the famous Galileo grown old, a prisoner to the Inquisition, for thinking in Astronomy otherwise than the Franciscan and Dominican licencers thought."[3] That Galileo, in his *Dialogue on the Two Chief World Systems* (1632), cautiously avoided identifying the Copernican view as his own did not safeguard him from prosecution. A nineteenth-century visual reconstruction of the meeting of Galileo and Milton survives in an oil painting by Annibale Gatti exhibited at Florence's History of Science Museum; in it a grimly animated Galileo leans forward to make a point, gesturing forcefully with outstretched hand to a callow-looking young man seated in front of the delicate little "optic glass" that revolutionized the history of astronomy. But we know nothing of the conversation that took place and must deduce through literary allusions the impact that Galileo's discoveries and Galileo's experiences made on England's apprentice epic poet. We can make a plausible guess at what Milton saw through Galileo's telescope because the event is memorialized in *Paradise Lost* in the comparison of Satan's shield to

> the moon, whose orb
> Through optic glass the Tuscan artist views
> At evening from the top of Fesole,
> Or in Valdarno to descry new lands,
> Rivers or mountains in her spotty globe. (I.287–91)[4]

This early evocation of lunar geography is part of a triple homage to the telescope in *Paradise Lost*. Milton also depicts Satan landing on the Sun and appearing like one of the sunspots Galileo was the first to observe through his "glazed optic tube" (III.588–90). But the shrewdest of the three Galilean passages appears as part of the account of the flight of the archangel Raphael to Earth. Raphael has a crisply focused view of the Earth, and of the garden of Eden on the Earth, glimpsed from the edge of outer space as he passes through the gate of Heaven. A simile captures the difference as well as the parallel between the unerring angelic eye and the more fallible telescopic lens:

Galileo and Milton, painting in oils by Annibale Gatti, late nineteenth century. Courtesy Istituto e Museo Storia della Scienza, Florence; photograph by Franca Principe

> as when by night the glass
> Of Galileo, less assured, observes
> Imagined lands and regions in the moon (V.261–63)

If Galileo's glass improved what the naked human eye could perceive, Milton intuited, it still might not approach the clarity and precision of a god's-eye view. The telescope was a visionary instrument and the images it disclosed might prove to be figments rather than accurate pictures of reality. Over the course of centuries, the "less assured" observations of the Moon would give way to still more problematic visions when astronomers tried to peer into the more distant world of Mars. Telescopes, trained on remote targets and beset by the turbulent and distorting atmosphere of our own world, were capable of creating illusory images—though sometimes quite visionary ones. Therein lay their usefulness to literature. Imaginary topographies would be a crucial by-product of the history of planetary astronomy throughout the era of Earth-based telescopes.

Paradise Lost was conceived in the century when the shape of the universe changed; when life outside the terrestrial sphere could be contemplated; when the aided human eye was exploring, with difficulty and not always with assurance, marvels never before visible or imaginable. In its account of Satan's flight through space, its vision of extraterrestrial travel by an evolved human species that could "winged ascend / Ethereal" (V.498–99), and its supposition of a plurality of Earth-like planets ("every star perhaps a world / Of destined habitation" [VII.621–22]), Milton's epic has some claims to be the first great anticipation of science fiction. In that respect, as in many others, Milton was a prophetic thinker and writer. As a younger man, he may have thanked his stars that England was a country without the institution of the Holy Office. But he endured his own Protestant version of the Inquisition in the aftermath of the failed republican revolution of 1642 to 1660, during which he published his notorious pamphlets on tyrannicide, divorce, and intellectual freedom. By the time he came to write *Paradise Lost* under the restored monarchy—middle-aged, blind, and in humbled station after being pardoned for crimes against the state—Milton perhaps had learned some Galilean caution in how he presented astronomical knowledge in his encyclopedic poem. In the often-neglected Book VIII, Adam asks Raphael a number of specific questions about the nature of the universe: Is there vegetation on the Moon? Is Earth at the center of things, or is it the Sun? Why are there so many stars? On the matter of geocentrism or heliocentrism, Raphael is so technically detailed in his noncommittal reply that the reader as well as Adam may feel less well-informed after the question has been answered. But it is the query about other worlds that draws the most revealing response from the angel. He tells Adam to restrain his imagination and leave such controversial issues to "God above":

> Heav'n is for thee too high
> To know what passes there. Be lowly wise:
> Think only what concerns thee and thy being.
> Dream not of other worlds, what creatures there
> Live in what state, condition or degree,
> Contented that thus far hath been revealed
> Not of earth only but of highest Heav'n. (VIII.172–78)

It is a fascinating and instructive moment in English literary history because it reveals a distinct boundary line between what could be envisioned and what was still unthinkable—or at least unprintable. Ideologically and theologically, the time was not yet right for the genre of science fiction to emerge from the realm of forbidden knowledge.[5] Still, one cannot help but wonder: What might Milton have had to say about Mars and the Martians had not he and his angel chosen discreetly to draw the curtain? Although such a question is both useless and unanswerable, the floodgate of speculation about life on other worlds would soon open. Once Copernicus had introduced the idea that Mercury, Venus, Mars, Jupiter, and Saturn were not wandering stars but Earth-like bodies orbiting the Sun, and once the seventeenth-century astronomers had the means to study those bodies, the question of their habitability became inevitable. As astronomers at their telescopes began picking out more details of the then-known planets, Mars eventually would be perceived as the most Earth-like of them all and therefore a prime candidate for habitation by intelligent life.

Only a dozen years after Milton's death in 1674, a twenty-nine-year-old French wit, Bernard le Bovier de Fontenelle, successfully crossed the line at which *Paradise Lost* had halted. Establishing himself on the side of the Moderns in the debate over the merits of Ancient and Modern literature and philosophy, and espousing without any reservation the Copernican view of the solar system, Fontenelle may have been fortunate that France was more tolerant of unorthodox thinking than either Galileo's Italy or Milton's England. He first published *Entretiens sur la pluralité des mondes* [*Conversations on the Plurality of Worlds*] in 1686, and continued to produce expanded and revised versions that incorporated new scientific information throughout his long life, which ended shortly before his hundredth birthday. In the preface to the first edition, Fontenelle confronted directly those "scrupulous people" who might feel that his speculations on extraterrestrial intelligence would pose a danger to religion, but "religion," he insisted, "simply has nothing to do with this system."[6] Although the Catholic Church listed *Conversations on the Plurality of Worlds* on its Index of Forbidden Books, that condemnation appears not to have inhibited readers, either in France or in England, where rival translations by John Glanvil and Aphra Behn appeared in 1688.

Fontenelle's series of five dialogues between a philosophical teacher and his pupil, the Marquise of G——, occupy five evenings in which the discussion moves progressively from the intimacies of the Earth to the distant galaxies, from Copernicus' revision of the Ptolemaic, Earth-centered universe to new astronomical discoveries of the death and birth of stars. Fontenelle celebrates the diversity of peoples, both on Earth and on the other planets, beginning with a remarkable fantasy in which the philosopher imagines himself suspended above the rotating Earth, observing a constantly changing diorama:

> I see passing under my gaze all the different faces: white, black, tawny, and olive complexions. At first there are hats, then turbans; woolly heads, then shaved heads; here cities with belltowers, there cities with tall spires with crescents; here cities with towers of porcelain, there great countries with nothing but huts; here vast seas, there frightful deserts; in all, the infinite variety that exists on the surface of the Earth. (20)

As on Earth, so in the heavens. As in the microcosm, so in the macrocosm. And for Fontenelle, it was not simply the diversity of human life on Earth that predicted a living cosmos, but the diversity of life in the smallest forms—microorganisms swarming in a leaf or a drop of water. Telescopic revelations of other planets complemented what the microscope was discovering in worlds below the threshold of the unaided eye's vision. For the time being, the human mind would have to rely on logical extrapolation from multiple forms of life on earth to life in the cosmos at large. But soon, Fontenelle argued, there would be direct confirmation. Humanity would not explore the heavens by Miltonic "winged ascent ethereal" but in airships that would cross space just as in recent centuries European ships crossed the Atlantic to the unknown Americas. "The art of flying has only just been born; it will be perfected, and some day we'll go to the Moon" (34).

Like Milton, Fontenelle refuses to be specific in picturing the beings who may live on other worlds—but his philosopher's reasoning is different from the Angel Raphael's. Fontenelle draws this curtain not because of a divine ban but because the pictures would not be empirically verifiable yet. "It is not proper for the imagination to go any farther than the eye can" (45). In contrast to Raphael's expunging of fantasy ("Dream not of other worlds"), the philosopher urges the Marquise to try to construct the inhabitants of other planets in her dreams. The experiment does not work, however, because, as she reports to him the next morning, her dreams "kept providing something that resembled what one sees here on Earth" (48). Instead, the Marquise and her mentor must content themselves with generalized fantasies about the inhabitants of other worlds: the likelihood that those on Mercury would be crazed by terrible heat unless they were cooled by tropical rains; that on Venus one might find a dark-skinned people, musical, poetic, and vivacious; that Jupiter with its four moons would enjoy a perpetually changing panorama in its night skies, and therefore the planet would be full of astronomers with telescopes; that on large, cold Saturn the people would be serious and phlegmatic. But Mars holds little interest for the Marquise and the philosopher. The few data generated by seventeenth-century science suggest that Mars is so similar to Earth that it "isn't worth the trouble of stopping there" (52). Martians, it would seem, are probably too much like us to afford many of the pleasures of novelty that other habitable worlds promised.

It would take almost another two full centuries from the time Fontenelle first set down his *Conversations* before Mars moved decisively to the central position among the plurality of worlds assumed to be inhabited. And when that change occurred, it would be based precisely on what Fontenelle thought was its least attractive quality: its apparent analogies with the Earth. If Fontenelle failed to prophesy accurately the coming Mars mania, his enormously popular and influential little book became a model for the genre of the extraterrestrial excursion—whether by mental or physical means—which took form in the eighteenth and nineteenth centuries. As the Victorian shapers of the scientific romance set to work, they repeatedly turned their readers' attention to the pioneering *Conversations on the Plurality of Worlds* as warrant for their fictional inventions. One of those writers even felt compelled to explain to readers that while he was inspired by Fontenelle, the resemblances in his narrative should not be construed as plagiarism.[7]

While Milton and Fontenelle were speculating about the heavens, astronomers began making the first significant observations of features of Mars in the early decades of the era of the telescope. In the 1660s, Giovanni Cassini, professor of astronomy at the University of Bologna, determined that the length of a Martian day was just a little longer than a terrestrial day; his figure of 24 hours, 40 minutes later would be fine-tuned to 24 hours, 37 minutes, 22.66 seconds, but his calculation was close enough to encourage thoughts of Mars as another Earth. In 1659, in Holland, the thirty-year-old Christiaan Huygens saw and sketched a large, dark area shaped like a V, later to be christened the Hourglass

Sea, and later still Syrtis Major. When Cassini became the first director of the Paris Observatory, Huygens often worked there, and in 1672 he drew a picture of Mars that showed the white cap on the south pole, another milestone in planetary observation. In the 1690s, in the last years of his life, Huygens fantasized about the conditions for life in the solar system; the posthumously published *Cosmotheoros* (1698) proposed that, while Mars was farther from the Sun than Earth and its climate colder, there was no reason to assume it lacked vegetable and animal life.

Almost immediately on publication, *Cosmotheoros* was translated from Latin into English as *The Celestial Worlds Discover'd: or, Conjectures Concerning the Inhabitants, Plants and Productions of the Worlds in the Planets*. The London publisher's brief preface records the translator's nervousness about "the Censures of learned Men" that might be visited on a book some would say "renders philosophy cheap and vulgar" while perverting both religion and science. The preface seems designed to perform a function similar to those cautious modern editorial disclaimers about the opinions therein expressed being those only of the author. And opinion—the weightiest and probably the most revolutionary scientific opinion of the seventeenth century—is the subject of the great opening sentence of Huygens' *Cosmotheoros*: "A man that is of Copernicus's Opinion, that this Earth of ours is a Planet, carry'd round and enlighten'd by the Sun, like the rest of them, cannot but sometimes have a fancy, that it's not improbable that the rest of the Planets have their Dress and Furniture, nay and their Inhabitants too as well as this Earth of ours."[8]

What Milton hesitated to say, Huygens trumpets without reservation: Once Copernicus's description of the solar system is accepted, not simply geocentrism but anthropocentrism must be called into question. "What a wonderful and amazing Scheme have we here of the magnificent Vastness of the Universe! So many Suns, so many Earths, and every one of them stock'd with so many Herbs, Trees and Animals, and adorn'd with so many Seas and Mountains!" (150–51). The new perspectives of the Copernican era both excite the imagination to contemplate the grand scale of the Creation and enable us to judge what matters and what is trivial on "this small speck of Dirt" that we inhabit (10). In *Paradise Lost*, Milton's Eve memorably articulates the innocent wonder of the amateur observer who beholds a multitude of glittering stars in the night sky: "But wherefore all night long shine these, for whom / This glorious sight, when sleep hath shut all eyes?" (IV.657–58). But if Eve's question implies one seventeenth-century response to the newly understood infinite universe, Blaise Pascal's famous outcry in Number 233 of his *Pensées* (1670) gives voice to the century's fear of the loss of a clean, well-lighted universe and of human centrality and domination within it: "The eternal silence of these infinite spaces terrifies me."[9]

Huygens is clever enough to insist that the newly subordinate place of the Earth in the scheme of the universe both humbles and exalts humanity. He disposes of the religious objection to Copernican theory by maintaining that Scripture's silence on other worlds is evidence that God refrained from enumerating all the sites of his creativity. But if God has chosen not to reveal knowledge of other worlds (as Milton's angel Raphael admonishes Adam), yet we have no cause to believe that God has set boundaries on human discovery. If we were so constrained, Huygens argues, Europeans would have remained ignorant of the existence of America, about which there had been no Revelation. Only human edicts, not divine ones, attempt to prevent discovery; only human interests, not divine ones, are threatened by new knowledge: "That vigorous Industry, and that piercing Wit were given Men to make advances in the search of Nature, and there's no reason to put any stop to such Enquiries."[10]

Cosmotheoros is most eloquent when Huygens is defending the pursuit of science and celebrating the infinite plenty of the Creation. Milton's Adam had been advised that the human race, if obedient and faithful to heavenly command, would naturally evolve ("Improv'd by tract of time") into a higher spiritual state and would be able to roam the cosmos at will.[11] Huygens also describes a divinely sanctioned form of evolution that God has entrusted to those rare individuals who have the self-discipline to pursue scientific study, or "natural philosophy" as it was then called. "God never design'd we should come into the World Astronomers or Philosophers; these Arts are not infus'd into us at our birth, but were order'd, in long tracts of Time, by degrees to be the rewards and result of laborious Diligence" (69).

Everywhere one looked at the close of the seventeenth century, there seemed to be evidence that the human species, led by its scientists, was poised to leap forward. Galileo's telescope, Leibniz's calculus, Newton's *Principia*, Harvey's study of circulatory systems, Brand's discovery of the uses of phosphorus—all promised stunning changes in how human beings understood themselves, their immediate world, their ability to manipulate their environment, and their place in the larger universe. Huygens' most delightful instance of the evolution of human knowledge is at the opposite pole from his own concern with mapping the stars. Like Fontenelle, he gave special attention to Leeuwenhoek's invention of the microscope, which opened a miniature world previously unglimpsed and unguessed: "that in the seed of the Male are discover'd, by the help of Glasses, Millions of sprightly little Animals, which it's probable are the very Offspring of the Animals themselves: a wonderful thing, and never before now known!" (99). In the midst of these stunning advances, astronomy was in both an exhilarating and a frustrating position, persistently locating new heavenly bodies but unable to have more than tantalizing glimpses of them through unwieldy tubes and warped lenses. Lacking a Pegasus to take us for a clear, close-up view of the other worlds being disclosed imperfectly by the telescope, we must resort, Huygens conceded, to conjecture, based on the best astronomical observations and logical deductions from them. Inevitably, perhaps, those conjectures, which constitute most of the second part of *Cosmotheoros*, are disappointing.

The working assumption behind Huygens' hypothetical exposition of life in the solar system is that "what's true in one part will hold true over the whole Universe" (43). If the Earth has rationally endowed animals, then so too must other planets; if the human hand with its opposable thumb is convenient for us, such a convenience could not be denied to other humanoid creatures; and if we have developed a science of astronomy, so too must the inhabitants of other Earths. "For supposing the Earth, as we did, one of the Planets of equal dignity and honor with the rest, who would venture to say, that no where else were to be found any that enjoy'd the glorious sight of Nature's Opera? Or if there were any fellow-Spectators, yet we were the only ones that had dived deep into the secrets and knowledge of it?" (62). In his survey of the solar system, Huygens actively rejects the earlier astrological conjectures of the Jesuit Athanasius Kircher in his *Ecstatic Journey* of 1656 because they offend against probability.[12] Kircher's Venus is pretty and pleasant, and the source of human health; his Mercury is brisk and airy and the provider of human wit and cunning; and Mars is "nothing but devilish, infernal, stinking, black Flames and Smoke," a hellish source of human plagues and mischiefs, according to Huygens (104).

But probability is a very relative yardstick. Huygens' own conjectures sometimes are shaped by European prejudices. He imagines, for instance, that the inhabitants of torrid Mercury, like terrestrial Brazilians and Africans, must have only a primitive science because people who live in tropical heat are "neither so wise nor so industrious as those that belong to colder and more temperate Climates" (107). What will strike readers as most arbitrary in Huygens' logic, however, is the degree to which he is impressed by sheer size and scale and by the number of attendant satellites a planet has. The magnitude of Jupiter and Saturn shames "this little pitiful Earth of ours," he laments (117). Assuming a direct correlation between a planet's dignity and the number of moons orbiting it, Huygens gives pride of place to Jupiter with its four known moons and Saturn with five. Both of the giant planets are described extensively in *Cosmotheoros*, but he provides little in the way of detailed conjecture about

Mars—even smaller than the Earth—save for a guess that its copper color is the result of soil darker than that of Jupiter or the Earth's moon. That neither of Mars's two tiny moons was discovered until 1877 (despite Jonathan Swift's famous lucky guess in 1726 about the pair of moons in "The Voyage to Laputa," part 3 of *Gulliver's Travels*) may partially explain why so little attention is paid to the planet, not only in *Cosmotheoros*, but in most imaginative and conjectural accounts of the solar system until the later nineteenth century.

While Mars stood in the shadows of the literary imagination, the planet continued to draw the attention of astronomers in the eighteenth century. At the Paris Observatory early in the century, Cassini's nephew Giacomo Maraldi not only confirmed his uncle's sighting of a white spot on the Martian south pole but detected one on the north pole as well. Maraldi observed changes in the size and shape of the south polar spot, the nature and significance of which it remained for later investigators to determine. The first of those investigators, by far the most important of the eighteenth-century scientists who studied Mars, was the German-born astronomer to England's George I, Friedrich Wilhelm Herschel. His success in advancing knowledge about Mars depended on his decision to use reflecting rather than refracting telescopes. Herschel's seventeenth-century predecessors used telescopes with single or multiple curved lenses—refractors. But observation was plagued either by distortion or by the unwieldiness of increasingly longer telescope tubes. Herschel knew that Isaac Newton had proposed a different kind of instrument—the reflecting telescope that used mirrors rather than lenses to gather and focus light. Devoting himself to making high-quality mirrors for his telescopes, Herschel began using his reflectors at the Martian opposition of 1777. His became the most systematic observations and calculations yet made about the physical nature of Mars. Herschel presented his findings in two papers read before London's Royal Society in 1881 and 1884. He determined more precise figures for the length of the Martian day, the axial tilt of the planet, and its diameter; he described the position of the poles and the shape of the planet as a flattened sphere; and he concluded that Mars had seasons similar in nature to, though twice as long as, Earth's, that the white spots at the poles that grew and diminished seasonally were ice masses, and that there was evidence of an atmosphere. As momentous for the history of astronomy as Herschel's data were, a single sentence in his second paper had the greatest impact on the ensuing literary history of Mars. Summing up the import of his findings on the rotation of Mars on its tilted axis, the existence of polar ice caps, and its sequence of seasons, he proposed, "The analogy between Mars and the earth is, perhaps, by far the greatest in the whole solar system."[13]

Herschel's presentations to the Royal Society were largely technical and mathematical, as he carefully laid out the bases for his deductions. But it is startling to find buried in the details of his 1784 lecture the casual assumption that there were Martians. Recording the appearance and disappearance of the north polar cap as he observed it at the 1781 opposition, he writes: "By a calculation, made according to the principles hereafter explained, its latitude must have been about 76° or 77° north; for I find that, to the inhabitants of Mars, the declination of the sun, June 25. 12h. 15' of our time, was about 9° 56' south." Elsewhere in the paper Herschel, makes additional matter-of-fact allusions to the Martian populace, including one in his striking final sentence, echoing the famous comment on the analogical relationship of Mars and Earth: "And that planet has a considerable but moderate atmosphere, so that its inhabitants probably enjoy a situation in many respects similar to ours."[14] The most scrupulous astronomer of his era, for whom the physical details of Mars required the patient accumulation and display of evidence, took it for granted that Mars was inhabited—and most probably by beings not unlike ourselves. Not surprisingly, writers with little or no scientific scruple or training made the same unexamined inference.

One of the curious cultural figures of the eighteenth century, who pursued interests in the natural sciences, philosophy, and mystical religion, combined Fontenelle's tour of the planets with the growing astronomical consensus that the planets of the solar system were analogous "Earths"—an idea first articulated by Huygens and at least partly confirmed by Herschel. Emanuel Swedenborg's De Telluribus in Mundo Nostro Solari (1758) was translated from the Latin in 1787 as Concerning the Earths in Our Solar System. It is a highly idiosyncratic application of the concept of a plurality of inhabited worlds that emphasizes the magnificence and plenitude of the Creator. The English translator acknowledged in his preface that for many readers Swedenborg's book would appear "merely visionary, groundless, and enthusiastic, and the Fruit only of a light or disordered Imagination."[15] Instructed by an angel, Swedenborg is informed that humanity is not confined to a single Earth, but that the inhabitants of various worlds are constituent parts of a universal humanity, "the Grand Man" (9). The narrative—if it can quite be called that—consists of an extended survey of the inhabitants of each of the known planets of the solar system and of the "Earths" in five other star systems.

Although Swedenborg maintained that the differences in the humanities of each of the Earths required separate, detailed presentations, for most readers the differences will appear so subtle that Concerning the Earths feels more tedious and repetitious than its modest length would suggest. The inhabitants of

Mercury are highly spiritual beings, enamored of abstract ideas and unconcerned with worldly necessities. Those on Jupiter enjoy long conversations over abstemiously nutritious meals, have a deep commitment to the education of children, and covet no one's property. The Martians have no governmental structure, are unacquainted with deceit or hypocrisy, and are, we are informed, among the best spirits in the solar system. And so on. Swedenborg's tour of other worlds is motivated by spiritual ideology rather than astronomical curiosity or fictional invention. All the extraterrestrial inhabitants seem to be telepathic, unconcerned with material goods, high-minded, self-improving, and glumly ill-adapted to vice. What William Blake, an errant disciple of Swedenborg, wrote about his master in The Marriage of Heaven and Hell has some relevance to the truisms and abstractions of Concerning the Earths: "Thus Swedenborg boasts that what he writes is new; tho' it is only the Contents or Index of already publish'd books."[16]

The arrival of Halley's Comet in 1835, for the second time since Edmund Halley calculated its orbit at the end of the seventeenth century and predicted the years of its return visits, inspired another survey of heavenly bodies. Not as self-consciously philosophical as Swedenborg, the anonymous author of A Fantastical Excursion into the Planets (1839) wrote for "fun and diversion" and deliberately sought "novelty, oddity, whim, and even extravagance," although he also expressed the wish that his fantasy might promote serious study of astronomy in young readers.[17] The author recites from a growing list of astronomical achievements: the confirmed sighting of four moons orbiting Jupiter, the discovery of Saturn's rings and moons, visible mountains on the Moon, the cyclical reappearance of comets. It is a measure of how much more liberal speculative license had grown since Milton's day that the author opens his excursion with an announcement that the solipsistic human-centered universe finally was disintegrating after two hundred years of scientific effort. He evokes the spectacle of the "illustrious Galileo" required to kneel "before the ghastly tribunal of bigotry at Rome" (4, 5). Most interestingly, he longs for a physical journey to other worlds—a journey he is confident will be available to future generations by air balloon. A fancied "Columbus in the ethereal ocean," he must content himself with a dream-excursion of the sort that the angel Raphael had denied Adam—and that religious wariness had dissuaded Milton from attempting (68).

Wafted into the heavens by the winged being Imagination, the narrator of the Fantastical Excursion is given a guided tour of each of the known planets as well as of the Moon. Extraterrestrial scenery is a chief focus of the excursion, and, making few pretenses to scientific plausibility, the author suffuses each world with the pictorial conventions of neoclassical and Romantic landscape painting. The alabaster and alpine glories of Venus seem straight out of Claude Lorrain, while the darkly monumental Martian landscape, with its blazing altars, "ponderous" temple gates and "unfathomable abyss," suggests the dark and grandiose illustrations of hell that John Martin painted for *Paradise Lost* in the mid-1820s (84–85). Despite the nod toward new scientific discoveries in the introduction, a reader looking for portents of nineteenth-century scientific romance in the *Fantastical Excursion* will find little that anticipates Jules Verne or H. G. Wells, or even the lesser accomplishments of Percy Greg or Gustavus Pope. The ethereal Columbus catches a glimpse of what "our astronomers denoted snow-capped poles" as he sails toward Mars, but that is the sole modern scientific ingredient in an otherwise old-fashioned mythological treatment of the planet (68). The Roman war god Mars and the fire god Vulcan divide Mars between them, with the latter overseeing the planet's extensive iron mining and weapons manufacture while the former presides over torch-lit military parades and inspires feats of martial heroism. The planet is a nightmare of blood and fire, cannon blasts and drumbeats, slaughter and mutilation from which the narrator finally flees in a state of horror and over-cooked rhetoric: "Oh! 'twas too much! Played my imagination here the coward? Methinks, I cannot deny it; as longer, no! longer I here could not abide; for strife seemed every moment on tiptoe, watching with lynx's eye the fit moment to rush forth" (96).

Whoever wrote *A Fantastical Excursion into the Planets* was no unsung rural Milton. There is so feeble a sense for style in the narration, such a stunning lack of authorial tact that it is no wonder that the book has long been forgotten. A skeptical or impatient reader might question whether I have performed any defensible service in resurrecting it even briefly. In one interesting respect, however, the *Excursion* does look forward to the ways in which "the matter of Mars" would become a vehicle and soapbox for authors who transpose terrestrial concerns to the Martian landscape. For this anonymous author, journeying to Mars is an occasion for reflecting both on the martial spirit of ancient Rome and, closer to home, on the Napoleonic wars of the first two decades of the nineteenth century. "Do not the instructors of our youth recommend always the Romans to our admiration, as a superior order of beings?" the author asks (93). The tour of the red planet exposes the barbarity of the Roman model of military heroism—of which Napoleon was a modern instance: "surely a hero of Roman stamp was he" (94). Using Martian fiction to mirror terrestrial politics would become, from the 1880s on, one of the hardiest conventions of modern science fiction, but unlike some later utopian novels about Mars, the

Fantastical Excursion does not condemn all wars or all military heroes. The author champions an alternative to the bloody victors favored by the Martian deity. "My readers will presently perceive that amongst this company, I found none of the Wellington stamp," he writes of the British general who defeated "conquest-infatuated Napoleon" at Waterloo (75). Without a paragon in Greek and Roman military history, Wellington—having served as prime minister and as foreign secretary in the years just before the *Fantastical Excursion* was published—exemplifies the hero whose "superiority of mind" is evidenced in the "loftiest deeds" performed off the battlefield (78):

> When yet, after performing hardly credited exploits, you see him, unconcer-nedly, re-enter private life, not ad interim, and but for a few weeks or months, no! holding steadily "the noiseless tenor of his way!" to me it seems indeed heroically great, it seems marvelous. (79)

Within a few decades, the journey to Mars would take several literary leaps, as astronomical knowledge of the planet leapt before it. Some of the coming fiction about Mars would be just as lame as the *Fantastical Excursion*, but among the good, the poor, and the indifferent early Martian novels there would be the same irresistible tendency to use Mars as analogous to and as allegorical of Earth and its concerns. Herschel's statement from his second Royal Society paper would become a mantra for scientists and imaginative writers alike in the later nineteenth century, governing their perceptions and their inventions of Mars: "The analogy between Mars and the earth is, perhaps, by far the greatest in the whole solar system." That sentence opened the chapter on Mars in Agnes Clerke's *Popular History of Astronomy during the Nineteenth Century* (1885); it anchors the discussion of Martian discoveries in John Ellard Gore's *The Scenery of the Heavens: A Popular Account of Astronomical Wonders* (1890); it is echoed in a chapter title of Richard Proctor's influential, often-reprinted popular work, *Other Worlds Than Ours* (1870): "Mars, The Miniature of Our Earth." Flammarion gave a nearly identical title to a chapter in his *Popular Astronomy* ("The Planet Mars, Miniature of the Earth") and reported how Mars appeared through the telescope. "It is the earth itself which we seem to see in space, with interest-ing varieties and novelties."[18] The verbal message of these historians of sci-ence was reinforced visually by the maps of Mars that appeared frequently in astronomy books designed for general audiences. While the telescope was the essential technology for creating knowledge about Mars, cartography, as K. Maria Lane has demonstrated effectively, was "the primary medium by which knowledge about Mars was communicated" in the second half of the nineteenth century.[19]

Martian mapmaking had become almost a cottage industry among nineteenth-century astronomers, from the first detailed sketches done by Johan Madler and Wilhelm Beer working from Beer's observatory in Berlin in the 1830s. The most commonly reproduced of subsequent maps were drawn in England by the Reverend William Dawes in 1864 and, following and expanding Dawes, by Richard Proctor in 1867; in France by Flammarion, who adapted Proctor's map but made the nomenclature for identifying the variety of supposed Martian continents, plains, and bodies of water less Anglocentric; on Madeira by Nathaniel Green in 1877; and in Italy, starting in 1877 and continuing over the next fifteen years, by Giovanni Schiaparelli. As the century came to a close, all such maps were superseded in the popular mind, though not in astronomical research, by the canal-dominated representations of Percival Lowell. More will be said of these maps in subsequent chapters, but perhaps at least as influential as the visual appeal of the maps of Mars was the nomenclature they introduced. In many ways, to name is to invest a thing with reality and to possess it. As Percival Lowell wrote in *Mars* (1895), "Everybody has tried his hand at naming the planet, first and last; naming a thing being man's nearest approach to creating it."[20]

The chief competing systems of naming the regions and physical features of Mars were the English and the Italian-Latinate. Under the former, people learned to look for and dream of locations named by Dawes and Proctor for astronomers: Kepler Land, Herschel Strait, Secchi Continent, and Tycho Sea became part of the familiar litany of Martian names. Schiaparelli's system, which eventually won out and was expanded by Lowell with his burgeoning roll-call of canals, drew on the ancient mythologies of Greece, Rome, and the Middle East for its evocative names. By the beginning of the twentieth century, many people could speak knowingly of Syrtis Major, Solis Lacus, Elysium, Margaritifer Sinus, and Mare Sirenum as if they had often holidayed there. And Schiaparelli's and Lowell's canals—Erebus, Protonilus, Euphrates, and the rest—became part of the small change of conversations about Mars and its inhabitants. Before the nineteenth century ended, many people, under the spell of the new lexicons, felt fully in possession of Martian geography—or areography as its most linguistically precise devotées liked to call it.

The visualization of Mars in nineteenth-century maps, with their continents and oceans cozily named, reinforced the analogical way of thinking, and facilitated the kind of political satire we can find in a *New York Times* tongue-in-cheek editorial of 1882. Having just reported three days earlier that Giovanni Schiaparelli—a name not yet familiar to American readers—had detected more than twenty canals on the surface of Mars, all of which the editorialist supposes have been constructed in the past winter, the *Times* suggests that an orgy of canal-building clearly would be in the planet's economic interest:

> The most careless glance at a map of Mars will suggest the thought that what Mars needs is ship canals, cutting the long promontories into which her continents are divided. Such canals would be of inestimable service to her commerce. If a steamer Captain wishes to sail from a port on the Tycho Brahe continent to another on the south shore of the Kepler continent, he is obliged—according to the most authentic charts—to sail three thousand miles down the Newton Gulf and twenty-four hundred miles or so up the Herschel Gulf; whereas were there a canal connecting the upper ends of the Newton and Herschel Gulfs the voyage would not be more than sixty miles in length. It is evident that with a proper system of intergulf canals, the Martians would be benefited to an almost incalculable extent; for what the Suez Canal has done for terrestrial commerce might be done for Martian commerce by any one of a hundred and thirty canals, the proper location of which can be seen on the map.[21]

The "Mars mania" of the 1890s was still a decade away, and the object of the editorial is not to stimulate speculation. The writer, in fact, has little interest in Martians or their canals whatsoever, except as an excuse for making an acerbic analogy to American foreign policy in Central America. James Blaine, recently resigned as Secretary of State, had taken a hard line on U.S. interests in the proposal to cut a canal through the Isthmus of Panama. "If we only had Mr. Blaine in charge of our foreign relations," the editorialist intones in mock-solemnity, "he would quickly convince the Martians of the error of their ways by writing an eloquent diplomatic note saying that the United States cannot view with satisfaction the construction of the Newton-Herschel Canal, and that either the canal must be closed or else we shall proceed in the interests of commerce to make war on Mars and incidentally to enforce a claim—now held by certain American citizens—to the coal-fields of the Tycho Brahe continent."[22]

If Mars was a world that physically resembled our own, then its use as a political, psychological, and cultural mirror was the next likely step in the evolution of the history of Mars in the human imagination. In the last decades of the nineteenth century, the dreamworlds suggested by the telescope two hundred years earlier were poised to come to life in fiction. The development of the genre of the scientific romance coincided with a new burst of astronomical discovery and excitement about Mars, and journeys to and from Mars were about to become commonplace in that new fictional genre. The prehistorical phase of the literary history of Mars came to a close in, very precisely, the year 1877.

Inventing a New Mars

In 1877, the planet Mars drew closer to Earth than it had been for more than thirty years—and as close as it would be again until 1892. Opposition would occur on September 5, and that impending event drew the attention of journalists. In mid-August, the *New York Times* reprinted from England's *Cornhill Magazine* a little article titled "Is Mars Inhabited?" It would be midsummer's day in the southern hemisphere of Mars just eleven days after the opposition, and the news report quoted what were then familiar lines from Oliver Wendell Holmes' philosophical fantasia on space travel, "Wind-Clouds and Star-Drifts":

> The snows that glittered on the disk of Mars
> Have melted, and the planet's fiery orb
> Rolls in the crimson summer of its year.[1]

The hope was that with snows melted and mists and clouds evaporated in the summer heat, a better view of the Martian surface than had yet been available to the increasingly powerful telescopes of the nineteenth century would be disclosed. The article does not go so far as Samuel Phelps Leland would a few years later when he predicted that the University of Chicago's 40-inch telescope might detect the Martian navy moored in its harbor and industrial smoke arising from Martian cities.[2] The more modest hope in 1877 was for a glimpse of green vegetation that would indicate the presence of life.

If the *Times* piece forecasts the burgeoning public curiosity about life on Mars in the coming decades, the scientific community was just as excited, in its own quiet fashion, about the opposition of 1877. Around the world, astronomers prepared for the event. On September 5, the Scotsman David Gill prepared his telescope on Ascension Island in the South Pacific, where he had set up a small observatory. His wife Isobel kept a daily journal. Both of them worried and fidgeted as they watched the sky cloud up, but late in the evening the clouds passed away "and the whole moonless heavens were of that inky blueness so dear to astronomers." In the early hours of September 6, Isobel Gill's attention was divided between the dazzling view of the Pleiades, with Mars glowing redly in the west, and the "sweet sounds" issuing from her husband inside the dome as he sang out his data. "Let not any one smile that I call these sweet sounds. Sweet they were indeed to me, for they told of success after bitter disappointment; of cherished hopes realised; of care and anxiety passing away. They told too of honest work honestly done—of work that would live and tell its tale, when we and the instruments were no more."[3]

Meanwhile, in the Atlantic, the portrait artist and amateur astronomer Nathaniel Green had set up a 13-inch telescope 2,200 feet above sea level on the island of Madeira. Using the nomenclature developed by Richard Proctor ten years earlier, augmented by a few new place-names of his own, Green published a richly pictorial drawing of Mars as he saw it. "It would be difficult to exaggerate the keen map-like appearance of the planet," he wrote, having viewed it in exceptionally transparent atmospheric conditions. His large, tinted, fold-out map, along with a dozen drawings of the Martian disc done between August 21 and September 29, tried to capture the rich colors that he perceived in his viewings of the planet: "a warm yellow, heightening into orange on some of the continents" and the "greenish grey" of those portions of the surface "supposed to be water."[4]

At the U.S. Naval Observatory, located less ideally than Gill's or Green's observation stations in Washington, D.C.'s Foggy Bottom, Asaph Hall struggled for a clear view of Mars. Although the Potomac mists ruined his efforts night after night, a few weeks before the day of opposition, Hall verified the existence of two small moons of Mars, Deimos and Phobos. Immediately, speculation began about possible miniature inhabitants of the tiny satellites, and whether natural selection might have rapidly and efficiently propelled their little worlds into the utopian state. A writer for the London Spectator thought it conceivable that "the law of 'conflict for existence' on so small a theatre" might operate to produce "far more select minds and powers and higher mental resources, than we can muster among the whole population of our globe."[5]

Scientifically, Hall's was the outstanding discovery of the 1877 opposition, but the news from Milan's Brera Palace would end up having the greatest impact on the literary history of Mars. The director of the Brera Observatory, Giovanni Schiaparelli, decided to draw a new map of Mars with a new system for naming its topographical features, based on what he could see during the period of opposition. In September 1877, Schiaparelli began to notice markings that he called canali. The term had been initiated by the papal astronomer, the Jesuit Angelo Secchi, when he observed Mars in the 1850s, but it had not

Nei problemi scientifici di grande complicazione e di
molta difficoltà sembra che la mente umana sia condan-
nata a non raggiungere il vero, se non dopo di aver
esperimentato un certo numero di combinazioni sbagliate
e percorso tutto un labirinto d'errori.

Giovanni Schiaparelli

Giovanni Schiaparelli, pen and ink portrait by Robert Kastor, c. 1900.
Courtesy Library of Congress, Prints and Photographs Division

been adopted or imitated by other astronomers and mapmakers until Schiaparelli took it up. Schiaparelli was color-blind, so the map he drew and published from his 1877 observations lacked the subtle gradations of coloring in
Green's map, but the dozens of *canali* he included in his drawing created both
excitement and some skepticism.[6] He offered no interpretation of these lines

nor did he suggest that they should be understood as feats of engineering rather than natural grooves or channels. But before long, the term was being translated into English as "canals," and the history of Mars in the human imagination was about to take a dramatic turn.

No other observer in 1877 could confirm the markings that Schiaparelli perceived, although the Italian astronomer was certain that he had recorded something objectively there on the planet's surface. "It is as impossible to doubt their existence, as that of the Rhine on the surface of the earth," he told Nathaniel Green in a letter that accompanied their exchange of drawings. Green insisted that at the 1879 opposition he could detect only "faint and diffused tones" in the places where Schiaparelli saw sharply defined lines, but Green had to admit that his urban observing station at St. John's Wood in London did not have the advantages of the steady air over Madeira that he had enjoyed two years earlier.[7] The impact of Schiaparelli and of his ambiguous, mistranslated, and ultimately illusory canali on the subsequent popular interest in Mars is one of the most often-told stories. Perhaps only the 1938 Orson Welles broadcast of The War of the Worlds is a more familiar (though, finally, less influential) fixture in the cultural history of Mars. Schiaparelli continued to note and name canali in the next several oppositions, and they became straighter and more numerous; they also began to "geminate"—that is, canals that Schiaparelli formerly had observed as single appeared double at some times. The canali became a subject of debate among astronomers, some of whom claimed that they too saw them (even the geminated ones), but many of the most prominent observers, using state-of-the-art equipment, could find no trace of them. But, for the time being, the disagreements among astronomers remained subdued and took place largely outside the notice of the press. Canals got only occasional brief mention in the newspapers of the 1880s. The earliest American notice that I have found is an unsigned piece reprinted in 1882 from the London Daily Telegraph. The opening sentences are constructed in such a way as to suggest that Schiaparelli's was not yet a household name and that the story of the canals had not often, if ever, been told in the mass media. The final sentence conveys with great succinctness, in its concluding allusion to the engineer who built the Suez Canal and was in 1882 drawing up a plan for a waterway across Panama, what tended to happen as soon as canali was translated as "canals." The article reads in its entirety:

A curious discovery, made by Signor Schiaparelli, Director of the Royal Observatory at Milan, seems to start again that old and unanswerable question, "Are the planets inhabited?" This Italian astronomer is one of the most assiduous watchers of the planet Mars. It was he who, in 1877–8, first detected the many dusky bands which traverse and sub-divide the ruddy portions of the martial orb. Again, in 1879–80, when the position of the planet was favorable, he re-identified these strange lines; but during last January and February he has been able to observe and map out in more than 20 instances duplications of the dark streaks "covering the equatorial region of Mars with a mysterious net-work, to which there is nothing remotely analogous on the earth." The Italian astronomer has styled them "canals," for they bear the appearance of long sea-ways, dug through the martial continents, as if a mania for short cuts had seized the inhabitants of the planet, and everybody residing there had become an active M. de Lesseps.[8]

Just ten days later, the New York Times reprinted from the Times of London a letter by the author of the period's most popular English-language books on astronomy. Richard Proctor urged caution on the subject of Schiaparelli's observations. Proctor reminded readers that a great many astronomers, including those using some of the largest telescopes, had been unable to corroborate the markings on Mars:

Until observers with such instruments as these have distinctly seen what Signor Schiaparelli has mapped we must not too hastily assume that these are real features of Mars. Mr. Nathaniel Green, whose fine lithographs of Mars adorn a recent volume of the "Memoirs of the Astronomical Society," considers that these narrow passages are due to an optical illusion (which he has himself experienced). Should it be proved that the net-work of dark streaks has a real existence, we should by no means be forced to believe that Mars is a planet unlike our earth, but we might perhaps infer that engineering works on a much greater scale than any which exist on our globe have been carried on upon the surface of Mars. The smaller force of Martian gravity would suggest that such works could be much more easily conducted on Mars than on the earth, as I have elsewhere shown. It would be rash, however, at present to speculate in this way.[9]

The fervor for Mars had not yet erupted, and Proctor's cool assessment of the difference between proof and surmise suited the decade of the 1880s. In fact, after the printing of this letter from Proctor, the New York Times remained silent for nearly ten years on the subject of Schiaparelli, the canals, and Martian speculations whether temperate or rash. The subject simply dropped out of the press until the eve of the close opposition of Mars and the Earth in 1892. When journalists took up the subject of Mars again in the 1890s, they did so with an eagerness and a volume of ink unlike anything seen earlier.

The period from Schiaparelli's 1877 observations until the next major op- position in 1892 saw the first important flurry of modern fictional writing about Mars. Because there was as yet little in the way of an ideological frame- work for imagining Mars, these early scientific romances are quite various in their ways of conceiving of the journey to Mars, the landscape of the planet, and the physiology and culture of its inhabitants. Mark Hillegas, one of the few scholars who has attempted to assess the range of Victorian-era fiction about Mars, suggests that the "Martian myth" was not in place until the middle of the 1890s.[10] None of the earliest romancers had to adopt a position on the canals, because as yet little visible professional debate and no public discussion had taken place on the question. In fact, canals are rarely mentioned in any of the works before 1892—and in the few instances in which they do occur the treat- ment is brief, incidental to the narrative, and peripheral to whatever agenda of ideas about Mars the novelist was developing. I have found only one work of fiction published before 1894 in which the name of Schiaparelli appears at all. Fictional Mars in the 1880s and early 1890s is defined by a few commonly known facts about the planet (that it has polar ice caps, seasons and a day just over 24 hours, low gravity, and a pair of recently discovered small moons) and myths that were thought to be fact or near-certainty at the time (that Mars had a thin but breathable atmosphere, oceans and continents, red or orange vegeta- tion, and intelligent inhabitants). The authors usually had consulted maps of Mars—rarely Schiaparelli's, and most often versions of the 1867 map made by the Rev. William Dawes and often reprinted in Richard Proctor's popular books of astronomy. They were cognizant of earlier discussions of the habitability of planets in the solar system—above all, Bernard Fontenelle's *Dialogues on the Plurality of Worlds* and the nebular hypothesis about the formation of planetary systems proposed by Pierre Simon Laplace in 1796.[11] But the two figures who without doubt most powerfully influenced the early fiction were Camille Flam- marion on the scientific side and Jules Verne on the literary side.

In the "open field" that constituted the subject of Mars at this time, writers began sketching out some of the major types of Martian fiction as they began deploying techniques, motifs, and plotlines that soon would have the status of conventions in the literary history of Mars. A half dozen of these books, three published originally on each side of the Atlantic, will suggest the new horizons that were opening: Percy Greg's *Across the Zodiac: The Story of a Wrecked Record* (1880); the Rev. Wladislaw Somerville Lach-Szyrma's *Aleriel, or a Voyage to Other Worlds* (1883); *Bellona's Bridegroom: A Romance* (1887) by the American freethinker

William J. Roe, writing under the pen name of Hudor Genone; Hugh MacColl's *Mr. Stranger's Sealed Packet* (1889); Robert Cromie's *A Plunge into Space* (1890); and, perhaps the most curious of this very curious body of fiction, *Messages from Mars, By the Aid of the Telescope Plant* (1892) by Robert D. Braine.

Fame among this group of texts is relative, since even the best-known of them are now read only by a small group of science-fiction historians and collectors. Only two of the six were ever reprinted in the twentieth century: *Across the Zodiac* and *A Plunge into Space*. And *Across the Zodiac*, while neither the best-written nor the most engaging of these romances, is the one that is cited most frequently in histories, bibliographies, and encyclopedias of science fiction. Hillegas thought only Percy Greg's work merited serious attention, the rest of the "crude romances," "inept satires," and "dull utopias" of the 1880s and early 1890s being "almost totally lacking in vitality."[12] On strictly artistic grounds, it is hard to fault this sweeping dismissal, although there may be more artful and thoughtful touches in Lach-Szyrma, MacColl, and Braine than in the over-valued Greg. But as examples of how the subject of Mars began to take shape in the popular imagination they are invaluable sources of information for the "pre-history" of the new Martian mythology that exploded into view in the mid-1890s.

It may be worth pointing out, as a minor footnote to the cultural history of the space age, that Greg's *Across the Zodiac* contributed a word to the English language: astronaut. Modeled presumably on the Argonauts, the sailors who worked Jason's ship the *Argo* on the quest for the golden fleece, the *Astronaut* was the name Greg gave to the spaceship on which his unnamed protagonist flew to Mars. (The Oxford English Dictionary does not record another occurrence of the word until 1929.) But the most significant of Greg's innovations, because it inaugurates an entire line of fiction, is the destination of the *Astronaut*. Earlier interplanetary romances either focused on the nearby Moon or made a Cook's tour of all or most of the known solar system. Greg selects a single planet. Although the protagonist says his preference would have been Venus, he acknowledges that because astronomers have been unable to penetrate the perpetual cloud-cover over Venus, too little is known about it to make it the destination of choice. "That Mars has seas, clouds, and an atmosphere was generally admitted," he writes in his manuscript, "and I held it to be beyond question."[13]

Like a great many early Mars narratives, *Across the Zodiac* imagines a space vehicle powered by harnessing gravitational forces of attraction and repulsion—here called "apergy."[14] Unlike most other authors of the late nineteenth century, however, Greg emphasizes the length and monotony of the voyage itself, which is described in great detail in an effort to achieve a Vernian technical plausibility. When the *Astronaut* lands on Mars, the traveler celebrates the momentous event with comparisons that would be invoked repeatedly in succeeding works of fiction (and in some astronomical writings as well). "All that Columbus can have felt when he first set foot on a new hemisphere," the voyager writes in his journal, "I felt in tenfold force as I assured myself that not, as often before, in dreams, but in very truth and fact, I had traversed forty million miles of space, and landed in a new world" (vol. 1, 76). The leap forward from earlier interplanetary romances also is signaled by the discarding of the dream-vision structure of Swedenborg and the author of the 1839 *Fantastical Excursion*. While visionary trips to Mars occasionally would resurface in the coming decades, especially in the "automatic" fictions written by supposed psychics and mediums, Greg points to the future in attempting the illusion of realism and technological credibility. Greg also initiates the practice of comparing the exploration of Mars with actual terrestrial explorations underway or planned, especially the European imperialist adventures in Africa and Asia and the multinational obsession with reaching the North and South Poles. "Of the perils that might await me I could hardly care to think," says the traveler as he prepares to disembark from the *Astronaut*. "They might be greater in degree, they could hardly be other in kind, than those which a traveller might incur in Papua, or Central Africa, or in the North-West Passage" (vol. 1, 76–77).

Such references are common enough in the book to form a pattern in which the extraterrestrial explorer wears the face of the British colonialist. When he joins a hunting adventure on Mars, he makes explicit connections between himself and Englishmen in India on tiger-hunts. Mounted on a saddled giant bird, part of a flock of domesticated animals used by Martians (or Martialists, as Greg calls them), he is impressed by the birds' strategy in pursuing their quarry, "whereof an Indian or African chief might be proud" (vol. 2, 19). As he engages in combat with the creatures called "thernee" he makes a further comparison. "This conflict reminded me singularly of an encounter with the mounted swordsmen of Scindiah and the Peishwah" (vol. 2, 20). And when he finally is brought in to meet the Camptâ, the king of Mars, he determines "to treat the Autocrat of this planet much as an English envoy would treat an Indian Prince" (vol. 2, 44). Here, as in so many fictions that would follow, Mars is simultaneously alien and familiar, at once both an exotic other world and a facsimile of the other countries and other cultures that EuroAmerican explorers and conquerors were encountering and subduing. For a British writer like Greg, Mars naturally enough becomes an extension of or parallel to Victoria's empire that had been metastasizing throughout the nineteenth century.

In fact, it was just four years before the publication of *Across the Zodiac* that Prime Minister Benjamin Disraeli had arranged the ceremony in which his queen was crowned Empress of India.

When Greg's traveler first appears on Mars and tells the story of his journey, the locals are puzzled and suspicious. Although physiologically indistinguishable from the inhabitants of Earth, the Martialists must first satisfy themselves that their visitor is in fact a human being. The chief obstacle to their acceptance of him is the perception that he is engaged in a fantasy or a lie in claiming to have traveled from another planet. Since Martian science, which has pronounced travel through space an impossibility, is taken to be infallible, the traveler is at risk of being confined to a hospital for lunatics. Taken under protection by Esmo, a Martialist iconoclast and leader of an underground movement for spiritual change on Mars, the traveler has an opportunity to learn at first hand what underlies the "material paradise" (vol. 2, 138) of a planet that has eradicated disease, maximized agricultural production, abolished poverty, and attained a high level of technological innovation and domestic comfort.

A price has been paid for the Martian paradise. The Martialists suffer from (as Greg's protagonist judges) a habitual indolence and solipsism, an inability to empathize with the joy or pain of others, hence a taste for torture (including the use of an electric rack and capital punishment by vivisection), an emotional frigidity that largely erases affection for spouses or for children, and disbelief in an afterlife or any metaphysical power. He concludes that "human nature in Mars" must be "utterly different from, perhaps, hardly intelligible to, the human nature of a planet forty million miles closer to the Sun" (vol. 2, 173). The persistent reflection on likenesses and differences between earthly and Martian practices gives Greg the framework, again a common feature in subsequent fictions about Mars, for critical analysis of the terrestrial issues of the moment. In *Across the Zodiac*, the pre-eminent issue is the status of women.

While Greg offers neither as comprehensive nor as wholehearted a feminist critique as Ella Merchant and Alice Ilgenfritz Jones do thirteen years later in their satirical *Unveiling a Parallel*, his narrative raises questions that anticipate the passions that would galvanize the suffrage movement in England. Greg, a utilitarian moralist in the spirit of John Stuart Mill, portrays Martian women as largely chattel in practice, although they have technical legal equality with male Martians.[15] For instance, they are able to divorce their husbands—and given the privilege taken by husbands to beat their wives, women have cause for divorce. But the women are so utterly dependent economically on men that they do not exercise their legal right to divorce. In their childhoods, girls are confined to sex-segregated schools where they are acculturated to self-effacing and self-sacrificing behavior; they have little to do except tend the garden, train pets, weep copiously, and prepare themselves for the marriage market. The traveler visits one such school and observes the girls preparing to display themselves to prospective husbands. The sight "reminded me," he says drawing a distinction that is as disquieting as it is precise, "of a slave market of the East, however, rather than of the more revolting features of a slave auction in the United States" (vol. 2, 166).

Greg's protagonist becomes enmeshed in the sexual politics of Mars in two interesting ways. When the life of Eveena, the daughter of his benefactor Esmo, is threatened by an accident, he forcibly enlists the aid of a Martialist aristocrat in rescuing her. Since no Martialist, following the creed of radical self-interest that governs male behavior, would consider putting his own life at risk for another man, let alone a woman, the visitor from Earth acquires a lifelong enemy in his unwilling partner in the rescue, who is determined to avenge his humiliation. More intimately, the protagonist falls in love with Eveena and marries her, but is required by the laws of hospitality to accept as a gift from the sovereign of Mars a harem of additional wives chosen for him. While Eveena comes slowly to appreciate her husband's un-Martialist respect for her views and insistence that she have complete freedom of movement in Martian society, his other wives see his refusal to give them orders or to discipline them as a contemptible sign of weakness. For the visitor, this daily encounter with the subjugation of Martialist women, including the internalized self-negation that keeps them intellectually and emotionally children in their own households, enforces his conviction that material progress on Mars has been accompanied by "a terrible moral degeneration" (vol. 2, 193).

Greg's romance ends in death and dissolution. One of the traveler's wives betrays him to an assassination plot and, when caught, herself becomes a candidate for vivisection; another of the wives is infected with a fatal disease whose germs the traveler unwittingly brought with him in the Astronaut; and the woman he loves, Eveena, his chief wife, dies in a final battle with the would-be assassin, the aristocrat who had been forced earlier to save her life. Finally, the traveler dies on his return to Earth when the Astronaut crashes and disintegrates in the South Pacific, with only the partially readable manuscript of his memoir—the wrecked record of the subtitle—surviving. The elimination of most of the cast of characters in Across the Zodiac may be taken as a signal that what matters most to Greg is not the fate of the explorer or even the discovery of another planet, but the critical examination of the nature of discovery and exploration and the application of the traveler's experience on Mars to the affairs of Earth.

In 1883, an Anglican priest, Wladislaw Somerville Lach-Szyrma, published *Aleriel, or A Voyage to Other Worlds*. In part, the narrative belongs to the excursion tradition of books that survey a plurality of inhabited worlds—the tradition descended from Fontenelle, Swedenborg, and the anonymous *Fantastical Excursion* of 1839. What *Aleriel* shares with that body of literature is a challenge to philosophical geocentrism; as Lach-Szyrma's preface states, "Our Earth is singular in nothing" and "Earth is not the Universe."[16] If the Earth is not unique, if the culture of terrestrial humanity represents only one distinct developmental possibility from a common human nature, then a journey to other worlds can function as a set of lessons for Earthly readers: inspiring or cautionary models for what we may become, sobering examples of what we once were or will one day decline to. In that spirit, Lach-Szyrma offers two utopias among the five visited worlds (Venus and Mars), two portraits of primitive and chaotic worlds less fully evolved than the Earth (watery Jupiter dominated by marine life, chaotic Saturn full of gigantic fungi and insects), and one dead world that predicts the ultimate fate of the Earth (the "magnificent and terrible" Moon [71]).

The most striking innovation in *Aleriel* is that the space traveler in this case is not someone from the Earth, since our species has not yet developed sufficiently to make such a journey. Lach-Szyrma uses a frame-story in which the title character, Aleriel, a winged inhabitant of Venus, has come to Earth in disguise as explorer, researcher, and teacher. In making the glum report of his findings, Aleriel tells his comrades on Venus that while there is great natural beauty on Earth, its minded inhabitants, despite occasional acts of nobility, are predominantly selfish, miserable, sometimes depraved, and always pitiable. He is particularly struck by the oddity that terrestrial humans cannot fly, yet risk going up in balloons, while the natural fliers on Earth—the birds—are in a primitive evolutionary state. "Earth is one vast prison-house," he concludes, "where all are bound to the surface" (88).

Astronomers on Venus construct a larger version of the "ether car" in which Aleriel has traveled to Earth so that he may be joined by several companions for the more ambitious tour of the whole solar system. Determined to try to improve the human lot on Earth, Aleriel has chosen a young Englishman, Hamilton, to receive the manuscript of the travelogue that records his circuit through the solar system. In the closing frame, Hamilton and his wife accept the manuscript but are interrogated by visitors from Venus. Struggling to account for the history of human vice and failure, they suffer the conventional embarrassments of human beings cornered into revealing an unfavorable portrait of their own kind. In his role as messenger, guide, and instigator of change, Aleriel prefigures the incarnations of a "Man from Mars" who appears in a number of late-nineteenth and twentieth-century works, from William Simpson's The Man from Mars (1891) and George DuMaurier's The Martian (1897) through Robert Heinlein's Valentine Michael Smith of Stranger in a Strange Land (1961) and Walter Tevis's Man Who Fell to Earth (1963). The beneficent extraterrestrial typically has angelic status in these narratives (the Greek "angelos" means messenger)—a link that Lach-Szyrma establishes almost literally with his winged visitor from Venus. That he is named Aleriel—perhaps derived from the Greek a + lereo, meaning not silly, not foolish—may suggest that the author intended a no-nonsense angel.[17]

In the account of his discoveries on Mars, near the region labeled on Camille Flammarion's map the Delarue Ocean, Aleriel sketches out a utopia that includes many of what became commonplace features in the portrayal of imaginary Martian societies designed for the edification and imitation of Earthly readers. In the lighter gravity of their planet, Lach-Szyrma's Martians are nine feet tall; they are large-chested because of the thin atmosphere; and they have more body hair than terrestrial humans as an adaptation to the cold. With war abolished after a "Holy One" brought the doctrine of love to Mars, the planet moved beyond nationalism. A Platonic system of government by the wise, chosen by competitive examination rather than popular election, achieves the Benthamite goal of "the greatest possible happiness to the greatest possible number" (143). A linguistic academy charged to develop a scheme "to establish a perfect language" produces a uniform written language, reminiscent of Egyptian hieroglyphics, and ensures that there will be no "diversity of speech" (116). Martians live in cities that are larger but less crowded than terrestrial cities. Each city is laid out with extensive parks for every neighborhood; roads are beautifully paved mosaics with gleaming rails along which electric cars move. All these garden-cities are full of "glow, and motion, and sound," Aleriel writes, unlike "sad and gloomy" Paris and London that so demoralized him on his sojourn on Earth (130).

Martians spend about a third of their day in work, including an hour of prayer; a third in amusement and recreation, which may consist of theater, sport, music, lectures, and reading; and a third in sleep. All are vegetarian and drink a mineral-rich, blood-colored fluid that provides the nutrients that meat used to supply in earlier eras. Religious ceremonies are flamboyant spectacles of blazing light and clamorous music—"a loud roar of song (too crushing to be melodious)," editorializes the delicate Aleriel—followed by worship in utter silence. Mars has neither money nor a barter system since all resources are understood to belong to the planetary community and all needs are met out of the common store. Martians live in communes rather than families and observe no gender distinctions or segregation in work and recreation. Selfishness and indolence have been educated out of Martian life, and anyone who fails to learn the basic moral lessons is punished. If they prove incorrigible, however, they are simply killed. "We pray for them, but we slay them. There is no room in our world either for liars or selfish people" (143).

It is not difficult to perceive the shadow of the clergyman on this pastoral paradise, including that touch of steel in summary capital punishment for moral shortcomings. Here is a world in which the ideals of Christianity and the Redeemer "took." However, while *Aleriel* has links not only to the extraterrestrial utopian romance of the 1839 *Fantastical Excursion* but also to the Christian allegories of earlier writers like Bunyan and later ones like C. S. Lewis, Lach-Szyrma has also incorporated something distinctive to his own historical moment. One of the clearest departures from earlier works is the explicit effort to keep the fictional speculations within the bounds of "established scientific discoveries" (vii) and to let fancy loose only on subjects about which science is currently silent. Lach-Szyrma prints a map of Mars using Flammarion's nomenclature, and he has a set of notes at the end of the narrative that cite his scientific and philosophical authorities—chiefly Flammarion, the popular astronomical writer Richard Proctor, and his most important older source, Bernard Fontenelle's dialogue on the plurality of worlds. So, for instance, when he depicts the "majesty and power in the colour of red" on Mars (103) and insists that the ruddy color seen through our telescopes is the result of vast crimson and orange forests, Lach-Szyrma was following Flammarion's theory that the redness of Mars came from vegetable life, not rock or sand. Prominent citations of contemporary scientific theory enforce the pious hope stated in Lach-Szyrma's preface—a goal stated as well in a number of other early fictions about Mars—that his imaginative inventions will encourage young readers to take up the study of serious works of astronomical science.

One piece of fiction from the 1880s that has no such educational pretensions is *Bellona's Bridegroom*, described by its author as both "romantic" and "flippant."[18] The pseudonymous Hudor Genone (actually William J. Roe) uses Greg's device of the found manuscript, but this one, composed by a get-rich-quick schemer named Archy Holt, receives more extensive editing and commentary from the bewildered narrator to whose care it is entrusted. In keeping with the flippancy that the narrative faithfully adheres to, the narrator's wife considers the author of the manuscript "manifestly deranged," and Archy's own wife Amelia thinks of him as a crackpot. The manuscript tells of Archy's decision, first, to put up $5,000 to finance development by an inventor, Professor Garrett, of an "ethereal disc"—in plain English, a flying saucer—to be powered by his newly discovered metal, hydrogenium, and then to accompany Garrett on what they believe will be the first human flight to Mars.

Mars, as the ether disc approaches it, "glowed like burnished silver" and revealed the familiar continents and small oceans of nineteenth-century maps. Flying through the sky over the carmine-colored land masses and the emerald waters are the two tiny moons discovered by Asaph Hall. But that is about as far as *Bellona's Bridegroom* goes in attempting to include authentic contemporary scientific data. Archy's first sight of a Martian is of a naked, toothless old man with long white hair who, Professor Garrett theorizes, has been exposed in the wilderness to die. The Malthusian professor assumes that Mars has begun to exceed its carrying capacity and is enacting the policy that economist Thomas Malthus predicted would in the future be required on Earth: "to suppress the surplus population" (61). But, Archy eventually learns, the wrinkled old man was being born, not dying, and the entire tale functions as a fantasy about a culture in which one is born old and ages backwards.

"I tell you," Archy writes in his manuscript at one point, "things were different in Mars from what they are in Indianapolis or Spidhank or Yonkers" (141). That is his way of justifying his engagement to the youthful-looking but actually quite elderly Bellona, although he already happens to have a terrestrial wife, the sharp-tongued Amelia. Martian women as depicted in *Bellona's Bridegroom* look strikingly like the models in pre-Raphaelite paintings: large and full-figured, with rich mouths and flowing robes. And that isn't the only resemblance of the Martians to terrestrial prototypes. The names Roe gives his Martian characters seem to come straight out of the dramatis personae of Restoration comedy: Mayor Bullymore, Lawyer Steelahl, Judge Helwriggle, and the newspaper editor Mr. Allfax. In an episode of inspired silliness, Archy is commissioned to go out into the woods to bring in Bellona's uncle, who is scheduled to be born. Cued by his early experience to look for a wrinkled old man, he finds one but becomes suspicious when he notices that the man is wearing "a pair of John Bean's shoes" (259). With footwear manufactured in Massachusetts, he can't be a Martian, and the old man is forced to reveal that he actually is an old man, a physicist who had traveled from Earth to Mars before Archy and Garrett did. Having taken all his clothes off for a swim to refresh himself from the voyage, he was taken for a Martian of magical powers who never aged (that is, never looked like he was getting younger). The physicist was only too glad to play the role and enjoy a godlike status among the natives.

The most striking of all Roe's flippancies is connected to one of the professor's pet theories: that "nature is always and everywhere the same" (124). Archy and Garrett make the startling discovery on their first contact with the inhabitants of Mars that they all speak English. The professor decides, in accord with Laplace's nebular hypothesis, that Mars as an older planet is farther along the evolutionary course than the Earth. Already, he says, in the latter years of the terrestrial nineteenth century English was becoming "the prevailing language of the entire globe" (126). And so with exquisite absurdity Roe takes one step further the conventional utopian assumption that a highly civilized world eventually will achieve a single global language. Not only will Mars have no linguistic differences, the Martians will have chosen English naturally as the best of all possible languages, the language toward which nature inevitably tends. Of all the Martian books of the 1880s and 1890s, *Bellona's Bridegroom* is closest to being pure whimsy. It never quite develops the potential Swiftian edge suggested by its evocation of Restoration satire, and it doesn't have the sustained manic invention of *Alice in Wonderland*. But it does lay out a direction for Martian narrative that will be pursued by E. V. Lucas and Charles Graves' parody of Wells's *The War of the Worlds* called *The War of the Wenuses* (1898) and such mid-twentieth-century writers as Fredric Brown and Philip K. Dick.

A far more ambitious work, and artistically the most impressive of the Martian books of the 1880s, is *Mr. Stranger's Sealed Packet*, first published in London in 1889 and followed by a second British edition and an American edition in 1890. Its author, Hugh MacColl, was known primarily for his writing on philosophical and theological subjects, including a translation he made from the Gaelic of James Erasmus Phillips' *Seven Common Faults* for the Society for Promoting Christian Knowledge. *Mr. Stranger's Sealed Packet* occasionally betrays MacColl's commitment to Christian proselytizing, but the narrative has a delicacy and melancholy that take it beyond the realm of the propaganda novel.

Appearing seemingly out of nowhere, a prematurely gray man is hired to fill the vacant post of science master at an English boys' school. Joseph Stranger (a name that suggests the degree to which he is both alien and alienated) turns out to be a spellbinding classroom presence, but on the day that he lectures on astronomy he grows increasingly disturbed as he outlines the analogies between Mars and Earth in landscape, atmosphere, and inhabitants. He concludes with a vow never to lecture on astronomical subjects again, and his peculiar agitation inclines some of his pupils to wonder if he is really of this world. Two months later, Mr. Stranger vanishes, and the next day a letter and sealed packet arrive at the home of his old friend Jones, the book's narrator. Jones is asked not to open the packet unless Stranger doesn't reappear within five years. After five years have passed, he may open the packet and do as he wishes with its contents.

The packet, as we expect, contains the manuscript of a narrative. From it we learn the life-story of Joseph Stranger, who was orphaned at an early age and, by the terms of his father's will, trained to continue the scientific investigations that his father had been quietly pursuing. When he turned twenty-one, Stranger received his own parcel of manuscripts explaining his father's research into that favorite subject of nineteenth-century scientific romances: how to harness the forces of attraction and repulsion to make it possible to escape from Earth's gravity. It takes young Joseph three years to complete the research and build a vehicle, the Shooting Star, that will explore the solar system. Feeling like Columbus in pursuit of a new world (as do so many other protagonists in similar romances), Stranger sets out to fulfill his father's aim of discovering a solution to the coming problem of Earth's overpopulation.[19] As in Bellona's Bridegroom, but in a more serious vein, Malthus presides over the journey to Mars.

Where Across the Zodiac went out of its way to describe the technical features of the space journey, in Mr. Stranger MacColl emphasizes the silence and the loneliness of the protagonist's solo ten-day flight. Stranger's first panoramic view of Mars as he nears the planet shows polar snows, mountain ranges, winding rivers, lush green vegetation, and rosy-pale land. As he descends into the Martian atmosphere, he discovers a world rich in animal life, with every variety of walking, creeping, swimming, and flying creature. "In no single instance did I see a form which exactly resembled any animal that I had seen on earth, though I frequently detected points of likeness or analogy" (48–49). The analogical view (what triggered his near-breakdown in the classroom) recurs throughout Stranger's manuscript, a perspective for which MacColl may be indebted to Sir William Herschel. Writing for the Royal Society of London in 1784, Herschel maintained, "The analogy between Mars and the earth is, perhaps, by far the greatest in the whole solar system." Considering the length of the day on Mars, its seasons, and what he took to be water vapor in its atmosphere, he concluded that the planet's inhabitants "probably enjoy a situation in many respects similar to ours."[20] Herschel's century-old analogical theory was at least as important to Victorian fictional conceptions of Mars as were any of the discoveries of contemporary astronomers. MacColl is unusual only in the overtness of his use of analogy as a central structural principle of the narrative. Joseph Stranger's manuscript spells out the Martian analogies in great detail—moving from its topography, climate, vegetable and animal kingdoms, and urban architecture to the climactic realization that Mars is inhabited, not by "creatures more or less *resembling* the human species, but by actual human beings—veritable men, women, and children, with unmistakably human features" (71).

Early on during his stay on Mars, the question arises for Stranger of *why* Martian and terrestrial humans should look so much alike. The only significant difference is a very pale blue hue to the complexion of the Martians of the city of Grensum among whom he lives (although another race from the region of Dergdunin has red skin); Stranger assumes that the color is related to diet, since he finds his own skin bluing after he has been on the planet a short time. When he puts his question to his Martian host, Kaflin, Stranger learns that the Martians believe that their ancestors originated on Earth when, many centuries earlier, a new star with a system of satellites entered the solar system, nearly collided with the Earth, and brought Earth and Mars into such close proximity that some of Earth's primitive human beings were transferred to Mars, through a process never clearly explained.

The story of Stranger's stay on Mars is organized around an exchange of services. If he will use the mechanical powers of his well-armed spaceship to help the citizens of Grensum repel an invasion of the "wild" red people, Kaflin will teach him Martian techniques for the management of planetary resources. Such an exchange would have the desirable effect of making it unnecessary for the people of Earth to immigrate to (or invade) Mars as their own population increased. After the first successful battle with the people of Dergdunin, Stranger marries Kaflin's daughter Ree and they take their honeymoon aboard the *Shooting Star* so that Ree can have a tour of her ancestral Earth (although Kaflin lays an injunction on Stranger not to leave the spacecraft or set foot on Earth's soil). She witnesses and learns about many of Earth's wonders, atrocities, and absurdities, from the spectacular view of the Amazon and its tributaries to the cruelty of the enslavement of black terrestrial humans, from the "huge size and din of the great modern Babylon" of London (286) to the unpleasant aftertaste of tobacco. "But smokheen is really nasty," Ree says in her accented English. "The taste is in my mouth now" (246). When the *Shooting Star* becomes encrusted with debris from the Cotopaxi volcano and needs to be cleaned, Stranger realizes he will have to break his promise to Kaflin not to alight on the Earth. Casuistically, Ree announces that *she* never promised to stay in the ship and volunteers to go out to clean it. That gives MacColl an opening for one of the few moments in the narrative that has the stamp of the Society for the Promotion of Christian Knowledge on it. Stranger comments, "Never before had I seen her so excited, and never before look so beautiful. She was a true daughter of Eve, though born on another planet. The forbidden fruit she *would* have" (252).

Partaking of the forbidden fruit has the usual consequence. On the return flight, Ree develops a fever that turns to delirium—presumably the result of infection developed when she was on the ground—and she dies enroute to Mars, though not before Stranger initiates her into Christianity and teaches her the doctrine of the soul's immortality. Back on Mars, Stranger finds himself again at war with the red people of Dergdunin, who this time are definitively beaten, but at the cost of the lives of Ree's father and brothers. In his grief, Stranger retreats to Earth after giving his promise either to return permanently to Mars or to return temporarily with a space vehicle for them to use, but in any case never to share the secret of the technology with his fellow terrestrials. That proviso becomes easier to fulfill when, on his return to his home in Scotland, his housekeeper and her daughter, despite his warnings to stay away from the *Shooting Star*, slip in, accidentally start it up, and fly off screaming, never to return. And the manuscript strikes the same sexist chord already heard: "Alas! the forbidden fruit seems ever to have an irresistible charm for women" (331).

While he is working to build a new spacecraft, Stranger is confined by relatives, aghast at his story of interplanetary travel, to an asylum. His manuscript stops at the point when he was released from confinement and took up his brief, two-month stint as a schoolmaster before making his final flight to Mars. In a closing discussion between the narrator-editor Jones and some friends, the credibility of the manuscript is debated. Is it a hoax, or the work of a madman, or a true story? To one reader it is "a story wilder than the wildest of the 'Arabian Nights'"; to another it is "not a whit wilder than the recent achievements of the phonograph" (335). All agree, though, that the Martian phenomena reported in Mr. Stranger's unsealed manuscript are in "perfect accordance" and "exact agreement" with scientific laws and theories (337).

It is a truism in discussions of science fiction, particularly of early scientific romances and "space operas," that it is a genre in which character matters less than an agenda. Like most truisms, it is a flatfooted approximation of the truth. In some of the most deeply engaging science-fictional narratives, ideas achieve their hold on readers because of the psychological subtlety of the characters that embody the book's agenda. Both Joseph Stranger and Aleriel stand out from the narratives they record as men of feeling, early examples of the figure of the alien—and in the case of MacColl's protagonist, the earliest instance in

Martian fiction of the alien who is alienated from himself. In his multiple journeys between worlds (first solo to Mars, then with his wife to Earth, back to Mars with his dying wife, to Earth as a mourning widower, back again to Mars to keep his bargain to return), Mr. Stranger's identity becomes increasingly problematic. Is he finally Martian or Scot? Were his students right that he was out of this world? Like later Martians or Terrestrials who become expatriates in space—George DuMaurier's Martia in The Martian (1897), C. S. Lewis' Ransom in Out of the Silent Planet (1938), Rex Gordon's Gordon Holder in No Man Friday (1957), Walter Tevis's T. J. Newton in The Man Who Fell to Earth (1963), Kim Stanley Robinson's Michel Duval in Red Mars (1993)—Joseph Stranger is an emblem of the isolation and disappointment that can flow from the dashed expectations of discovery, of the would-be Columbus who ends up an Orpheus, if not an Icarus. Some of the finest narratives about Mars have at their heart a deep, modern melancholy, and Mr. Stranger's Sealed Packet is the first of those books.

In A Plunge into Space, Robert Cromie describes a journey markedly different from that of the lonely voyages of MacColl and Greg. The seven-man crew that Cromie sends into space is the largest extraterrestrial expedition in any nineteenth-century romance until The War of the Worlds and brings a cross-section of professional talents to the exploration (and exploitation) of Mars. Henry Barnett, the hermit-inventor of the fabled new theory of gravitation, is constructing a large globe-shaped vehicle in the Alaskan wilderness. He chooses to staff the expedition with a seasoned explorer and adventurer who has braved "bears in the Rockies, blacks in the Congo, simooms in Arabia"; a businessman prepared to invest in Mars; a journalist who will record the details of the sojourn; a novelist; a painter; and a politician. Their first glimpse of the steel globe elicits a pair of comments that nicely capture the way in which this book, like others of the period, straddles ancient fantasy and modern science, the fabulous and the technological. The journalist says of the vehicle, "It beats the 'Arabian Nights,'" but the politician, choosing a contemporary reference point, finds that it "certainly beats the Eiffel Tower."[21]

Cromie dedicated his book to Jules Verne, who wrote a short preface to the second edition, praising the "weird and wild" invention of his English "pupil," but wishing that A Plunge into Space provided "more details, more facts and figures in connection with the stupendous phenomena" (5). In at least one respect, A Plunge into Space has much less of the Verne manner than Greg's Across the Zodiac, which is full of facts, figures, calculations. Where Greg had his traveler take a month and a half to reach Mars, during which he made minute records of times, temperatures, weights, distances covered, diameters, and radii, Cromie imagines a 13-hour flight at 50,000-plus miles per hour along an "ether line," as simple and uneventful as an overnight train journey. His seven travelers enjoy a sumptuous picnic dinner of fish and game, delicacies from the London shops, freshly brewed tea, and whiskey; only pipes and cigars have to be foregone in the interests of keeping the air supply fresh. There are glorious views of the stars out the window, but weightlessness is never acknowledged at all. Cromie himself suggests the analogy with luxurious train travel when at the conclusion of the flight the spacecraft "sank to the surface of the planet, and rested upon it with a shock no greater than that of a shunting locomotive" (85). In the mechanics of space flight, A Plunge into Space actually is closer to the Arabian Nights' methods of transport than it is to the scientific plausibility that Verne attempted in From the Earth to the Moon (1865) and Around the Moon (1870).

But Cromie shines in his account of the initial landing site on Mars in the Secchi Continent (as the region was called in Flammarion's map). The crew reacts with horror to the "dead waste" of red sand and dull red sky, "fitting landscape for the well-named planet Mars, the god of war, desolation, and death." The antiromantic first view of the planet prompts feelings of anti-climax: "And is this Mars?" the professional explorer in the group asks (87). The narrator elaborates, "Well might the bitter exclamation pass from lip to lip. Was this what they had done and dared so much to see? Was this sorrowful wilderness the reward of a venture more gallant and audacious than ever man had yet achieved? Was this all?" (87). The writer and the painter, surveying the monotonous, nearly featureless equatorial plain, conclude, "For literature and art there was practically nothing in it" (94). A description follows of the misery of contending with the ubiquitous sand, a description of a sort that would not be surpassed for its uncompromising sense of the alienness of Mars until Kim Stanley Robinson's novels more than a hundred years later:

> It was almost impossible to walk in the soft fine sand. Besides, every foot-step stirred up little clouds of it which rose in blinding wreaths, and filled their eyes, ears, and nostrils. There was no protection against its penetrating particles. It was everywhere; irritating and inflaming every pore. (88)

The dust clouds through which the expedition must make its way cause Barnett to make the only commentary on the canali that I have discovered in fiction published before 1892: "I am convinced that the canals which Schia-parelli observed from Milan in '77 are in reality simooms crossing the great central continents of Mars. If he was observing Mars at this moment he would draw a canal in his chart in the exact course we are traveling" (92–93). Here is the first, and far from last, theory offered by literary and scientific writers in the

1890s to account for the lines that Schiaparelli and his followers detected on the Martian surface.

When Barnett and his crew move into an inhabited region in the south temperate zone and discover a "paradise" of lush fruit trees, silvery (but shallow) seas, verdurous mountains, and blue skies in which the large-headed Martians have established a progressive society, the romance becomes abruptly more predictable. Cromie provides the usual genderless costumes, absence of titles, universal language, single nation, and comely young woman with whom both the writer and the politician become infatuated. The Earthmen give her, as they do everyone they meet on Mars, a terrestrial nickname that approximates the true Martian names they have trouble pronouncing. In her case, it is "Mignonette"—the French equivalent to Cutie Pie. As the title of chapter 12 suggests, all this is just "The Old Story" transferred once more to Mars. The highly automated Martial civilization harnesses the "beneficent giant" of electricity (168) to see to every human need from public transport to climate control, and an array of domestic mechanical devices has replaced any need for servants: coat racks that disappear with one's coat, beds that sing lullabies to put one to sleep, polite machines that serve meals and clear the table.

But even more than most utopias, this one is above all defined by what it lacks. The Earth visitors find the food wanting in seasoning and the wine weak, the theatrical entertainments so empty of content that the painter dismisses them as "bosh" (149). A litany of negatives informs us that Mars has no government, no money, no soldiers, no navy, no judges, no lawyers, no police, no trains or buses, no crowds or slums, no disease, and no strife. In this inventory of its deficits, the Mars of A Plunge into Space seems to merit Hillegas' label of a "dull utopia," but just as clearly, Cromie intended that the reader weigh the achievements against the losses and ask whether insipidity is an acceptable price for progress. When the travelers propose some examples of terrestrial literature to young Martian women who have indicated their curiosity, a guardian turns down nearly everything as falling too short of perfection: Scott is too bloody; Tennyson too sentimental; George Eliot too tedious; Tolstoy too brutal; Hugo too morbid; Thackeray too bitter. In the Martians, we are told, "the hell of human passion is calmed and still" (180) and "the animal had been suppressed and supplanted by the intellect" (112). The effect is chilling—and H. G. Wells capitalized on this horrific notion a few years later in The War of the Worlds with his heartlessly intellectual Martians who are "heads—merely heads."[22]

The original intention of Barnett was to have his group of seven remain on

Mars for two years to conduct a full survey of the planet, until the next opposition of the two planets enabled them to take a short, direct route home. But after only two months, the Martians are eager to be rid of the corrupting influence of their visitors and the Earthmen have become sick and tired of Mars. However, Mignonette has fallen in love with the writer, and she stows away on the steel globe. And here, in the final chapters, Cromie reveals fully the ironic and anti-romantic perspectives that have been percolating beneath the surface of the whole narrative. Not realizing that the supply of oxygen has been calculated carefully for the needs of seven, not eight, passengers and accidentally causing a leak in the oxygen tanks when she went into her hiding place, Mignonette precipitates a crisis. Someone has to be thrown overboard for the common good—and everyone but the writer agrees that the logical person to be sacrificed is the stowaway herself, and if not her then the writer who flirted with her. When the men cannot bring themselves to forcibly expel Mignonette from the spacecraft, they seize on the writer. But then Mignonette does "the right thing" and casts herself out to die in space. In a conclusion that C. S. Lewis may have borrowed for the ending of *Out of the Silent Planet*, the ship makes it back safely, though just barely, with the crew on the edge of asphyxiation. The vehicle lands in Guinea, but the writer—crazed by love and loss—blows it up with Barnett and himself inside and the secret of space travel is blown up with them.

A Plunge into Space has some of the whimsical inventiveness of *Bellona's Bridegroom*, but its Irish author offers dark and bitter undertones unlike anything we find in the other Martian fictions of this period. The faintly gloomy romanticism of *Aleriel* and *Mr. Stranger's Sealed Packet* gets a bracing corrective in Cromie's challenge to the doctrine of progress. The portrait of an overripe world on Mars in which there is nothing left to invent or explore, in which the decadence of the natives is matched by the crudity of the terrestrial expedition, in which a Martian wasteland and a Martian material paradise coexist uneasily may have had its most immediate impact on a scientific romance that had nothing to do with Mars at all—Wells's *Time Machine* (1895), with its witless and insipid Eloi and its creatures of the night, the Morlocks, sharing a grim lost paradise. But in the direct line of fiction about Mars, it may be Ray Bradbury's *Martian Chronicles* (1950) that carries the blending of romanticism and ironic criticism that Cromie pioneered to its richest possibilities.

The final example among this group of early Martian narratives is, from one point of view, anomalous. It has no space craft—neither ether car, nor ethereal disc, nor steel globe. There is no Martian visitor to Earth and no terrestrial expedition to Mars. Interplanetary travel is never even a possibility. *Messages from Mars, By the Aid of the Telescope Plant* has a ridiculous title and is probably the most obscure Martian romance of the 1880s and 1890s—and the most difficult for a contemporary reader to obtain. Three noncirculating copies are held in rare book libraries in the United States, and the most practical, though uncomfortable way to read it is on microfilm at the Library of Congress. The life of the author Robert D. Braine is a blank in history; he seems never to have published anything else, and he was not well-served by the publisher of *Messages from Mars*. The book was wretchedly produced, and seems hardly to have been copyedited or proofread at all, with numerous printing errors, misspellings, verbs and subjects lacking in agreement, words repeated, and words omitted. On the surface, it appears hardly worth the trouble of spooling through the machine.

And yet this book is often astoundingly inventive and it offers as complete a demonstration as one could desire of where the literary history of Mars stood in the crucial year of 1892, the year of the first close opposition between Mars and Earth since Schiaparelli's and Hall's dramatic observations in 1877, and just two years before Percival Lowell entered the scene and transformed the subject of Mars in the popular imagination. The missing space ship aside, *Messages from Mars* includes nearly all the major icons characteristic of the early phase of Martian romance. It is dedicated to Camille Flammarion. It contains, within the narrative itself, an extensive, detailed discussion of the fiction of Jules Verne. The favorite childhood readings of its protagonist, a sailor from Chicago named Victor Nordhausen, were the *Arabian Nights*, Defoe's *Robinson Crusoe*, and adventure stories set in "the wilds of Central Africa."[23] The protagonist, shipwrecked on the uncharted island of Roxana in the Indian Ocean, is saved from execution by a priestess-princess named Raimonda with whom he falls in love. The island, which is simultaneously and improbably at once Edenic, technologically progressive, and sociologically brutal, is in direct communication with Mars, whose utopian society is presented in full. Nordhausen, aided by Raimonda, is drawn into this communication and, a latter-day Gulliver, he has an often deliciously satirical exchange on Martial and terrestrial cultures with the Brobdingnagian king of Mars. To crown all, there is the central nineteenth-century image for understanding Mars. The giant telescope on Roxana, with an enormous lens derived from the fabulous telescope lily alluded to in the subtitle, somehow manages to combine fantasy with realism. As absurd as the idea of a telescope plant is, it comes closer than all those ether ships running on antigravity to the definitive mode of interplanetary travel in the nineteenth century—which was mental rather than physical, telescopic rather than astronautical.

When Nordhausen washes up on the island of Roxana, the sole survivor of his wrecked ship, he accidentally breaks a stalk of a large and peculiar plant growing near the beach and is threatened with death by the island's inhabitants for sacrilege, since the telescope-plant is an object of worship. Under the protection of the young priestess Raimonda, Nordhausen learns that "the secret of the habitation of the starry worlds had been solved here in this out-of-the-way island, by the simple people, isolated from all the world—a secret which had been the despair of the greatest philosophers and astronomers in our own country, and Europe" (62). Communication between Roxana and Mars (whose actual name, we learn, is Oron) was established by signal lights of many colors flashing in complex patterns. Visual contact with the Oronites was made fifty years earlier when two European astronomers (one of whom was Raimonda's father) built a great Starion (the Roxanian word both for the telescope plant and the actual telescope constructed by the astronomers using the gigantic lens of the exotic plant). When Nordhausen sees the great Starion of Roxana, he rhapsodizes on the telescope, as Percival Lowell would just a couple of years later, as the distinctive modern instrument of exploration, a vessel of discovery with which an explorer could descry new lands as surely as Columbus had from the Santa Maria. "Was it possible," Nordhausen asks, "that that little tube before me would lay bare the secrets of another world?" (72)

On Oron, astronomers have even larger telescopes, and when Oronite and Roxanian observers train their instruments on each other, they are able to see one another and communicate, with the aid of another device that the Martians have taught the islanders to construct: a chromograph, which seems to combine the principles of the color television and the fax machine to reproduce the eye-language of color used on Oron. When Nordhausen gets a close-up view through the telescope, he sees that the Oronites do not look like terrestrial human beings. They are ten feet tall, have very large eyes that constantly and subtly change hue as they "speak," and enjoy ten fingers to each hand and ten long finger-like toes on each foot (all of which, he later learns, come into play in their complex musical performances). The Oronites have no mouths but do have a three-foot-long proboscis, abundant tawny hair resembling a lion's mane, and a pointed white horn growing from their foreheads. All food is liquid, taken once a day from a special elixir of nutrients stored in a gigantic reservoir, and sucked through the nostrils of the proboscis.

If Braine's Martians are clearly more alien physiologically than the terrestrial simulacra common in other narratives of the period, they are nonetheless reliably utopian in their social arrangements. Having eradicated disease-carrying bacilli, they typically live to about the age of six hundred. They have achieved universal comfort and prosperity and practice population control to ensure that their numbers remain stable at twenty million, which they have determined is the carrying capacity of their planet. Technological inventions include the cerebellograph and the vitalometer, which measure fitness of mind and body and are used to determine all social choices, from which citizens will be granted the privilege of reproduction, to which are qualified to pilot the airships, to which are suited for public office.

Many features of Martian society are the familiar stuff of utopian convention. Private ownership of land or houses is unknown; work is indistinguishable from pastime and typically takes up no more than two hours a day; there is neither war nor capital punishment; and crime is understood as a rarely occurring form of insanity that is treated in a hospital or asylum. Unlike most other Martian utopias, however, this one is not urban in organization. There are no cities on Oron because technology—including especially the airships and the chromograph—make it unnecessary for people "to live cooped up by thousands when they could live just as comfortably and conveniently in a larger space" (169). Braine goes farther than any of his contemporaries in making his utopia a litany of subtractions:

> The Oronites have no money—no banks, no burglars—no absconding bank cashiers—no stocks—no bonds—no stock companies—no railroads, no ships—no sailors—no cities—no wharves—no boats—no canals—no bridges—no horses—no wagons—no vehicles of any description.
>
> They have no fashions—no shoes—no hats—no distinctive dress for men and women—no personal ornaments—no paint—no powder—no hair pins— no barbers—no hair dressers.
>
> They have no stores—no hotels—no restaurants—no meat—no vegetables . . . (162–63)

The catalogue runs for a page and a half, concluding with "no envy—no spleen— no avarice—no jealousy—no purse-proud people—and no aristocrats" (163). Mars seems a Thoreauvian paradise in which the advice to "simplify, simplify" has been taken fully to heart.

Most of the second half of *Messages from Mars* follows the standard format for a utopian dialogue. Nordhausen, in telescopic visual contact with the Raon [or king] of Oron while Raimonda on the chromograph acts as translator of the eye-language, will ask a question, such as "May I ask how the people are educated?" (182). Nordhausen's question will then generate a chapter of exposition by the Raon, interrupted by comments or questions from Nordhausen and rejoinders from Raon, often eliciting damaging information about how matters are conducted on Earth. One of the most intriguing subjects, since it indicates some artistic self-consciousness on Braine's part, is literature. Nordhausen is surprised to learn that very few books are written on Oron and innocently asks, "Is it possible that you are without the great army of novelists and romancers which with us fill every nation with their stories?" But the Raon has no concept of fiction, and Nordhausen must define for him the practice of novelists: "authors whose sole business is to cudgel out of their brains a string of incidents which might possibly have happened, but which never did happen" (210). To illustrate the terrestrial taste for fantasy ("the more impossible the incidents related, the better the readers like them"), Nordhausen chooses a contemporary example about a spaceship, and goes on to explore the relationship between the literary imagination and scientific study:

> I told him that a native of France had written a book in which he told how a huge ball of hollow metal had been fitted up as a room, and fired by the explosion force of gun cotton from an enormous cannon built in the earth with prodigious labor; that its flight had been watched with one of the largest telescopes on the earth and it had been seen to travel until it reached the sphere of attraction of the moon, when it was drawn into the orbit of that body, and immediately commenced to revolve around it. I told him that the same man had written a book called a "Journey to the center of the Earth," in which a story was given of how several inhabitants of the earth had descended in the extinct crater of a volcano and penetrated to the regions of fire near the center of the earth. Both these books described things which are clearly impossible, and yet they were read with the greatest interest by the people of the earth. I further told him that these works of imagination were so popular on the earth that they vastly exceeded in number the works on philosophy, geography, chemistry, science, etc., and that many people during their entire lives never read anything else than these books which describe these impossible and false events. I told him that so great was the preference for these works of fiction as we call them, that many of our greatest men have written works of science and serious instruction in the form of these romances, since in that form many more people will read them than if they had been announced as sober works of science. (210–11)

The Raon is flabbergasted. Here, he concludes, is further evidence of the insanity of the terrestrials, since no one on Oron could conceive of writing or reading anything but the absolute truth. The Oronites almost never read history because it is full of errors that have since been corrected, and when scientists discover something new or revise a previous understanding, all the books are immediately changed and the parts that are no longer true are removed. Nordhausen is moved to reflect on "what magnificent bonfires there would be if every book containing the least grain of falsehood in my country" had to be destroyed (213).

As with many utopian dialogues, the satire in this instance can cut both ways, since both author and reader of *Messages from Mars* are actively colluding in the kinds of imaginative pleasures and imaginary events denounced by the Oronites. But the sharpest satire is usually reserved for terrestrial practices. The Raon hears approvingly of the outlawing of various kinds of torture that had once been condoned on Earth, but he is shocked to learn about the prevalence of alcoholism in Nordhausen's own country. "By some queer crook of the Orontic intellect," Nordhausen observes in his best imitation of Gulliverian naïveté, "the Raon could not see the very obvious distinction between killing a man after poisoning his mind and body with whiskey, and stabbing him slightly every day for a year, until he finally died of the injuries. These Oronites have curious ways of looking at things, which are considered so simple on the earth that a boy of ten can understand them" (237). Then, when they discuss the draconian regulation of marriage and reproduction on Oron, Nordhausen's "bosom swelled with patriotic pride when I dwelt on the absolute liberty we enjoy in free America" (238). But the Raon is unimpressed with American individualism and freedom from government regulation. The absence of forethought about how the country will support and improve the lot of children born into disease and poverty strikes the Raon as most unenlightened. He gets Nordhausen to admit that most such children will end up, if employed at all, in the most menial jobs "so that in reality they are little better than slaves to the rest of the people" (239).

By the time he has concluded his sessions with the Raon, not only is Nordhausen ready to return home to try to reform his country's social practices, he asks for instructions on how to design a cerebellograph so that it can be manufactured in the United States. "The American Congress was greatly in need of some such instrument," he explains to the Raon, "in order to ascertain that the brains of the congressmen who made speeches, and were about to introduce important measures, were in proper condition. I also told him I thought that it would prove useful in examining the heads of lecturers, authors, etc., before they appeared before the public" (240–41). But Nordhausen's resolve to return to America precipitates a final crisis on the island of Roxana.

Raimonda warns him that as they become aware of his intention to leave, the Roxanians are determined to carry out their earlier plan to execute Nordhausen, despite the Raon's orders to spare him. The islanders fear that if he goes on a proselytizing tour in the United States, he will end up returning to Roxana "with ships and soldiers to enslave them, take their island, and rob them of their homes" (244). This specter of American imperialist adventure turns out, perhaps, to be warranted by what happens when Nordhausen escapes from the island and makes his way back to Chicago. His mother, to whom he tells the whole story, persuades him "to acquaint my fellow countrymen with my wonderful discoveries through the medium of this book" (256). The decision to write the book is in keeping both with his promise to the Raon to try to convert the people of Earth to more enlightened behavior and with his own argument that works of fiction have greater power than factual treatises. And Nordhausen certainly does seem to be of the Raon's party. Just as Gulliver at the end of his *Travels* has identified so strongly with the rational Houyhnhnms that he ends up sleeping in the stable to be near the horses, so Nordhausen has begun twitching his eyes and pulling on his nose in semi-conscious imitation of the Oronites' linguistic eye-movements and their habit of tugging on their probosces. But the identification is not quite complete. Ominously, at the end of his narrative Nordhausen appeals to any wealthy readers of his memoir who might want to finance an expedition to Roxana to get the use of their great telescope. "Or if the U.S. Government should wish to organize such an expedition, I should be glad to put myself at its head" (257–58). And so we are left with the image of a possible invasion by the United States Army, with Nordhausen as conquistador-in-chief. It may be worth remembering that 1892 was not only the year of a close opposition of Mars and the Earth, but the four hundredth anniversary of Columbus's "discovery" of the Americas.

Robert Braine's Martian narrative, for all its crudity of execution and production, ends up being a remarkably transparent example of the intersection of fantasy and cultural history, richly representing and interrogating terrestrial and specifically American nineteenth-century values. And a fascinating final note is appended to the narrative, which we must presume was added while the book was in press—perhaps as a result of the new attention to Schiaparelli's observation in newspaper accounts in the summer and autumn of 1892 as the opposition approached. In the long list of utopian deficits on Oron, "no canals" is tucked unobtrusively into a long list of other artifices not present on Mars. But canals were suddenly in the public awareness when *Messages from Mars* was about to appear, and so Braine adds this paragraph to his book, stimulated by what I take to be, but what needn't be, an imaginary reader:

NOTE.—I have a communication from Jas. Farmaque of Milwaukee, Wis., asking for an explanation of the canals, or supposed canals which have been seen by several astronomers in Mars. In reply I will state that in all my observation of the planet by the aid of the Great Starion of Roxana, I never saw anything like a canal. All transportation is done by the electric air-ships. What the astronomers took for canals were no doubt the flower forests of Mars. These consist of immense trees which are covered at certain seasons of the year with gorgeous flowers. Some of these forests form a vast strip of verdure and flowers from one side of the continent of Rabiggia to the other. These are no doubt what the astronomers have seen and mistaken for canals. Observers have noted the fact that these supposed canals disappeared and changed at certain times. This was probably due to the fact that the trees forming the flower forests only bloom at certain periods.— V.N. (259)

Here is a line of demarcation in the early history of Martian narratives. After Braine, and indeed after the opposition of 1892, it is increasingly difficult for all but the most single-mindedly oblivious romancers to ignore the public discussion of the *canali*. Either the canals are included in the portrait of Mars, with or without acknowledgment to Schiaparelli and later to Lowell, or they must—as here—be subjected explicitly to an alternative fictional explanation. Braine's decision to take the canals as an illusion may have been partly a convenience to avoid revision of a completed manuscript, but it is also an opening shot in the controversy that was about to erupt in fiction, in scientific journals, and in the popular press over the next two decades.

The opposition of 1892 turned out to be largely a disappointment for astronomers, since Mars appeared so low in the sky in the northern hemisphere that, despite its relative nearness to the Earth, few features could be discerned clearly and no major new discoveries were made. Even so, newspapers had picked up on the sense of expectancy that scientists had felt and communicated that anticipation to many members of the reading public. Asaph Hall, who had discovered the two Martian moons in 1877 when almost nobody was paying attention to astronomical research, professed amazement at the change in 1892, telling a *New York Times* reporter that "he did not understand why there should be such general popular interest taken at this time in the opposition of Mars."[24] But while Ralph Waldo Emerson's wistful vision in the 1830s of a day when there would be a telescope in every street never came to pass, by the 1890s there was a news stand at nearly every street corner. The combination of fiction writers who had discovered the subject of Mars and Martians and the aggres-

sive interest that journalists had begun to take in the scientific debate about Mars stoked a new public curiosity. From 1892 on, Mars occupied a visible and audible place in popular discourse, and every twenty-six months, as the solar orbits of Mars and Earth drew into alignment, the conversation intensified.

The year 1892 saw one other important contribution to the history of Mars. In that year, Camille Flammarion, to whom Braine dedicated his romance, published volume one of his massive study of the history of observations of Mars, *La Planète Mars*. His preface spoke of the discovery of a Mars "incomparablement plus différent du notre que l'Amerique de Christophe Colomb n'était differente de l'Europe" [incomparably more different from our {Earth} than the America of Columbus was different from Europe]. And yet Schiaparelli's use of "le nom des *canaux*," the French astronomer conceded, inevitably would encourage analogical thinking. To a considerable degree, Flammarion himself, the most outspoken champion of a living Mars among European astronomers, gave analogy a new lease. Commenting on the limitations of Herschel's famous statement on the similarities of Mars and Earth, Flammarion wrote, "Mais l'explication par analogie est evidemment la première que la nature nous offre elle-même. Lorsqu'elle suffit *completement* pour expliquer un phenomene observé, il n'y à pas de raison pour chercher une autre" [But the explanation by analogy is obviously the first that nature itself offers. When it is *complete* enough to explain an observed phenomenon, there is no reason to seek another].[25]

In America, at least, the few readers of La *Planète Mars* would be specialists, since the book was not translated from French, and the common reader would get his ideas about Mars and its canals primarily from the newspapers or from Flammarion's more popular, translated works—including his novel about Mars, *Uranie*, which had appeared in English translation in 1890. But one amateur who did read La *Planète Mars* in French is the subject of the next chapter, and his impact on the representation of Mars in science and in fiction altered the landscape. After 1892—and still more, after Percival Lowell entered the field at the opposition of 1894—came the first great burst of canal-mania and the beginnings of a large body of fiction that took the existence of intelligent life on Mars as a scientifically sanctioned certainty.

percival lowell's mars

No figure is more central to the cultural and literary history of Mars in the twentieth century than Percival Lowell. Born in 1855 into a Massachusetts family with a famous intellectual pedigree, Lowell emerged with stunning suddenness as a major player in the excitement and controversies about Mars when he was nearly forty years old. He completed a bachelor's degree at Harvard in 1876 and took on a role in the family investment business, one element of which was the Lowell textile mills. Between 1883 and 1894, however, he spent only about half his time in Boston, making four extended trips to East Asia. These journeys shaped the first phase of Lowell's writing career. His essays on Japanese and Korean art and society appeared not only in specialist journals but, with considerable regularity between 1886 and 1891, in the *Atlantic Monthly*. Lowell collected many of his observations, reflections, and photographs from his three extended trips in several widely read books, including *Choson: The Land of the Morning Calm: A Sketch of Korea* (1886), *The Soul of the Far East* (1888), *Noto: An Unexplored Corner of Japan* (1891), and *Occult Japan* (1894). But in the early months of 1894, his name surfaced in connection with an altogether different locale, though to New Englanders one nearly as remote and exotic, not in the Orient but in the American West.

Lowell was featured in stories in the *Boston Herald* that portrayed him as the financial backer of a new observatory, to be constructed under the auspices of Harvard University in the clear, unpolluted air of the Arizona Territory. He was not pleased by the newspaper coverage. Repeated allusions to the planned building as an outpost of Harvard—references encouraged, maybe planted, by the director of the Harvard College Observatory, Edward Pickering—angered Lowell, who quickly made it known to the paper's editor that he was more than just an underwriter, that Harvard would have no control over or affiliation with the observatory, and that he would direct operations and set the observatory's agenda. He telegraphed his assistant, Andrew Ellicott Douglass, who was scouting the sites from which Flagstaff finally would be selected, with instructions on how to respond to press inquiries about the project: "Simply call it the Lowell Observatory."[1]

Journalists might have been pardoned for assuming that the enterprise belonged to Harvard, for while the Lowell family fortune was a very public fact and the family's ties to Harvard were prominent (poet James Russell Lowell had been on the modern languages faculty), few people knew of any credentials that Percival Lowell had as an astronomer. He possessed a solid foundation in mathematics, but was largely an autodidact in astronomical research, with almost no professional connection to the scientific community outside his circle of acquaintances at Harvard. Both of his assistants in setting up the Lowell Observatory were men on leave from the Harvard Observatory, the young A. E. Douglass and William Henry Pickering, professor of astronomy and brother of the director. But official Harvard paid little attention to him. In all the annual reports that Edward Pickering wrote during his more than forty years as director of the Harvard Observatory, the name of Percival Lowell scarcely ever appears, save for a terse announcement in the 1894 report that must have been prompted by Lowell's complaint about the press coverage. Pickering's text certainly reads as if uttered through clenched teeth: "Leave of absence, without salary, was granted on April 1st, 1894, to Professor W. H. Pickering and Mr. A. E. Douglass, in order that they might join the Lowell Observatory in Arizona. The 12-inch telescope and its stand were leased to Mr. Lowell from May 1st. No connection, however, exists between the two observatories."[2]

Abbot Lawrence Lowell, who would become Harvard's president in 1909 and his brother Percival's first biographer in 1935, later described him, in a metaphor suggestive both of the frontiersman and the canal-digger, as a man who "plowed his own furrow largely by himself in the spirit of a pioneer."[3] Late in his career, Lowell offered a prickly assessment of his status as an amateur astronomer. Lecturing before the Harvard Union, he recalled an unwelcoming educational environment thirty-five years earlier. Professors did not take the trouble to introduce undergraduates to scientific work because it would have "interfered with original research," he charged. "In my day at Harvard absolutely no instruction in astronomy was given, and even access to the observatory was denied though I managed to squeeze in by special favor to sit by [painter E. L.] Trouvelot while he sketched the planet Jupiter." And then he added, with undisguised glee, "*Tempora mutantur*; Harvard now asks to visit Flagstaff."[4] In a career marked by public celebrity but scanty academic respect, Lowell took his revenges when he could.

Until recently, it was assumed that Lowell's career change from gentleman-author of travelogues on Asian arts and customs to builder and director of a major private observatory was inexplicably abrupt. An often-repeated anecdote, credited to his friend George Agassiz, has Lowell discovering, while in Japan in 1893, that Schiaparelli's deteriorating eyesight was forcing him into retirement; then and there, the story goes, Lowell determined that he would take up the Schiaparelli legacy.[5] But there was more to the decision than an opportunistic response to Schiaparelli's health. David Strauss's painstaking research into papers at both the Lowell Observatory Archives and Harvard Archives has demonstrated that Lowell's astronomical interests persisted from his undergraduate days and began to get "more systematic" in the early 1890s. Before leaving for his final trip to Japan in 1892, for instance, he requested a tour of the facilities at the Harvard Observatory and asked Edward Pickering for copies of Schiaparelli's maps of Mars.[6] Presumably, those maps (if he received them) were in his luggage along with the telescope that he said he took with him to search, unsuccessfully, for good viewing locations in the Far East.[7]

Two Christmas presents, spaced twenty years apart, hint at how a durable though latent passion for astronomy and, especially for the study of Mars, suddenly possessed Lowell as 1893 turned to 1894. When he was seventeen, his mother had presented him with a Christmas gift of the book that was probably more responsible than any other publication for stirring an interest in the stars and planets among the young throughout the later nineteenth century: Richard Proctor's *Other Worlds Than Ours*. Then, in 1893 when he returned to the United States for good from his ten-year sojourn in Asia, Lowell's Aunt Mary Putnam gave him another Christmas book, this one perhaps symptomatic of a change in professional interests already underway: Camille Flammarion's *La Planète Mars*. This exhaustive compendium, by the astronomer who had become the chief European popularizer of solar-system astronomy, would have brought Lowell fully up to date on the state of the question about Mars up through the opposition of 1892. His copy is full of penciled marginalia, many technical and mathematical annotations, a few more informal asides ("a jaunty remark!" he writes of one of Flammarion's more flamboyant statements), and some corrections of mistakes.[8]

Nevertheless, if curiosity about Mars was longstanding, something in the mid-1890s stirred that quiescent interest into a passion. The trigger seems to have been as much cultural as personal. The small world of Boston intellectuals gave Lowell easy access to a crucial person who shared his enthusiasms and had the connections needed to translate them into action; at the same time, the larger world served by the mass media was at the beginning of a feeding frenzy on things Martian. Popular interest came fully awake in a decade when Mars was frequently in the newspapers, increasingly the subject of fiction writers, and the focus of a team of astronomers using the largest telescope in the world at the newly founded Lick Observatory in California. At the August 1892 opposition, and still more at the next opposition in 1894, Mars became a hot topic throughout Europe and North America. The heat was generated, in part at least, by a few astronomers who, shortcircuiting the usual scientific procedures of publishing their findings after careful reflection and verification in refereed journals, were writing colorful popular books about Mars or were eagerly seeking out the press to report immediately on their observations and conclusions. Of all who wrote on the subject of Mars none had the world-wide impact of Camille Flammarion, and in 1894, Americans with no French could read from a new translation of his *Popular Astronomy*:

> Henceforth the globe of Mars should no longer be presented to us as a block of stone revolving in the midst of the void, in the sling of the solar attraction, like an inert, sterile, and inanimate mass; but we should see in it *a living world*, adorned with landscapes similar to those which charm us in terrestrial nature; a new world which no Columbus will ever reach, but on which, doubtless, a human race now resides, works, thinks, and meditates as we do on the great and mysterious problems of nature. These unknown brothers are not spirits without bodies, or bodies without spirits, beings supernatural or extra-natural, but active beings, thinking, reasoning as we do here.[9]

In Europe, Camille Flammarion was the exemplar of the new breed of astronomer, and the bane of more conservative scientists. In the United States, the most prominent case was someone whose path was intersecting with Lowell's: William Pickering.

In the summer of 1892, Pickering sent a series of cables full of his latest discoveries to the *New York Herald* from Harvard's Arequipa Station high in the Andes, where he had trained his telescope on Mars (despite the fact that he had been sent there primarily for stellar observations). The result, to the dismay and embarrassment of William's older brother Edward, the Harvard Observatory Director and his boss, was a sensational account of forty new lakes on Mars that Pickering claimed to have sighted and weather reports detailing the dates and locations of snowfalls and melts on the planet. The younger Pickering came in for a blistering interrogation by Edward Holden of the Lick Observatory. "How does he know the dark markings are lakes? Why does he not simply call them dark spots? And is he sure there are forty?"[10] Pickering made the lame and defensive reply that cables have to be condensed, that editors sometimes inaccurately fill out the outlines of a telegraphic dispatch, and that he had stated things more precisely in an 1892 article in the journal *Astronomy and Astro-Physics*. His response sidestepped the real question that Holden was posing—and that later would be raised repeatedly about Percival Lowell's dealings with the press: Why was Pickering communicating to "the newspaper readers of the whole world" before vetting his claims with scientific colleagues?[11]

William Pickering had first met Lowell, home from one of his Eastern voyages, shortly before setting out for the Andes in 1890; and it was Pickering, the first American translator of Schiaparelli, with whom Lowell talked just after New Year's 1894 and concocted the venture to Arizona. Their close collaboration did not last very long; by 1896 they had parted company and Pickering returned to Harvard. But they both seemed to have a temperamental affinity for sensation and controversy. Throughout Lowell's life and even after his death in 1916, when most astronomers expected the Lowellian theories of Mars would die with him, Pickering remained committed to the canals of Mars. He continued single-mindedly to send in reports from Harvard's observing station in Jamaica about new canal sightings, of which his brother Edward took dutiful, though undoubtedly pained notice in his annual reports. Until 1930, he continued writing regularly about the canals for *Popular Astronomy* and he died in 1938, embittered, as William Sheehan has revealed, by the lack of recognition for his work.[12]

When Lowell moved from Boston to the Arizona Territory in the spring of 1894 to open his observatory on a steep bluff a mile west of the little downtown of Flagstaff, which he named Mars Hill, he did not so much initiate a revolution in the popular perception of Mars as give it shape and definiteness and conviction. For the next two decades, he would be both point man and cheerleader for the pro-life faction among astronomers studying Mars and the icon of the public and the press as interest in Martian matters accelerated. The Mars that Lowell championed was big, exciting, romantic, and richly textured. Lowell's vision was extraordinarily artful and literary in presentation. Nevertheless, it was more creation than discovery, and his contribution to the science of Mars was in many respects retrograde. Lowell saw himself as the successor of Schiaparelli, but, in strictly scientific terms, he did little to advance the study of Mars beyond where Schiaparelli had taken it. If anything, the effect of all Lowell's telescopic surveys of Mars, from 1894 until 1916, was to institutionalize a few features of Schiaparelli's Mars—above all, of course, the *canali*—and to assemble a vast speculative theory about Mars and Martians that rested on, reinforced, and overreached the Schiaparelli observations. Lowell wrote the most vivid and influential—and profoundly erroneous—chapter in the history of Mars in the human mind, but as Michael J. Crowe concluded in his monumental study of two centuries of debate over extraterrestrial life, the result for the scientific profession was largely disastrous. The effort spent resisting and correcting the Lowell legacy entailed a huge expenditure of time and resources, as well as a loss of public confidence in astronomical research.[13]

The chief elements of Lowell's theory were already present in his first book on the subject, the 1895 *Mars*—composed and published with remarkable speed after his initial series of telescopic observations at Flagstaff in the summer of 1894. While the later *Mars and Its Canals* (1906) and the lectures collected in *Mars as the Abode of Life* (1908) push the theory more aggressively and in more detail, by 1895 Lowell already had begun making his case for a Mars peopled by highly civilized and ingenious beings who were staving off extinction with a global irrigation system. He claimed "proof positive" for a Martian atmosphere, evidence of an "astonishingly mild" climate, the likelihood of little in the way of winds, storms, or mountains. The aging, desiccated planet, he argued, was seasonally greened along the banks of the extensive network of canals constructed to bring water from the melting reservoirs at the poles. Because of the straightness of the lines he saw, some running for thousands of miles, he concluded that these were "cases of assisted nature," not natural geological features. Aware that a line visible from Earth would have to be at least 30 miles in width, he proposed that the term "canals" was a misnomer only in the sense that the lines he observed crisscrossing Mars were not themselves the channels through which the water moved but the belts of vegetation growing on either side of the waterways. Larger dark spots where canals appeared to intersect he called "oases," suggesting a canal system built on a hub-and-spokes principle. Acknowledging that he had no data to make a physical description of the Martians who performed this engineering feat, Lowell deduced that the Martian mind was mathematical, comprehensive, inventive, cosmopolitan, and technically superior to our own. Like later writers of science fiction, he used his imagined alien beings as an instrument for chastening anthropocentric vanity. "Man is merely this earth's highest production up to date. That he in any sense gauges the possibilities of the universe is humorous."[14]

In *Mars*, Lowell cast himself in the role of adventurer and explorer. Mindful of planned expeditions to the Earth's as-yet-unreached Antarctic pole, he positively gloated over the knowledge that he had acquired telescopically of the Martian south pole: "It is also pleasing to remember that during this our polar expedition we were not frost-bitten for life, nor did we have to be rescued by a search party. We lived not unlike civilized beings during it all, and we actually brought back some of the information we went out to acquire."[15] He dedicated his next book, *Mars and Its Canals*, to Schiaparelli, hailing him as "the Columbus of a New Planetary World." Lowell seems to have set his own sights on becoming Mars's Magellan and Mercator, circumnavigating the planet telescopically and mapping it as exhaustively as he could on paper and in the exquisite three-dimensional globes of polished wood he fashioned at each opposition from 1894 forward, adorning them with fine black and red lines to mark the canals that he had most lately sighted (see color plate 4).[16] In a long, unfinished narrative poem, probably composed during his early days at Flagstaff in 1894, he revealed his ambitions more starkly. Titled simply "Mars," the poem is loaded with nautical images. It opens with a statement of his yearning to make the "Voyage beyond the compassed bound / Of our own Earth's returning round." And its final verse paragraph depicts Lowell, the lonely mental traveler in his observatory on Mars Hill, contemplating the future of actual space travel:

> Yet still I sit in my silent dome
> Wharf of this my island home
> Whence only thought may take passage to
> That other island across the blue
> Against hope hoping that mankind may
> In time invent some possible way
> To that longed for bourne that while I gaze
> Through the heaven's heaving haze
> Seems in its shimmer to nod me nay.[17]

The limping versification does not cancel the eloquence and the frustration of a man who lived and died before the coming of the Space Age.

Lowell compensated for what the historical moment denied him with a visionary commitment that verged on pigheadedness. One of the chapters on Lowell in *Planets and Perception*, William Sheehan's invaluable psychological study of three hundred years of telescopic observation, is titled "The Visions of Sir Percival." It is a title that neatly captures the degree to which Mars was Lowell's Grail. The last decade of the nineteenth century was an era of medieval revival, and Lowell's hometown of Boston was building a public library with an enormous set of murals by Edwin Austin Abbey depicting the Quest of the Holy Grail. Nowadays one is tempted to look for the connections between Lowell's Martian writings and later science fiction—indeed, to find Lowell writing a form of science fiction without knowing it. But a backward glance to the old chivalric romances is also relevant. Lowell's books may have a deeper relationship to late Victorian medievalism than to modern planetary astronomy. Cer-

tainly, one of Sheehan's most intriguing contributions to the history of interpretations of Lowell's fascination with Mars is his comment on how Lowell
recalled his childhood fantasies while surveying feudal ruins in Japan: "All
tended to carry my thoughts back to the middle ages, or was it only to my own
boyhood when the name *middle ages* almost stood for fairy land?" Sheehan
wonders if, in envisioning a Martian populace desperately shoring up a threatened civilization on an old planet, "Lowell discovered yet another world that
was, if not in ruins, well on the way to it."[18]

Lowell as Sir Percival is also a reminder of how quests can be not just
inspirational but obsessional. Arthur's court, after all, came to disaster in part
because of mass hysteria among the knights seeking the Grail. In Lowell—
isolated, zealous, defensive, and unwaveringly loyal to what he *saw*—we may
have a case of both illusion and delusion. "Good seeing" is the perpetual,
elusive pursuit of all Earth-bound, atmosphere-plagued astronomers, and it is
what led Lowell to the high desert air of Flagstaff, far away from the pollutions
of light and smog that were making observatories in Paris, Washington, Milan,
Cambridge, and other cities obsolete. The lines taken from *Mars and Its Canals*
and engraved on his mausoleum of Massachusetts granite, built on Mars Hill
next to the dome that houses his most famous telescope, evoke eerily both neo-
Arthurian notions of the spiritually cleansed knight and the classic symptoms
of neurotic egotism:

> Astronomy now demands bodily abstraction of its devotee. . . . To see into
> the beyond requires purity . . . and the securing it makes him perforce a
> hermit from his kind. . . . He must abandon cities and forego plains. . . .
> Only in places raised above and aloof from men can he profitably pursue his
> search. He must learn to wait upon his opportunities and then no less to
> wait for mankind's acceptance of his results . . . for in common with most
> explorers he will encounter on his return that final penalty of penetration
> the certainty at first of being disbelieved.[19]

With his talent for popular expression, a spellbinding tone both on paper
and in person, and ready access to the country's newspapers and magazines,
Lowell was an irritant to and the envy of other astronomers. His fiercest and
most determined critics were his rivals at California's Lick Observatory. Its first
director, Edward S. Holden, launched an effort to undercut public enthusiasm
for Lowellian Mars in an 1895 newspaper article. Without ever using Lowell's
name, Holden castigated the "reckless theorizing" that was having a harmful
effect on "non-professional readers." Flammarion was identified as a culprit,
but with Lowell's *Mars* just reaching bookshops, Holden singled out the pro-

nouncements issuing from "an observatory [that] has recently been founded, devoted chiefly to 'an investigation into the condition of life in other worlds, including their habitability by beings like man.' " Hoping to curb the taste of journalists and "non-professional readers" for sensationalist accounts, Holden attempted a lesson in public education about proper scientific procedures:

> I remember I was asked, in 1890, to telegraph my opinions as to the land and water on Mars, etc. I replied that our observations at the Lick observatory up to that time enabled us to construct an accurate map of the dark and of the bright regions of the planet; but that neither I nor any one could say which regions were land and which were water. This telegram was received with a certain air of disappointment, natural enough, I suppose, to those who had been fed on (alleged) certainties, and who could not conceive that such fundamental matters were still unsettled. They were not settled then, and we have but just obtained a little satisfactory light on them. "I do not know," is a scientific answer, though it is, undoubtedly, a disappointing one when it replies to a question in which the whole world takes a vivid interest. But scientific men are in honor bound to make this answer in so far as it is true, and to be scrupulously exact in their dealings with the public which supports observatories and which has a right to know where certainty ends and speculation begins.[20]

It was a splendidly reasoned and articulate case for caution in making scientific announcements. And Holden had a poignant if naïve faith in the self-respect of a public that would not want to be thought gullible ("But there is room, one would think, for a well-grounded protest on the part of the public against the pertinacity with which conjectures have been presented as facts"). But the only outcries continued to come primarily from scientists.

If Holden thought his article could influence Lowell to temper his public statements and adopt the professional ethos expected of a scientist, he greatly overestimated the ability of the hermit on Mars Hill to be a team player and he had not reckoned with Lowell's immunity to embarrassment. In 1908, when the craze for Mars was in full bloom, William Wallace Campbell, who had succeeded Holden as director of the Lick Observatory, pronounced Lowell "a trial to sane astronomers."[21] With few exceptions, most astronomers continued to dispute and reject Lowell's arguments about the Martian canals, and they were galled that they had little success in dislodging the Lowellian images from people's minds. Lowell rarely submitted his findings to the leading academic journals of astronomy (which were largely under the control of his professional rivals); most of his technical articles appeared in either in-house publications of the Lowell Observatory or *Popular Astronomy* and *Popular Science Monthly*. Reviewers with scientific standing shredded the reasoning in all of his books about Mars—most famously, the former colleague of Charles Darwin, the now-elderly Alfred Russel Wallace, who wrote a book refuting the arguments of *Mars and Its Canals*.[22]

None of this mattered to the popular image of Mars, though the hostility of fellow astronomers to his ideas and their blackballing him from their club embittered Lowell. Not only his three big books but his contributions to the *Atlantic Monthly* and other mass-circulation magazines, his eagerly attended lectures in a number of U.S. cities, on college campuses, and abroad, and the publicity generated in lavishly illustrated magazine supplements to the Sunday newspapers in Boston, St. Louis, New York, Los Angeles, Chicago, and other large cities guaranteed enthusiastic adherents to his theories. Indirectly, Lowell's theories insinuated themselves into the mental texture of many people who didn't follow the scientific news but who read the steadily growing body of fiction, written for both adults and children, that portrayed Lowell's Mars as matter of fact. One of the most interesting of those books was the gorgeously produced *To Mars Via the Moon: An Astronomical Story*, whose author, Mark Wicks, gave it a disciple's dedication:

To
PROFESSOR PERCIVAL LOWELL
A.B., LL.D.
Director of the Observatory at Flagstaff, Arizona
To Whose Careful And Painstaking Researches,
Extending Over Many Years, The World Owes
So Much Of Its Knowledge Of
THE PLANET MARS,
This Little Book Is Respectfully Inscribed By
One Who Has Derived Infinite Pleasure From
The Perusal Of His Works On
The Subject[23]

Lowell lost the debate with the scientists whose recognition as a peer he craved; his consolation was a Pyrrhic victory with the common reader and the community of science fiction writers, a victory sustained well into the middle of the twentieth century.

Much of Lowell's success with the public (and some of his disfavor with scientists) can be traced directly to his rhetorical skills. An astronomer at the Allegheny Observatory wrote to a colleague about some of Lowell's earliest writings on Mars, "I dislike his style. . . . It is dogmatic and amateurish. One would think he was the first man to use a telescope on Mars."[24] But it was precisely that ability to convey an impression of freshness and youthful excitement that connected Lowell to nonspecialist readers. Here is Lowell taking his reader (or listener, since the first incarnation of this passage was in a public lecture) on a fantastic voyage into the heavens:

> Viewed under suitable conditions, few sights can compare for instant beauty and growing grandeur with Mars as presented by the telescope. Framed in the blue of space, there floats before the observer's gaze a seeming miniature of his own Earth, yet changed by translation to the sky. Within its charmed circle of light he marks apparent continents and seas, now ramifying into one another, now stretching in unique expanse over wide tracts of disk, and capped at their poles by dazzling ovals of white. It recalls to him his first lesson in geography, where the Earth was shown him set ethereally amid the stars, only with an added sense of reality in the apotheosis. It is the thing itself, stamped with that all-pervading, indefinable hall-mark of authenticity in which the cleverest reproduction somehow fails.[25]

What the grumpy Allegheny astronomer failed to grasp—and what Lowell never forgot—was that such word-pictures were as close as most members of his audience would ever get to a telescope. Lowell offered what no other Anglo-American astronomer of the era was prepared to give readers: a vicarious experience of the thrill of planetary research. Like the other formidable charmer of the era, France's Flammarion, he mastered the art of instructing novices, though at the expense of fuzzing the boundary between fact and speculation. Unlike his French counterpart, spoofed as Flimflammarion in an American cartoon (see illustration in chapter 7), Lowell steered his romanticizing prose clear of the mystical and (most of the time) the rhapsodical. To the layperson, his words always sounded sensible, his reasoning plausible.

Taking note of the extraordinary fury that Lowell's pronouncements on Mars generated among astronomers, a New York literary review speculated, bitingly and probably accurately, that Lowell had a greater feeling for the power of words than most academic scientists. "If a gracile and limpid style, always comprehensive [sic] to the layman, were the earmark of the charlatan, a good many illustrious ears would be marked—practically all the Frenchmen and William James. But Dr. Lowell's style is more, always consciously picturesque, often passional, occasionally quaint with an agreeable eccentricity. It suggests a poet lost, a joint artistic inheritance with his sister, Amy Lowell, the exceedingly subtle artist in words who is leading the free-verse cohorts."[26] The

Percival Lowell
lecturing, c. 1900.
Courtesy Lowell
Observatory Archives

reviewer, himself so evidently drawn to fustian, manages to capture exactly what must have appealed to late-Victorian middle-class readers of Lowell and exactly what may now strike many readers as an overripe style.

For those who heard Lowell speak, his charismatic presence at the lectern complemented his highly colored vocabulary. Elegance of phrasing and witty metaphors combined to invest cosmological abstractions with compelling human interest. With the faultless diction of his social class, leavened by a common touch, he conveyed an impression of intimacy even in a cavernous lecture hall. Of all the platform presentations of his work that Lowell gave, none is more easily documented than the series of eight slide-lectures under the auspices of Boston's Lowell Institute that he delivered in 1906. Later collected in his third book on Mars, *Mars as the Abode of Life* (1908), the twice-weekly series was so popular that the entire set of Monday and Thursday lectures had to be repeated on Tuesdays and Fridays to accommodate the crowds. Lowell's secretary, who wrote a worshipful memoir of Lowell after his death, reported that the spectacle of crowds in Boylston Street outside Huntington Hall in 1906 made it seem "as if it were grand opera night."[27] Louise Leonard's adulation is confirmed by the extent of coverage in the Boston press, with one newspaper providing lengthy summaries and reviews of each of the eight lectures as they were given. The *Boston Post* called him "an earnest, magnetic speaker" and the *Evening Transcript*'s reviewer wrote of the final presentation, "The lecture as a literary production was of the highest order, abounding with those epigrammatic phrasings which mark Mr. Lowell's productions."[28]

Lowell pursued his mission at Flagstaff in the conviction, from which he never wavered, that Schiaparelli's *canali* constituted "the most startling discovery of modern times."[29] But while Schiaparelli, from the time he first began mapping the *canali* during the opposition of 1877, remained carefully neutral about interpretations of the straight lines he drew, Lowell found it hard to live with ambiguity. In his unpublished narrative poem "Mars," Lowell captured the mood of popular curiosity about Mars in the aftermath of Schiaparelli's publications: "We know just enough to long to know more."[30] Lowell's ambition to fill in the blanks was matched by a public appetite for images of Mars that would turn the *canali* from hypothetical data into an epic story. Lowell celebrated and gratified that appetite. At the close of *Mars and Its Canals*, he linked his fantasies with his audience's in a first-person plural assertion of the compatibility of desire and evidence:

> We have all felt this impulse in our childhood as our ancestors did before us, when they conjured goblins and spirits from the vasty void, and if our energy continues we never cease to feel its force through life. We but exchange, as our years increase, the romance of fiction for the more thrilling romance of fact.[31]

Lowell's gift for transmitting his passion to others was remarkable. Everywhere, people accepted his fiction as fact, and the romance of Mars seized the collective imagination. A visit to the Lowell Observatory in 1906 provides a telling glimpse of the kind of spell Lowell could cast. The zoologist Edward S. Morse, director of the Peabody Museum in Salem, Massachusetts, came to Flagstaff a professed skeptic about the Martian canals. He spent more than a month observing Mars through Lowell's renowned 24-inch Clark telescope. Although Morse insisted that neither Lowell nor his assistants gave him any clues about where to look for markings on the disc, it is not hard to imagine the suggestibility of an old Boston friend and a house guest on Mars Hill— where the usual talk of the canals and the civilization that produced them would have been intensified by the fact that *Mars and Its Canals* was then in page proofs. Moreover, as Strauss has argued, Lowell skillfully maneuvered acquaintances from his Boston network into making public defenses of his

Martian theories when they came under concerted attack by academically affiliated astronomers. Morse, in particular, became Lowell's "bulldog"—and his protestations that he was a converted skeptic may have been disingenuous. In any case, by the end of his stay, Morse announced that he had become a true believer. He had seen lines "geodetically straight, supernaturally so" at Flagstaff and had become convinced that "there can be no question" that those lines were the work of engineers on Mars. Morse wrote, with a convert's breathless zeal, a first-person narrative of his observations and conclusions that began:

> Is Mars inhabited? Unquestionably. It is a world in many respects like our own. It has its sunsets and sunrises. Winds sweep over its surface. Dust storms roll over its deserts. There are snow flurries that leave the Martian landscape white. There are polar snows, rivers and torrents and vast expanses of vegetation.[32]

"A world in many respects like our own." This was not a new theme. Herschel had introduced the analogical mode of Martian description more than a century earlier, and its effective bridging of the known and the unknown, the terrestrial and the extraterrestrial, was an essential ingredient in the popular acceptance of Lowell's suppositions about the *canali*. "Mars, it has been found, is like Holland," one 1895 news report begins. "Its inhabitants appear to have drained nearly the whole of its surface as a measure of protection against encroaching waters, which threaten an invasion when summer's heat melts the polar ice and snow."[33] Mars persistently was conceived and described analogically, both by those who had made first-hand observations of the planet and by those who reported, more or less accurately, on the work of Lowell and his disciples. Fiction writers thrived on the analogical mode of representing Mars. In his didactic novel *Uranie*, Flammarion wrote reassuringly of Martian weather: "A country of Mars situated on the borders of the equatorial sea differs less in climate from France, than Lapland differs from India."[34] Louis Pope Gratacap's 1903 *The Certainty of a Future Life in Mars* likens the experience of floating along a high-banked Martian canal to passing through the Palisades in New York's Hudson River Valley.[35]

Common as the analogical conception of Mars was, Lowell gave it endless variations, despite his own warnings in *Mars and Its Canals* that "offhand analogy with the earth" is risky.[36] The Sunday supplements of American newspapers, which gave full and frequent play to his pronouncements in the first decade of the twentieth century, often used pictorial analogies (drawn directly from Lowell's books) to suggest that the canals were artifacts rather than natural topographical features. A typical layout of the supplement page would feature photos of both Lowell and his Clark telescope, a summary of his latest evidence for the canals, and depictions of one of Schiaparelli's gridded maps and one of Lowell's globes with their long, arcing lines traced across the Martian surface. Ranged alongside the maps would be drawings of terrestrial artifacts: railroad lines in Illinois; a street plan for Montreal; irrigation canals in Arizona; Dutch canals at Groningen. Readers would be left to draw their own analogical conclusion that the lines on Mars were the design of purposeful intelligence.

Lowell himself likened the so-called geminated canals—the lines that appeared both to Schiaparelli and to him to run in tandem—to the tracks of the intercontinental railroad, "stretching off into the distance upon our Western plains," along the route he traveled so often between Boston and Flagstaff.[37] When he defended *Mars and Its Canals* from the attacks of critics, he used an extensive analogy to unfold his theory that the *canali* are fertilized strips of land that border either side of a narrower channel of water:

> What, then, it will be asked, are these so-called canals? The best answer consists in pointing to the Nile. What we call the canals are narrow belts from ten to twenty miles wide on the average. They behave as strips of vegetation would, and such beyond much question is their character. Seen from space the Nile would look not otherwise. It, too, threading its way across a desert, fertilizes a ribbon of country which is some fifteen miles wide. Once each year it grows green after the fashion of the Martian canals, and then in due time lapses again to ocher. The river itself would escape detection from a Martian distance, and still more remain invisible if, as probably on Mars, the fertilizing conduit were smaller still. Canals, then, these lines may with propriety be called, although there is no ground for supposing them to be of herculean description, any more than there would be for deeming the water supply of our cities to be indebted to anything larger than two-foot pipes.[38]

If his habitual analogical reasoning nullified, or at least imperiled, the scientific credibility of his arguments, Lowell deployed it with striking success in popularizing the romance of Mars. He wanted desperately to be right about Mars, but he also was deeply committed to the kind of engaged imagination he brought to his own work and encouraged in others. If we ask what might be the value of the history of an error as massive as Lowell's erroneous conception of Mars, part of the answer must be that he showed that it was possible to persuade people that other worlds mattered, that in constructing images of

Mars and Martians, human beings inevitably constructed images of themselves and their own world. In many of his writings, Lowell took not simply an analogical view of Mars but an exemplary one. In one of his earliest expositions on the subject, he asserted that he had evidence from "the so-called canals" that Mars was not only habitable but actually inhabited by a race whose subordination of provincial self-interest to the larger planetary welfare betokened rational and moral capacities worth our admiration and imitation:

> Of course we cannot be sure that they are our intellectual superiors, but mortifying to our vanity as it may be to do so, we must, however grudgingly, admit that such is altogether probable. For their system of public works is one to which in its marvelous adaptability to its end no earthly system of public works approaches. Young Martians must be born mathematicians and then never outgrow the faculty. In the second place the system betrays a wonderful unity of purpose for it girdles the planet from pole to pole. Race prejudice, national jealousy, individual endeavor are there all subordinated to the common good. The net-work is harmoniously one, from one end of the planet to the other, each line running into the next in the most effective manner all round the globe.[39]

From the imagined geometry of the Martian canals, Lowell drew the imaginative conclusion of a utopian planet on which the fractious Earth might begin to model its own potential for achieving the common good.

In nearly all his speculative writing about Mars, and in the uses to which he urged his readers to put his speculations, Lowell put into practice his principles of education. "To learn to read, to write, to cipher should be changed to learn to re-read, re-write and decipher," he said in 1902. And, further, "To learn to decipher the world about us is the ultimate aim of all education."[40] Lowell's undoing consisted in his singleminded attachment to deciphering something that simply wasn't there. From his first lectures and publications about Mars in 1894 until the 1905 opposition, Lowell was dogged by persistent suggestions from astronomers that the lines he had been seeing and dutifully cataloguing were the product of optical illusion. His responses to all such skeptical reservations were variations on three themes: He used a more suitable telescope, worked from a better location for observing, and had a more acute eye than other astronomers enjoyed. While some other observers confirmed Lowell's sightings, their suggestibility was strongly suspected. Lowell longed for some more objective confirmation, and in 1905 it looked as if he had finally secured it. One of his assistants at the Flagstaff Observatory, Carl Lampland, attempted to photograph Mars during the opposition and capture the canali. Lowell seized on the outcome of Lampland's experimental photography as the long-awaited definitive corroboration of the Martian canals. Surely, however fallible or prejudiced the human eye might be, the camera lens would tell the truth.

The news of the photographing of the Martian canals caused a sensation. In England, the Royal Photographic Society awarded a medal to Lowell and Lampland for their technical breakthrough. One news account spoke of "a distinct epoch in the study of Mars" having been reached.[41] Eugène Michel Antoniadi, whom Flammarion had hired as an assistant at his observatory at Juvisy-sur-Orge, thought the picture of the canal of Iuventae Fons "the greatest triumph ever obtained in planetary photography, and . . . an achievement above praise." But there was less there than met the eye. In later essays and in his 1930 book on Mars, Antoniadi would take a strikingly less charitable view of Lowell's pictorial representations of Mars. "Quelques auteurs sarcastiques ont qualifié les cartes de Mars de Lowell de 'toiles d'arraignée' et de 'terreurs des mouches.' La comparaison n'était guère immeritée." [Some sarcastic writers have described Lowell's maps of Mars as "spider webs" and "the terrors of houseflies." The comparison was hardly undeserved.] Recently and more dispassionately than Lowell's antagonists, psychologist and astronomer William Sheehan has explained how in planetary observation the fleetingness of stable images is actually captured more accurately and sharply by the human eye than by the slow exposure time required by a photographic plate, particularly given the state of the art a hundred years ago.[42] Lowell liked to boast that he was gifted with a quick eye that could detect, in those brief fractions of a second when the telescopic image was stable, features on Mars "with copper-plate distinctness."[43] Because the view through the telescope wouldn't hold still for the slower camera eye, the resulting printed image inevitably looked badly out of focus, indistinct. Mars appeared as if seen by an extremely near-sighted viewer who could make out nothing but the vaguest shapes. Lampland's photographs provided "proof" that could satisfy only those who already had faith in the canals' existence.

That Lowell was unsuccessful in getting the canals to show up clearly in book or magazine reproductions of the photographs was a setback on which he chose not to dwell. The public was now sold on the reality of the canals and on the certainty of the existence of Martians who had built them. When the tiny, blurry Lampland pictures were put on display at the Massachusetts Institute of Technology early in 1906, they drew awed, if somewhat baffled, crowds. "All day long yesterday, singly and in groups, people came to gaze upon the little photographs. So some who came thinking to look upon photographs showing something resembling those of the Erie canal or the 'Soo' were disappointed, but mostly even they gazed learnedly at the pictures, read the rather technical explanations with a grave air, and passed on."[44] In the popular judgment, the controversy over the canals was settled in Lowell's favor. The hypothetical Martians became actual ones. Within a year, a London newspaper could dramatize, in an unqualified headline, the "Tragic Struggle of the Dying Martians." And a writer for the New York Times in 1909 could assert, "The hypothesis of canals on Mars has already emerged from its progress through the usual stages of skepticism, ridicule, and denial which every new advance in science has to encounter."[45]

As the years passed, Lowell continued to issue bulletins with his latest confirmations of his theory. And the press came to anticipate bombshells from Flagstaff each time Mars was in opposition. "Will the New Year Solve the Riddle of Mars?" a full-page illustrated article asks in December 1906. A sphinx is inserted into a drawing of the solar system, above photos of Lowell and the Clark telescope and an excerpt from Mars and Its Canals.[46] Lowell told a Chicago reporter early in 1910 that the opposition of 1909 furnished the "final proof" that Mars was actually inhabited and that the canal system was continuing to grow. He saw "a new canal spring into being last Summer," showing that it "had just been completed by the Martians, water had just been turned into it, and vegetation had just sprung up in a hitherto uninhabitable part of the great desert which comprises most of the planet's surface." The newspaper's front-page headline obligingly took this fiction for a statement of fact: "New Canal Built by Martians."[47] Ironically, it was the 1909 opposition that provided the evidence that astronomers were seeking to put Lowell's claims to rest. A seventy-page analysis for the British Astronomical Association of data amassed from observing stations throughout the southern hemisphere—where the best views of Mars were to be had in 1909—concluded: "The alleged existence of a geometrical network of canals on Mars has received a lasting and unanswerable confutation."[48]

Lowell, with the complicity of credulous (or savvy) journalists, continued to appease the public hunger for new tidbits about Mars, while the rejection of his work by academic scientists became more pointed and more personal than ever. The harshest criticism ever leveled at his work came in the first of a six-month series of extended letters to the editor of the journal Science in 1909 on the theme of scientific ethics. Eliot Blackwelder, Professor of Geology at the University of Wisconsin, assailed Lowell's sins against professional ethics and questioned whether he deserved the title of scientist at all. Leaving astronomical errors to others, Blackwelder confined himself to matters of geology in the recently published *Mars as the Abode of Life* and, in a relentless two thousand-word catalogue, blasted the fallacies in Lowell's understanding of terrestrial geology and the lack of foundation for his Martian extrapolations. The summation is devastating:

> I think enough has been said to show what kind of pseudo-science is here being foisted upon a trusting public. "Mars as the Abode of Life" is avowedly a popular exposition of a science, not a fantasy. Its author is a highly educated man of distinguished connections and some personal fame. He writes in a vivid, convincing style, with the air of authority in the premises. The average reader naturally believes him, since he can not, without special knowledge of geology and kindred sciences, discern the fallacies. He has a right to think that things asserted as established facts are true, and that things other than facts will be stated with appropriate reservation. This is precisely the same as his right to believe that the maple syrup he buys under that label is not glucose, but is genuine. The misbranding of intellectual products is just as immoral as the misbranding of the products of manufacture. Mr. Lowell can not be censured for advancing avowed theories, however fanciful they are, for it is the privilege of the scientist; nor for making unintentional mistakes in fact, for that is eminently human. But I feel sure that the majority of scientific men will feel just indignation toward one who stamps his theories as facts; says they are proven, when they have almost no supporting data; and declares that certain things are well known, which are not even admitted to consideration by those best qualified to judge. Censure can hardly be too severe upon a man who so unscrupulously deceives the educated public, merely in order to gain a certain notoriety and a brief, but undeserved credence for his pet theories.[49]

The sense of deep professional offense in Blackwelder's tirade is augmented by his galled realization that almost none of the general readers enamored of Lowell's Martian fantasies would ever read these words.

The public clung to Lowell and he to the public. When the academic critics turned up the heat on Lowell, journalists took his side and made him the subject of flattering, illustrated articles in the Sunday supplements. One such article, dismissing any criticism of Lowell's work for being "unscientific" or "trivial," makes plain that it was Lowell's literary gifts that were decisive: "Here was a man of science whose logical deductions were as full of fascination as Jules Verne's romancing."[50] As he got older, Lowell, never a thin-skinned controversialist, wore his popular acceptance like armor, impervious to any effort by scientists to get him to modify his core beliefs about Mars. In the face of growing contrary evidence, he simply became more shrill, more derisive in his counterblasts. Paradoxically, the greater a crank he seemed to other astronomers, the more devoted his public became. He announced in *Mars as the Abode of Life* that the "revelations" at Flagstaff had been "decried as baseless views and visions by the telescopically blind. So easily are men the dupes of their own prejudice." Later in the same volume, he deplored "the clerkage of science" that amassed data without putting them into an interpretative framework. "A theory," he declared, "is just as necessary to give a working value to any body of facts as a backbone is to higher animal locomotion." So at once Lowell assailed his critics for spinelessness while he claimed an indisputable victory for a "theory" that had become his creed ("now, assurance of actuality no longer needs defense").[51] The very arrogance of his treatment of those whose approval he once sought and still coveted simply reinforced his heroic status in the eyes of the common reader.

Some letters in his archive reveal the intensity, and sometimes the oddity, of Lowell's following among the public. Correspondents repeatedly praise his gift for explaining abstruse scientific concepts in language both accessible and exhilarating. A billiards expert opened a lengthy letter of inquiry by saying, "I hardly know which to admire more: your profound knowledge of your subject and the lucid and logical nature of your reasoning or the beautiful and even sublime language with which you have clothed your theories and facts."[52] For a landscape painter from Cincinnati, Lowell's Martian books "have certainly furnished rich food for the imagination; and to me it is specially fine, because of the perfect foundation of truth upon which the imagination can play."[53] In the era of the Chautauqua and other exercises in self-improvement, Lowell's books were a staple in adult reading groups. "An unscientific reader" who had been assigned to lead discussion on *Mars as the Abode of Life* at a meeting of her book club wrote anxiously to Lowell to ask how she should go about refuting Alfred Russel Wallace's charges against Lowellian Mars.[54] A watchmaker in Schenectady sent him a draft of a short story, "The Martian," along with a request to use his enlargement of one of Lowell's maps of Mars if the story were published. To the story-writer's surprise, Lowell wrote back not only granting permission but enclosing suggestions for revising the draft.[55] Touchingly, some letter-writers assume that Lowell is worshipped as fervently by scientists as by themselves. "I know that the admiration of the whole world is at your feet," an English nurse writes, "and that words as poor as mine have no weight, compared with those of all the great men of science who wholly understand the laws of nature and therefore appreciate your book from other points of view than mine."[56]

Not all Lowell's fan mail was prompted by literary interest in his writing. A building-materials dealer in Delaware asked for copies of the photographs of Mars that appeared in *Nature* in 1910 and appealed for anything Lowell could tell him about Martian hydraulics. "When you get so far along as to be able to give me particular information as to the pumping system employed there, I shall receive the information with great interest."[57] An irrigationist in Australia ruminated on the flatness of the Martian terrain and offered a counter-hypothesis for the construction of the canals, proposing that they might not have been dug but have been designed by building parallel banks to enclose a ribbon of plains.[58] The only favorable responses to his work that seemed to disconcert Lowell came from psychics and mediums. Although at a younger age he had studied various occult practices and phenomena in Asia, he was uneager—at a time when his methods were decried as unscientific—to have his Martian observations "verified" by spiritualist visions. One author sent an autographed copy of her novel, *Journeys to the Planet Mars*, which she claimed was the product of automatic writing under the direction of a Spirit. Another wrote to inform him ("this is confidential," she cautioned) that she had been "working telepathically on Mars"; she enclosed a clipping with her discoveries and offered her services to "aid your mechanical devices in investigation." On this letter there is a terse pencil note in Lowell's hand: "Return clipping. No Ans[wer]."[59]

When he died suddenly in the fall of 1916, Lowell still enjoyed wide public acceptance. He had just had a triumphal tour in the Northwest, and among his final writings were four lectures he prepared for venues that included the Universities of Washington, Idaho, and California. At that last stop, he particularly relished his reception in the seat of his old nemeses from the Lick Observatory. He wrote to his secretary, "Lick and Berkeley have now reached the very respectful stage, shown by their distinguished consideration of the Martian ambassador. One could not expect more of mere mortals educated in the Martian dark ages."[60] Not that the Martian ambassador had begun soft-pedaling his message. One of his last lectures was widely cited and partially reprinted in news accounts of his death. It opens with a sentence of uncompromising severity in his career-long crusade: "That Mars is inhabited we have absolute proof."[61]

In 1916, much of Lowell's impact on the writing of fiction about Mars was still to come, but some discerning journalists foresaw that legacy. At his death, published obituaries were less adulatory than news coverage of the previous twenty years might have predicted; they displayed a measure of reserve about how durable Lowell's conjectures about Mars would prove to be, but they also contained thoughtful acknowledgments of the contributions that he had made to the public romance with Mars. The *Kansas City Star* wrote of his Martian theory: "It opened up fascinating possibilities for speculation, and most persons did not observe how slight was its foundation, and a vast amount of interesting fiction has been based upon its possibilities. So the theory has come to be so widely accepted that it is almost a pity to recall the fact that it is still only a theory, with no convincing evidence behind it." "His announcements took an enormous hold on popular imagination," a literary journal in New York pointed out in likening his stature to that of his sister Amy in the imagist school of contemporary poetry. "They did more to popularize the study of astronomy than all the college courses could have done in a hundred years."[62]

An editorial in the Paterson, New Jersey, *Guardian* may have been the most astute of all the obituaries and commentaries that appeared in the weeks following his death: "Professor Lowell gave untrained men the freedom of the skies, turned the imagination of nations starward and enlarged our conception of what the life of the universe may be. This is really a greater achievement, though a poetic achievement, than the exact discovery of what the bluish markings on Mars indicate."[63] It would have been a bitter pill for Lowell to have acquiesced in the judgment that his successes were more literary than scientific, but it is a verdict that does rough justice to his place in the history of imagined Mars.

Mars and Utopia

By the later nineteenth century, cartographers had little room left on their maps of Earth for the hidden valleys, lost kingdoms, and uncharted islands that were the favored locations for Utopia. With the coming of the airplane at the beginning of the twentieth century, Utopia became an even more endangered destination; that peculiar American Utopia of Oz, in L. Frank Baum's series of children's books, finally had to be cloaked in invisibility to keep it concealed from the eyes of aviators.[1] But as terrestrial sites for Utopia became harder to portray convincingly, writers turned increasingly to a Martian locale. In post-Schiaparelli Mars, especially as adumbrated by popular scientific writers like Flammarion and Lowell, the literary imagination could people a habitable planet with ideal societies that served the traditional critical and creative functions of utopian romance.

In the classically derived nomenclature for his maps of Mars, Schiaparelli actually included the place—or more precisely, the no-place—for which terrestrial maps no longer had room. Unlike most of his other Martian place names, Utopia did not come out of the legends and history of the ancient world. The word was invented in the sixteenth century by Thomas More as a punning title for his satirical fable of an ideal society, *Utopia*. Had it been an actual Greek word, it would have been spelled either *ou-topia* (no place) or *eu-topia* (good place)—exactly the sort of sly ambiguity that More aimed for in designing a good-place-that-was-no-place-at-all. A hundred years after Schiaparelli named this vast region of plains in the northern hemisphere of Mars, at about the sixty-fifth parallel, the *Viking 2* lander began testing for signs of Martian life and sending data back to Earth from Utopia Planitia. Long before that historic event, fiction writers with a social and political bent had discovered the usefulness of Mars as a utopian locale.

Over the course of the late nineteenth and twentieth centuries, many dozens of works of utopian fiction were inspired by Schiaparelli or Lowell, both of whom are often memorialized by having Martian cities or space vehicles or, of course, canals named after them. The earliest of these is the anonymous *Politics and Life in Mars*, published in England in 1883, the preface to which announces that "Mars is now seen to be completely covered with canals" and is likely to be inhabited.[2] The author takes the new canal hypothesis so seriously that the Martians are depicted as living in the water, amid lush submarine vegetation. Although for the most part an uninspired and conventional account of the socialist arrangements of the Martian utopia—the abolition of war and poverty, the dissolution of the monarchy and a hereditary legislative body, colonial divestiture, the reclamation of criminals, workers' ownership of the means of production—*Politics and Life* does rise to a higher level of pointedness and eloquence in its ninth chapter, devoted to women's rights to suffrage and education, to professional employment, and to autonomy within marriage, including the right to divorce. This dramatic shift may suggest that the anonymous author was an English woman, but if so, *Politics and Life in Mars* falls far short of the wit and edgy charm of the American feminist utopia set on Mars, *Unveiling a Parallel*, published ten years later and discussed below.[3]

While Schiaparelli is cited respectfully in many early Martian utopias, one narrative actually is dedicated to Lowell and glosses his ideas about Mars in lavish and even idolatrous terms: the 1911 *To Mars via the Moon: An Astronomical Story*, by Mark Wicks. Remarkably little can be learned about Wicks, a Briton who published just one other (often reprinted) book in 1887, *Organ-Making for Amateurs*. But if the pipe organ was the subject of his professional expertise, it appears that astronomy was his great avocation and Lowell a cultural hero to him. *To Mars via the Moon* is a book of mixed genre: partly a textbook exercise in popular astronomy in fictional guise, partly a traditional utopian exploration of an imagined ideal society, partly a romance of reincarnation, partly a hagiographic tribute to Lowell who is invoked frequently in the narrative and who actually makes an appearance in the book's closing chapter. Published in both the United States and England, *To Mars via the Moon* is an elaborate piece of bookmaking, with a gold-stamped illustration on its spine of airships hovering over a Martian city and canals, a detailed gilt map of Mars on the front cover—complete with the dark wedge of Syrtis Major, north polar ice cap, and Lowellian single and double canals with shaded oases—and, inside, sixteen glossy plates, nearly all of which are identified as Wicks's own illustrations, of astronomical charts, maps, globes, and an aerial view of the capital city of Mars with its canals.

The first half of the three hundred-page narrative is essentially a walk through "the most recent and reliable scientific information respecting the moon and Mars" in the form of lectures by the sixty-three-year-old narrator, Wilfrid Poynders, to his two companions, the young engineer John Claxton and a

Scottish mechanic McAllister.[4] The lectures are delivered aboard the *Areonal*, a sleek 95-foot spaceship constructed secretly under Poynders' supervision at his home in Croydon. The journey past the Moon and to Mars is for the most part cozy, with all the comforts of home. ("We were all sitting together in our living-room on the 9th of September, whiling away the time in a game of whist," the narrator opens one chapter. [113]) The only significant crisis—one that was to become a staple of fictional voyages to Mars—is a meteor strike en route, but the ship's special metallic alloy of "martalium" is able to hold up under the assault (114). All the while, Poynders offers his auditors the gospel of Mars according to Lowell. Anti-Lowell arguments are put up and then knocked down; "a target for captious critics," Lowell is represented as a longsuffering victim of jealous and ignorant opponents (153). The book's final chapter is an addendum, in the form of a lengthy lecture that surveys the results of observation of Mars at the 1909 opposition. Reports are heard from Schiaparelli, Eugène Antoniadi at France's Meudon Observatory, and George Ellery Hale of the Mount Wilson Observatory, telling us where each of them now stands on the canal controversy. Lowell himself comes to England to lecture on the subject, and we get a detailed portrayal of his platform style, complete with a characteristically unrepentant, unqualified reassertion of his core views: "I have never made any retractation [sic] as to the reality and geometricism of the canals; they are marvellous beyond conception, and are only doubted by those who never observed the planet itself sufficiently well" (319).

Once the *Areonal* reaches Mars, the novel takes a different turn, though it remains heavily didactic. With its telepathic Martians and the use of reincarnation as a plotting device, *To Mars* has some elements of the romance of the paranormal (which will be on view in chapter 7). But the chief interest in the book's second half is in its effort to portray a Mars that illustrates Lowell's theories, including his supposition that the Martian technology of the canals would be the product of an advanced, utopian, pacifist, one-world society. The terrestrial visitors are taken to see the canals for themselves and learn of their history. The narrator tells his Martian hosts about Schiaparelli's original sightings of the *canali* but informs them that "the greatest exponent of the idea that there were really canals was, however, Percival Lowell, an American astronomer" who has endured the calumnies of "the older school of astronomers, who are not very receptive of new ideas" (187, 188). When Poynders is shown the clever way in which the canals are shaded by arching willowy trees to prevent evaporation of the water, he pounces on this detail as the definitive answer to Alfred Russel Wallace's well-known dismissal of Lowell's supposed 100,000-mile irrigation network passing through the bone-dry atmosphere and desert conditions of Mars as "the work of a body of madmen rather than of intelligent beings."[5] As he ticks off the revelations of his tour of Mars, Poynder can say, with a smugness worthy of his idol Lowell, "Thus the mysteries connected with Mars were being cleared up one after the other" (229).

Wicks gives the greatest attention, however, to pursuing Mars as a Lowellian utopia, and in so doing adopts the characteristic literary strategies of utopian romance. We are offered an inventory of the various social, medical, ethical, and technical advances that the Martians have achieved, including excellent housing for all citizens, full employment, political unity, rational urban planning, chaste and loving courtships, total care for elder citizens, radiation treatments for diseases, and nominal equality of the sexes. The standard list of utopian absences also appears: of poverty, social classes, war, hereditary privileges, prisons, tariffs, divorce, and alcoholism. When the question of artistic accomplishments on Mars arises, the Earthmen are taken to witness a dazzling son et lumière show in the sky, as Martian airships with multicolored lights move in elaborate kaleidoscopic patterns synchronized to electronically generated music. Although later readers will be reminded of the climactic spectacle in Stephen Spielberg's film *Close Encounters of the Third Kind*, those who have read other examples in the utopian tradition being mined by Wicks, from Thomas More through Charlotte Perkins Gilman, will recognize how often performance art in Utopia takes the form of visual spectacle and pageantry.

Wicks's narrator suffers the characteristic embarrassments of the visitor to Utopia when he must explain his own society's shortcomings. Interestingly, when a question very much at the center of cultural debate in 1911 comes to the fore, Wicks reveals his own ambivalence about the movement for women's voting rights. Terrestrial antifeminism is deplored on Mars, but when a Martian woman hears about the demonstrations and actions taken by suffragists she objects. "Surely there are other and proper means of obtaining their rights and privileges without resorting to such childish and unwomanly tactics as chaining themselves up, pestering high officers of state, and forcing their way into your council chambers" (222). Here, obviously, the anxious male author peers out from beneath the threadbare fictional disguise of his female Martian mouthpiece.

Wicks's Mars is a planet in physical decline and social ascendancy. When Poynders asks his hosts how they face the prospect of eventual catastrophe when the planet's resources of air and water are finally exhausted, he is told that the eminently rational Martians will practice absolute birth control as a means of racial suicide in their final century. "Thus the race will gradually die out naturally, and become extinct long before the conditions of our world can make life a terror" (202). With such examples of Martian ingenuity, nobility, and fatalism, Poynders concludes, in a strong echo of Lowell's theory, that Mars "pictures to us what must as inevitably be the fate of our own world ages hence" (299). In both its utopianism and its heroic canal-building to stave off planetary deterioration, Mars is model for and prophetic omen of the future of Earth.

Of all the early Martian utopias, *To Mars via the Moon* is exceptionally detailed in its use of the scientific information and speculation of Schiaparelli, Flammarion, and Lowell. Many other utopias set on Mars do little more than invoke the names of the great popularizers of the subject of Mars, and the problem of *how* human beings would travel to Mars is often finessed. Fantastic and preternatural devices of visions, dreams, hypnotic sleeps—standard narrative dodges in nineteenth-century utopias like Bellamy's *Looking Backward* and Morris's *News from Nowhere* for bridging the present and the future—often serve to bridge the distance between Earth and Mars. A popular stage work (later the basis for both a novel and a silent film), Richard Ganthony's *A Message from Mars* (1899), is structured on a dream in which the self-centered protagonist is visited by an armor-clad giant from Mars who teaches him, through a series of humiliating encounters with friends and relatives, the Martian values of "otherdom." Like Dickens' "A Christmas Carol," on which it clearly is patterned, *A Message from Mars* uses the supernatural to stimulate a conversion experience. In H. G. Wells's story "The Crystal Egg" (1897), televisual communication between Mars and Earth occurs by means of the titular crystal found in a shabby London antique shop. Probably the most famous preternatural device for bypassing the problem of how to get to Mars occurs in a romance that is anything but utopian: the hypnotic trance that Edgar Rice Burroughs used in *A Princess of Mars* (1912) to send his hero John Carter from Arizona to Mars. In some cases, however, the method of passage to Mars is ignored altogether. The narrator of one of the first American utopias set on Mars, Alice Ilgenfritz Jones and Ella Merchant's *Unveiling a Parallel: A Romance* (1893), announces that his journey to Mars occurs in a not-yet-invented aeroplane, but he gives the reader no account of the trip "since you are more interested in the story of my sojourn on the red planet than in the manner of my getting there."[6]

The unnamed narrator of *Unveiling a Parallel*, a privileged young New Yorker with decidedly unprogressive social views, alludes at the outset to the Mars fervor of the 1892 opposition. He says that his arrival was not unexpected by the Marsians—as Jones and Merchant call the inhabitants—because they had observed him in transit. "A college of astronomers in an observatory which stands on an elevation just outside the city [of Thursia], had their great telescope directed towards the Earth,—just as our telescopes were directed to Mars at that time" (2). Even though Jones and Merchant choose one of the younger astronomers to play the conventional utopian role of chaperon and guide for the visitor, the authors of the romance indicate by their title that their chief interest is not in astronomical issues but in devising a parallel Martian society that will invite comparison with terrestrial social practices. The essential cultural context that *Unveiling a Parallel* reflects, therefore, is not the debate over the Martian *canali* but the debate over the suffragist movement and women's social status. Characteristic utopian and feminist gestures appear in the representation of Marsian society: the absence of titles like Mr. and Miss; the absence (or reversal) of gender distinctions in social roles; the use of the dialogue form, familiar from Plato's *Republic* and More's *Utopia*; and a blandly assured, often doltish narrator whose answers to his hosts' queries persistently and unwittingly expose the contradictions, parochialism, and wrongheadedness of his own culture.

From the moment the narrator blushes over the "womanish" white garments the Marsians offer him to replace his trousers, Jones and Merchant make clear their intention to use the unveiled parallels to challenge and ridicule the practices of terrestrial, and particularly American, masculinist culture. As with the better-known utopianists who would follow them in the next twenty years—H. G. Wells and Charlotte Perkins Gilman—for Jones and Merchant the thinnest line is drawn between utopia and satire. The women of Mars do not occupy pedestals and are not angels in their houses. They have all the privileges and all the flaws of terrestrial men: They get drunk, they belong to silly clubs, and they tell risqué stories; through a special pipe they smoke an addictive mixture of alcohol and valerian; they engage in boxing matches; they have lovers, they visit male prostitutes, and they acknowledge having children out of wedlock.

When the narrator tells his guide Severnius of his shock and distaste at the excesses of Marsian women and insists that such behavior would violate terrestrial women's natural antipathy to coarseness, the Marsian uses biology to counter any claims for the special spiritual status of Earthly women:

> You have shown me in the case of your own sex that human nature is the same on the Earth that it is on Mars. You would not have me think that there are two varieties of human nature on your planet, corresponding with the sexes, would you? You say "woman's" spiritual fibre and fine moral sense, as though she had an exclusive title to those qualities. My dear sir, it is impossible! you are all born of woman and are one flesh and one blood, whether you are male or female. (47)

As the Marsians acquire an education about terrestrial mores through their relentless questioning of the narrator, they are stunned to realize that simply because of their physical strength the men of Earth have amassed all the power while practicing noblesse oblige to the women who depend on them. Finally, the Marsian woman Elodia invents "a vision of your Earth" that functions as an explanatory myth about how terrestrial males got their privileges:

> In the Beginning . . . there was a great heap of Qualities stacked in a pyramid upon the Earth. And the human creatures were requested to step up and help themselves to such as suited their tastes. There was a great scramble, and your sex, having some advantages in the way of muscle and limb,—and not yet having acquired the arts of courtesy and gallantry for which you are now so distinguished,—pressed forward and took first choice. Naturally you selected the things which were agreeable to possess in themselves, and the exercise of which would most redound to your glory; such virtues as chastity, temperance, patience, modesty, piety, and some minor graces, were thrust aside and eventually forced upon the weaker sex,—since it was necessary that all the Qualities should be used in order to make a complete Human Nature. Is not that a pretty fable? (107)

Initially smitten with the beauty and—though he cannot admit this to himself—the intellectual independence of Elodia, the narrator turns "sick at heart and angry" when he realizes her low standard of "virtue"—a standard about on a par with that of terrestrial males in the United States (110). Severnius does not attempt to defend the lax Marsian behaviors that so distress the narrator, but he insists that immorality is not specific to either sex and that the city of Thursia that has furnished all the examples of conduct for the visitor is conscious of its vices and still has some distance to go on the road to Utopia. He tries, without much success, to convince the narrator of the more serious and fundamental contradiction in the neochivalric dual standard of terrestrial male behavior: simultaneously elevating women to an angelic status and demeaning them, demanding absolute purity and rectitude of them while reserving a more flexible morality for themselves. "That—pardon me!—is the fault I find with your civilization; you make your women the chancellors of virtue, and claim for your sex the privilege of being virtuous or not, as you choose" (109). In the last portion of his sojourn on Mars, the narrator is invited to visit another part of the planet where sexual equality is complemented by more enlightened social mores. In the Caskian city of Lunismar, the narrator finds a society that, without having experienced either Christian revelation or redemption, has adopted principles that are parallel to the precepts of terrestrial Christianity and has integrated them fully into the fabric of people's lives.

Despite the pallid didacticism of the final episode in Caskia, the entire romance of Jones and Merchant operates, in Elodia's term, as a "pretty fable"— with teeth. The parallel world of Mars has no "Adam's curse" hanging over it, and therefore none of the gender dualities that came in the wake of sin in the Garden of Eden. This implication is made explicit in an exchange late in the narrative when the man from Earth grows irritated with the Marsians' belief in their own perfectibility. "Don't you believe in the Fall of Man?" he asks of a spiritual teacher in Caskia. To that the Marsian replies, in typical utopian fashion, rejecting the postlapsarian nostalgia for a state of imagined perfection in the irrecoverable past, "No, I think I believe in the Rise of Man" (150). In *Unveiling a Parallel*, Jones and Merchant, while displaying almost no interest in the scientific controversies of their day about Mars, inaugurated a tradition of using Mars as a utopian experiment in criticism and simulation, a model for terrestrial contemplation and action. Their romance is the ancestor to the later utopias of Alexander Bogdanov and Kim Stanley Robinson and not unlike the antiscientific critical romances of C. S. Lewis and Ray Bradbury.

Of all the utopian romances about Mars from the 1890s, *Unveiling a Parallel* is the one that still has the most residual energy. Henry Olerich's *A Cityless and Countryless World*, also appearing in 1893, is more a manual or catechism—the author calls it an outline rather than a novel. Or, one might say that it fits the Percival Lowell formula of a "romance of fact" since, as its Martian narrator Mr. Midith claims, "My history is a romance in which every event is a reality."[7] Because "the fundamental laws of nature" are identical on Mars and Earth (40), Olerich can concentrate on the social arrangements on Mars without the bother of characterization. The book has a simple question-and-response structure, reminiscent of the dialogue tradition of Plato and More, but with none of the energy of the Platonic inquiry or the wit of More's repartée. With its explicit thesis, repeatedly invoked—"social and economic prosperity and har- mony can be attained only in a system which recognizes extensive voluntary co- operation as its fundamental principle of production and distribution"(6)— and its various architectural and planning diagrams, *A Cityless and Countryless World* advises, in practical detail, how to reform American society. That the reformer whose principles are being urged is a "Marsite" is incidental; he could just as easily be from Holstein, Iowa—Olerich's own hometown.

Olerich's is one of several narratives of the period that solve the transporta- tion problem by having a Martian (or in his case, Marsite) come to Earth, by either advanced mechanical or spiritual means. Olerich's Mr. Midith arrives in the Pacific Ocean via a never-described "projectile." In William Simpson's frequently reprinted *The Man from Mars* (1891), the unnamed Martian stranger appears in California by "reflection"—a process of spiritual transference that leaves his body on Mars.[8] That Simpson's majestic and dignified Martian is present only in spirit suits the disembodied quality of the book's exposition, which offers even less in the way of narrative and romance than Olerich's. Mars is the grindstone on which Simpson sharpens his ideological axe. His seventy-page preface is actually more readable than the first-person narration, since it promises nothing more than it is: a frankly committed argument about the chief obstacle to utopian progress on Earth, the churches. The "deadly texts" of Scripture, especially from the Old Testament (51), for much of the previous nineteen hundred years, stifled the mood of inquiry and intellectual independence inaugurated by the ancient Greeks. Christianity, Simpson proposes, was in origin a socialistic, bottom-up movement of political reform and universal brotherhood; when it became institutionalized, it pressed creed into the service of persecution and demonized any challenge to its authority. The heretics that the churches—both Catholic and Protestant—hated and feared most were scientists. But, he believed, the religious influence on social and political life was dead or dying in the last decade of the nineteenth century and "the clutches of superstition compelled to relax its hold upon the throats of many a worthy human enterprise" (12).

The decisive battle for Simpson was over evolution, and science had emerged triumphant. The doctrine of the Fall of Mankind from a Golden Age in Eden had inhibited utopian progress by diverting attention from the future to the past. Darwinism reordered views of the world and of time. "The fact that man has ARISEN from a condition of brutality, instead of FALLEN from a state of perfection is, to ecclesiasticism, a raking blow from stem to stern" (34). Christianity could yet be a positive force for social and economic change if it recovered its original purpose and if it "set science on its right hand" and abjured superstition (59). Already, as science became liberated from theological constraint, new technologies in the nineteenth century were transforming the quality of everyday life: electricity, railroads, urban sewage systems, domestic heating systems. Nevertheless, as the Martian visitor tells the narrator, terrestrial culture is still in an early stage of development, and paleolithic by comparison with Martian culture.

Simpson makes a gesture toward the new astronomical fascination with Mars by setting the encounter with the Martian at the opposition of 1892. The hermit-like narrator has a telescope at his mountain-top cabin in California and he goes sleepless many nights in the hope of satisfying himself on the several current controversies about the physical nature of Mars. But when the golden-bearded Martian appears at his cabin, he reveals that his world has long been studying Earth, its inhabitants, its customs, and its history. "You have only measured us as a planet. We have measured you as a people" (87). That statement determines the narrator not to waste any of his time with his visitor asking about Martian landscape or marvels, not to question him about the truth or falsity of astronomical theories, but to learn about the "inner lives" of Mars's people and to gain a contrastive analysis of Martian and terrestrial societies. As it frequently does in utopian narratives, that noble purpose results in a relentlessly professorial style; it also results, and this is not always the case in the best utopian literature, in exposition conducted almost exclusively on the plane of generality and abstract principle, with few particulars and no personalities. There is a Martian proverb that dismisses theories that are not anchored in experience and knowledge: "He who gets his feet in the air is lost" (245). Simpson's narrative would have profited from better-grounded feet.

Simpson's *Man from Mars* exhibits features common to late nineteenth-century utopias, whether set on this world or another: a horror of war, defined as "sending masses of your people into deadly combat for the settlement of political and religious questions" (100); a vegetarian ethos that abjures the killing of animals for food or clothing; a reduced work-day and expanded leisure for everyone; rational city planning; legal and cultural equality of women and men; common ownership of land, with parcels available for the use of individual citizens; a government that provides light, heat, water, insurance, and funeral costs for all its citizens; a notion of the planet itself as "a bequest which has been delivered into our hands" for stewardship and improvement (260). Also, in standard utopian fashion, the Martians refuse to venerate the past: "We let the dead ages rest. We can find nothing in their ashes to compare with the living. The present is better than the past, as the future will be better in exact measure with the new truths discovered, and the old fallacies set aside" (134).

The only apparent gesture toward the past is the Martians' reverence for the greatest citizens of Earth—Kepler, Newton, Darwin—and their dismay at our failure to value highly enough their intellectual accomplishments. For Simpson's Martians, scientific experiment and speculation are never threatening: "a triumph of science with us is a triumph of religion" (126). In one of the rare but interesting moments when the Martian visitor descends from the general to the particular—though even here with a touch of allegory reminiscent of Bunyan's *Pilgrim's Progress*—he tells of his own residence in a Martian city named Good Will. The city's domestic architecture has the stylistic look of classical

Greek temples, but all the roofs are glass-domed to light the entire house. His top floor, the visitor explains, is full of plants and is used for sun-bathing. By night, it is a place to observe the stars and planets. The spectacle of the night sky "is the altar upon which we worship the great unseen" (251).

The figure of the "Man from Mars"—benevolent in nature, a source of gentle moral instruction and correction to benighted earthlings—became the most long-lived phenomenon of the sentimental Martian utopia, with outcroppings as late as 1940 in J. W. Gilbert's peculiar parapsychological romance The Marsian. The most popular example of this figure, however, first appeared in Richard Ganthony's play A Message from Mars. First produced in London, where it ran for over five hundred performances during the 1899–1900 season, it was revived frequently (especially at Christmas time), exported to New York with most of its original cast, adapted as a novel by Mabel Winfred Knowles, and twice filmed (in 1913 and 1921). In the early 1920s, Ganthony's script was issued in the Samuel French series for professional and amateur productions. In Ganthony's "fantastic comedy," the Martian visitor is a dream figure who reforms a selfish London plutocrat and amateur astronomer named Horace Parker. In the pages of the fictional journal The Astronomer, Parker has read, in a favorite simile of the era, that the "advent of a messenger or an army from Mars should not seem to us of the twentieth century a greater marvel than did the shining sails of Columbus to the aborigines of America."[9] In what was designed as a feel-good dramatic conversion of the sort that popular plays and later films turned out regularly and smoothly, Parker turns from cad to saint in the course of a single night under the influence of his dream of the man from Mars in which he learns the lesson of "Otherdom": "philanthropy, benevolence, altruism" (74).

A decade after the first publication of Simpson's Man from Mars, another utopian story of a Martian visitor with a similar title appeared. Henry Wallace Dowding's The Man from Mars, Or Service for Service's Sake (1910) opens in Rome in August 1909, just before the closest Martian opposition since 1892. It is an awkwardly designed narrative that revolves around an assassination plot against a general (the Martian visitor, it turns out), stolen papers that include a copy of the Martian constitution, and a mass of concealed identities worthy of a Jacobean play where nearly all the leading characters prove to be related to one another. If a reader sets aside the author's penchant for highflown formulas for conduct (the Vision Beautiful and Service for Service's Sake are invoked repeatedly) and the contortions of a plot that often seems headed to no relevant place, Dowding's Man from Mars offers interesting variations on the Martian utopia, a revealing critique of the prospects for astronomical discoveries about

Mars in the twentieth century, and a more mysterious and troubling version of a messenger from Mars than can be found in Ganthony's play.

The 1909 opposition contended for public attention with the competing claims of Robert Peary and Frederick Cook for first reaching the North Pole—a competition ultimately settled in Peary's favor by the U.S. Congress. At the same time, one of the most often-reported ventures during the year of the opposition was the campaign to communicate with Mars by using mirrors to flash signals to the planet's inhabitants. There had been talk for twenty years about beaming a signal-light to Mars or drawing a gigantic geometrical figure in the Sahara desert that Martian astronomers would be able to observe.[10] But interest in signaling Mars reached a crescendo at the end of the first decade of the new century. In 1909, William H. Pickering, the longtime associate of Percival Lowell and one of the few professionally trained astronomers of his era who never gave up on the *canali* or the notion of an inhabited Mars until his death in 1938, lobbied unsuccessfully for ten million dollars to construct an elaborate network of huge mirrors. There was even a popular piano "march and two step" by Raymond Taylor, "A Signal from Mars," whose published sheet music had a five-color lithograph cover depicting Martian astronomers flashing their light signal to Earth (see color plate 2).[11]

Small wonder, then, that Dowding's narrative is interrupted at one point by a telegram announcing, with amusing irreverence, that the Stars and Stripes is "floating around the Pole somewhere on a cake of ice."[12] This news is dismissed immediately by General Moraine as an empty achievement by comparison with "the discovery of another planet upon which there might be found a civilization vastly superior to our own, and from which it might be possible for us to learn lessons of social, civic, and moral righteousness which all the centuries of the past have failed to teach us" (63). And later at a dinner party where the subject of Mars "naturally" comes up in conversation, one acerbic guest remarks, "I wonder if Pickering has succeeded in signaling Mars by his hand-mirror?" (92)

The general's account of the Martian utopia is riddled with Dowding's own unfounded and often absurd notions of the planet's topography and climate and of the conditions of space travel. When he sets out for Mars in his zeppelin at the novel's close, he packs just enough oxygen to navigate a "dangerous zone" three miles above the Earth; beyond that point, he assures his companion, "oxygen abounds" [378].) But his portrait of Martian society is both appealing and odd. Most oddly, Mars is a Christian world, a Redeemer having been incarnated four hundred years after the appearance of the terrestrial Jesus. But Christian principles seem to have taken firmer root in Martian soil. The "one great principle" taught by the Martian Messiah, "Service for Service's Sake," is enshrined in Martian law and, the general explains, "service" has the same standing on Mars as "liberty" has in the United States. Service is to be preferred to liberty as "a more fitting symbol of universal greatness, a word better calculated to draw forth all that is noble in the race, a word with a larger meaning and a wider mission" (215, 216). Nearly as important to Martian cultural identity is the valuing of sexual equality. The Martian version of the Eden story says that woman was created prior to man, but on Mars the story is not used to claim women's superiority to men. "The equality of sex, next to the idea of service for service's sake, has done more for the planet Mars than anything else." It has resulted in an exaltation of domestic life so perfect that "the subterfuge of modern life known as the club" does not exist at all in Martian society (238). The principles of service and equality also entail putting a large share of the planet's resources into education; public schools on Mars have facilities and equipment that outstrip what is found in the most elite terrestrial universities. Martian education is founded on the development of values and the application of principles, while terrestrial schooling aims only "to see how many facts can be stored away in the brain as apples are packed into a barrel" (251).

What gives Dowding's *Man from Mars* a special place in the literary history of Mars is that it is the first frankly anti-scientific narrative of its kind. Others like Merchant and Jones's *Unveiling a Parallel* had been nonscientific, but Dowding actively promotes a skepticism about the usefulness of astronomy to our understanding of Mars. The general suggests that in fifty years most of the conjectures made by recent astronomers will be shown to be unfounded because the planet will be explored in person, not by telescopic observation. "The scientists have done their work in the discovery of Mars; but be sure that it will not be a scientist who will depart from his theory and make communication possible" (334). The practical thinker, "the mechanical man," the technician, and the generalist will open up Mars in the future. In a melding of fiction and fact, the prime instance of Dowding's brief against scientific theory is the case of Lowell. The general interrupts a conversation late in the novel by reading aloud from an article by Eugène Antoniadi, based on his work in September 1909 using the 33-inch "Grand Lunette" at the Meudon Observatory, announcing that "there was no trace of a geometrical network of canals" (330). Antoniadi, probably the finest astronomical writer on Mars in the first third of the twentieth century, made precisely that rejection of Lowellian Mars in a series of eight reports on the 1909 opposition in the *Journal of the British Astronomical Association*.[13] The scientists, Dowding's general insists, "are expecting too much from their instruments" and inevitably would suffer delusions (331). Until Mars is seen with the naked eye by actual visitors, it will remain a region constructed of myth and fancy. In the unlikely event that astronomers like W. W. Campbell, Edward Barnard or Antoniadi himself ever came across *The Man from Mars, or Service for Service's Sake*, it would have confirmed the worst fears of the scientific community that the amateurs and cranks like Lowell had tarred the entire profession.

Two works in the utopian tradition belong among the hardiest and most culturally significant of early fictions about Mars. The first was an invasion fantasy written in German and it had a profound influence on European readers throughout the early twentieth century, including a principal architect of the American space program, Wernher von Braun; the second was written in Russian by a leading Marxist intellectual and displaced the coming Bolshevik Revolution to the red planet. Kurd Lasswitz' *Auf zwei Planeten* was published in 1897 and was quickly translated into a number of European languages, though an English text (*Two Planets*), based on an abridgment by the author's son, did not appear until seventy-five years later. In 1908, amid the disappointments of the unfulfilled 1905 revolution, a press in St. Petersburg issued *Krasnaya Zvezda*. Alexander Bogdanov's utopia was reissued several times after the Bolshevik revolution of 1917, translated into German and Esperanto, and adapted for the Russian stage, but, like Lasswitz's novel, it had no English translation until it appeared as *Red Star* seventy-five years after its original publication. *Two Planets* and *Red Star* together constitute the peaks of the first wave of utopian writings about Mars.

As Percival Lowell had done before him and Henry Dowding would do a decade later, Lasswitz evoked the context of the turn-of-the-century polar expeditions in launching his Martian romance. While the great and terrible contest between British and Norwegian teams to reach the South Pole was gearing up at the end of the nineteenth century, Lasswitz imagined that the North Pole already had been reached and a base established there—by colonizing Martians. With an orbiting space station just outside the terrestrial atmosphere as a transfer point for journeys to and from their home planet, the Martians have both exploratory and philanthropic, though perhaps also imperial, aims. The entire Earth operation, the narrator of *Two Planets* remarks somewhat mysteriously, is "a complicated and important chapter in the cultural history of the Martians."[14] Visualized as big-headed and platinum-haired with large eyes covered by protective dark glasses on the sun-drenched Earth, the Martians have reached the pole using the highly favored nineteenth-century fantasy of a special gravity-harnessing material, known here as "Stellit." The announced intention of the Martians is to teach the inhabitants of Earth not only advanced scientific techniques but the politics of global peace.

Scientific information permeates *Two Planets*, and the influence of the Schiaparelli-Flammarion-Lowell conceptions is palpable in Lasswitz's design. Mars, called Nu by its inhabitants, is an aging, water-poor world whose inhabitants have been challenged by their environment to develop "a technology to dominate nature" (41), highlighted by the building of a canal network to bring meltwater from the poles. The 100-kilometer-wide belts of vegetation around each canal are a distinctly Lowellian touch. In investing his Mars with a history, Lasswitz imagines a monolinguistic global civilization, organized by more advanced Martians from the southern hemisphere, that has replaced separate tribal and national cultures. The novel explicitly raises the question of whether it is appropriate for one to think of oneself first as German or English or American, or simply as a terrestrial human. While the narrative seems clearly to advocate such a primary sense of global identity, it also acknowledges the threat that Martian politics poses to terrestrial politics in the intensely competitive context of late nineteenth-century imperialism. That "there is suddenly an intellectually and materially superior foreign supernation in our era of nationalism" (104) provokes resistance, especially from the British and American empires.

The decision of the British navy to order an attack on the Martian base causes the Martians to reevaluate humanity—and causes them, against their instincts, to resort to force. The Martians, it appears, made errors in imagining Earth that were at least as consequential as Flammarion and Lowell's misapprehensions of Mars. "Those humans are out of their minds," says a leader of the polar colony. "I had imagined them in a different way. I hear the humans have named our planet after the god of war. We wanted to bring peace. But it appears that the encounter with this wild species throws us back to barbarism" (165). Until the final battles with the United States near the end of the novel, only Britain ever goes to war with the Martians, and the British are defeated soundly. The temptation to see this outcome as Lasswitz's amused (and jingoistic) comment on the growing Anglo-German tensions as the new century loomed is irresistible. Eventually, the Martians occupy most of the Earth and establish the benevolent dictatorship of a "Protectorate." The United States is one of the last regions to be colonized, and America begins practicing passive resistance while secretly building its own air fleet in Central America to prepare for guerilla warfare. In the climactic episode, while the Martian occupation forces are gathered at Washington, D.C., the Americans launch a surprise tactical strike against the Martian polar base. "The unbelievable had occurred, what no one had really thought possible: the power of the Martians had been trapped in their own fortress. A comparatively small group, by careful thought, long-range planning, energy, boldness, willingness to sacrifice, had brought about this result" (360). The peace treaty that follows requires the Martian warships to return to Nu, although the space station and the polar base are retained by the Martians, but subject to American jurisdiction. As the novel closes, a new era of terrestrial peace is being ushered in; a more formal interplanetary trade relationship between Earth and Nu is anticipated; and the militarist forces on Mars, who had contemplated using bacterial warfare to wrest a final victory over Earth, are defeated in elections.

Two Planets finally puts the greater emphasis on the utopian renovation of the Earth. The Martian expedition is exposed as an imperial venture masquerading as a humanitarian one, and ultimately the potential tragedy of the dying world of Mars is left unresolved and forgotten. Lasswitz uses his romance of Martian invasion in a way similar to what H. G. Wells was contemplating in the same year: to teach humanity a different way of thinking about itself, its status in the universe, and the requirements for survival in an increasingly crowded planet and solar system. The centrality of a change in perception can be seen in one of the most striking scenes in Two Planets, when a group of human beings travels on the Martian spaceship for the first time. As the ship ascends, they have a vision of Europe from outer space, "a sight which no Earthly eye had ever beheld." The lesson in humility is one that would be repeated in many other scientific romances about Mars, and famously in C. S. Lewis' Out of the Silent Planet when its protagonist glimpses Earth from the vantage point of Mars. Here in Two Planets is the initiation of humanity into a new planetary and philosophical awareness: "More clearly and more overwhelmingly than ever before, they realized what it meant to be whirled about in space on a small particle named Earth. Never had they seen the sky underneath them. How great was the temptation of pride and triumph—how humble and awe-stricken they felt!" (93).

Bogdanov's Red Star is a very different kind of utopian text. There is far less romance here than Two Worlds offers, and a much more overtly didactic narrative design. Red Star is built on the traditional utopian tour of an alternative society, like Unveiling a Parallel, but Bogdanov forgoes Jones and Merchant's use of satirical humor for a more sober and theoretical presentation. The narrative is presented as the manuscript of the terrestrial scientist Leonid, whose research has been on the properties of matter, including—of course—antigravity. He meets a Martian traveling incognito on Earth and who looks much like one of Lasswitz's Martians—macrocephalic, slender, soft-voiced, and wearing dark glasses. But there the resemblance to Lasswitz ends. The Martian, Menni, has been searching for someone who will be "a living link" between Martian and terrestrial cultures, and Leonid has been chosen for an invitation to take a round-trip voyage to Mars in the egg-shaped "etheroneph" (literally, air-cloud).[15] With a touch of scientific smugness, Menni explains that the etheroneph is powered by atomic energy rather than by the method imagined by Jules Verne in *From the Earth to the Moon*. "As for the 'cannon shot' method I have read about in your science fiction novels, it is of course simply a joke, because according to the laws of mechanics there is practically no difference between being hit by the shot and being inside the projectile at the moment it is fired" (37).

As the etheroneph approaches Mars, Leonid goes to the vessel's observatory, where he has a sight of the planet, 100 kilometers away, both wonderful and familiar: "the contours of the continents and the seas and the canal networks, which I recognized from the maps of Schiaparelli" (41). As a scientist, Bogdanov took some pains to ensure that the Mars he imagined in *Red Star* was consistent with the new Mars that popular astronomy at the turn of the century seemed to be revealing. (A medical researcher, rather than an astronomer, Bogdanov was not likely to know—or to care—about the controversies within the astronomical community about the Mars of Schiaparelli and Lowell.) So when Leonid tells Menni of his surprise that such huge canals were constructed, wide enough to be seen through terrestrial telescopes, Menni's response comes straight out of Lowell. "The canals are indeed immense, but they are not dozens of kilometers wide, as they would in fact have to be for your astronomers to be able to see them. What they see are the broad bands of forest we have planted along the canals in order to maintain an even level of humidity in the air and prevent the water from evaporating too rapidly. Some of your scientists seem to have guessed as much" (56).

The effort at scientific credibility is most apparent in the early chapters of *Red Star* where Bogdanov is describing how "minus-matter" (43) and radioactive decay work, why nausea and disorientation, not euphoria, accompany weightlessness in space, and how the two moons Deimos and Phobos move differently through the Martian sky. But once Leonid has arrived on Mars, Bogdanov drops any pretense that the narrative is to be primarily an astronomical primer or a travelogue:

I lack the time and space to describe the peculiar Martian flora and fauna, nor can I devote much attention to the atmosphere of the planet, which is pure and clear, relatively thin, but rich in oxygen. The sky is a deep, dark green, and the most prominent celestial bodies are the sun—much smaller than it appears on Earth—the two tiny moons, and two bright evening and morning stars, Venus and Earth. All of this was strange and foreign to me then and seems splendid and precious to me now as I look back upon it, but it is not essential to the purpose of my narrative. The people and their relationships are what concern me most, and they were the most fantastic and mysterious of all the wonders of this fairy-tale world. (60)

From that point forward, with its steady emphasis on the social arrangements on Mars and the persistently invited comparisons with terrestrial society, *Red Star* clearly defines itself as a utopia rather than a scientific romance. Geological, chemical, and ecological data about Mars are introduced instrumentally to explain social phenomena. Leonid, who had fancied himself "the Columbus of this world" crossing "the Ocean of the Ethereal" (59) settles into the more prosaic role of pupil instructed in Martian history, economics, and ideology. Even one of the rare jokes in *Red Star* signals a shift in perspective. When Leonid is surprised to find (as Flammarion had long theorized) that Martian plants are red-leaved, he immediately links the color to the revolutionary emblem of Marxism: "I shall have to get used to your socialist vegetation" (60).

In shaping the narrative, Bogdanov makes his own adaptation of Laplace's nebular hypothesis, since the eighteenth century a staple in theories of the origin of the solar system and of the relative ages of the planets. Lowell had used the nebular hypothesis as the basis for his own theories of the evolution of worlds, with Mars having a longer geological history and an older culture than Earth's.[16] Bogdanov retunes Laplace's theory in a Marxian key, and Leonid first encounters it in a children's outline of history that he reads while learning the Martian language on his outward journey on the etheroneph. There he learns that Mars is geologically twice as old as Earth, four times older than Venus; the evolution of life therefore began much earlier on Mars. When creatures of human status evolved, they went through phases of development and social organization similar to those of terrestrial human beings. But the parallelism was not exact. The social evolution on Mars was "gentler and simpler" (53), with wars playing a minor role. Slavery as an institution never existed on Mars, there was little militarism, class struggles played out in less violent forms, and nation-states died out more quickly. The weaker gravity on Mars led to ease of self-transport, and the smallness of mountains and lack of large oceans hastened the development of a single planetary language and made for more effective communication. "Nature," Menni explains to Leonid, "has erected far fewer walls and barriers between our peoples than she has between yours" (54).

The turning point in Martian history was the drying up of the planet's water resources, which had been occurring gradually over tens of thousands of years but reached a critical stage a thousand years before the events of *Red Star*. The crisis of climate caused a political renovation on Mars. The Great Canal Project, initially financed by private enterprise, led first to capitalist consolidation of land resources and ultimately to a proletarian revolt against the power of the landlords. In his manuscript, Leonid summarizes what he learns from the children's book: "Thus the famous canals served as a powerful stimulus to economic development at the same time as they firmly reinforced the political unity of all mankind" (55). The revolutionary socialist utopia that terrestrial Marxists foresaw as Earth's future already had come to pass on Mars. For much of his time there, Leonid then becomes the quintessential utopian tourist, visiting factories, museums, hospitals, and schools; attending public meetings, scientific conferences, and theatrical performances; reading Martian literature; and always and everywhere asking questions about how life is organized on Mars.

But the Martian utopia is far from perfect, and the great engineering and political feat of the global canal system does not represent a permanent solution to the planet's ability to sustain a large population. The final third of Red Star is devoted to that crisis and to a secret debate occurring among scientists about where to locate a new habitat for Martian civilization. Leonid gets his first inkling that all is not well on Mars when he learns that the favorite genre of drama on Mars is tragedy—an art form seemingly at odds with utopia. On Mars, tragic theater focuses especially on the subject of humanity versus nature and the struggle for existence in an era of ever-diminishing resources. These environmental tragedies enact the hard choices that Martians have had to make, such as the cutting down of most of their large forests when the coal ran out, a desperate measure that resulted in the disfiguring of the planet and the degradation of its climate. "The tighter our humanity closes ranks to conquer nature," Leonid's guide explains to him, "the tighter the elements close theirs to avenge the victory" (79).

At last, Leonid comes to realize that the Martian interest in Earth is not simply a matter of pure research conducted for its own sake. In a library, he discovers the records of closed meetings about the "colonial expedition" to Earth (107). Scientists have concluded that an impending food shortage on Mars will mean huge losses of life in about thirty years' time unless there is a mass resettlement to either Venus or Earth. Conditions on Earth are much more favorable than on hot, undeveloped Venus, but a preliminary visit to Earth—the very one that ended with Leonid's journey to Mars—has convinced researchers that terrestrial humanity would not voluntarily share its resources or its space with outsiders. "Such reluctance," the harshest of Earth's critics insists, "derives from the very nature of their culture, which is based on ownership protected by organized violence" (110). Because coexistence with patriotic, xenophobic, violence-prone Earthlings is impossible, "*colonization of Earth requires the utter annihilation of its population"* (113). While another faction on Mars argues for an intensive education and conversion of the terrestrial population to socialism, the hardliners are unconvinced that the "semibarbaric Earthly variant" of socialism will be able to avoid being compromised and exploited by the superior power of the ruling classes (116). Eventually, a compromise resolution is passed to make a first attempt on Venus, despite the miserable conditions and the dangers involved, but if that fails it is clear that the proposal to attack Earth will be back on the table.

Leonid returns to Earth, shattered by the revelation on Mars. Afflicted by melancholia and by what doctors regard as hallucinatory fantasies about Martians, he is treated in a mental hospital. But at the end of his manuscript, Leonid accepts what he now perceives as his necessary historical role and is planning a revolutionary act that will begin "to erase the hated boundary between the past and the future" (136). An epilogue to his manuscript, written by a doctor to whose hospital the wounded Leonid is brought, provides a hopeful coda. A "first great victory in the great battle now in progress" has been won (137). Leonid, whose injury is not fatal, vanishes from the hospital, presumably to join his comrades in the next struggle and to make the Earth a fit place both for its terrestrial occupants and for its likely future immigrants from Mars.

Bogdanov returned to his Martian materials five years later, with a sequel entitled The Engineer Menni (1913), set hundreds of years before Red Star and focused on the career of the mastermind behind the canal system. The engineering project is the narrative peg on which Bogdanov hangs the history of the development of union movements on Mars and an incipient workers' revolution. With an economic prophet in the background named Xarma, Engineer Menni is even more polemical and more pointedly referential to Earthly Marxism than Red Star. One of the characters in Engineer Menni offers a definition of utopia that captures Bogdanov's strategy in displacing the as-yet-unrealized socialist revolution to another planet: "Utopias are an expression of aspirations that cannot be realized, of efforts that are not equal to the resistance they encounter."[17] In a period of frustration and apparent defeat for Russian Marxists, before the 1917 revolution, the hoisting of the socialist banner on the red star of Mars might serve as inspiration and motivation, an antidote to disheartenment. Even if, finally, the good place is no place at all, as Thomas More suspected, a place of unrealizable aspirations, as Bogdanov himself seems to acknowledge, aspirations and models are necessary to the effort to reconstruct the world. The Mars that still remained mostly unknown, mysterious, and controversial to astronomers had just the right proportion of those qualities to make it a suitable setting for the social experiments of visionary fiction-makers.

H. G. WELLS
and the Great
Disillusionment

The genre of the celestial voyage is an old form of storytelling, going back at least to Lucian of Samosata's second-century *True History* in which a hurricane lifts up a ship and carries it to the Moon. Until the Schiaparelli era, the most favored destination for extraterrestrial travel remained the Moon, followed more distantly by the Sun. Almost always, it was a terrestrial voyager who went to the heavenly body; invasions of the Earth by moon-men were not part of the tradition.[1] In the nineteenth century, under the literary influence of Jules Verne's series of *Voyages Extraordinaires*, begun in 1863, as well as the scientific influence of new astronomical discoveries, the interplanetary voyage took on fresh life. Verne's only voyages to take place off-world were a pair of throwbacks to earlier fantasies, though brought up to date technologically: *From the Earth to the Moon* (1865) and *Around the Moon* (1870). But in the last decades of the nineteenth century, a discernible shift of locale took place. Fictional goings and comings between Earth and Mars took precedence over all other forms of the interplanetary romance. As in earlier celestial voyages, the interest was most often in what the views of other worlds and other inhabitants of those worlds had to suggest about human and terrestrial concerns. The scientific romances of Percy Greg, Hugh MacColl, Camille Flammarion, Robert Cromie, Alice Ilgenfritz Jones and Ella Merchant, and Robert Braine, during the period from 1880 to 1896, represented an impressive if uneven group of narratives of expeditions to a Mars conceived, for the most part, solidly within the traditions of utopianism and adventure fiction. Late in 1897 came a strikingly original variation on the extraterrestrial voyage, and for the first time the new subject of Mars was in the hands of a great thinker and a powerful writer.

No one would have believed in the last years of the nineteenth century that this world was being watched keenly and closely by intelligences greater than man's and yet as mortal as his own; that as men busied themselves about their various concerns they were scrutinised and studied, perhaps almost as narrowly as a man with a microscope might scrutinise the transient creatures that swarm and multiply in a drop of water.[2]

The opening of H. G. Wells's *The War of the Worlds* is justifiably celebrated for the economy of its cadenced language and the frosty postmortem it offers on the end of human hegemony in the universe. It isn't true, of course, that nobody at the end of the nineteenth century was prepared to believe in extraterrestrial intelligences; it was precisely the new mood of wondering and believing that made possible the striking success of a work of fiction like *The War of the Worlds*. At the time of the 1892 opposition, proposals were being floated to try to establish communication with Mars by signs that could be detected by Martian astronomers. England's leading eugenicist Francis Galton advocated setting up a line of mirrors twenty-five yards long to flash a beam of sunlight that would be visible from Mars "if seen through a telescope like that at the Lick Observatory in California." If the Martians had such a telescope, Galton figured, they "would speculate concerning the beam and would wish to answer."[3]

Throughout the 1890s, there were flurries of excitement about the possibility that the inhabitants of Mars themselves might be attempting to initiate contact with the third planet. "The mere suggestion of such a thing sends a thrill of fascinated expectancy through the whole academic system of Europe," the London correspondent for the *New York Times* reported.[4] Some of the conjectures about Martian signaling were as bizarre as it is possible to imagine, none more so than that of a Washington, D.C., Orientalist who, studying one of Percival Lowell's first maps of Mars, found in the patterns of the canals the outlines of the Hebrew letters for "God."[5] Even as sober a journal as the British *Nature* weighed in cautiously on the question of signals. Reporting that luminous projections from the disc of Mars had been seen from the Nice Observatory in July of 1894, just before that year's opposition, *Nature* observed that the light could be of natural origins (perhaps a vast forest fire) or the product of purposeful intelligence. "Without favouring the signaling idea before we know more of the observation, it may be stated that a better time for signaling could scarcely be chosen."[6]

It was a shrewd move on Wells's part, therefore, to build the first paragraph of *The War of the Worlds* on the global preoccupation with telescopic surveillance.

Much of his romance's originality depends on a persistent focus throughout the narrative on the eyes of observers, but in the opening paragraph these are not the eyes we might have expected to encounter, peering through the telescopic lenses at the major European and American observatories, all trained on Mars. Those observatories and the dispatches emanating from them throughout the 1890s are indeed mentioned repeatedly in the opening chapter, but the dominant theme, at the outset, is of our world under scrutiny. The human role is displaced from the surveyor to the surveyed as the Earth's inhabitants fall under the envious gaze of Martian observers. So powerful are the Martian telescopes that the terrestrial objects of their study are revealed with the detail that we associate with specimens under a microscope. This startling reversal of perspectival images leads to an equally startling makeover of the biblical injunction to "increase and multiply." To the Martian eye, human beings appear not as the crown of God's creation but as aimlessly skittering microbes that "swarm and multiply in a drop of water." In The War of the Worlds, for the first time, the inhabitants of Mars are depicted not as kindlier and nobler versions of ourselves but as monsters of intellect—"vast and cool and unsympathetic," as the narrator memorably characterizes the Martian mind. And, like Kurt Lasswitz in Germany, Wells was not imagining an expedition to Mars by terrestrial explorers and missionaries, ambassadors and curious adventurers. Mars comes to us in the shape of invasion and imperialist expansion. The result— even though the invasion is ultimately a disastrous failure for the Martians—is "the great disillusionment" of the human species (51).

Wells had been interested in the subject of Mars from his student days in the teacher preparation program at London's Normal School of Science. In 1888, he took up the issue of extraterrestrial life in the School's Debating Society and proposed a strong case for living beings on Mars. Five years later, in collaboration with his friend Richard Gregory, a future editor of Nature, Wells wrote a textbook, Honours Physiography, in which he speculated about both Martians and their canals. In 1897, he published a fantasy, "The Crystal Egg," whose images of the eyes of Martians staring back through their crystal lenses at the intrusive eye of the Londoner Mr. Cave (Latin for "beware") adumbrate the more brilliant and complicated opening of The War of the Worlds. The final paragraph of another short story from the same year, "The Star," depicts Martian astronomers—"for there are astronomers on Mars, although they are very different beings from men"—studying the Earth.[7] But the most revealing anticipation of his great romance is an 1896 Saturday Review essay, "Intelligence on Mars," on the supposed similarities of Mars and Earth in climate, physical and chemical composition, and geography. Unlike writers who had

Photographic portrait of H. G. Wells, undated, 1890s. Courtesy Library of Congress, Prints and Photographs Division, George Grantham Bain Collection

imagined Martians as nearly indistinguishable physiologically from terrestrial human beings, Wells—schooled in evolutionary theory by Darwin's disciple T. H. Huxley—proposed that it was more likely that natural selection and the "evolution of protoplasm" on Mars would have taken a different course than it had on Earth. "No phase of anthropomorphism," he concluded, "is more naïve than the supposition of men on Mars. The place of such a conception in the world of thought is with the anthropomorphic cosmogonies and religions invented by the childish conceit of primitive man."[8]

That last remark suggests two things that separate Wells from most of the other early imaginative writers about Mars. He does not conceive of the Martians as human look-alikes—maybe a little smaller or taller, longer-lived or more aesthetically inclined—but as emphatically alien. And his conceptions of Martian anatomy and culture are governed less by planetary astronomy than by biology and anthropology. Darwin, not Lowell, is the key intellectual influence on Wells's Martians. Although Lowell's *Mars* appeared in 1895 in the United

States, a British edition was not issued until the following year, when Wells's drafting of *The War of the Worlds* was already well under way. Possibly Wells read Lowell during the course of his writing or revisions, and if he hadn't read *Mars* itself, he certainly would have heard about Lowell's ideas and likely read the review of the book in *Nature*. But there is little evidence of any substantial impact Lowell's theory of a heroic, utopian race of beings had on Wells's Martians.[9] Lowell was always careful to insist that there was no way to predict the physical appearance of Martians, and one sentence in *Mars* echoes or anticipates the close of Wells's "Intelligence on Mars." "To talk of Martian beings," Lowell cautioned, "is not to mean Martian men. . . . What manner of beings they may be we lack the data even to conceive."[10] Wells's writings certainly conform to that proposition. Nevertheless, it is doubtful that Lowell, as he speculated about the inhabitants of Mars from his observation post in Flagstaff, ever imagined the naked, oily-skinned octopods that Wells's narrator describes in near-hysterical detail:

> They were, I now saw, the most unearthly creatures it is possible to conceive. They were huge round bodies—or, rather, heads—about four feet in diameter, each body having in front of it a face. This face had no nostrils—indeed, the Martians do not seem to have had any sense of smell—but it had a pair of very large, dark-coloured eyes, and just beneath this a kind of fleshy beak. In the back of this head or body—I scarcely know how to speak of it—was the single tight tympanic surface, since known to be anatomically an ear, though it must have been almost useless in our denser air. In a group round the mouth were sixteen slender, almost whip-like tentacles, arranged in two bunches of eight each. (149)

And so on. That these Martians are also imagined as lacking bone or muscle or an alimentary tract, as asexual and producing their young by budding, as feeding vampirically on the blood of living creatures, preferably of the two-legged sort, further separates Wells's creatures from any benign Lowellian model.

The canals of Mars are hinted at in the first chapter of *The War of the Worlds* when the narrator alludes to the appearance of the planet in the telescope ("so bright and small and still, faintly marked with transverse stripes"), and to the "fluctuating appearances of the markings" mapped by astronomers (53), but the canals are at the periphery of Wells's imagination. Another indicator of the absence of Lowell from *The War of the Worlds* is the depiction of the redness of Martian vegetation—a detail that is vividly elaborated in chapter 5 of book II, when Earth appears Martianized by the growth of a red weed accidentally seeded by the invaders. It was central to Lowell's theory about the irrigation of Mars that the vegetation was observably blue-green and that the red hue of the planet came from its deserts. Wells almost certainly picked up the notion of red flora from Camille Flammarion, who promoted the idea in his widely read *Astronomie Populaire* (1880), translated into English in 1894 as *Popular Astronomy*.[11]

Lowell's name never appears at all in *The War of the Worlds*, although Schiaparelli, the research at the Lick Observatory in California and Henri Perrotin's work at the Nice Observatory during the 1894 opposition, and the report from *Nature* on possible signal lights coming from Mars are all cited in the opening chapter. A lengthy and astute review of *The War of the Worlds* early in 1898 supposed that recent astronomical findings lent an air of plausibility to Wells's fictional inventions. "The view that the Martians—it is less unreasonable to think that Mars is inhabited than that is not—would look towards our earth with longing eyes is thus quite within the bounds of legitimate speculation; and the fact that Mr. Wells put it forward before Mr. Lowell had brought before the attention of British astronomers the reasons for thinking that Mars at the present time is mostly a dreary waste from which all organic life has been driven, is a high testimony to his perceptive faculties."[12] So, if Lowell did not influence Wells's imaginings, he could be brought in after the fact to validate them.

The plot of *The War of the Worlds*—in which technologically advanced inhabitants of Mars arrive in England, sweep to quick, stunning victories against panicky mobs and ineffectual armies, only to succumb just as suddenly to bacterial disease for which they have no immunity—is too familiar for extensive summary. But it is a misfortune of literary history that a later adapter of Wells's romance had a homonymic name. Many people now actually identify Orson Welles as the author of *The War of the Worlds* or assume that Welles's melodrama adequately translates Wells's vision. Orson Welles's notorious characterization of his 1938 radio broadcast as a Hallowe'en prank—the Mercury Theatre's "version of dressing up in a sheet and jumping out of a bush and saying Boo!"— has retrospectively colored perceptions of H. G. Wells's intentions.[13] In fact, the seventy-two-year-old Wells was angered when he learned of the American radio adaptation of the novel that he had published forty years earlier. He thought, with some justice, that it coarsened a serious political allegory into a sensational hoax. But the radio script also highlighted an aspect of *The War of the Worlds* that has made it a central text in the cultural history of Mars. In shifting the locale from London and its suburbs to New York City and rural New Jersey, Orson Welles was participating in a century-long series of adaptations of Wells's novel that paid homage to its mythic universality by altering its local particularity in order to make the geographical details of the imagined invasion familiar to various audiences. Even well-informed U.S. Anglophiles sitting by their Philco radios in 1938 might have been vague about the location of the Chobham Road, Horsell Common, Putney Hill, and other places designed by Wells to be instantly recognizable to British readers. Orson Welles sought American equivalents to that sense of journalistic immediacy with dispatches from Princeton University, reports of black smoke pouring through Times Square, and the view of a gigantic Martian machine in Central Park.

Welles's kind of alterations became the standard for later adaptations of *The War of the Worlds*. A 1944 broadcast in Chile put the invasion in South America and in 1949 a radio adaptation in Ecuador moved events to Quito; when Hollywood adapted the novel in Byron Haskin's 1953 film, the invasion, appropriately enough, was centered in southern California.[14] But Welles didn't initiate this practice. From the very moment of its first public appearance, *The War of the Worlds* underwent such scenic changes. Before it was published in book form, Wells sold the story in serial installments to *Pearson's Magazine* in England and to *Cosmopolitan* in the United States. When the *New York Journal* and the *Boston Post* requested the right to republish the serial in their newspapers in late 1897 and the first month of 1898, Wells agreed, not knowing that the geographical details would be altered. New Yorkers reading their evening papers learned about the Martians' sacking of such landmarks as the Brooklyn Bridge, St. Patrick's Cathedral, Columbia University Library, and Grant's Tomb. In Boston, readers could track the invasion from Concord to Lexington to Waltham before the Martians headed for Boston Harbor and the industrial center of the city.[15]

On learning about the *Boston Post* version, Wells raged helplessly from London at the violation of his work. Although the results were crude and clumsy, this beginning of a century's worth of geographical metamorphoses of *The War of the Worlds* (culminating in the 1997 parodic film *Mars Attacks!*, centered in the post–Cold War era in Washington, D.C.) attests to the attraction of Wells's fantasy for a number of historical moments and cultural settings. Among fictions that straddle the literary and the scientific imaginations, only Mary Shelley's *Frankenstein* looms larger as a modern myth susceptible of endless reworking and new applications. Like *Frankenstein*, *The War of the Worlds* achieves its special status by an effective combination of intimacy and generality, archetypal storytelling and open-ended allegorical possibility, a richly specific sense of time, place, and occasion, and an interrogative mode that transcends circumstantial detail.

Frankenstein's conceptual and emotional framework is the series of questions the nameless artificial creature asks as he searches for his parent, his own identity, and the purpose of his life: "Who was I? What was I? Whence did I come? What was my destination?"[16] Wells chose as the epigraph for The War of the Worlds questions attributed to the astronomer Johannes Kepler and drawn from Robert Burton's seventeenth-century Anatomy of Melancholy: "But who shall dwell in these Worlds if they be inhabited? . . . Are we or they Lords of the World? . . . And how are all things made for man?" (47) These are questions that also address identity, purpose, and the human role in the scheme of things. Kepler's questions are brought down to the simplest, most colloquial level in what may be the single most important exchange of dialogue in The War of the Worlds. A neurotic young clergyman, distraught at the scale of destruction in the first days of the invasion from Mars, meets the narrator, himself suffering from acute thirst and the loss of his wife in the chaos. The curate, invoking Biblical images of the end of the world visited upon a sinful humanity, asks, "What are these Martians?" The narrator answers him only with this question: "What are we?" (103). In the history of fiction about Mars, this is the first great articulation of a central motif in the tradition: the representation of Mars as a mirror and of Martians as reflections of human beings. That Wells introduced this motif of seeing ourselves in the Martians in the first novel to portray them as monsters rather than as human facsimiles is startling but also characteristic of what he later described as his impulse at the time to make "an assault on human self-satisfaction."[17]

The complacency that Wells targeted is partly a matter of human vanity, as suggested by the anthropomorphism he chided in "Intelligence on Mars," or the anthropocentrism that has been a chief preoccupation of the genre of science fiction as it has emerged over the past hundred years. But the assault on self-satisfaction in The War of the Worlds was also directed quite specifically at late-Victorian cultural assumptions of superiority in the context of the British Empire. For Wells, Mars was not to be used as a utopian model but as a satirical instrument for exposing the philosophical pretensions and the political crimes of his contemporaries. The anthropocentric fallacy puts a human face on all intelligence, assumes that only those beings created in our image have status equivalent to ours, cannot conceive of a civilization that is other than our own. Wells exposes this fallacy in the early chapters of The War of the Worlds in the persistent assumption, expressed by the narrator, other unnamed characters, and the national newspapers, that the cylinders that have landed on Earth contain "men from Mars." As the first capsule finally starts to open the narrator comments, "I think everyone expected to see a man emerge—possibly something a little unlike us terrestrial men, but in all essentials a man. I know I did" (63). The narrator's sense of disgust at the shape that appears is outdone by a neighbor who, like the mechanical voice in a child's toy, keeps reiterating his conviction that the Martians, because they do not look human, must be savages: " 'What ugly brutes!' he said. 'Good God! what ugly brutes!' He repeated this over and over again" (65).

The War of the Worlds relentlessly links such moments of grotesque comedy to larger cultural perspectives on British xenophobia and colonialist policies toward subject peoples.[18] The ultimate destination of the Martian invaders is London, capital city of the most powerful country on the planet, headquarters of an empire with colonial operations on every continent except Antarctica. And part of that continent had even been claimed and christened Victoria Land as early as 1840. In 1897, as the serial version of The War of the Worlds was appearing in print, new expeditions in search of the South Pole were being readied. When the narrator of The War of the Worlds first lays out the broad interpretative framework for the true story that he is about to record, he urges his readers to resist condemning the Martians for their act of war unless they also are willing to engage in self-condemnation: "And before we judge of them too harshly we must remember what ruthless and utter destruction our own species has wrought, not only upon animals, such as the vanished bison and the dodo, but upon its own inferior races. The Tasmanians, in spite of their human likeness, were entirely swept out of existence in a war of extermination waged by European immigrants, in the space of fifty years. Are we such apostles of mercy as to complain if the Martians warred in the same spirit?" (52)[19]

Such passages may suggest that Wells is as didactic in his assault on human self-satisfaction in its personal and political manifestations as the utopian writers had been in their exposition of Mars as a model society. But Wells was a far subtler artist than William Simpson or Jones and Merchant. He traced his literary pedigree to the satirical geniuses of Swift, Voltaire, and Gibbon, and they stand behind the scathing indictment of humanity in The War of the Worlds. In some of his later works of utopian fiction, Wells, like the Duchess in Alice in Wonderland, could dig his chin into the reader's shoulder while intoning, "And the moral of that is . . . ." But not in this book. In The War of the Worlds, Wells thought and composed in scenes; he used spectacle to display folly and arrogance without finger-pointing; he understood that sometimes the fastest route to the brain is through the nervous system, and therefore played on readers' dreads and anxieties to shock them into thought. Let me focus attention on just two extraordinary moments that represent Wells's prodigious gift for turning the invasion of Mars into powerful and artful social prophecy and psychological analysis.

The sixteenth chapter of The War of the Worlds is titled "The Exodus from

London." It is an account of the northward evacuation of millions of Londoners as word reaches the city of the advancing Martian military operation from the southwestern suburbs. Any associations with the dignity and order of the exodus of the Israelites from Egypt are canceled immediately as the narrator describes "the roaring wave of fear that swept through the greatest city in the world" (121). We witness chaos at the railroad stations, wanton looting of bicycle shops by people desperate for a means of transport, police "breaking the heads of the people they were called out to protect," roads crammed with every imaginable vehicle: "cabs, carriages, shop-carts, waggons, beyond counting; a mail-cart, a road-cleaner's cart marked 'Vestry of St. Pancras,' a huge timber-waggon crowded with roughs" (121, 126). On the road to St. Albans, these vehicles are splashed in blood and there is a tumult of screaming, quarreling, exhausted voices: "Push on!"; "Clear the way!"; "I can't go on!" A mother calls in desperation for her daughter lost in the mob; a Salvation Army man bawls out monotonously "Eter-nity! eter-nity!"; and, repeatedly, frightened voices from the pushing crowds invoke the terror at their backs: "They are coming!" (126, 127). There is little heroism or kindness; there is scarcely any sanity. Human beings under pressure do not behave well. As they flee for their lives, they abuse their horses and slash at each other with whips; someone being trampled by horses bites the hand of his would-be rescuer; a man in evening dress suffers a nervous breakdown in the highway, "one hand clutched in his hair and the other beating invisible things" (125). In crisis, humanity reveals what it is made of. What are these Martians? What are we?

The narrator of the history of the Martian invasion claims (and it surely would be the claim of Wells himself, conscious of the originality of his representation) that chaos on this scale was unprecedented:

> Never before in the history of the world had such a mass of human beings moved and suffered together. The legendary hosts of Goths and Huns, the hugest armies Asia has ever seen, would have been but a drop in that current. And this was no disciplined march; it was a stampede—a stampede gigantic and terrible—without order and without a goal, six million people, unarmed and unprovisioned, driving headlong. (131)

To grasp the enormity would require a wholly different perspective than an Earthbound narrator could achieve. Paradoxically, distance and impersonality are needed to convey an adequate impression. "If one could have hung that June morning in a balloon in the blazing blue above London every northward and eastward road running out of the tangled maze of streets would have seemed stippled black with the streaming fugitives, each dot a human agony of terror and physical distress" (131). If such a sight and such an angle of vision were novelties in 1897, they would become fixtures of the century to come. Photographic images of refugees and forced marches of evacuees, of civilian war victims and genocidal atrocities haunt the twentieth century, and the new century's altered understanding of the scale of human suffering and human depravity is prophesied in the texture and details of Wells's imagined war.

If the catastrophe on the road to St. Alban's captures Wells's brilliance at conveying mass hysteria and the physical and moral collapse of society, the narrator's experiences in the second, third, and fourth chapters of book II of *The War of the Worlds* give us a parallel rendering of the psychology of the individual under extreme stress. The narrator spends those chapters, amounting to fifteen days, trapped as a virtual prisoner of war in a portion of a collapsed house next to a pit in which one of the cylindrical Martian spaceships has landed. Dirt and debris from the landing have piled up against the one side of the house from which an exit might have been made. Here Wells returns, with astonishing versatility and shrewdness, to the motifs of eyes and vision with which he opened the novel. A vertical aperture in the kitchen wall provides a peephole through which the narrator and his unwelcome companion—the timorous young curate—can observe what is happening in the Martians' pit. What is revealed in the pit is dreadful, gruesome, profoundly frightening, occasionally nauseating—and absolutely irresistible to the two prisoners. Each struggles for his share of time at the peephole, grotesque versions of the patient astronomer at his eyepiece, for "that horrible privilege of sight" (154).

From that vantage point, the narrator makes clinical observations of Martian physiology and watches how the Martians construct and use their various war machines. He notices how the machines seem more vital and muscular than the Martians themselves. The machines are like prosthetic devices that replace the largely useless Martian limbs, and the Martians, whenever disconnected from the mechanical extensions of themselves, are burdened by and alienated from their own ungainly bodies. The narrator—in yet another Wellsian variation on "What are these Martians? What are we?"—deduces that the invaders have reached a plateau of cultural evolution toward which human beings at the close of the nineteenth century were just beginning to climb:

> We men, with our bicycles and road-skates, our Lilienthal soaring-machines, our guns and sticks and so forth, are just in the beginning of the evolution that the Martians have worked out. They have become practically mere brains, wearing different bodies according to their needs just as men wear suits of clothes and take a bicycle in a hurry or an umbrella in the wet. . . . It is

remarkable that the long leverages of their machines are in most cases actuated by a sort of sham musculature of discs in an elastic sheath; these discs become polarised and drawn closely and powerfully together when traversed by a current of electricity. In this way the curious parallelism to animal motions, which was so striking and disturbing to the human beholder, was attained. Such quasi-muscles abounded in the crab-like handling-machine which, on my first peeping out of the slit, I watched unpacking the cylinder. It seemed infinitely more alive than the actual Martians lying beyond it in the sunset light, panting, stirring ineffectual tentacles, and moving feebly after their vast journey across space. (152–53)

The narrator's most disturbing visions through the peephole are of Martian feeding practices. One night he crouches at the opening and observes a starkly illuminated construction site in the pit where aluminum is being manufactured. A Martian is sitting in the hood of one of the machines:

As the green flames lifted I could see the oily gleam of his integument and the brightness of his eyes. And suddenly I heard a yell, and saw a long tentacle reaching over the shoulder of the machine to the little cage that hunched upon its back. Then something—something struggling violently— was lifted high against the sky, a black, vague enigma against the starlight; and as this black object came down again, I saw by the green brightness that it was a man. For an instant he was clearly visible. He was a stout, ruddy, middle-aged man, well dressed; three days before he must have been walking the world, a man of considerable consequence. I could see his staring eyes and gleams of light on his studs and watch-chain. He vanished behind the mound, and for a moment there was silence. And then began a shrieking and a sustained and cheerful hooting from the Martians. (156)

Earlier, the narrator had noticed the cage-like contraption attached to the Martian machines, wondering what its purpose might be. Only at this moment does he grasp that it has the function of a picnic hamper. In the sort of reversal that characterizes the satirical method of The War of the Worlds, the plump suburban consumer becomes the consumed, as the British colonizers of the Earth have become colonized by invaders from another world. With a single word—"cheerful"—Wells captures the indifference of the Martian invaders to the suffering of their victims, and in so doing reminds his readers of their cheerful obliviousness to the human costs of the empire whose fruits they enjoy.

Very early in the narrative, before the enormity of the threat has become evident, an engineer, given a description of the mollusc-like Martians, pronounces them outside the moral law: "It ain't no murder killing beasts like that" (78). It was a sentiment, as Wells knew, that had been used to excuse, if not justify, the genocide of the Tasmanian aborigines by British colonists. In *The War of the Worlds*, the Martians, with their vast, cool, and unsympathetic intellects, take exactly the same stance. What horrifies the onlooker inside the collapsed house is simply matter of fact to the Martian consumer; this is not murder but only the satisfaction of need. And to the Martian eye, the human form looks remarkably like the familiar food products of his native world. After the invasion, scientists had discovered on board the Martian space vehicles the remnants of the food supply the invaders had brought to sustain them on their voyage:

> Their undeniable preference for men as their source of nourishment is explained partly by the nature of the remains of the victims they had brought with them as provisions from Mars. These creatures, to judge from the shrivelled remains that have fallen into human hands, were bipeds with flimsy, silicious skeletons (almost like those of the silicious sponges) and feeble musculature, standing about six feet high and having round, erect heads, and large eyes in flinty sockets. Two or three of these seem to have been brought in each cylinder, and all were killed before earth was reached. (150)

Perhaps somewhat meatier and tougher than their counterparts on Mars, the human bipeds in other respects are little different from Martian "beasts" that it would be no crime to kill. No wonder that the narrator, when he finally escapes from his imprisonment in the wrecked house and surveys the altered landscape of a planet under occupation, is moved to reflect on the relationship of human beings to the animal kingdom on Earth:

> I touched an emotion beyond the common range of men, yet one that the poor brutes we dominate know only too well. I felt as a rabbit might feel returning to his burrow and suddenly confronted by the work of a dozen busy navvies digging the foundation of a house. I felt the first inkling of a thing that presently grew quite clear in my mind, that oppressed me for many days, a sense of dethronement, a persuasion that I was no longer a master, but an animal among the animals, under the Martian heel. With us it would be as with them, to lurk and watch, to run and hide; the fear and empire of man had passed away. (165)

Wells's greatest achievement in *The War of the Worlds* is his critical examination of what it means to colonize another world, another species, another race.

The popular fascination with Mars furnished him with an opportunity to expose the delusions of grandeur and the moral callousness in England's pursuit of its imperial goals. For Wells, a "great disillusionment" is good medicine for a culture sick from an overdose of its own colonialist comforts and illusions. Critics have sometimes scoffed at the subtitle of book II, "The Earth under the Martians," when the depicted invasion is confined to metropolitan London. Wells intended that his scientific romance, appearing in the Diamond Jubilee year celebrating Victoria's sixty years as queen, twenty of them as "Empress of India," would strike home in the most immediate and powerful way. And because it had a local target—the Englander and his bloodily achieved empire— rather than the gaseous abstractions of most of the utopian novels about Mars written in the same decade—The War of the Worlds earned its larger applicability to human nature and history.[20] That was a lesson that Wells effectively learned from his masters in the satirical tradition, as a minor fellow novelist observed in writing to him about his Martian romance:

> This is a wonderful yarn. And absolutely the finest thing in it to me is the lack of sympathy between a superior & inferior order of creation. This would probably be inevitable. There is a grand [pattern?] about those poor muddle-headed men creeping up with their cut & dried normal life of the suburbs while the abnormal is knocking at the door. . . . As a result the verisimilitude is like Swift's. I can give it no higher praise from my standpoint.[21]

But the great Enlightenment satirists were not Wells's only cultural inheritance. The telescope, with its power to excite the imagination, to reveal but sometimes to misread realities, contributed essential perspectives to The War of the Worlds. Telescopes didn't always tell the truth any more than fiction did—but both the romancer and the astronomer have something to teach. In a little essay aptly titled "From an Observatory," Wells described how unselfcritical the human species would have been if the accidents of atmosphere had kept the stars invisible to us in the night sky. And were the stars for the first time to appear to human eyes, "How suddenly—painfully almost—the minds of thinking men would be enlarged when this rash of stars appeared." The unknown, he believed, was good for us, and "the starlit night," with its Pascalian immensities and terrors, enables us to "see in its true proportion this little life of ours with all its phantasmal environment of cities and stores and arsenals, and the habits, prejudices, and promises of men."[22]

That principle was put into practice in Wells's contribution to the literature of Mars. The epilogue to The War of the Worlds has more visionary telescopes, in the aftermath of the failed Martian invasion, once again panning the skies in "eager scrutiny of the Martian disc" (192). Such sights as are disclosed, the narrator insists, will contribute to "the broadening of men's views," to finer visions and healthier self-questioning (193). In *The War of the Worlds*, richly endowed with altered perspectives, proportions, and moral measurements, Wells initiated the most profound alternative to the Lowellian line in the twentieth century's traditions of imagining Mars.

Wells's story of extraterrestrial invasion spawned over the course of the next hundred years a variety of imitations, parodies, and adaptations. But one reply to *The War of the Worlds* deserves particular attention, since it appeared immediately on the heels of the Americanized serial installments of Wells's romance in the United States. No sooner had the last installment of these rewrites of *The War of the Worlds*, complete with the destruction of metropolitan New York and Boston, appeared in the *New York Evening Journal* and the *Boston Post* than a serialized sequel began to run. The author was a science journalist named Garrett Serviss and he called his sequel (never published in book form until 1947) *Edison's Conquest of Mars*. As fiction it is hackwork; as a commentary on *The War of the Worlds* it is astonishingly impervious to Wells's anti-imperialist motive; but as an example of how cultural and national values get drawn into the Martian myth it is both instructive and appalling.

Serviss's narrative, with an establishing shot of the ruins of the eastern United States after the departure of the few surviving Martians from the first invasion, opens with reports of new signal lights seen on Mars, presage of a second expeditionary force being readied for an assault on the Earth. A coalition of terrestrial scientists, headed by Thomas Edison, is organized to prepare a defensive strategy against "those terrible men from Mars"—a phrase that immediately indicates Serviss's failure to understand a crucial element of Wells's critique of anthropocentrism.[23] Edison, in a triumph of "American inventiveness" (9), comes up not only with an electric spaceship propelled by the favored nineteenth-century fantasy of gravitational forces of attraction and repulsion but with an early version of the staple of twentieth-century space fantasies, a ray-gun, here called a "disintegrator." Serviss appears to take literally the nickname that journalists had given Edison, "the Wizard of Menlo Park." Perhaps the earliest manifestation of the scientist-as-hero in Martian fiction, Edison prefigures the comic-book scientist Dr. Zarkov, whose technological expertise underpins Flash Gordon's fistfights and derring-do and the altogether different band of professional scientists who become the heroic centers of the Martian fiction of the 1990s.

Under Serviss's Edison, the defense of the Earth is transformed quickly into a counteroffensive against Mars, with an armada of a hundred electric ships, staffed by a multinational force under Edison's command. But despite the narrator's claim that "all racial differences and prejudices" have been set aside in the common global endeavor, the ethnocentrism that Wells chastised is not so easily suppressed. At a celebratory ball in Washington on the eve of the armada's departure, the Prince of Wales expresses his satisfaction that "the champion who is to achieve the salvation of the earth has come forth from the bosom of the Anglo-Saxon race" (30). Indeed, the entire contingent of scientific brains behind the expedition (Kelvin, Roentgen, Rayleigh, Moissan, and Sylvanus Thompson are named specifically along with Edison) is uniformly EuroAmerican.

Percival Lowell is never named in *Edison's Conquest*, but his imprint is on the book, and Serviss was an outspoken proponent of his ideas about Mars. As head of the astronomy department at the Brooklyn Institute, he had invited Lowell to lecture there in the fall of 1895, and in *Harpers* in 1896 he published a detailed and illustrated "conjecture" about a journey to Mars by "electric liner" to which, he says, Lowell's theories "lend probability." The liner, he imagined, would be fully booked with tourists and adventurers and would be dominated by "the Anglo-Saxon race, which has furnished most of the great travellers."[24] In *Edison's Conquest*, the vision of Mars is superficially—that is, topographically—Lowellian, although in his moralistic insistence that its inhabitants are depraved, Satanic, the embodiment of "evil" (68), Serviss follows neither Lowell's theory of heroic and utopian Martians nor Wells's scrupulously amoral vision of the products of an advanced evolutionary state pursuing a biological imperative. As the terrestrial fleet approaches Mars's southern hemisphere, exclamations of wonder burst from the crews. Both the soil and the vegetation are visibly red; the buildings are gleamingly metallic; there are numerous large fortifications, befitting the planet named for a war god; but the most prominent features are the canals. "From the earth about a dozen of the principal canals crossing the continent beneath us had been perceived, but we saw hundreds, nay thousands" (106). Serviss uses the canals as the critical plotting device in this second war of the worlds. While the small terrestrial force is unable to defeat the far more massive Martian air fleet, a team of saboteurs, including Edison and a former American army colonel, enters the plant that controls the whole irrigation system's floodgates and unleashes a Noachian deluge that ruins the planet and kills an estimated 90 percent of the population.

With the constant move west of white Americans from the Atlantic seaboard, frontiers, like utopias, were in search of a new locale. The turn towards Mars is already evident in Serviss's narrative in the character of Colonel Alonzo Jefferson Smith, who had fought "in many wars against the cunning Indians of the West" (119) and saw Martians as no different from Apaches. It is the colonel who shows others in the terrestrial force how to outflank the enemy by sneaking around them under cover of the tall Martian grasses. In a characteristically clumsy locution, Serviss has him say, "We can get close in to the Indians—I beg pardon, I mean the Martians—without being seen" (125). And it is he who, in an echo of the "white maiden" conventions of Indian captivity narratives, arouses American outrage and gallantry over a young woman slave, the descendant of captive Earth people imported to Mars many centuries earlier. In Colonel Smith, Serviss has sketched the archetype of the pistol-packing cowboy-soldier-romantic who populates American narratives about Mars from Edgar Rice Burroughs' adventure stories to the Flash Gordon movie serials of the 1930s to Robert Heinlein's juvenile fictions. As we will see in chapter 8, a line of men's and boys' fiction about Mars took shape between 1890 and 1920, and Serviss's *Conquest* is connected more strongly to those masculinist escapades than to Wells's political fabulation.

H. Bruce Franklin, the most astute interpreter of *Edison's Conquest of Mars*, links the aggressive expedition against Mars to the events of 1898 that were leading to the Spanish-American war. He points out that the very issues of the *New York Evening Journal* in which the installments ran contained news reports on American anxieties about a possible invasion by Spain as well as on the belligerent posturing by the United States and preparation of its warships for a preemptive strike. "MAINE MAY SAIL FOR HAVANA AT ANY MOMENT," a *Journal* headline announced.[25] Garrett Serviss' riposte to H. G. Wells has little to offer as a comment on Wells's devastating accounting of the wages of British colonialism, indeed seems quite oblivious to the targets of Wells's satire. But *Edison's Conquest of Mars* is a revealing portrait of the raucous and bullying imperialism that was the American cousin to England's more suavely managed conquests. Throughout the twentieth century, though especially during the Cold War era, American fictions about Mars frequently would play variations on the frontier motifs, the ideology of manifest destiny, and the depiction of Martian aliens as facsimiles of America's enemies that Serviss crudely introduced in his Edisonian fantasy.

Wells had not quite finished imagining Martians with *The War of the Worlds*. A decade later, he wrote for *Cosmopolitan* an essay titled "The Things That Live on Mars," designed to revisit his earlier speculations in the light of "much valuable work [that] has been done upon that planet" since his novel first appeared. By 1908, he had read Lowell, whom he names in his essay "my friend." Perhaps they had even met, since each had crossed the Atlantic on lecture tours in the other's country. In 1898, Wells brought Martians to the Earth; in 1908, he reverses the journey, but unlike Serviss he looks at a "world we are invading in imagination." Despite the fact that by then Lowell's theories were considered dubious, if not absurd, by most reputable astronomers, Wells takes the generous view that he had made a "very convincing case" for an inhabited planet in *Mars and Its Canals* (1906). Noting that Lowell had refrained from any conjectures about the physical make-up of Martians, Wells decided to exercise the novelist's license to imagine while trying to remain within the framework of "definite knowledge" and "facts" established by Lowell.[26]

Starting from the differences in gravity and atmosphere, Wells makes the deductions that flora and fauna on Mars will be slenderer, lighter, taller, and more tolerant of dryness than their terrestrial counterparts. Interestingly, Wells adopts Lowell's belief in green vegetation on Mars since "if there is life, chlorophyll will lie at the base of the edifice" (336). He does not remind his readers that in *The War of the Worlds* he had translated into fiction Flammarion's guess that Martian vegetation would be red. But the heart of the essay is Wells's depiction of the "ruling inhabitants" of Mars. "Unless Mr. Lowell is no more than a fantastic visionary," Wells writes as if to hedge bets, those are the beings who designed and built the enormous irrigation network that had become the subject of so much public curiosity. The things that live on Mars do not look, in this iteration, quite as monstrous as they did in Wells's portrait in 1898. Now he is willing to grant that the Martians may have "a quasi-human appearance" and be of "quasi-mammalian" descent (340) but he still does not expect them to look like our extraterrestrial cousins. Their prehensile organ may not be a hand but a proboscis or—as he had imagined in *The War of the Worlds*—a set of tentacles. They are more likely to be furred or feathered than bare-skinned. And, again as in his earlier novel, if the Martians are technologically advanced, one could plausibly expect them to be outfitted with an assortment of mechanical prostheses that may or may not look much like the "artificial aids" that terrestrial humans have developed: "clothes, boots, tools, corsets, false teeth, false eyes, wigs, armor, and so forth." At nine or ten feet tall and with big heads, deep chests, perhaps a variety of "knobs and horns and queer projections," the Martians may appear a caricature of humanity and provoke "a kind of disgust of the imagination" (342).

Lowell may have softened the edges a bit, but this is still the same Wells who doubted in 1898 that there were "men on Mars." And it is still the same Wells who enjoys tweaking human complacency and self-centeredness. The Lowell legacy would get passed down well into the twentieth century. But so would the equally durable Wellsian legacy. By the late 1930s—when Wells published his last, and least-known, Martian fiction, *Star-Begotten*—C. S. Lewis could create a character in his own novel about Mars who would say, with great certainty and anxiety, as he arrived on the planet:

> He had read his H. G. Wells and others. His universe was peopled with horrors such as ancient and mediaeval mythology could hardly rival. No insect-like, vermiculate or crustacean Abominable, no twitching feelers, rasping wings, slimy coils, curling tentacles, no monstrous union of superhuman intelligence and insatiable cruelty seemed to him anything but likely on an alien world. . . . He saw in imagination various incompatible monstrosities—bulbous eyes, grinning jaws, horns, stings, mandibles. Loathing of insects, loathing of snakes, loathing of things that squashed and squelched, all played their horrible symphonies over his nerves. But the reality would be worse: it would be an extra-terrestrial Otherness—something one had never thought of, never could have thought of.[27]

The things that lived in Wells's imagination no longer are a living part of our visions of Mars, but they have not yet entirely vanished from cultural memory or from the imagery of other worlds.

Mars and the paranormal

One of the most peculiar instances of symbiosis in the cultural history of Mars is the one that developed in the late nineteenth century between astronomy and parapsychology. As the fervor for Mars grew in the final two decades of the nineteenth century and into the twentieth century, there was a parallel explosion of interest in telepathy, reincarnation, and theosophy that was a cosmopolitan outgrowth of the provincial spiritualist movement that had begun in New York State in the mid-nineteenth century. In an intriguing historical conjunction, the Society for Psychical Research (SPR) was founded in London in 1882, just half a dozen years after the modern phase of Martian observation had gotten underway with the events of the 1877 opposition. Three years later, the American SPR opened in New York, under the presidency of one of the harder-nosed American astronomers, Simon Newcomb, who was determined to use his position to expose spiritualism as phony science. It was not unusual for astronomers to sign up as members of either the British or the American SPR, whose lists included both committed spiritualists and more dispassionate psychical researchers.[1] Percival Lowell—as his biographer, David Strauss, has explored in some detail—was intrigued by psychic research in his earlier years traveling in Japan, and consulted with members of the American SPR and with William James, who began a two-year term as president of the British SPR in 1894. The sequence of Lowell's career as both a scientific researcher and a popular writer who was "drawn to exotic topics—trances and extraterrestrial life," as Strauss has commented, itself demonstrates the links between psychic phenomena and Martiana. Lowell moved from investigating Shinto mesmerism and cases of possession, recorded in his 1894 *Occult Japan*, to planetary studies begun at his observatory at Flagstaff in that same year.[2]

In fact, one hundred years ago, the two most popular scientific writers who engaged with questions about the habitability of Mars—Lowell in the United States and Camille Flammarion in France—both combined interests in psychic research and astronomy, although their interests in the paranormal were sharply different in nature. Lowell always remained a materialist and looked for physical explanations for psychical practices. When he was approached by spiritualists hoping to use his Mars research in their cause during the period of his fame as proponent of an inhabited Mars, Lowell made it clear that he had little patience with table-rappers and clairvoyants who sought to find in him a kindred spirit.[3] Flammarion, on the other hand, was as devout about parapsychology as he was about Mars, and the two subjects often commingled in his books. His learned La Planète Mars (1892) was the definitive summation of three hundred years' worth of telescopic observations of the planet. But this volume, as well as his more populist works about astronomy, alternated with spiritualist narratives such as the 1893 Uranie (discussed below) and essays like his "Spiritualism and Materialism," originally published in 1900 as an open letter to Camille Saint-Saëns, in which he claimed that clairvoyance "is proved by such a considerable number of observations that it is incontestable."[4] Flammarion's espousal of spiritualism was lifelong. As a teenager, he became a member of La Societé Parisienne des Études Spirites, and in 1923, two years before his death, he became president of the international SPR. Telepathy, he asserted in his inaugural address, is "as much a fact as are London, Sirius and oxygen."[5]

In his study of the history of telepathy, Roger Luckhurst has proposed that modern scientific ideology and intellectual networks took hold in the late Victorian era, becoming increasingly multidisciplinary and at last independent from the authority of the church: "The emergence of a scientific culture consequently produced other, less predictable effects: strange, unforeseen knowledges, hybrid and ephemeral notions, that emerged as compromise formations melding apparently discrete systems."[6] Certainly, Lowell's ability to persuade vast segments of the public to his views of Mars as irrigated and inhabited depended significantly on the hybrid science he called "planetology" and on the multiplex nature of his arguments, which were based not only on telescopic observation but also on evolutionary theory, geology, paleontology, and social science.[7] Many spiritualists, with their own antagonistic relationship to mainstream religion, may have assumed that, as boundaries between fields of knowledge blurred, they would have reliable allies among natural scientists. But while many scientists were deeply interested in psychical phenomena as a subject of investigation, few were inclined to be partisans. At the beginning of the twentieth century, psychical research still seemed capable of being brought under the umbrella of scientific research and of coexisting comfortably with psychology. But the case was not made, and before long the term "parapsychology"—that is, beside or outside psychology—came into usage.[8]

Similarly, the Martian canals championed by Lowell and Flammarion came under increasingly severe attack in the early twentieth century, denounced as being based on what Eliot Blackwelder deemed a "kind of pseudo-science."[9] A cartoonist, depicting a vaporizing "Flimflammarion," suggested that the canals were the product not of investigative science but of hallucinogenic fantasy.[10] The critique made of the spiritualists could, with only minor adjustments in phrasing, be applied equally to the Lowellians: "No amount of rationalization can write away the discrepancy between empiricist ways of knowing (as the professional sciences understand them) and occult knowledge."[11]

The conjunction of Martian studies and the paranormal is most visible in a number of narratives published by mediums over the space of about fifty years from the late nineteenth century through the early decades of the twentieth. Psychologists and philosophers—at a time when psychology was still considered a branch of philosophy rather than a scientific discipline—were particularly drawn to investigation of séances and of the experiences and the claims of mediums, including those who offered accounts of their visions of Mars in the form of travelogues that were, de facto, works of science fiction. The most celebrated instance of the intersection of Mars and the paranormal appeared at the turn of the twentieth century, when Théodore Flournoy, professor of psychology at the University of Geneva and a psychical researcher, published Des Indes à la Planète Mars (1899), his extensive case study of a Swiss medium who called herself Hélène Smith. Smith's supposed visionary experiences, manifested in her paintings of the Martian landscape, inhabitants, and artifacts and, centrally, in the Martian language that she spoke and wrote, attracted the attention of linguists and psychopathologists, dream analysts and surrealists.[12] Smith's visions and the fascination they generated can be more fully understood in the context of other narratives from the 1880s to the 1920s that combined the subject of Mars with psychic experience.

A surprising number of early novels about Mars and Martians are either framed by or deeply imbedded in spiritualist practices. The two most famous Mars narratives in English from the fin de siècle and the early twentieth century glancingly incorporate psychic phenomena into their fiction. H. G. Wells's Martians in The War of the Worlds communicate telepathically, although the narrator clearly reflects Wells's own deep and public skepticism about paranormal phenomena: "Before the Martian invasion, as an occasional reader here or there may remember, I had written with some little vehemence against the telepathic theory." And indeed Wells did write a hostile review for Nature of Frank Podmore's 1894 Apparitions and Thought Transference.[13] In A Princess of Mars (1912), Edgar Rice Burroughs depicts a disembodied John Carter standing

1906

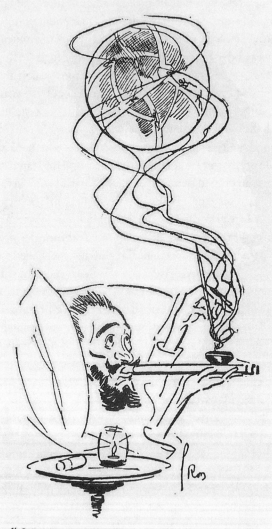

"July First: Camel Flimflammarion Announces
that He Has Distinctly Seen People Swim-
min' in th' Canals iv Mars."

Cartoon of Camille
Flammarion as
Flimflammarion,
by Gordon Ross,
illustrating F[inlay]
P[eter] Dunne, "Mr.
Dooley Reviews the
Year 1906," *New York
Times Magazine*,
30 December 1906,
19; found in the
scrapbooks of Percival
Lowell. Courtesy Lowell
Observatory Archives.

naked over his clothed double, and then being transported instantaneously from a cave in Arizona to the surface of Mars as he "felt a spell of overpowering fascination" with the red star in the night sky. "My longing was beyond the power of opposition; I closed my eyes, stretched out my arms toward the god of my vocation and felt myself drawn with the suddenness of thought through the trackless immensity of space."[14] While there is no evidence of any research by Burroughs into psychic phenomena, it is plausible that he picked up the notion of astral projection of a double from the culture at large. But it is not clear, in any case, that this is a case of astral travel. When Carter returns to the cave in similarly mysterious fashion at the end of *Princess*, he finds the mummy of an ancient woman, a charcoal brazier with an unidentifiable green powder, and a row of human skeletons. Carter's trip to Mars may have been accomplished by old-fashioned witchcraft as much as by newfangled teleportation. While it is of interest to find in Wells and Burroughs reflections of the popular interest in telepathy and astral bodies, to get a fuller appreciation of the interconnections between narratives of Mars and the paranormal it is necessary to examine some much more unfamiliar writers and texts.

The earliest example I have discovered is Henry Gaston's *Mars Revealed, or Seven Days in the Spirit World* (1880), an account of a journey by psychic projection whose publication is dictated by a spirit guide, said to be John of Patmos, author of the Book of Revelation. Some later psychical narratives of journeys to Mars would make at least a nominal effort to tie their accounts to the maps of Schiaparelli and the theories of Lowell, but *Mars Revealed*, published before the surge of publicity over the "canali," depicts an exotic fairy-tale landscape, "a world in ruby, emerald, and silver," a planet lush and full of water in its rivers, lakes, seas, and falls.[15] Gaston includes a prefatory letter that traces the genealogy of his narrative to the doctrines of Swedenborg, a tenable line of descent for many subsequent ventures that link psychic apparatus to interplanetary travels. The preface also makes explicit what is often an ambiguous boundary in paranormal narratives between the factual and the factitious. "Some may consider it a beautiful romance," we are advised, but thoughtful readers will find in it "the very essence of spiritual philosophy" (8).

Mars Revealed, like many of its later paranormal brethren and like earlier "fantastical excursions," offers a hodge-podge of utopian vignettes of communal life, spiritualist propaganda, earnest moralizing, highly colored sentiments and descriptions, and unintended farce. Utopian hygiene and grooming tumble into this latter category when we hear that Martians "give their teeth and mouths a thorough cleansing" each morning and "comb their hair, as do all decent people on the Earth." Men and boys, we are reassured, "part theirs upon the side, like all men of sense on Earth" (200–201). Much of Gaston's Martian imagery appears to derive not from scientific texts but from visionary descriptions of the New Jerusalem. The Mars revealed by John of Patmos is "a miniature heaven" (106) adorned in gold, sapphires, emeralds, and other precious materials. In a curious wedding of astronomy and the numerology of the Book of Revelation, Martian temples are topped with telescopes—including one monster with a lens 144 feet in diameter—and they are guarded carefully, since one must be exemplary in virtue in order to look through one. At the end of the account of the journey to Mars, the narrator acknowledges that he would like to go to Saturn next, but only if readers show a proper appreciation of his Mars narrative. They are exhorted to talk the book up with other potential readers and "then write to the publishers of this book, and encourage them by many purchases" (208). This campaign seems not to have prospered; there was no Saturnian sequel.

In many turn-of-the-century Martian fictions, science and spiritualism coexist uneasily. The plot of Mark Wicks's 1911 To Mars Via the Moon is a veritable encyclopedia of astronomical lore and a fictional homage to Lowell and his Martian writings, but its plot turns on the narrator's discovery on Mars of his reincarnated son (whose name, strangely, is also Mark). Wicks's Martians are both telepaths and prodigious canal builders, and the narrator takes pains to indicate how his journey to Mars—by spaceship, it should be noted, not by astral projection—and his experiences on the planet confirm the maligned theories of Lowell and Flammarion. When, for instance, the Martians reveal that they have no fear of death because of their confidence that they will be reborn on any one of an infinite number of habitable worlds, the traveler has a sudden epiphany. "There are some upon our world who hold very similar ideas, he tells his interlocutor, "notably a great French astronomer named Flammarion."[16]

A more mainstream instance of the incorporation of the paranormal into the literature of Mars is a posthumously published novel by the well-known illustrator for Punch, George DuMaurier. The Martian (1897), despite the alien sound of its title, is for most of its length a conventional and uninspired bildungsroman. It is the account of the growth, intellectual development, and artistic successes of Barty Josselin, a fantasy-version of the author's career. Late in the novel, however, it is revealed suddenly that Barty's consciousness is inhabited by someone named Martia, who has been steering his life since birth. Through Martia's long letter, apparently composed "automatically" in Barty's hand while he was asleep and just before she leaves his body forever, the reader is offered a brief account of Martian geography (only partly informed by current scientific views). Mars is inhabited now only near the equator, with winters there even more brutal than in Spitzbergen. Amphibious, seal-like, furry, vegetarian, and naked, the Martians have highly developed senses, including a sixth sense that is both magnetic and telepathic. Mars has been rid of nearly all its fauna, except for some large fish and bat-like birds, in order to conserve its dwindling resources for the humanoids. The Martians have become "the Spartans of our universe" who are "near the end of their lease" on their native world and perhaps will soon migrate to Venus.[17] But before their extinction or migration, the Martians take a missionary interest in the benighted inhabitants of Earth. Incarnating themselves in "promising unborn though just begotten men and women," as Martia has done with Barty Josselin, they stir their terrestrial hosts with dreams and visions that can open up humanity to the aesthetic and philosophical delights that the inhabitants of Mars know as part of their daily lives. "According to Martia, most of the best and finest of our race have souls that have lived forgotten lives in Mars" (674).

Once a well-known novel, The Martian is not a satisfying work of fiction—longwinded, self-absorbed, awkwardly straddling the realistic and the preternatural modes. It is not in itself a psychic novel, nor does it operate as propaganda for the spiritualist movement. But in its odd importation of telepathy, reincarnation, astral traveling, gender-switching, and automatic writing, it works in some of the leitmotifs that were beginning to appear in paranormal fictions about Mars and it represents the growing popular fascination at the close of the nineteenth century in the connection between the world of Mars and the world of the séance. While DuMaurier seemed to have no program that he was pursuing in The Martian other than an indirect exploration of the shaping of his own professional and emotional life, other authors of Martian "romances of fact" (to use Lowell's term), or their publishers at least, were often eager to advertise an explicit affinity between the psychical content of their narratives and the new astronomical research centered on Mars.[18]

Some of the most dogmatically spiritualist Martian narratives are zealous, even obsessive, about invoking supposed astronomical authority for their visions. One of Schiaparelli's papers on "The Planet Mars" (in the 1893 translation of Lowell's associate, W. H. Pickering) is printed as an appendix to the narrative of Louis Pope Gratacap's The Certainty of a Future Life in Mars (1903). Sara Weiss's 1905 Journeys to the Planet Mars is full of homages to both Schiaparelli and Flammarion. In the most curious example of all, the true author of The Planet Mars and Its Inhabitants (1922), we are told by the purported "amanuensis" J. L. Kennon, is Iros Urides, a Martian. The narrative is punctuated by numerous references to the work of Percival Lowell, sometimes with extensive footnotes summarizing his views and comparing them with the visions of Mars that have been conveyed to the amanuensis by a medium, and it concludes with a ten-page appendix with extensive summaries of the leading ideas of *Mars and Its Canals* and *Mars as the Abode of Life*.

Of all the works of fiction that incorporate spiritualist structures or motifs, none was as influential as Flammarion's, for the obvious reason of his dual status as an astronomer and a popular writer. Because Flammarion was so attached to his theories, both on the habitability of the planets and on reincarnation, his fiction is extraordinarily didactic and autobiographical, as much personal essay as narrative. *Uranie*, published in 1889 and translated into English in the following year, is named for the muse of astronomy. A summary of the organization of this book may suggest how stubbornly the author seeks a seamlessness between astronomy and parapsychology and between romance and fact. In part I, the first-person narrator (we eventually learn that his name is Camille) tells of his apprenticeship at the Paris Observatory at age seventeen where, Pygmalion-like, he becomes obsessed by a statuette of Urania. In a dream, Urania comes alive to take him on a tour of the universe and to introduce him to the infinite diversity of worlds and species. The narrator's friend, twenty-five-year-old astronomer George Spero, is the protagonist of part II. After Spero and his fiancée Iclea are killed in a ballooning accident, the narrator goes to a séance and the savant has a vision of a place with cliffs and foaming seas, sandy beaches, and reddish vegetation. The landscape is Martian, and in the vision, the savant sees Spero and Iclea, who somehow have ended up on Mars after their deaths.

The major portion of part III is devoted to case histories—what Flammarion italicizes as *facts*—that purport to validate claims of communication between the living and the dead. Some of the cases are documented in the text from publications of the Society for Psychical Research. Alternating these "authentic" stories of telepathy with passages on the telescopic observation of Mars, the narrator insists that "astronomy and psychology are indissolubly connected."[19] The narrator falls asleep under a tree and awakens to the sight of two small moons in the sky. He, too, is now on Mars. He feels astonishingly light on his feet, discovers that he has acquired a sixth sense (magnetism), and observes the Earth appearing as the evening star. This last sight leads him to meditate on the failures of most terrestrials to appreciate the beauty of their planet as they indulge in soldiering and nationalist wars: "Ah! if they could behold the earth from the place where I am now, with what pleasure would they return to it, and what a transformation would be effected in their ideas" (166).

The narrator surveys Martian physiology (delicate, winged, six-limbed, and luminescent at night); customs (vegetarian, pacifist, sexually sublimated); and terrain (flat and, of course, networked with irrigation canals). His claim that all his visionary experiences are "completely in accord with the scientific notions we already have of the physical nature of Mars" (175) is true in some respects, if one grants that many astronomers of the period applied the nebular hypothesis to predict that a Martian civilization, if one existed, would be older and more highly developed than terrestrial civilization. Similarly, when he intimates that the climate of Mars would be livable for human beings, he says no more than many astronomical writers of the nineteenth century suggested; however, the graceful analogy he makes manages to downplay the fact that life at the Martian equator would be *very* chilly: "A country of Mars situated on the borders of the equatorial sea differs less in climate from France, than Lapland differs from India" (190).

But *Uranie*'s narrator goes well beyond "scientific notions" about Mars when he starts to pursue some of Flammarion's pet spiritualist fantasies. He has a conversation with his friend Spero, now reincarnated as a woman while his fiancée has emerged in male form. Spero undertakes to enlighten the narrator about the philosophical and spiritual character of life on Mars, and the narrative takes a turn from the improbable to the ludicrous. The Martian body is etherealized and Martians take their nourishment from the atmosphere, freeing them "from the grossness of terrestrial wants" (182). Because their planet is not very "material," the reader is urged to conceive of the Martians as "thinking and living winged flowers" (185). The Martian standard of beauty is highly refined and they view (using telephotographic technology to film and study terrestrial history) "the Apollo Belvidere and the Venus de Medicis [as] veritable monstrosities because of their animal grossness" (188–89). Sexual passion has atrophied (hence Spero and Iclea seem unfazed by their metamorphoses). And the physiology of reproduction has been so spiritualized that the narrator is hard-pressed to find words to describe the process. "Conception and birth take place there in an altogether different manner, which resembles, but in a spiritual form, the fecundation and blossoming of a flower" (185). And for reasons just the reverse of those put forward by Jones and Merchant in *Unveiling a Parallel*, Mars is ruled by the feminine sex because of the delicacy of their sensations and therefore their "incontestable superiority over the masculine" (79).

The most surprising feature of *Uranie* is not that it is fiction with a message, and not even that it is strikingly unsuccessful fiction. Like many more strictly literary, though not necessarily more artistically talented, writers who would follow him, Flammarion used Mars as an excuse to pursue a cultural agenda.

What we might expect of a novel about Mars written by one of the astronomers most closely identified with the popularization of Martian discoveries in the nineteenth century is a thinly disguised paean to science, as the title seems to promise. Instead, this miscellany of "episodes," "researches," and "reflections" that are "brought together in a sort of *Essay*," as Flammarion accurately describes the mixed genre of the book (252), has the distinction of being one of the earliest examples of the fictional misappropriation of scientific research on Mars.

Uranie is in the vanguard of a group of books and pamphlets, published over the next several decades, in which Mars becomes the domain of spiritualists. In such narratives, the link between paranormal experience and astronomical research is often made explicit and visible. Gratacap's *Certainty of a Future Life in Mars* is a reincarnation fable narrated by Bradford Dodd, a young innovator in "interplanetary telegraphy," whose father Randolph—in a move reminiscent of Lowell's journey from Boston to Flagstaff—leaves New York's Hudson River Valley to build his own observatory on Mount Cook in New Zealand. With an echo of Lowell's Mars Hill, Randolph Dodd calls the locale of his observatory "Martian Hill."[20] Throughout the early parts of the narrative, frequent knowledgeable references are made to the Martian drawings of Herschel, Johann, Schroeter, and Schiaparelli, as well as to reports from more recent astronomers, including Henri Perrotin, Francois J. Terby, and Edward S. Holden.

The narrative oscillates between the presentation of then-standard information about Martian climate, topography, and habitability—often buttressed with notes from current numbers of *Scientific American*—and Randolph Dodd's fantastic notions of the evolution of souls through successive reincarnations and streams of transference of life from one plane to another in the solar system. The motive behind his observations of Mars and, more importantly, his efforts to establish wireless contact with Mars, is to communicate with his dead wife who, he believes, may have been "transplanted" (53) to Mars. The sickly father passes on to his son the ambition of achieving "the union of our world with others by magnetic waves" (40). Shortly before his death, the father receives a message of dots and dashes, but in an untranslatable form. He concocts a plan to send a message himself in Morse Code from his future *post mortem* home on Mars and enlists his son to monitor the apparatus in the observatory. A year after Randolph Dodd dies, long transmissions in Morse Code begin to arrive, telling of a Mars full of reincarnated terrestrials—the great majority of them scientists.

The expectation that the era of Edison and Marconi would be a ripe time for communication with Mars and its inhabitants was a notion that the new interest in parapsychology encouraged. If the technology of transport had not yet reached the stage that would gratify the human desire to visit the worlds being disclosed by the telescope, emergent mental powers might do the trick. Just ten years after the publication of Gratacap's narrative, the young Olaf Stapledon, at the beginning of his long epistolary courtship of his cousin, craved a telepathic shortcut: "Writing is such a slow way of conveying thought. Speaking is bad enough. I should like some method of wireless telepathy. If Marconi and Mrs. Eddy and Brahms were to get into partnership they might discover the thing."[21] But Stapledon's whimsy is treated with high seriousness in *The Certainty of a Future Life in Mars*, which is largely absent of intentional humor, save for one irreverent Martian transplant who finds some other Martians "a trifle heavy in style, just a suggestion of a kind of sublimated Bostonese about them" (158).

For Gratacap, Mars has become "a sort of Paradise" (128) or, at least, a "stepping stone" to a "higher beatitude of living" (172). Like Flammarion's Mars, this one also celebrates immateriality and registers its distaste for terrestrial grossness. Its center is a City of Light and its primary aesthetic delight is the most disembodied of the arts, music. There is a ghostly vapidity to the planet and its reincarnated inhabitants: the newly reincarnated are, we are informed in the Morse Code dispatches, "little more than gaseous condensations" (79); the human body is so distilled and etherealized that not only is sexual passion absent but "evaporation replaces defecation" (99). And when death finally comes to the reincarnate, it too is "like evaporation" (104). In many respects, the Mars of Gratacap is less like a heavenly paradise than a Dantean Limbo of the Virtuous in which Randolph Dodd can attend a dinner party where the great physical scientists of Earth's past—Galileo, Isaac Newton, Antoine Lavoisier, Joseph Priestley, Humphry Davy, Léon Foucault, Mary Somerville, Alessandro Volta—engage in scintillating conversation.

There is little of the classic utopian tour in Gratacap's book, although he does address the question of how the reincarnated Martians manage to find the leisure to enjoy their apparently endless delights of travel and music and talk. There are almost no labor-saving technologies in this immaterial culture, save those machines that are used in engineering the canals and manufacturing telescopes. Nevertheless, the reincarnates are fortunate in having "prehistoric" native Martians who cheerfully perform other arduous tasks like mining the marble that is used in constructing the cities. "Where hard labor on a mammoth scale is necessary," the disembodied father reassures his son, "the little race of *prehistorics* serves all their purposes" (183). That the indigenous Martians are brown or copper-colored while all the reincarnates are white makes commentary on the significance of the class division superfluous.

As a novel, *The Certainty of a Future Life in Mars* has little to recommend it. Gratacap tries to generate suspense with an approaching comet that will collide with the capital city of Mars, and by having the son grow fatally ill as he rushes to complete the manuscript based on his father's messages. He also makes an effort to achieve a domestic resolution to the slender plot when, just before the coded messages abruptly end, Dodd discovers his reincarnated wife on Mars. The son's death is reported by his executor, who has been given the charge of having the manuscript published. But the concluding note from the New York editor of the volume we have been reading tells us what may not entirely surprise us—that the manuscript was rejected repeatedly by other publishers before it fell into his hands. At the close, the reader is primed to anticipate a full family reunion on Mars, when the son will also pass through the immigration hall for newly arrived souls. The tenuous narrative, however, has long since deliquesced into little more than the vaporish abstractions that Gratacap's Mars celebrates as human destiny.

The blurred line between fable and factual report suggested by the editorial apparatus in Gratacap's novel is a structural feature common within the tradition of utopian allegories. But the relationship between truth and fiction becomes even more attenuated in Martian narratives that are self-proclaimed "psychic revelations." The authors of such narratives claim only to be amanuenses who record, as faithfully as possible, the communications they receive through their spirit advisors. Take as an example the complete title of one such book published in 1903:

> *Journeys to the Planet Mars or Our Mission to Ento (Mars), Being a record of visits made to Ento (Mars) by Sara Weiss, Psychic, under the guidance of a Spirit Band, for the purpose of conveying to the Entoans, a knowledge of the Continuity of Life, Transcribed Automatically by Sara Weiss Under the Editorial Direction of (Spirit) Carl De L'Ester*[22]

And to enforce the claims of authenticity, Sara Weiss includes thirteen botanically detailed illustrations of Martian flora, a prefatory note on the pronunciation of and gestural accompaniments to the Martian language, and an extensive glossary including tables of specific words for colors, numbers, and personal pronouns.

Like many of the psychical accounts of Mars, Sara Weiss's *Journeys* lacks any principle of narrative selection. At well over five hundred pages, it is a kind of encyclopedia of spiritualist doctrine. Digressions sprout up everywhere, occasioned by any chance sight or comment during the various tours of Mars on which the medium is taken by the company of spirits (led by Carl De L'Ester and including Giordano Bruno, Louis Agassiz, Charles Darwin, Bulwer-Lytton, and Alexander von Humboldt). A visit to the unpopulated Martian poles, for instance, prompts an exposition of the dogma that evolved peoples on all planets gravitate away from inhospitable arctic climates, which leads the medium to ask for—and to get—an account of "the origin of the Eskimos and other polar races of our planet" (439). The references to evolution here and in Flammarion's *Uranie* and Wicks's *To Mars via the Moon* have led Robert Markley to observe that Martian fictions centered on reincarnation and spiritualism are efforts at "reconciling evolutionary theory and Judeo-Christian theology" and at providing comforting reassurance in the face of Wells's more malevolent images of highly evolved Martians in *The War of the Worlds*.[23]

The impact of Lowell's canal hypothesis, with its attendant suppositions about the heroic Martian race and deteriorating planetary environment, is evident in Weiss's frequent observations of and explanations of the "Waterways, Irrigating System, Embankments and other stupendous works" of civil engineering (387). But because the astral journeys to Mars supposedly occurred in 1893 and 1894, Lowell himself is never mentioned (although Sara Weiss made sure to send him a copy of the book on its publication).[24] Instead, late in the book, Carl De L'Ester, in instructing the medium about the words she is to use, makes an explicit reference to other terrestrial astronomers whose work can now be, as it were, "validated" by the psychic testimony:

> Through telescopic observations, one of Earth's foremost astronomers is inclined to believe that the Entoans (Martians) have resorted to irrigation. To him and to another illumined scientific man, who, I am proud to say, is my countryman, you will convey this message: "Gentlemen, to your vision your telescopes convey faint, and generally misleading gleams of what may be facts, but in the instance mentioned, I assure you that the surmise is entirely correct, and inevitably a period will arrive when Earth, like Ento, will require the same treatment. (475–76)

The identity of the two "illumined" scientists is revealed in subsequent extended panegyric apostrophes to Schiaparelli and Flammarion. And a further effort to bring the revelation into line with scientific research is evident in the book's physical design: the front board is stamped with what is labeled "Schiaparelli's Map of Mars."

In 1906, Sara Weiss published a second automatic transcription from Ento, *Decimon Huydas: A Romance of Mars*, again with floral illustrations and—a rarity in such mediumistic narrations—a photograph of herself as frontispiece. This "romance" does have a narrative unity absent from the earlier book, being the sustained story—communicated to Sara Weiss by an Ento spirit with the assistance of Carl De L'Ester—of a domestic tragedy supposed to have occurred hundreds of years earlier on Ento. It is a numbingly tedious recital, interrupted occasionally by a statement of spiritist doctrine about the evolution of life in the solar system. One such statement by the spirit-narrator of the romance details the expectation that at some point in the twentieth century the psychic link between the spirits on Mars and terrestrial mediums will be augmented by the invention of technology for more material telecommunication with Martians. Such a prediction rested on the two-fold faith that Mars was certainly inhabited and that wireless telegraphy would soon open up Mars to exchanges of messages with Earth. Those messages, it was confidently believed, would confirm the stories told by Sara Weiss:

> No other inhabited planet of our solar system presents, in all directions, correspondences so noticeable as those which exist between Ento and Earth; and were I a prophet, or the son of a prophet, I would predict, that ere the close of the present century communication, on a scientific basis, will be established between the two worlds known, astronomically, as Earth and Mars.[25]

For sheer imaginative brazenness, a 1922 text, The Planet Mars and Its Inhabitants, said to be the work of "Iros Urides, A Martian, Written Down and Edited by J. L. Kennon," outdoes even Sara Weiss's narratives. Iros Urides was on Earth two thousand years ago, and Kennon—under the editorial supervision of an angel named Gaston Sergius—takes shorthand dictation from a psychic, Mrs. X——, whose messages come "direct from a disincarnated intelligence of Mars."[26] More interesting than the standard parapsychological apparatus, however, is the omnipresence of Lowell in Kennon's book. Not only is there a drawing of a canal-gridded Mars, but the book has frequent footnotes to popular scientific articles—chiefly by Lowell—as well as an appendix on Lowell with an abstract of fifty-six points taken from Mars and Its Canals and Mars as the Abode of Life. Mrs. X——, we are solemnly assured in the foreword, "knows nothing of astronomy and has never read anything concerning Mars." The fact that the revelations she conveys jibe almost perfectly with Lowell's ideas about Mars is a matter for wonder. The crowning marvel, however, is the book's frontispiece. Kennon receives not only a verbal portrait of a utopian Mars but a series of clairvoyant pictures, one of which is reproduced as a photograph of a

Martian plateau with a large city "built of white stone" (40). No matter that to the ordinary reader's eye the city appears to be nothing more than a cloud or fogbank and that the mountain looks suspiciously terrestrial. It was, after all, a given in psychic narratives about Mars that the similarities among the planets were more important and far more numerous than their differences.

The paranormal periodically cropped up as an ingredient in Mars fiction through much of the first half of the twentieth century, even after the discrediting of both Lowell's Martian theories and the scientific basis of spiritualism. Early in World War II, for instance, an odd hybridization of the utopian and the spiritualist romance appeared in J. W. Gilbert's *The Marsian*. The narrator, a devotee of telepathic experiments and psychic phenomena, is visited by a splendidly angelic being who has heard a "cry of woe" coming from Earth and has experienced "radiations of sadness" in the ether waves.[27] These cosmic signals of the new world war on Earth are the occasion for the narrator's being projected psychically into space. First, he orbits the Earth, explaining terrestrial history, economics, and religion to the incredulous "Marsian" and touring places like the Ford auto plant in Detroit. Then, in part II, he is taken to Mars for a standard utopian excursion and homily on Martian social practices. Gilbert inserts a few inspired moments into the narrative, as in the account of the stunning glassed-in gardens that, helped out by the improvements of "a utopian Burbank," provide bountiful, oversized fruits and vegetables for the Martian population (147). Intensive farming is not the only key to the survival of the Marsians in a deteriorating planetary environment. They also practice population control—a "superstitiously tabooed" subject on Earth, the narrator explains to the Marsian. "One of our good women has almost made a martyr of herself by persisting in the wisdom of birth-control," he says in an apparent reference to Margaret Sanger (142).

Despite such glimmers of inventiveness when Mars holds up a mirror to terrestrial issues, *The Marsian* is an old-fashioned and often ill-written book. Gilbert's earnest collectivism is so heavy-handed that the narrator never even puts up a decent argument in the fashion of the classic utopian dialogues. Obligingly, he capitulates at once to each socialist image on Mars. "My dear brother," he confesses to the visitor from Mars, "to look upon your people makes me feel that my own people are a race of runts" (108). The narrator is a Gulliver-figure of neither charming innocence nor stubborn opinions nor inappropriate sentiments; he is simply a pushover. And the Marsian himself lacks the gravity and complexity of Hugh MacColl's 1889 Mr. Stranger, the theatrical hijinks of Richard Ganthony's messenger from Mars, and the suggestive otherworldliness of other earlier versions of the type. In any case, by 1940, the "man from Mars" figure had long since run its course, and the creakily proselytizing psychic frame of The Marsian guaranteed few readers. Before much longer, the spiritualist fringe of extraplanetary travel literature would be replaced by the fad for alien abduction, and the humanitarian man from Mars would be supplanted by extraterrestrial kidnappers.

Few of these psychic Martian fictions deserve re-reading, although two others that could be said to be late developments in the Flammarion line of a spiritualized Mars are among the literary masterpieces about other worlds. Olaf Stapledon's Last and First Men (1930) and C. S. Lewis' Out of the Silent Planet (1938) will be discussed in chapter 9, but it is worth noting here that both of them use humor to skewer psychical fads. Stapledon's cloud of intelligent Martian viruses are advanced enough to communicate telepathically but are so delusionary that they totally misconstrue the human culture of Earth, associating intelligent life not with the upright bipeds roaming the planet but with the electromagnetic energy transmitted by radio stations: "Here at last was the physical basis of the terrestrial intelligence! But what a lowly creature! What a caricature of life!"[28] Lewis' delightful representation of the physicist Weston's blustering insistence that the telepathic communication of the spiritual being who governs Mars is mere ventriloquism epitomizes the debunking of voices from beyond in séances.

In still later works set on Mars, the indigenous inhabitants sometimes are granted telepathic powers in keeping with their imagined cultural advancement. In his boys' book Red Planet (1949), Robert Heinlein invents Martians that go into trance states while they commune with "the other world"—and Heinlein, despite his reputation for hardheadedness, seems just as comfortable with a dose of parapsychology as he is with including Lowell's canals in his Martian landscape. Ray Bradbury's case is more interesting. He revels in the paranormal in The Martian Chronicles (1950), but far from wanting to advance spiritualist dogma, he is drawn to a fantastic Mars out of which he can create cultural satire and political allegory. The casual gestures made by the Martian girl in this bit of dialogue with the captain of the second American expedition to Mars—a far cry from the solemnity with which parapsychological experience is represented in the committed spiritualist narratives earlier in the century— gives away Bradbury's ironic stance:

"We're Earth Men," he said. "Do you believe me?"

"Yes." The little girl peeped at the way she was wiggling her toes in the dust.

"Fine." The captain pinched her arm, a little bit with joviality, a little bit with meanness to get her to look at him. "We built our own rocket ship. Do you believe *that*?"

The little girl dug in her nose with a finger. "Yes."

"And—take your finger out of your nose, little girl—I am the captain, and—"

"Never before in history has anybody come across space in a big rocket ship," recited the little creature, eyes shut.

"Wonderful! How did you know?"

"Oh, telepathy." She wiped a casual finger on her knee.[29]

Fiction founded on uncritical deployment of psychical phenomena on Mars could not really survive either the casual ironies that come so readily to Bradbury or the definitive death knell to Lowellian Mars that the space age tolled. But however impoverished its literary legacy, the phenomenon of spiritualism in Martian fiction, especially as it was manifested just before and after the turn of the century, is worth some thought. It is almost as if the pseudoscience of the psychics was drawn irresistibly to the faulty science emerging from some of the astronomical observatories. Just as the late 1930s saw an instance of mass hysteria in the United States generated by Orson Welles' broadcast of a Martian fantasy, so the early twentieth century was a ripe time for paranormal delusions. Mars furnished a convenient, and for many people, credible destination for spiritual journeying. And as Freudian and Jungian psychological research and experimentation was beginning to flourish, the claims of psychics who said they had traveled to Mars, observed its people, and even learned its language provided a fertile field for investigators. By far the most famous of the professional studies, published in the last days of the nineteenth century, was Théodore Flournoy's *From India to the Planet Mars*, a case study of the Swiss medium known as Hélène Smith.

The case of Hélène Smith, born Élise Müller, provides a useful perspective on the various published Martian narratives that celebrate paranormal experience. Hélène Smith did not herself publish any of her Martian visions, but in his richly detailed study of her—written with her cooperation, though disowned by her when she saw the published version—Flournoy pays ample attention to what he called her "Martian romance" as well as her "Hindoo romance." A contemporary reviewer of Flournoy's 1899 book wrote shrewdly, "Today, with the great interest that there has been among the spiritists for the writings of Flammarion on the planet Mars and the revelations of the theosophists on the Hindu Masters, it's Mars and the Orient which are fashionable."[30]

As the editor of the 1994 reissue of *From India to the Planet Mars* points out, the case of Hélène Smith today would be classified as an instance of multiple personality. Believing that she was the reincarnation of the fifteenth-century Princess Simandini and of Marie Antoinette, during her séances Smith also adopted the personality of Marie Antoinette's admirer and court magician Cagliostro; him she renamed, in his "discarnate" spirit-form, Léopold, the mentor for all her paranormal experiences. But it was not Smith's ability to take on Cagliostro's personality and voice, complete with male bass and Italian accent, that most fascinated Flournoy, who was himself drawn into what he called her "Hindoo romance" when she informed him that he was the reincarnation of Prince Sivrouka on whose funeral pyre the historical Simandini was cast alive. It was Hélène Smith's glossolalia, the phenomenon of speaking in tongues that was a common behavior of mediums during a séance, which took the unusual form of her speaking at length—and sometimes writing as well—in Martian.

For Flournoy, and for the pioneering linguist Ferdinand de Saussure who was drawn to the Hélène Smith case, the mystery to be solved was where this Martian language, with its elaborate vocabulary and syntax, came from. As a psychologist, Flournoy searched diligently for internal sources of Smith's visions; he believed that the smallest external source, buried in her subliminal memories, could trigger the elaborately creative inventions. While an external source of the Hindoo romance could be traced, circuitously, to historical documents that Smith could have read or heard about, Mars seemed an entirely different matter. Flournoy was inclined to believe that the Martian romance must be a matter of "pure imagination" (87), since no hard historical data existed from which a vision of Mars could be extrapolated. But as Flournoy acknowledges—and as the reviewer quoted above insists—theories about Mars were everywhere in the culture in the last decade of the nineteenth century. A medium's imagination about Mars, far from being pure, was likely to be thoroughly broken in, if not by the books and scholarly articles on the subject of Mars then by news reports and conversations on the Martian debate. And the French-speaking Smith and her acquaintances in the psychic circles in Geneva would above all be aware of Flammarion's writings, interweaving as they did astronomical and parapsychological notions about Mars.

One of the most suggestive discoveries of Flournoy, who attended many of the séances during which Smith "visited" Mars or described Martian scenes in transcriptions from their spiritual "author" on Mars, is something absent from her Martian romance:

He [the supposed spirit-author] shows a singular indifference—possibly it may be due to ignorance—in regard to all those questions which are most prominent at the present time, I will not say among astronomers, but among people of the world somewhat fond of popular science and curious concerning the mysteries of our universe. The canals of Mars, in the first place—those famous canals with reduplication—temporarily more enigmatical than those of the Ego of the mediums; then the strips of supposed cultivation along their borders, the mass of snow around the poles, the nature of the soil, and the conditions of life on those worlds, in turn inundated and burning, the thousand and one questions of hydrography, of geology, of biology, which the amateur naturalist inevitably asks himself on the subject of the planet nearest to us—of all this the author of the Martian romance knows nothing and cares nothing. (120)

What, then, *does* Hélène Smith—or the "author" who is one of her several submerged personalities—care about in her visions of Mars? A single word will do: communication. What is absolutely central to the work of Smith, as to all mediums, is the forging of a link between the living and the dead, the material and the spiritual. It is her voices more than her visions that are primary, and Mars as a site for the reincarnated and the discarnate—as we saw in the narratives by Flammarion, Gratacap, Weiss, and Kennon—is the crucial interest of the turn-of-the-century spiritists. Fifty years later, in strikingly different contexts, the neo-Romantic science-fiction writer Ray Bradbury would have a character say, with exuberant sentimentality, "Mars is heaven."[31] The spiritists, starting with Henry Gaston in *Mars Revealed*, believed something like that, and quite literally.

As Flournoy analyzed the evidence in the case of Hélène Smith, he discovered that almost no technological invention, architectural scheme, social arrangement, costume design, or any other cultural artifact in the Mars that she envisioned ventured beyond what already existed or could be anticipated in the near future on Earth. Even her Martian language, the greatest of the mysteries, turned out to be modeled on French; although Hélène Smith remained of interest to linguists for her extraordinary gifts of mimicry, the Martian language itself was about as innovative as pig Latin. Only in trivial details (eating on square rather than round plates) does Smith's Martian anthropology differ from terrestrial practice; in fact, Mars in its external forms looks a good deal like Asia, as imagined by a European. The jacket illustration for the new edition of *From India to the Planet Mars* is one of Hélène Smith's own oil paintings of

Mars—but anyone who makes a casual study of the details of pagoda-like buildings, hanging gardens, and tunicked figures in turban-like white hats will be reminded instantly of Persian carpets and Indian tapestries. That is, the picture, with what Flournoy calls its "clearly Oriental stamp," could as easily have emerged from Smith's Hindoo romance as from the Martian romance (122).

The psychics who made their astral voyages to Mars, had clairvoyant images of its cities, transmitted messages from both its incarnate and discarnate inhabitants, and reunited grieving terrestrial mourners with their reincarnated families and friends living happily as Martians were not as different from Percival Lowell as one might at first think. Like him, they believed they had proceeded from mere fantasies about other worlds to the higher level of romance of fact. They too thought their methods were scientific, or at least advance forays into the new science of the twentieth century—and they too found in Mars exactly what they expected to find, exactly what their theories told them they would find. For them, too, Mars was a mirror in which they saw their own ideological reflections.

MASCULINIST
FANTASIES

Nobody was shrewder than C. S. Lewis in analyzing how readers' (and writers') desires are gratified by the locale of stories. Other worlds, he liked to say, are treasured locales because they offer satisfactions difficult to achieve in the familiar and quotidian settings of realistic narrative. When Lewis wrote stories of his own set on other worlds—including his Mars novel—the possibilities and satisfactions that he particularly sought were spiritual, even theological. But he could acknowledge other uses for alternate worlds as well.[1] Some of these uses we have already encountered in late nineteenth-century fictional treatments of Mars: the utopian, the mystical, the prophetic, and the corrective pleasures that an invented Mars served.

Now our focus shifts to a simpler, less intellectual, often more vulgar, and certainly more popular set of pleasures. In an era when our native planet was increasingly deromanticized and demythologized, when the American frontier had been declared officially closed, when exotic (that is, non-EuroAmerican) locations already had been fully explored and exploited, Mars provided an opportunity for recovering the pleasures of romance. While not utterly neglecting the new information and theories developed by telescopic observers, the popular romancers were drawn to the red planet in all its ancient associations with war, blood, and male prowess—to which they often added the modern baggage of colonialism and racism. For such writers, Mars tended to be less a futuristic setting that opened new horizons for speculation than a nostalgic and provincial one. This Mars would have princesses. And swords and beasts, fistfights and magic, slaves and treasure, but especially princesses. A group of narratives written over a twenty-five-year period will illustrate this first modern outcropping of masculinist fantasies about Mars, starting with Gustavus Pope's 1894 *Journey to Mars* and concluding with Marcianus Rossi's 1920 *A Trip to Mars*. This body of fiction includes Ellsworth Douglass' *Pharaoh's Broker* (1899), George Griffith's *A Honeymoon in Space* (1901), Edwin Arnold's *Lieut.*

Gullivar Jones (1905), and the book that more than any other typifies this sub-genre, and that has gathered the largest (predominantly male) audience for the past century, Edgar Rice Burroughs' A Princess of Mars (1912). At the end of the chapter, we will take a side trip to the one significant group of masculinist fantasies about Mars without princesses: some early boys' adventure books.

To call such books masculinist is an anachronism. A construct of the 1990s, masculinism is a defensive assertion of male worth in the face of a perceived threat from feminism. The men who wrote Martian romances between 1894 and 1920 did not feel besieged by feminism—the term had only just barely come into use in that period—although there is plenty of evidence of irritation at and contempt for demonstrating suffragists.[2] But anything as formal as a philosophical or activist men's movement would have been perceived in 1917 as both unnecessary and incomprehensible. Nevertheless, there is a need for some terminology to characterize what is distinctive about what may be ag-glomerated loosely as Burroughsian fiction about Mars. These books stand out as fundamentally opposite to feminist utopian fiction of the same era, such as Mary Bradley's Mizora (1890), Ella Merchant and Alice Ilgenfritz Jones' Mar-tian utopia Unveiling a Parallel (1893), and—now the best-known of them all—Charlotte Perkins Gilman's Herland (1914). The masculinist Martian fictions are peopled with princesses and slave-girls, and virtually no other female charac-ters. The male travelers expect to find princesses on Mars and devote much of their time either to courting or to protecting them. Isidor Werner, the feck-less Midwestern grain agent with the Chicago Board of Trade in Douglass's Pharaoh's Broker, becomes infatuated with a languid, blank-eyed woman whom he encounters on Mars, and addresses her in language he seems to think ap-propriate to a royal figure: "If thou art the queen, command me but by a look or sign, and I obey. And if thou art not the queen, then they should make thee one."[3] The one book in this group with no Martian princess at all—Grif-fith's Honeymoon—has an American one, the new spouse of the aristocratic English protagonist. Lilla Zaidie Rennick, the conservative product of new-world wealth who spends her honeymoon touring the solar system, enjoys life on a pedestal. She cannot endure the thought that she might be descended from an ape and chooses to see herself as the daughter of the original queen of the Earth. "Darwin was quite wrong when he talked about the descent of man—and woman. We—especially the women—have ascended from that sort of thing, if there's any truth in the story at all; though, personally, I must say I prefer dear old Mother Eve."[4] The ubiquitous princesses, actual and putative, of Martian romance translate the antifeminist cultural assumptions of the authors into extraterrestrial fantasy.

The division of all women on Mars into royalty and servants mirrors the dichotomies that were characteristic of prefeminist thought. The woman on the pedestal and the woman on her knees were two positionings of the same person, as the male habit of worship shifted gears into a habit of dominating. The first husband of Charlotte Perkins Gilman once wrote about her, ominously, "She was innocent, beautiful, frank. I grasped at her with the instincts of a drowning heart—was saved for the time. I loved all I saw pure in her."[5] Walter Stetson later would take fictional form in the nightmare image of the suffocating husband of the autobiographical crawling woman in Gilman's masterpiece, *The Yellow Wallpaper*. In the Martian romances, the baldest acknowledgment of the struggle for sexual equality that is taking place in real time, outside the fictionalized Mars, occurs in what is on the surface the most mild-mannered of the masculinist fantasies about Mars, Douglass's *Pharaoh's Broker*. The protagonist, who has accompanied a German physicist-inventor on the first journey to Mars, makes a deal with the Martian Pharaoh to acquire huge amounts of surplus grain in exchange for gold. The Pharaoh is so pleased by the agreement that he gives the broker a slave-girl as a gift. Nonplussed, the broker offers the slave her freedom, but she begs not to be degraded and turned out into the world masterless. "This age," observes the physicist, "is not ripe for the grand idea of freedom which dominates our own."[6] Here we have the inverse of Merchant and Jones's unveiled parallel. The eager return of the Martian slave to her bondage operates as a cautionary fable about the dangers and unhappiness that rebellious terrestrial women bring on themselves.

In the masculinist treatments of Mars, the element of fantasy is shaded in very different ways from the scientific romances we have already examined. Consider a moment in Burroughs' *Princess of Mars* when the protagonist, trying to find his way around the landscape of Mars (called Barsoom by its inhabitants), asks the titular princess if she can help him with a map:

> "Yes," she replied, and taking a great diamond from her hair she drew upon the marble floor the first map of Barsoomian territory I had ever seen. It was crisscrossed in every direction with long straight lines, sometimes running parallel and sometimes converging toward some great circle.[7]

To any observant reader who had seen one of the numerous newspaper illustrations of Percival Lowell's maps and globes of Mars, this would be a moment of recognition. But Burroughs has no abiding interest in Lowellian Mars, and the brutal, fractious Martian culture he imagines is antithetical to Lowell's conception of a utopian global community. The diamond and marble materials for mapmaking engage Burroughs more than scientific issues; his imagination is exotic, not astronomical; his artistic sensibilities run more to primary colors than to subtle tints. Inoculated against criticism, Burroughs viewed with suspicion those he once characterized as "scholars and self-imagined literati." That defensive put-down was part of his response to Q. D. Leavis's questionnaire to best-selling authors for her famous study of literary taste and expectations, Fiction and the Reading Public, where she took up Burroughs' romances as examples of "light reading," reading for "mental relaxation" and the pleasures of "day-dreaming." Such fiction, Leavis argued, "for very many people is a means of easing a desolating sense of isolation and compensates for the poverty of their emotional lives."[8]

It is doubtful that Burroughs made much effort, if any, to read Lowell carefully in dreaming up his narrative. As Brian Aldiss has observed, Burroughs was impatient with scientific fact and his Martian fiction "reports on areas which cannot be scrutinized through any telescope."[9] The scattered references in A Princess of Mars to "so-called canals," the moons Phobos and Deimos, strips of vegetation, and dead sea bottoms could have been gotten second hand from many popular accounts of Lowell's ideas.[10] Astronomical images are incidental to the hormonal mayhem that runs the battery of Burroughs' plot. By contrast, for earlier writers like Robert Cromie in A Plunge into Space and Wells in The War of the Worlds, the new knowledge about Mars led to a kind of romance of ideas, a romance in which scientific discovery and theory were not merely departure points for adventure but central subjects for imaginative analysis.

In the Martian fiction of Americans Pope, Douglass, Burroughs, and Rossi, as well as that of British writers Griffith and Arnold, a more old-fashioned sort of romance comes into play. The naval hero of Arnold's Lieut. Gullivar Jones: His Vacation is likened to Sinbad the Sailor, and he calls his experience on Mars an "incredible fairy tale of adventure."[11] As a group, the masculinist narratives recall the "fantastical excursions" of earlier eras, suggested by the presence in the titles of tourist terms like "journey," "vacation," and "honeymoon." The tenor is often an exotic mix of the luxurious and the outlandish: jeweled architecture, costumes of silk and fur, fabulous creatures drawn from terrestrial prehistory or from legend, scenic landscapes of a lushness quite incompatible with an arid Mars. Fantasy easily crosses the line into the grotesque, as in the "piscatorial pandemonium" in Pope's account of a sea battle between the Leviathan and aggressive swordfish.[12] The strain for gorgeous effects leads to composite absurdity in Rossi's description of a Martian girl with "brilliant gold-fish skin, vivid azur [sic] eyes, beautiful green hair, shining pearl teeth, paradise bird feathers on her wings."[13] At the other extreme, there are insipidities drawn from the thin soup of romance conventions. The opening paragraph of a chapter in Pope's *Journey to Mars* has nothing specifically Martian in it. In its archaic pastoral generality, even in the name of the prince who presides over the landscape, the scene belongs more to Versailles than to Mars, and the passage might have graced an eighteenth-century Gothic romance rather than an extraterrestrial one:

> A charming rural scene was displayed. A broad and level plateau extended along the river's banks and ornamented with magnificent trees interspersed with bowers and open glades. Along the greensward were hundreds of tents and pavilions decorated with banners and occupied by the invited guests. We entered the Duke's *maison de campagne*, a beautiful chateau embowered amid a grove; the ducal party had arrived a short time before. We retired to our apartments and having made our toilettes for the festival, passed out to the lawn where the guests were assembled. The Princess with her suite of beautiful young ladies were clad in rustic attire, as flower girls, nut and berry gatherers, dairy maids and shepherdesses. Prince Altfoura with his friends, as foresters, hunters, horsemen, farmer boys and fishermen.[14]

What sets the Martian romances discussed in this chapter apart from others of the era, however, is not the canned romanticism of their styles, a feature of many late Victorian works of popular fiction. The literary inheritance these romances can claim is derived principally from neo-Arthurian codes of honor and *Arabian Nights* wonders. To Pope's traveler to Mars, the buildings of the capital city look Moorish and the planet's giant birds recall the fabled roc of Islamic fantasy; Arnold's Lieut. Gullivar Jones is actually transported to Mars by flying carpet; and the otherwise technologically advanced Martians of Pope, Burroughs, and Rossi prefer fighting with swords and bows. But this is a heritage already detectable in earlier books such as Percy Greg's *Across the Zodiac* and Robert Braine's *Messages from Mars, By the Aid of the Telescope Plant*. The distinctive ingredient in the Martian stories of Pope, Burroughs, and company is a narrative focus and a targeted audience that are resolutely male. To the Orientalist and neomedievalist flourishes of Greg and Braine, the masculinist romancers of Mars add the frontiersman ethos of American westward expansionism and the tawdry glamour of European colonialist adventures.

It has been a shibboleth of middle and late twentieth-century popular culture that outer space—and, with increasing specificity, Mars—constitutes a new frontier. But the imaginative redrawing of the frontier boundary actually began to occur in 1890, when the U.S. Census announced that so many pockets of (white) settlement had been found in regions previously unsettled (by whites) that the term "frontier" no longer could be considered operative. In 1893, at the Columbian Exposition in Chicago, in observance of the four hundredth anniversary of Columbus's landing in the new world, Frederick Jackson Turner took the closing of the frontier as the springboard for his famous address on "The Significance of the Frontier in American History." Turner argued that American ideals and behaviors had been shaped by the process of fresh beginnings in new places under difficult conditions. "This perennial rebirth, this fluidity of American life, this expansion westward with its new opportunities, its continuous touch with the simplicity of primitive society, furnish the forces dominating American character."[15] Near the end of his essay, Turner inventoried the traits of the American intellect—we might call them the cowboy virtues—that had evolved from the conditions of frontier life: coarseness, strength, acuteness, inquisitiveness, practicality, inventiveness, materialism, energy, individualism, buoyancy, exuberance, freedom. Turner made no attempt to prophesy how, exactly, Americans would function without the presence of a geographical frontier. The cowboy painter Charlie Russell, in a verse written in 1917 (the year of the book publication of A Princess of Mars), foresaw a revival of the frontier ethos in literature—although it is unlikely that he (or Turner, for that matter) would have thought of Martian fiction as a probable venue:

The west is dead my Friend
But writers hold the seed
    And what they sow
    Will live and grow
Again to those who read.[16]

When Edgar Rice Burroughs opened A Princess of Mars in the year 1866 with his hero wafted from a tomb-like cave in the Arizona Territory and reborn on the surface of Mars ("prone upon a bed of yellowish, moss-like vegetation"), it is as if the author were announcing that the dying frontier of the American West was being removed to and reconfigured on another world.[17] There is no space vehicle to take the hero from Arizona to Mars; there appears simply to be a permeable border between the two places. Arizona, and specifically Mars Hill in Flagstaff, was the location of the Lowell Observatory, but perhaps even more significantly, Arizona was the last major western territory to achieve statehood, becoming the forty-eighth state in 1912, when Burroughs published the first magazine version of his Mars book with the title "Under the Moons of Mars." In that year, the end of Arizona's frontier status became definitive. Before long, it would become a commonplace in the literature of Mars that no place on Earth looked more like the red planet than northern Arizona. Already in 1920, the hero of Rossi's *A Trip to Mars* sets up a communications link with the directors of Earth's major observatories to report to them on Martian topography: "The Prairies are like our Western American deserts."[18]

In *A Princess of Mars*, the connections to the American Wild West are pervasive. Burroughs' protagonist John Carter, an Indian fighter being hunted by Apache warriors, is conveyed magically from his cave in Arizona to a hot and arid landscape that he knows, immediately and instinctively, must be Mars. There, encountering giants armed with spears and rifles, Carter remarks, "I could not disassociate these people in my mind from those other warriors who, only the day before, had been pursuing me."[19] Throughout his adventures on Mars, Carter repeatedly connects the Martians—especially those with red skins—to their terrestrial counterparts in the American West. "I could not but be struck," he says of a group of mounted and befeathered Martian troops, "with the startling resemblance the concourse bore to a band of the red Indians of my own Earth" (142). And the Martian princess, Dejah Thoris, is linked obsessively by Carter, whose mind runs on torture and sexual violation, to captive white pioneer women in the Amerindian West.

An even eerier evocation of the white occupation of the American West can be found in Griffith's *Honeymoon in Space*, where a Martian "chief," dazzled by the beauty of the protagonist's new wife (a term and concept unknown on Mars), tries to acquire her. Immediately, the husband-hero goes into a frenzy of destruction with pistol and Maxim gun. Instead of showing anger or seeking reprisal, the chief blandly accepts that he and his fellow Martians are not "convenient" for the terrestrial visitants; nevertheless, when the Chief steps toward her, the disgusted woman, with the cool remark "That's not a man," shoots him in the head.[20] Her husband quietly reassures her that "he's better dead," and advises his wife to have some cognac and a nap (164). The entire episode— written by an Englishman, with an American heroine who is "a daughter of the younger branch of the Race that Rules" (18)—suggests a smoothly allegorical justification of the removal, by death and relocation, of the indigenous people of the American prairies for the convenience of Anglo-Saxon pioneers—and rich honeymooners.

Even more important than the Western frontier to the ambience of the masculinist romances of Mars is the Africa of British colonialism. When Arnold's Lieutenant Gullivar Jones enters an outlying Martian town, he offers his reader a literary shortcut: "If I said it was like an African village on a large scale, I should probably give you the best description in the fewest words."[21] If the *voyages extraordinaires* of Jules Verne inspired many of the first Martian scientific romances, then the African adventure stories of H. Rider Haggard can be regarded as the standard model for the masculinist fantasies of Mars. The famous dedication of Haggard's *King Solomon's Mines* (1885) "to all the big and little boys who read it" is about as transparent an instance of masculinism as one could wish for. But even without that advertisement, the book has the mark of male all over it, from the loving catalogue of armaments to be used in Allan Quatermain's expedition to present-day Zimbabwe ("Three heavy breechloading double-eight elephant guns," "three double .500 expresses," "one double No. 12 central-fire Keeper's shot-gun, full choke both barrels," "three Winchester repeating rifles," "three single-action Colt's revolvers") to Quatermain's battle-eve redaction of the King's anxieties the night before Agincourt in Shakespeare's *Henry V*:

> I shook my head and looked again at the sleeping men, and to my tired and yet excited imagination it seemed as though death had already touched them. My mind's eye singled out those who were sealed to slaughter, and there rushed in upon my heart a great sense of the mystery of human life, and an overwhelming sorrow at its futility and sadness. Tonight these thousands slept their healthy sleep, tomorrow they, and many others with them, ourselves perhaps among them, would be stiffening in the cold; their wives would be widows, their children fatherless, and their place know them no more for ever.[22]

Perhaps nowhere is the line connecting Haggard's Africa to the masculinists' Mars drawn more clearly than in the scene in which Quatermain intimidates a tribe by claiming that he and his companions come from outer space: " 'It is granted,' I said, with an imperial smile. 'Nay, ye shall know the truth. We come from another world, though we are men such as ye; we come,' I went on, 'from the biggest star that shines at night.' "[23] The colonial con-man has a good deal in common with the extraterrestrial imperialist. The two Earthmen in Douglass' *Pharaoh's Broker*, professing peaceable intentions on Mars, nevertheless behave like Haggard's Englishmen in Africa. With disdain for the "primitive" inhabitants, whom they easily cow with guns and terrestrial technology, they casually kill several Martians and try to induce the rest to see them, descended from their spaceship, as "Thunder-gods."[24] Griffith's American heroine Zaidie Rennick christens an open area in a beautiful Martian city "Central Park" and urges her English husband, "If we don't find these people nice, I guess we'd better go back and build a fleet like this, and come and take it." Her husband, Rollo Lenox, Earl of Redgrave, who knows that Britain has no monopoly on colonialist habits of mind, labels that sentiment "the new American imperialism."[25]

In addition to the assumption about the inherent right of Americans and Europeans to do as they like with "inferior" peoples and their land, *King Solomon's Mine* adumbrates other recurrent motifs in the masculinist fictions of Mars: the celebration of the ethos of war and the warrior; a preoccupation with hierarchical conceptions of race; a paradoxical (for the American writers, at least) infatuation with royalty and aristocracy; social Darwinism; and the definition of manliness. Even more than Haggard's African fiction, the mode in which these Martian narratives are written tends toward the high preposterous—great helpings of what in Pope's *Journey to Mars* are called "whimsical conceptions and monstrous absurdities" decked out in a style that mingles strut and bluster with rhetorical archaisms.[26] The self-consciously masculine hero is likely to leaven his bloodthirstiest assertions with a sprinkling of gentlemanly beholds, nays, and 'twases. In the pursuit of his captured Martian princess, named Heru, Edwin Arnold's Gullivar Jones gives a ludicrous tongue-lashing to the native Martians who fail to live up to his standards of bravery: " 'What!' I roared, 'Heru taken from the palace by a handful of men and none of you infernal rascals—none of you white-livered abortions lifted a hand to save her—curse on you a thousand times. Out of my way, you churls.' "[27] Later, he will confess, "Well, I am no fine writer," an admission Jones shares with Haggard's Quatermain, "more accustomed to handle a rifle than a pen."[28] How much the willfully anti-literary bent of the masculinist writers about Mars rationalizes a slenderness of talent may be a matter of opinion, but the unjust reputation of science fiction for artistic sloppiness and carelessness with language owes a large debt to writers of this school.

The earliest of this group, Gustavus Pope, makes the most revealing display of the artistic insecurity that characterizes many of the masculinist romances of Mars. His narrative of over five hundred pages is peppered with quotations from English poets, particularly Shakespeare, Pope, and Byron, although it is Milton who haunts his *Journey to Mars*. Many chapters have epigraphs from *Paradise Lost*, and Milton's angels, devils, hell, and paradise are frequent reference points for the exposition of Mars. The pedigree this tissue of allusion seems calculated to provide for his narrative is belied by the relentlessness of cliché and stylistic flatfootedness when Pope writes in his own voice—purportedly the manuscript of Lieutenant Frederick Hamilton, an American naval officer. When Hamilton must describe his Martian princess, Suhlamia, he announces grandly that her beauty cannot be expressed in terrestrial language because our highest aesthetic canons fall so far below the Martian standard. Having said that, he goes on to itemize her assets in the most conventional princessly terms: luxuriant hair, delicate complexion, small hands and feet, magnificent eyes that are "perfect mirrors of her pure noble soul," elegant carriage, sweet expression.[29]

Almost nothing is known of Gustavus Pope's identity, save for the bare information contained in his title-page and preface that he was a Washington, D.C., physician. But if the contents of *Journey to Mars* are an index of his personality, we can deduce a patriotic sentimentalist with a classical education and a preoccupation with matters of race and color. At the beginning of his manuscript, when Hamilton is rescued from an ice-cavern on a floating berg by a young stranger not yet identified as a Martian, he is astounded that his savior is unfamiliar with the United States of America. "Can it be possible that you have never heard of the greatest and most glorious Republic on the face of the Earth, whose name is honored in every land and whose Star Spangled Banner floats over every ocean on the globe?"[30] That American chauvinism is celebrated repeatedly throughout the narrative. At one point, Hamilton is overcome with tears when he sees the American flag flown from a naval flagship on another planet and hears a Martian band, with innumerable trumpets and drums, blaring out the American anthem. Lieutenant Hamilton's naval colleague, Arnold's Lieutenant Gullivar Jones, displays a similar jumble of soft-headed and fierce-hearted patriotism. Finding in a remote polar region of Mars a shore full of jewels—the kind of landscape that comes straight out of the *Arabian Nights*—Jones exults, " 'All ownerless, and with so much treasure hidden hereabout! Why, I shall annex it to my country' . . . I whipped out my sword, and in default of a star-spangled banner to plant on the newly-acquired territory, traced in gigantic letters on the snow-crust—U.S.A."[31]

In Pope's *Journey*, the new militarism of the United States in the decade of the Spanish-American War sits side-by-side with the old militarism of classical myth. Pope emphasizes the bellicose character of the war-god's planet: omnipresent helmets, swords, champing steeds, fiery-spirited warriors, and naval vessels that "bristled with military engines whose terribly destructive power is unknown on Earth."[32] In his burnished armor, the Prince Altfoura whom Hamilton befriends, "looked like a young Mars fresh from Olympus."[33] When Hamilton also observes a Martian chariot, its prow decorated with a Neptunian figure armed with a trident, he is astounded by the resemblance of Martian to Grecian mythology. The puzzle is resolved by a Martian doctor who explains, just as Fontenelle had done two centuries earlier, that humanity is basically the same on every planet.

None of the other masculinists is quite as explicit as Pope about the convergence of planetary mythologies, but nearly all of them create similarly striking cultural parallels. Douglass's Martians speak Hebrew; Rossi's, Latin; and

Griffith's, English. In *Pharaoh's Broker*, Douglass explains that each habitable world passes through the same historical phases, and Mars is running a bit behind the Earth; at the end of the terrestrial Victorian Age, the Martians are re-enacting the Jewish captivity in Egypt. Rossi's Martians speak Latin because a Roman forcibly emigrated in A.D. 79 when Vesuvius erupted and blew him to Mars, where he instructed young natives in his own language. Absurd as these two rationales are, Griffith manages to outdo his colleagues. In *A Honeymoon in Space*, we learn that the preference on Mars for English is the sign of a highly developed civilization since the Martians are clever enough to recognize that English is, obviously, the "most convenient" of all languages.[34] Besides, the aristocratic Rollo Lenox tells his wife, Earth itself is moving into a similar one-language-fits-all stage of development when a dominant English will eliminate all other languages. Griffith naïvely enshrines precisely the kind of Anglo-centric illusions that H. G. Wells had taken pains to satirize just three years earlier in *The War of the Worlds*.

Pope's enthusiasm for combat, and his resurrection of the mythological identification of the planet Mars with the male god of aggression, is avidly taken up by the other masculinists. The military hero becomes a fixture of Burroughsian romance, with *A Honeymoon in Space*'s Lenox (an aviator in whom "the thousand-year-old Berserker awoke"),[35] Arnold's Gullivar Jones (another Navy lieutenant), and, most emphatically, Burroughs' own John Carter (Confederate war veteran, Indian fighter, mercenary in several kingdoms and re-publics, and anointed "warlord" of Mars). As Hamilton in Pope's *Journey to Mars* disdains the "philosophical idiots" and "brainless fops" of polite American society as well as the "royal swells, fops, dudes and weaklings" he finds on Mars, so Carter scourges "the weakling and the saphead."[36] Even the most effete of the masculinist heroes, Rollo Lenox, casually rams several Martian airships with his spacecraft simply because he believes the first Martians he encountered behaved "absolutely caddishly."[37] When Zaidie mildly protests the death of all the crew members, Lenox condescends to his new wife (her body mass on the pedestal noticeably shrinking): "When you are dealing with brutes, little woman, it is sometimes necessary to be brutal."[38]

The outstanding instance of the self-consciously martial hero is Burroughs' John Carter who, in the moment before his mystical transit across outer space, looks into the Arizona sky and sees the "large red star": "As I gazed upon it I felt a spell of overpowering fascination—it was Mars, the god of war, and for me, the fighting man, it had always held the power of irresistible enchant-ment."[39] Mars, or Barsoom, turns out to be full of humanoid males whose every waking moment is devoted to provoking conflict and then wallowing in the bloodletting that inevitably follows. But the men who come from Earth bring their own reserves of fury to the angry red planet and often outdo their Martian counterparts not only in the amount of damage they do but in their sheer exuberant enjoyment of it.

Burroughs' hero is the pattern of all the attributes of male aggression celebrated by the masculinist romancers. "Through Carnage to Joy" is the title of the climactic chapter 26 of A Princess of Mars in which Carter wins the hand of the princess, and it is clear that without carnage there can be no joy. The ecstasy of slaughter surpasses every other pleasure. Sexual desire has largely atrophied on Burroughs' Mars, and Carter adjusts easily to both the martial and the anti-erotic aspects of Barsoomian culture. Naked throughout his sojourn, he dispatches Martians with abandon on the battlefield, in the throne room, at the arena, along the canals, but his attachment to the similarly naked Princess Dejah Thoris is strangely formal, chivalric, almost unsexual. Burroughs' preference for Mars over Eros is made explicit in Carter's algebraic credo of masculinism: "I verily believe that a man's way with women is in inverse ratio to his prowess among men."[40]

Male honor in the masculinist fantasies even asserts its primacy over the neochivalric principles of protecting female virtue and safety. Gullivar Jones displays an ambivalence toward Ar-Hap, king of the barbarians on Mars, reviling him as the ravisher of Princess Heru but admiring his manliness and foreseeing with satisfaction Ar-Hap's ultimate conquest of the pretty "Hither Folk," "those triflers, those pretences of manhood."[41] Similarly, Burroughs' Carter refrains at one point from killing the would-be torturer of his princess because of another warrior's long-standing grievance (and therefore prior title to vengeance) against the villain. "I could not rob him of that sweet moment," he decides.[42] The knightly tenets of Camelot undergo marked revision on the fields of Barsoom. A princess may be an object of obsessive devotion for the adventurer on Mars, but if he has to make a hard choice between the rival claims of the princess and a comrade-in-arms, the male bond umpires the conflict. The privileges of the soldier matter more than a woman's vulnerability to danger, even when the woman in question is the much-rhapsodized-over Princess Dejah Thoris.

As the male writer imagines his female characters' reactions to this heroic revisionism, the new system of values is gratifyingly endorsed by all the women concerned. "Was there ever such a man!" Dejah Thoris exclaims of Carter.[43] And the female slave assigned to take care of him is even more gushing. "John Carter, if ever a real man walked the cold, dead bosom of Barsoom you are one."[44] Even the flexible masculinist ethics of the old American South suits her:

"I trust you because I know that you are not cursed with the terrible trait of absolute and unswerving truthfulness, that you could lie like one of your own Virginia gentlemen if a lie would save others from sorrow or suffering."[45]

The preoccupation with the "real man" illuminates one of the most striking cultural displacements to Mars in fiction at the turn of the century. Alpha-males in the Martian romances are all committed believers in the survival of the fit, biologically and socially. "I'm a hopeless Darwinian," says Rollo Lenox, and Isidore Werner's first sight of Martians in *Pharaoh's Broker* reassures him of his own superiority since they are "just fat, puffy, sluggish men."[46] Carter strongly approves of the eugenical policies on Barsoom that regulate breeding and permit the shooting of defective offspring. In Pope's *Journey to Mars*, despite the glamorizing of hereditary aristocrats and princesses that it shares with the other masculinist romances, Hamilton refuses to "toady to royalty on Mars," invoking American democratic values, "as I fancy any officer in Uncle Sam's Navy would have done."[47] But all these compulsive fantasies of cultural superiority go beyond simple assertions about rugged American individualism and the then-fashionable notions of social Darwinism. What receives the most pervasive and repeated attention in these works, and what links them once again with Haggard's African fiction as well as with the "Yellow Peril" literature of the late nineteenth century, is the subject of race.

In her study of the imperial theme in Rider Haggard's fiction, Wendy Katz has observed that "racism is more a given of the African scene than a preached doctrine" and that a "combination of asserted tolerance and practised racism" characterizes Haggard's narratives.[48] Similarly, the most blatant illustrations of racism in the Martian romances coexist blandly with platitudes about universal human nature, like the one Gustavus Pope makes in his prefatory "To My Readers": "It may be assumed, in strict accordance with the spirit of Science, Philosophy and Religion—as well as analogy,—that, Humanity, created in the Image of God, must necessarily and always be the same in *Esse*, in essential Being and Nature, on whatever habitable planet of our Solar system it may find its home, sphere of action and environment, and it is wholly contrary to reason to assume otherwise."[49] The hollowness of the sentiment is exposed at the end of *Journey to Mars*, when Hamilton, returning to Earth in a vehicle staffed by a Martian crew, observes a boat full of Chinese "coolies" capsize in a storm. When the Martians want to rescue them, Hamilton dissuades them because the coolies are "ignorant and superstitious" and must be left to their fate.[50] A few moments later, however, Hamilton spots a man, woman, and baby among the wreckage and is nearly beside himself: " 'Great God! I exclaimed; 'they are of my race—white men,—quick,—lower the ship.' "[51]

Pope makes color a visible fact of life on Mars, with yellow-, red-, and blue-skinned races in a carefully maintained hierarchy. Miscegenation is considered abhorrent, and Pope goes so far as to include a lengthy footnote approving Martian laws against racial mixing: "The laws of heredity are inexorable. The moral, mental and physical degeneracy of the greater part of our semi-civilized and barbarous races is due to these admixtures. It is also seen in our own country, in Mexico, and in parts of South America, in the mongrels of indian and negro, white, indian and negro, as is shown in our half-breeds, mulattoes, quadroons, etc. This, of course, does not apply to the alliances of different nationalities of the same race."[52] In *Honeymoon in Space*, the expedition by Lenox and his new American wife is endorsed formally by the United States President as an opportunity to demonstrate Anglo-Saxon superiority in the universe.[53] The Martian tour-guide for the terrestrial voyager in Rossi's *Trip to Mars* shows him representatives of "our inferior race, the same as your terrestrian negroes."[54] Burroughs, as usual, is even more expansive. Like Pope, he imagines several different colored races on Mars, all portrayed as in various stages of degeneracy. The evidence of a superior civilization, now mostly in ruins, is finally explained when John Carter observes murals depicting the creators of high Martian culture: "people like myself . . . fair-skinned, fair-haired people."[55] In his foreword to *A Princess of Mars*, Burroughs claims to have met Carter, "a typical southern gentleman of the highest type," at his father's house where "our slaves fairly worshipped the ground he trod."[56] It is not surprising, perhaps, that in the aftermath of the Confederate defeat, Carter identifies himself with the extinct white rulers of Mars.

The era of the masculinist romances coincides with the first boys' books of science fiction, and two of the earliest—the Englishman Fenton Ash's *A Trip to Mars* (1909) and the American *Through Space to Mars* (1910) by "Roy Rockwood"—lay out the paradigms for fictional treatments of Mars intended explicitly for teenaged boys. The line between Martian narratives whose intended audience is adult and those read primarily by children and teenagers is not always readily definable. Some scholars think Mark Wicks's textbookish romance *To Mars via the Moon* (1911), for instance, may have been designed to introduce young readers to current scientific theories about Mars, but its themes and structure seem too sober and dull to appeal to teenagers and none of its three voyagers to Mars is young enough to encourage a juvenile audience's identification.[57] Certainly, however, Burroughs' *Princess of Mars* became a staple adventure book for male teenagers throughout much of the twentieth century, even though Burroughs made no use of youthful protagonists. A distinctive marketing phenomenon developed in the late nineteenth century as a set of conventions and formulas took shape for the mass production of scientific romances "intended chiefly for boys," as Fenton Ash stated in the preface to *A Trip to Mars*.[58] In the United States, the formulaic nature of the writing was institutionalized in the notorious Edward Stratemeyer publishing syndicate, which produced children's books in series: The Hardy Boys, The Bobbsey Twins, Nancy Drew, and—for adventures with a technological theme—the Great Marvel Series. Among the latter was *Through Space to Mars*, written, like all the Great Marvel volumes, to an outline by Stratemeyer by a freelance author who used the syndicate name "Roy Rockwood." The Roy Rockwood for the Mars volume in the series was Howard R. Garis.

Boys' books of this kind had protagonists—usually in pairs, often siblings or cousins—who were themselves teenagers, but with opportunities for adventure and permissive parent-figures that project the wishful longing of the boy-reader. In Ash's *Trip to Mars*, the teenaged heroes are called Gerald and Jack. "The two chums," as they are tagged on nearly every page, are hardly distinguishable except that one is a dreamer and the other practical-minded. Individualizing is not a concern of the author; more to the point, the chums are "stalwart, well-grown, clean-limbed British youths."[59] Both Gerald and Jack are orphans being raised (though little supervised) by an astronomer and two working-class, dialect-speaking "attendants" on a remote South Sea island. The Roy Rockwood Mars book has its Jack and Mark—also described in the opening chapter title as "two chums" and, with a convenience to match their British counterparts, orphans under the guardianship of a scientist on the coast of Maine. The American chums are students at the Universal Electrical and Chemical College, although this does not prevent them from nearly blowing up the lab at their guardian's house (where *in loco parentis* oversight is as lax as on Ash's South Pacific island). The Rockwood boys also have their American equivalent of Gerald and Jack's servants in a hunter named Andy Sudds and a cook named Washington White, who speaks in "colored man's" dialect and refers to the boys as Massa Mark and Massa Jack.[60] The parallels are so close that one might almost suspect plagiarism, except that the formulas were already so widely available in magazines like the *Boys' Own Paper* and *Chums*.

Both *A Trip to Mars* and *Through Space to Mars* can be read as junior versions of stories like Pope's *Journey to Mars*, *Lieut. Gullivar Jones*, and *A Princess of Mars*, initiations for the teenaged reader into the ethos of masculinism. The Ash and Rockwood fantasies are cut from patterns that are also discernible in the most influential of all boy's books of the period, Baden-Powell's *Scouting for Boys* (1908), a primer for turning boys into men by insulating them as much as possible from the polluting influence of the feminine. Much of what may strike a twenty-first-century reader as astonishing and risible in Ash and Rockwood was, in fact, typical of an era that had "discovered" male adolescence, institutionalized it, and was doing everything it could to try to tame it. Boys' clubs for children of the poor, the Boy Scout troop for middle-class boys, private boys' academies for the sons of wealth constructed separate male universes. In those cozy confines, a sentimentalized boyhood could be prolonged under adult male guidance and authority, clean-mindedness could be encouraged and sexual experimentation deterred through a combination of discreet preaching and outdoor distractions, and boys could be schooled in the masculine virtues. David Macleod has neatly summarized the paradoxes of the early twentieth-century movement to build boys' characters: "boys must be manly but dependent, virtuous without femininity in a culture which regarded women as more moral than men."[61] To achieve that goal, organizers of the male youth movement had to look backward. Baden-Powell's Scouting for Boys made Camelot the British model for apprentice masculinists. "One aim of the Boy Scouts scheme," the founder admonished instructors in the movement, "is to revive amongst us, if possible, some of the rules of the knights of old, which did so much for the moral tone of our race."[62] Baden-Powell's chivalric refrain was adapted for the American version of the movement in the familiar enumeration of the Scout's attributes: trustworthy, loyal, helpful, friendly, courteous, kind, obedient, cheerful, thrifty, brave, clean, and reverent.

Boys' adventures on Mars are full of daring exploits and rescues by youths who are invariably good-hearted and well-bred, but whose actions flow out of a pervading spirit of aggression. Ash's Jack and Gerald pack pistols on their trip to Mars and don't hesitate to use them; Rockwood's Jack and Mark travel in a spaceship called "the Annihilator." The chief difference from the adult masculinist romances of Mars, the one striking omission, is the absence not only of princesses but of any female characters, young or old, terrestrial or Martian. Neither queen nor witch, mother nor sister nor girlfriend appear in these monastic narratives. Although even as late as 1970 the prize-winning German children's novel about Mars, The Earth Is Near (Die Erde Ist Nah), functioned entirely without female characters, later generations of Martian fiction for young readers have tended not to draw so stark a picture of a single-sexed universe. Still, the women and girl characters have only marginal or secondary roles in later masculinist boys' books such as John Keir Cross' The Angry Planet (1945), which includes one girl among the four males who fly to Mars; Robert Heinlein's Red Planet (1949), which quickly disposes of mothers in the early chapters to set up a world in which two buddies and their Martian critter can have comfortably girl-free adventures; and the first of the Tom Corbett Space Cadet series, *Stand By for Mars!* (1952) by the pseudonymous Carey Rockwell, in which nearly all the action focuses on the male initiation rites of the Space Academy.

Authors of children's books about Mars often claim to use their fiction to instruct young readers on the current state of the scientific question about the planet. Sometimes this takes the form—in common with Martian romances of the 1880s and 1890s intended for adult readers—of potted paragraphs of information about the seasons, the moons, the atmosphere, and the terrain of Mars. But the books seldom dwell long on these data, and the authors do not always bother to do any more research than what they could get out of popular magazines or the Sunday newspaper. In his foreword to *A Trip to Mars*, Fenton Ash emphasizes his desire to "combine amusement with a little wholesome instruction" and to construct the adventures on "some quasi-scientific foundation." Observing a "deference to the known prejudices of young people," Ash aimed to keep scientific interruptions of the narrative to a minimum:

> I am conscious that I have set myself a difficult task, for it is not an easy matter to give verisimilitude to a story of a visit to another planet about which we necessarily know so little. Yet astronomy as a study is so fascinating, its mysteries and possibilities are so wonderful, so boundless, its influences so elevating and ennobling, that little apology is needed for any effort to attract the attention of youthful readers to it by making it the subject of a romance.[63]

Despite Ash's pieties, little astronomical instruction actually appears in *A Trip to Mars*—or, for that matter, in Rockwood's *Through Space to Mars*. In neither, for instance, do young readers learn that anything like scientific disagreement muddies the question of the canals. The professor who leads the expedition in *Through Space to Mars* is a Lowellian who has studied Schiaparelli's maps and his chief interest on Mars is to learn how the canals were dug. A conversation between a Martian and the "chums" in *A Trip to Mars* glibly confirms Lowell's theory about the spreading deserts on Mars and the imminent extinction of its inhabitants:

> "Ha! You have deserts, then, as we have?" said Gerald.
>
> Malto looked at him in surprise.
>
> "Why, of course; I thought everybody knew that! Fully one-third of our globe is waterless desert, and, what is worse, the tract is gradually extending. Our scientific men prophesy that the proportion will grow larger and larger until the whole planet becomes a dried-up waste. That is the cheerful sort of doom they predict for future generations!"

"Curious, isn't it?" murmured Jack, glancing at Gerald. "That is exactly what our earthly scientists have prophesied as likely to happen to Mars in the future!"[64]

A later American boys' book, The Mystery Men of Mars by Carl Claudy, with its standard pair of boy heroes (one representing Brawn and the other, Brains) who accompany a professor to Mars, continues the tradition of enshrining the canals of Mars, laid out like "gargantuan railroad tracks." But Claudy cannot resist tossing in some Wellsian insectile aliens, modeled on the Selenites of The First Men in the Moon.[65]

Still, the more pervasive didactic subject in all these stories is not astronomy but gender. Like Scouting for Boys and the Boy Scout oath, both preoccupied with gender but bereft of sex, the romances of Fenton Ash and Roy Rockwood operate as manuals of the male virtues. Baden-Powell, invoking the British military experience at the garrison of Mafeking in the Boer War, insisted on the importance of marksmanship as an essential accomplishment of the Scout. "We ought really not to think too much of any boy, even though a cricketer and a footballer, unless he can also shoot."[66] If the Boy Scouts of America gave guns a less prominent role in character formation, the American fiction-factory for boys offered a rousing endorsement of Baden-Powell's principle. The teenagers and their mentor in Mystery Men of Mars depart their home planet with little in the way of baggage but with a bulging arsenal: "Automatics, 38, 3. Ammunition, 900 rounds. Knives, belts, 3. Dynamite, small cartridges, 1 case. Large cartridges, 2 cases. Portable battery and switch, 1. Fuses, one box." Even so, the boy who personifies Brawn, and who is always eager to resolve every difficulty on Mars with firepower, grumbles that this isn't enough. "Should have machine guns!"[67]

But one of the earlier books is even more revealing of how the masculinist ethos insinuates itself into boys' adventures on Mars. In the final two chapters of Through Space to Mars, Mark and Jack regret having to fight against the Martians who have been hospitable to them but have balked at the terrestrial adults who insist on carrying away a mineral resource unique to Mars. (To the Martian curator of this substance who asks for the return of whatever has been stolen, the German scientist who has led the expedition says in surprise, as if the assertion needs no further justification, "But we came here to get it"!)[68] With considerable enthusiasm, the American chums obey the orders of their adult authorities to "man the guns."[69] In a blaze of electric cannonfire that leaves the ranks of the Martians antiseptically "thinned," and with never a mention of bloodshed or pain or death, Mark and Jack and the others return to

Earth with their captured loot, full of the satisfactions of fulfilled adventure and without a moral qualm.[70] It is hard to know whether the story is better read as a coda to the American saga of the rough riders of the Spanish-American War or as an unwitting forecast of the doubtful glories that American youth soon would experience while adventuring "over there" in Europe's Great War. Certainly it was the down payment on a literary patrimony of fresh-faced, weapon-toting boy-heroes from which writers and filmmakers could draw freely in a long line of descent from Tom Corbett to Luke Skywalker.

QUITE IN THE
BEST TRADITION

9

By 1920, Percival Lowell and the scientific controversies that he inspired were dead. H. G. Wells had largely abandoned the pioneering science fiction that had made him famous in the 1890s. The fashion for idealism and utopianism that had led to such disparate early Martian fictions as *Unveiling a Parallel*, *Red Star*, and *The Man from Mars, or Service for Service's Sake* had passed, the victim of World War I and a cynical worldliness that had come in its aftermath. The most memorable Martian art of the war years was not a literary narrative but part of a musical composition, Gustav Holst's *The Planets* (1914–1916); tellingly, it was not in the least influenced by recent astronomy but harkened back to the astrological significance of Mars as "the bringer of war." During and after the war, Edgar Rice Burroughs ground out the many popular sequels to *A Princess of Mars* and Richard Ganthony's 1899 play *A Message from Mars* was reprinted as a working script for amateur productions in 1923. But despite a continuing romance with Mars that was played out in the press, the immediate postwar years were not a period of great literary innovation in "the matter of Mars."

In the 1920s and 1930s, most astronomers wanted to turn down the temperature on the subject of Mars. The canals, when they were accepted at all, were considered topographical features rather than engineered artifacts. The hypothesis of some form of plant life on Mars was still entertained, even into the 1960s, but for newspaper readers, vegetables did not carry the same dramatic charge as advanced, intelligent living beings. Although the opposition of 1924 would bring Mars closer than at any other time in the twentieth century, scientists at the Mount Wilson Observatory in southern California professed indifference to the event. They opened their facilities to the visiting public, but the staff announced that they themselves were "not even going to look for evidences of life on Mars" when the planet came within 35 million miles of Earth. "Realizing that Mars is of special interest to the lay mind," the *New York Times* reported, "the astronomers said they would lend one of their big telescopes—the largest has a 100-inch lens—to any one who will climb the 5,000-foot mountain in the hope of seeing a Martian or two. . . . Photographs will be taken of it as a matter of observatory routine, but the astronomers insist they do not expect their plates to show anything startling."[1] On the eve of World War II, at the time of the 1939 opposition that rivaled that of 1924, *Time* magazine reported, with a hint of frustration, that to "the old and battered question—does intelligent life on Mars exist—astronomers good-naturedly gave some old answers and a few new ones."[2] But the new answers were quite unsensational lessons in chemistry and optics. Clearly, one thing the astronomical profession had learned from the Lowell era was the strategy of lowered expectations.

With rare exceptions, astronomers paid little attention to and avoided public discussion of Mars in the interwar years. William Pickering, banished from Flagstaff and from his brother's observatory in Cambridge, continued studying Mars from Harvard's outstation in Jamaica; in 1921, he published a collection of his Martian studies from 1890 to 1915. While distinguishing carefully between data and surmises, Pickering still left it clear that he continued to find the hypothesis of intelligent life on Mars likely.[3] Flammarion, the last of the surviving giants among the amateurs and popularizers of the pre–World War I era, had not bowed to the new mood of caution. He continued to expatiate on his two favorite subjects—Mars and the paranormal—until his death in 1925. With characteristic factual jugglery, he asserted that "we know the general geography of Mars better than we do that of our own planet."[4] While remaining doubtful, as he had been for many years, about the practicalities of space travel, Flammarion looked forward to the use of "psychic waves" to achieve contact with the inhabitants of Mars: "Telepathy will overcome space." That declaration prompted the *New York Times* to editorialize on the "pathetic" state into which he had fallen in old age. Noting that "M. Flammarion always has been inclined to mistake his imagination for his judgment," the editor pointed out that Percival Lowell, for all his other shortcomings, at least confined his speculations to what he saw through the telescope.[5] Even if, in its own lofty way, the *Times* still partook of the sensational in its coverage of Mars—after all, it printed a long piece on Mars by Flammarion just three months after its editorial rebuff—respectable astronomers wanted to distance themselves from the Martian brouhaha.[6]

Applied scientists—engineers, inventors, and radiotelegraphers in particular—were another matter. They remained intrigued by Mars, and not incidentally also were becoming avid consumers of pulp science fiction. But even at Flagstaff, where Lowell's disciples still carried on his investigations, Mars was somewhat less prominent on the agenda, and a major effort was made to fulfill Percival's *other* great astronomical quest: confirmation of the existence of a ninth planet in the solar system. In 1930 there was success. Word came from the Lowell Observatory that Clyde Tombaugh had located the elusive Planet X that its founder had been searching for. It was named Pluto—its astronomical abbreviation, PL, becoming Percival Lowell's posthumous badge of honor, despite Pluto's demotion to "dwarf planet" status in 2006 by the International Astronomical Union.

In spite of the scientific turn away from Mars, the planet continued to live in the imagination, but the astronomy that appeared in Martian fiction of this period was mostly old stuff, relics of the Schiaparelli-Lowell years. Even in 1907, the science journalist Garrett Serviss was praising Lowell's work on Mars for being "as fascinating as a dip into the 'Arabian Nights' or the stories of Theseus and Hercules."[7] By the 1920s and 1930s, the canaled and inhabited Mars certainly had passed into popular mythology, trailing clouds of Low-ellian, Wellsian, and utopian glory in its passage through the decades that led up to the Second World War. At the beginning of that war, a fiction writer introduced her Martian fantasy with an airy headnote: "Astronomy and Science have been treated altogether imaginatively."[8]

Many other writers could have said the same. As the author of one of the most gorgeously drawn but scientifically perverse portraits of another planet ever written would acknowledge, astronomical research now had little to do with how Mars was portrayed. "There is thus a great deal of scientific false-hood in my stories: some of it known to be false even by me when I wrote the books," C. S. Lewis admitted in a reply never actually mailed to a hostile critic of his extraterrestrial romances. "The canals in Mars are there not because I believe in them but because they are part of the popular tradition."[9] Lewis, as we will see, may not have been unusual among the post-Lowell writers of the 1920s and 1930s in bypassing science and trying to squeeze some life out of the old Lowellian fantasies about Mars. Like others in that interwar period who imagined life on Mars, including Olaf Stapledon, Stanley Weinbaum, John Wyndham, and Orson Welles, he also included a measure of tongue-in-cheek humor, sometimes whimsical and sometimes cutting, at the expense of scien-tists, journalists, and a suggestible public.

As early as the lightweight novel of 1912 A *Message from Mars* by Mabel Winfred Knowles (writing under a pseudonym and adapting Richard Gan-thony's 1899 play of the same title), knowing winks started to be cast at the reader. Her central character, a clubman and regular reader of the journal *Astronomer* who presumes himself a sophisticated scientific amateur, is derided

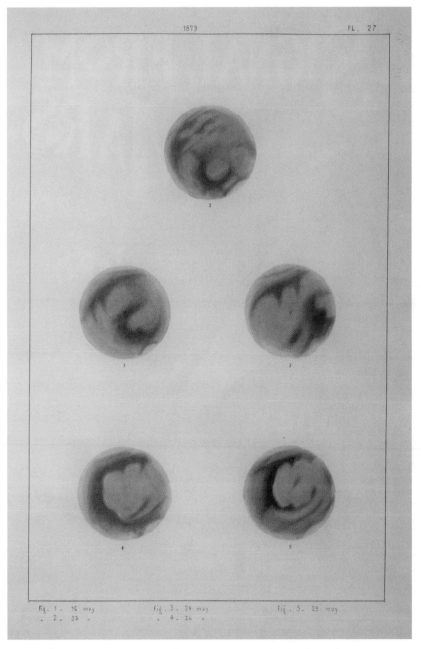

PLATE 1. Étienne Lêopold Trouvelot, five pencil and gouache drawings of Mars, spring 1873. From his unpublished sketchbook. Courtesy Wolbach Library, Harvard Smithsonian Observatory

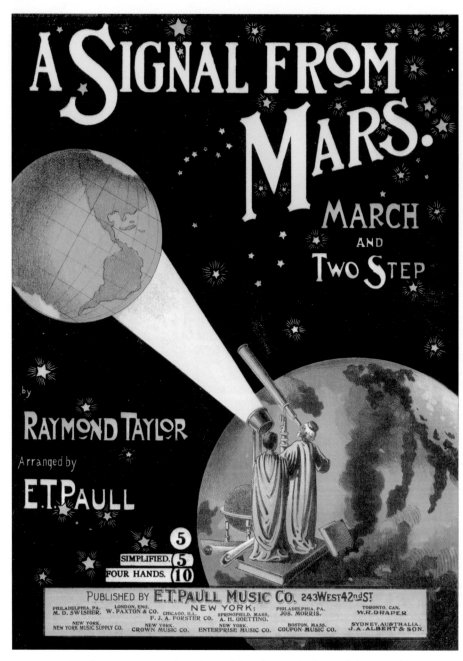

PLATE 2. Martian astronomers observing and signaling Earth. Cover of sheet music for Raymond Taylor's march and two-step, "A Signal from Mars," arranged by E. T. Paull, 1901. Courtesy Parlor Song Association, Inc.

PLATE 3. Percival Lowell and the "First Word of Science as to Life on Mars," Sunday Supplement to the *Boston Herald*, 18 November 1906. Courtesy Boston Public Library Newspaper Collection

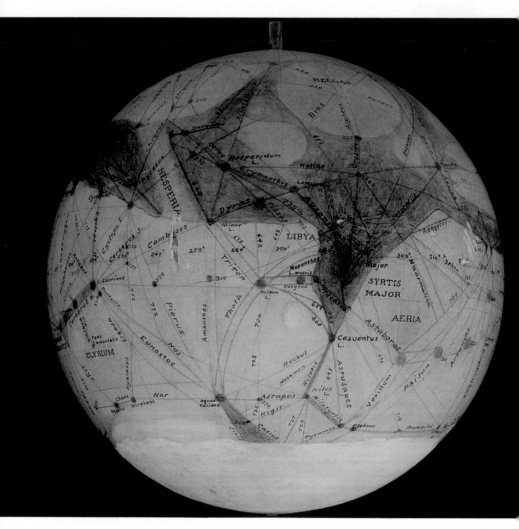

PLATE 4. Percival Lowell's hand-carved and hand-painted globe of Mars, 1911.
Courtesy Lowell Observatory Archives, Coleman/Kennedy Collection

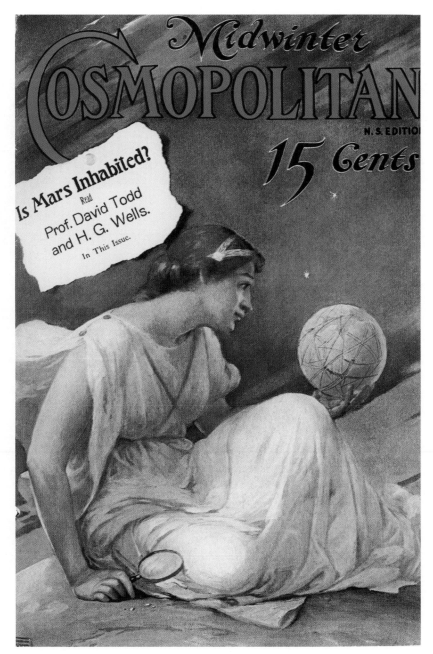

PLATE 5. The Muse of Astronomy contemplates Lowell's Mars. Cover of *Cosmopolitan* by Frederick Lincoln Stoddard, March 1908. Courtesy Boston Public Library

PLATE 6. H. G. Wells, *The War of the Worlds*, serialized in Hugo Gernsback's *Amazing Stories*, August 1927, cover by Frank R. Paul. Courtesy Popular Culture Library, Bowling Green State University and the Estate of Frank R. Paul

PLATE 7. *Approaching Mars*, Ron Miller's 1991 reconstruction of *The Grand Flotilla to Mars*, a lost painting by Chesley Bonestell illustrating Wernher von Braun's *Marsprojekt* for the cover of *Collier's*, April 30, 1954. Courtesy private collection

PLATE 8. Drilling into underground aquifers on Mars. Acrylic painting, *Our Place on Mars*, 2006, © William K. Hartmann. Courtesy of the artist

by a professional astronomer for his dated knowledge: "He has some fantastic idea about life on the planet Mars. Now, all scientific men of any standing are quite agreed on this point. There is no such thing as life on the planet Mars."[10] While Knowles may have exaggerated the degree of scientific consensus in 1912 on the habitability of Mars, her send-up of the pompous Horace Parker points the direction for a line of popular seriocomic images of Mars that culminate in Orson Welles's notorious Hallowe'en radio prank of 1938. Perhaps more importantly, we begin to see scientific Mars and literary Mars growing increasingly apart—as they would for much of the twentieth century. The old nineteenth-century ideal of using narratives about Mars to stimulate interest in astronomical research and to teach readers the state of the scientific question ceased to have much bearing on the literary imagination. The Mars of fiction became a predominantly mythic place, and with few exceptions remained so until the 1980s.

The beginning of 1920 brought a new fad for attempting to send signals to Mars—or perhaps, more accurately, a new version of an old fad. The 1890s witnessed a first round of signaling mania, touched off by several observations of mysterious flashes of light seen on the Martian surface; the opening chapter of Wells's *The War of the Worlds* capitalized on reports from the Lick and Nice Observatories of such lights during the 1894 opposition. A hypothesis that Mars's inhabitants were trying to communicate by light with the Earth led to various ingenious proposals in that decade from what a *New York Times* editorialist waggishly called "philosophers and noodles." Ideas included the use of giant mirrors to reflect sunlight from Earth to Mars, the digging of geometrical forms in the plains of the western United States or in the Sahara desert that could be observed through Martian telescopes, and the construction of a lighting system in Siberia to send answering signals to Mars.[11] Several people, including the Croatian-American inventor Nikola Tesla, proposed wireless telegraphy to get in touch with the Martians. At the century's turn, Tesla provoked widespread ridicule for his claim that some noises that he could not account for on his wireless apparatus in Colorado constituted a message from "the inhabitants of Mars."[12] For three decades Tesla kept the drumbeat going for this pet project of interplanetary communication, but his credibility never recovered from the chorus of laughter in 1901.

The signaling craze had a second major incarnation at the time of the 1909 opposition, when William Pickering dominated the news with his proposal that the United States spend ten million dollars to build a system of reflecting mirrors. The *New York Times* followed up its front-page report on the scheme by sending a reporter to interview Pickering in Cambridge and making him the subject of the cover story of its *Sunday Magazine*, of a feature story on another Sunday, and of a rather more skeptical editorial that questioned "the accuracy of our own Boston dispatch" that a Mars peopled by canal-diggers and astronomers pointing beacon-lights at Earth was a generally accepted proposition.[13] A flurry of letters to the *Times* editor followed, most of them doubting the practical efficacy of Pickering's idea and one suggesting that the public infatuation with signals to Mars was escapist. "The solution of the problem of the unemployed and the sweeping away of the deplorable conditions on the east side, where little babies gasp and die in the fetid atmosphere of the tenements, would be of infinitely greater benefit to humanity than a successful communication with the inhabitants of the planet Mars."[14]

When proposals to initiate wireless signals to Mars emerged again after the 1918 Armistice, the recent war experience was added to the mix. Charles Steinmetz, chief engineer for the General Electric Company in Schenectady, argued that technical and financial resources were up to the challenge of attempting to confirm a guess by Guglielmo Marconi that inexplicable wireless signals he had detected might be coming from Mars:

> If the United States, for instance, should go into the effort to send messages to Mars with the same degree of intensity and thoroughness with which we went into the war it is not at all improbable that the plan would succeed. To do so would mean the consolidation of all the electrical power in the country into one great plant or sending station. Lofty towers would have to be erected, 1,000 feet high or more, and the cost of the attempt might be a billion dollars.[15]

And if a response came to the American signal, there were experienced military code-crackers who could apply their skills to the problem of the Martian language. Others argued for a return to the notion of signaling with light, including Elmer Sperry whose Brooklyn company had developed high-powered searchlights for the war effort. By grouping together a number of Sperry searchlights, a single beam of one billion candlepower could be directed at Mars. "The combined power of 150 or 200 of our searchlights would equal the light of a star of the seventh magnitude," Sperry said, making the signal readily discernible to the Martians, assuming that they knew how to use telescopes. Even Einstein weighed in on the debate, reportedly declaring that he was inclined to light rather than telegraphy as the more practical means of communication.[16]

Eventually, the United States Army Signal Corps was drawn into the effort to listen in for signals from Mars, and radio stations were asked to shut down

operations at the 1924 opposition so that there would be no possible interference with transmissions from Mars. (The Radio Corporation of America
declined to suspend broadcasts.) While public interest in the signaling effort
was high, the scientific community was skeptical and irritated. British astronomer Arthur Eddington branded the whole enterprise "absolute nonsense" and
a group calling itself the Society for the Prevention of Believing What Ain't So
urged its members, in an uncanny foretaste of the great Orson Welles hoax of
1938, not to get excited by unusual sounds on their radio, "especially if they
happen to live near an amateur broadcaster with a practical sense of humor."[17]

Unfazed by the failure of any of the efforts to contact Martians by telegraph
or radio, Flammarion proffered an explanation. The civilization of Mars, he
reminded his readers, was very much older than ours, and the Martians had
probably simply given up on us. "Perhaps they tried 200,000 or 300,000 years
ago, before the appearance of man, at the time of the cave-bear or the mammoth. Perhaps they addressed themselves to our planet at the time of the
Iguanadon and the Dinosaurus." After repeated unanswered signals sent to us,
the Martians may have concluded that Earth had no intelligent life. And Flammarion was not so senile that he was incapable of a mordant suggestion that
the Martians might have been right about intelligent Earthlings since "we do
not know how to behave and three-quarters of our resources are employed
for feeding soldiers."[18] But strange as Flammarion's pronouncements always
were, the strangest case of all in this episode is Marconi's. In early 1919, he first
suggested that mysterious signals he was picking up on the wireless might
have an extraterrestrial origin. In 1921, in what was a front-page news story, the
manager of his London telegraph company told New Yorkers that Marconi was
"sure" these continuing mysterious signals were coming from Mars. But as
evidence mounted that the sounds—which many other telegraphers were also
hearing—were probably the result of interference from the proliferating number of radio stations being built, Marconi distanced himself from the debate.
By 1924, he put out word that he "never has attempted communication with
Mars nor given it serious thought" and that wireless signals from Mars were "a
fantastic absurdity."[19]

The extensive newspaper attention to signaling efforts may have been responsible for the publication in 1922 of a little-remembered narrative, *Yezad: A
Romance of the Unknown*. An incredible mishmash of a book, drawn out of
Lowell's *Mars and Its Canals*, Zoroastrian religion, utopianism, Miltonic angel-
ology, feminism, reincarnation, and potted encyclopedia articles on everything
from lunar topography to the court jesters of Charles the Bold and Cardinal
Wolsey, *Yezad* must be one of the most peculiar novels ever conceived for a

Martian setting. Among other imponderables in its plot is a very long story-within-the-story of the emigration of ten thousand Martians to, of all places, Earth's moon when the waters of Mars dry up. The author of *Yezad*, George Babcock, acknowledges in an appendix that the book actually was written between 1912 and 1915 but did not secure a publisher until late in 1922. Perhaps in that oppositional year, when wireless transmitters were focused on Mars, a central message of *Yezad* seemed timely. For many millennia, we are told, Martians have been patiently awaiting the historical moment when scientists on Earth would have advanced sufficiently to attempt communication with Mars. When that event occurred, the Martians would generously share their age-old wisdom with terrestrial humanity and "relieve Earth's people of all laborious toil."[20] Babcock's protagonist, a dead aviator who is to be reincarnated after his spiritual instruction on Mars, is urged on his return to Earth to tell scientists to keep on working at their wireless telegraphy projects!

A more significant foray in Martian fiction was being made in Russia in the same year that *Yezad* was published. Alexei Tolstoi's *Aelita, or The Decline of Mars* appeared in three installments in the most prestigious of the revolutionary magazines, *Red Virgin Soil*. An account of a sojourn on Mars by the lovelorn engineer Los and his fiery companion Gusev, a veteran of the Red Army, *Aelita* is framed by the signaling craze of the early 1920s. In recruiting Gusev for the journey, Los recalls the stories of radio stations throughout Europe and North America hearing mysterious signals and explains his expectation that they will find people on Mars:

> Somebody wants to communicate with us. Where from? On the planets, except Mars, there's no evidence for life. The signals must come from Mars. See this map—Mars looks like a network, it's covered with canals. Apparently it would be possible for them to establish powerful radio stations. Mars wants to communicate with the earth. At the present time we can't answer their signals. So we'll fly there to answer their call. It's hard to imagine that the radio stations on Mars could be constructed by monsters, creatures not resembling us.[21]

Armed with his Lowellian map as well as Lowellian notions of utopian human inhabitants of Mars, Los also takes with him a notebook in which he will record his experiences because he has pre-sold the story of his voyage to an American newspaper correspondent. Although Archibald Skiles does not accompany Los and Gusev on their egg-shaped space vehicle, he forecasts the increasingly prominent role of journalists as real-world instigators of as well as fictional characters in postwar Martian fiction.

While *Aelita* has some of the ideological commitments of Bogdanov's *Red Star*, published fifteen years earlier, the books are also quite different from each other intellectually, structurally, and psychologically. Bogdanov imagined a socialist Mars as prototype for the Bolshevik society that had not yet come into being in Russia. In *Aelita*, the Bolshevik revolutionary principles and tactics are exported to Mars. Tolstoi, writing in the early years of the Leninist experiment, had been more ambivalent about the revolution and his duality is reflected in his two principal characters. Los is, or attempts to be, apolitical; he is motivated in part by curiosity but even more by the need to escape from personal loss, the recent death of his wife. "I am a coward, a fugitive, I am driven by hopeless despair," he confesses to Skiles the newspaperman (41). By contrast, Gusev is fiercely political, a life-affirming and risk-embracing activist. Los spends most of his time on Mars dedicated to, and paralyzed by, his growing love for Aelita, daughter of the despotic ruler of Mars, but Gusev insists on exploring the planet's social arrangements. Less convinced than Los that Mars has achieved something like utopia, Gusev grumbles, "The bastards live well, but what a bore" (92). He tours factories and locates the proletariat's living quarters and discovers that despite the tidiness of their clean, well-lighted homes, the Martian workers live without hope and as slaves of the state. Always eager for a battle and instinctively identifying with the oppressed workers, Gusev becomes the leader of a Martian revolt.

What Tolstoi had in mind in this novel full of contradictions isn't obvious. The revolution fails, Aelita—who has committed the crime of surrendering her virginity to Los—is sentenced to death, and Los and Gusev flee to Earth. After a brief period of celebrity and a monetary windfall from their published "Travel Notes," Los and Gusev resume life in a busy Soviet society in which "the sound of hammers all over the country, the whine of saws, the hiss of sickles, the whistle of scythes" obliterates fanciful speculation about "countries beyond the clouds" (172). Los takes up mundane work in a factory but hardheaded Gusev becomes the romantic eccentric, founding "The Society for the Transport of Military Units to the Planet Mars with the Purpose of Saving the Last of its Working Population, Incorporated" (173). The novel returns to the opening frame with renewed journalistic sensationalism: radio signals "of extraordinary power" are being detected at a station in St. Petersburg (175). Los hurries to listen to the signals, and hears the voice of Aelita in Martian repeating over and over, "Where are you? Where are you? Where are you?" (176).

Tolstoi's *Aelita* is full of thrilling spectacle and romantic charm, and that combination made it a natural text for cinematic adaptation. Yakov Protazanov's 1924 film *Aelita, Queen of Mars*, the most important science-fiction film from the silent era apart from Fritz Lang's indispensable *Metropolis* two years later, uses expressionistic sets and costumes that reflect Kasimir Malevich's Constructivism to capture the spectacular elements of the novel. The allegory of the revolution against a corrupt monarchical regime on Mars is treated comically and satirically and, in the final frames, the entire journey to Mars is revealed, in that worst of cop-outs, to be nothing more than a dream. "Enough daydreaming," Los says in the final scene as he burns his plans for a spaceship. "We have different work to do." Socialist realism triumphs over fantasy, and Moscow displaces Mars. Despite its popularity with Russian audiences and despite the director's effort to wrap his film in Leninist principles, *Aelita* was soon withdrawn from circulation by Soviet authorities who found its politics too compromised. But in that respect, the film merely reflected its source. Tolstoi returned to his muddled story after the appearance of the film and he attempted to make it more ideologically correct in succeeding years until he produced a revised text in 1939.

Although flawed, *Aelita* is a fascinating harbinger of the state of the Martian novel in the 1920s and 1930s. It looks both backwards and forwards. *Aelita* is conscious of the growing body of Martian literature. It is clear that Tolstoi has paid almost no attention to then-current scientific studies of Mars, but he is acutely aware of literary tradition. The influence of the Lowell-Flammarion romance of Mars is evident in the landscapes of the narrative, starting with the moment shortly after the landing on Mars when Los observes mussel shells in the dusty track that he and Gusev are pursuing and realizes that they are walking in the bottom of a dried-up canal. As they mill around the bonfires in the first stage of the revolt led by Gusev, the Martian workers chant, "Ulla, ulla" (144), echoing the dying Martians in Wells's *The War of the Worlds* whose re-peated lament "ulla, ulla, ulla, ulla" resounds throughout the chapter titled "Dead London." Tolstoi's American translator suggests that the representation of various red-skinned, blue-skinned, and olive-skinned Martian races also indicates an awareness of Burroughs' *Princess of Mars*. But in Aelita's retelling of a Martian foundation-myth, Tolstoi looks even farther backward. The giant reservoirs and the canal system, we learn, were far beyond the engineering skills of the indigenous Martians. Intelligence on Mars was on the verge of extinction twenty thousand years earlier when the planet was colonized by humans fleeing from the advanced but doomed civilization of Atlantis. Perhaps it was such mind-boggling extravagances that led to a contemporary Russian critic's blunt dismissal of *Aelita*: "Martian novels aren't worth writing."[22] But a more sympathetic reader may conclude that Tolstoi grasped that the subject of Mars had entered the arena of modern mythmaking.

For the imaginative writers of the 1930s, the Mars myth already had a history about which one could have a sense of ironic self-consciousness. Consider a plot synopsis offered by a character in a 1937 novel:

> Some of you may have read a book called The War of the Worlds—I forget who wrote it—Jules Verne, Conan Doyle, one of those fellows. But it told how the Martians invaded the world, wanted to colonize it, and exterminate mankind. Hopeless attempt! They couldn't stand the different atmospheric pressure, they couldn't stand the difference in gravitation; bacteria finished them up. Hopeless from the start. The only impossible thing in the story was to imagine that the Martians would be fools enough to try anything of the sort.[23]

One of the jokes here is that the author of this novel, Star-Begotten, is H. G. Wells, who knew all too well and to his chagrin, that some reviewers used to call him the English Verne. The other joke is about the laughableness of a premise that had struck readers as horrifying just about forty years earlier. Nevertheless, Wells could still feel justifiably confident that The War of the Worlds remained culturally alive, even if the precise identity of its author among "those fellows" who were writing fantastic fiction was in doubt.

In Star-Begotten, the last of his fictional visits to the subject of Mars, Wells actually moved as far away as is conceivable from the monstrous images of Martians he had invented four decades earlier. As John Huntington has astutely observed in introducing this "Biological Fantasia," as Wells subtitled the book, the author turned inside out the genre of the scientific romance that he had defined almost singlehandedly in his fiction of the 1890s (25–26). No Martians ever appear in their own form in Star-Begotten (if they exist at all), and if an invasion occurs here it is a mental rather than a physical event, an intervention designed to accelerate the evolution of Homo sapiens into Homo sideralis (108), a kind of telepathic tutorial for moving certain susceptible terrestrials along the road to Utopia. With references to coded "extra-terrestrial radiations" (97) that may be stimulating human brains, the narrative voice in Star-Begotten draws on the period's interest, heightened by the mass media, in possible communications between Mars and Earth. But for Wells, that "Martian fever" (109) is only a pretext for a philosophical fable, the fictional genre that preoccupied him in his old age. In pursuing the speculative possibility "that one might possibly Martianize even ordinary people by a saner education" (122), Wells, through his fictional mouthpiece Professor Keppel, has turned Mars into a metaphor for a progressive future. He makes enough sly allusions to his earlier Martians of 1898—dark-eyed and "cool-brained" (90, 123), observing human beings like amoebae under a microscope (63, 68)—to suggest the tradition of Martian fiction that was descended from Wells's original invention. But acerbic references to "all these pseudo-scientific story writers who write about Mars" (80) suggest his subversive intentions. Working simultaneously with and against the grain of the line of Martian fiction that he had established, Wells turns *Star-Begotten* into an instrument for promoting, through his biological fantasy, a discussion of the necessity of changing mental habits on a global scale—the cause that became the hallmark of his fictional and nonfictional writing from the 1890s forward. In many ways an elusive novel and one marginal to the science-fictional development of "the matter of Mars" in the 1930s, *Star-Begotten* remains the intriguing and provocative farewell to the genre from one of its greatest practitioners.

In fact, the mythology of Mars in 1937 retained a distinctly more Wellsian than Lowellian flavor. The ghost of Sir Percival still hovered over the imaginations of those who depicted a canal-crossed Martian landscape, but it was Wells's legacy that mattered more. In 1931, Olaf Stapledon, who staged a Martian invasion and occupation of the Earth in his 1930 *Last and First Men*, told Wells that the only one of his book-length scientific romances he had ever read was *The War of the Worlds*—and its influence shows in his depiction of Martians as invading viruses, a roundabout homage to the bacteria that made victims of Wells's Martians.[24] In one of the best Martian fictions of the 1930s, *Planet Plane*, John Wyndham's weightless astronauts bounce off the walls of the *Gloria Mundi* on the first trip to Mars. The journalist on board (a character whose inclusion on the voyage speaks to the role of the mass media in the growing Martian mythology) tells an embarrassed crewman, "You were quite in the best tradition, Wells' and Verne's people biffed about just like that."[25] A revealing instance of the persistence of the Wellsian tradition in the 1920s and 1930s is the case of the American pulp-fiction editor Hugo Gernsback. Originator of the term "science fiction" in its clumsy initial form of "scientifiction," Gernsback depended on Wells's literary reputation in launching his monthly magazine *Amazing Stories* in 1926. Much of the best fiction in the early years of *Amazing Stories* was in the form of serialized reprinting of Wells's most famous scientific romances. Wells himself had a running intercontinental argument about royalties with Gernsback, who requested "a complete library" of Wells stories for his magazine. "Watch these cads," he wrote at the top of one of Gernsback's many letters that alternated between wheedling flattery and protests over the fees that Wells required.[26] But if Wells was short-changed by the Gernsback enterprise, the magazine reprints—often with striking and dramatic cover art, as in the August 1927 issue of *Amazing Stories* that featured *The War of the Worlds*—introduced the great tradition of British science fiction to younger American readers (see color plate 6).

The definitive statement on the legacy of Wells can be found in C. S. Lewis's *Out of the Silent Planet*. Sending his professorial hero, "who had read his H. G. Wells," on a journey to Mars in 1938, Lewis equips him with a Wellsian repertoire of fearful images. "No insect-like, vermiculate or crustacean Abominable, no twitching feelers, rasping wings, slimy coils, curling tentacles, no monstrous union of superhuman intelligence and insatiable cruelty seemed to him anything but likely on an alien world."[27] The key phrase here—the phrase that separates Wellsian Mars from Lowellian Mars—is "alien world," so strikingly different in imaginative effect from the conception of the Schiaparelli-Flammarion-Lowell triumvirate (and their forebears, Fontenelle and Herschel) of a world whose inhabitants are essentially like us, only older, smarter, and nicer. The most frequently invoked testament to the staying power of the Wellsian image of alien, bellicose Mars is Orson Welles's radio broadcast of an adaptation of *The War of the Worlds*, which for a brief time engaged the terrified belief of up to a million people, but it was a culminating, not a unique, instance of the perverse appeal of Wells's notion of Mars as a threat to terrestrial hegemony.

While the decade of the 1920s was a comparatively quiescent period for new fiction about Mars, at the end of 1930, with the publication of Stapledon's *Last and First Men*, an exciting new round of fictions about Mars and Martians began. Characteristically, these works adopted a Wellsian conception of the alien and, while often strikingly innovative in some respects, showed a new self-consciousness that there *was* already a tradition of Martian representation that needed (often ironic) recognition. The Martians in *Last and First Men*, like Wells's, are invaders, but placed as they are in the midst of one of the most persistently inventive philosophical romances ever written, Stapledon's Martians could hardly *not* be original creations. *Last and First Men* is an outline of the future history of the human species—and its chronicling structure may be indebted to another of Wells's works, his bestselling *Outline of History* (1920). Starting at the close of the Great War, *Last and First Men* continues the history of humanity until the final dissolution of the eighteenth and last mutation of *Homo sapiens*, in exile from its home planet on Neptune two billion years from now. The wave of Martian invasions occupies a fifty thousand-year blip in that future history, at a point ten million years after the twentieth century and during the epoch of what the author calls "the Second Men." Stapledon's

Martian invasions constitute an ongoing war of the worlds in which both planets are left in spiritual and physical ruin.

The Martians in *Last and First Men*, as I've indicated, recall the germs that defeated Wells's Martian monstrosities in *The War of the Worlds*. They appear as nearly gaseous entities, green-hued clouds that can either spread into a thin fume or congeal into a jelly. Each cloud is composed of submicroscopic viral units that are united electromagnetically to form a group mind that receives and transmits messages by radiant energy. Like Wells's Martians, they have no sexuality, are coldly reasonable, and go to Earth because of their need for a water supply for their dried-up planet. But the desire to exploit Earth's resources in order to survive is only one of the motives for invasion by the Stapledonian Martians. The other—and utterly unWellsian—motive is religious. Being themselves almost unsubstantial beings, they venerate material rigidity—and the hardest and most rigid of all minerals, diamonds, they regard as sacred. When their telescopes reveal that Earth's diamonds are not treated with appropriate reverence by Martian standards, they conceive of their invasion, in part, "in a crusading spirit, to 'liberate' the terrestrial diamonds."[28] Like many a colonialist and crusading enterprise, the Martian invasion wraps self-interest and its destructive behaviors in the protective ideology of a religious imperative.

Stapledon, with a reputation for daunting austerity in his fiction as in his philosophical writings, is rarely thought of as a humorist. Yet that phrasing about liberating the diamonds has an absurdist quality that in fact permeates his imagined Martian wars. Perhaps the slyest comedy in *Last and First Men* comes at the expense of the wireless signaling efforts that had been a running sideshow in the decade that preceded publication of Stapledon's book. The cloudlike Martians themselves are likened to "mobile 'wireless stations' " (160) and, invading forces tending always to look first for intelligence in facsimiles of themselves, they report back to the home planet the disappointing news that terrestrial clouds have no minds at all. They do discover some erect bipeds who inhabit buildings (which also contain a few pitifully uncherished diamonds). The bipeds, however, have no sensitivity to electromagnetic radiation and they die as soon as they are pulled apart; they are evidently both unintelligent and unconscious. During their survey of the Earth, the Martians are accidentally assaulted by wireless radio beams that derange their electromagnetic systems. Here is evidence of some terrestrial intelligence, but for some time the Martians are unable to find the creatures from whom this power emanates. The "solution" to the mystery is rendered in an exquisitely comic reversal worthy of Jonathan Swift:

Presently the Martians discovered the sources of terrestrial radiation in the innumerable wireless transmitting stations. Here at last was the physical basis of the terrestrial intelligence! But what a lowly creature! What a caricature of life! Obviously in respect of complexity and delicacy of organization these wretched immobile systems of glass, metal and vegetable compounds were not to be compared with the Martian cloud. Their only feat seemed to be that they had managed to get control of the unconscious bipeds who tended them. (177)

The Stapledonian satire cuts at least two ways. The Martian egotism that leads the invaders to condescend to the deplorable earthly mind that inhabits radio towers served by stupid bipeds is a mirror of the similar egotism of the much-maligned "bipeds" themselves. Earth's human inhabitants are equally blind to the identity of the Martian invaders, whose destructive power they perceive all around them as they suck up the planet's water and vegetation, but they do not stop to consider that the greenish clouds might actually be extra-terrestrial. "Some had jokingly suggested that since the strange substance had behaved in a manner obviously vindictive, it must have been alive and conscious; but no one took the suggestion seriously" (176). But the sheer silliness of the episode may also reflect Stapledon's pleasure in making fun of the follies of the wireless-signals-to-Mars advocates.

In the United States, a celebrated story originally published in 1934 in a pulp magazine, Stanley Weinbaum's "A Martian Odyssey," gave further impetus to the tendency to shift Mars out of the realm of the familiar and into alien, sometimes Dadaist, territory. With a combination of inventive playfulness and attention to the mutual incomprehensibility of Martian and human minds, Weinbaum takes Stapledonian humor to even giddier levels. An account of the first human expedition to Mars aboard the *Ares* in the twenty-first century, Weinbaum's narrative catalogues several indigenous Martian species, each as bafflingly and hilariously alien as the next: a Wellsian tentacled monster that lives in the ground and traps its prey by projecting illusory images, a silvery, long-armed creature whose biology is silicon-based and produces bricks from its mouth, creatures shaped like four-legged barrels that ceaselessly push carts full of rubbish into a crushing machine and then calmly commit suicide by casting themselves into the same machine. The crowning Martian alien is an ostrich-like intelligence that expresses pleasure by flying into the air and making one-point landings with its beak buried in the sand. The terrestrial crew member who encounters all these Martians reports back to his comrades that while friendly and clearly the most intelligent of the aliens, the feathered, nose-

diving Martian, to whom he assigned the name Tweel, had a mind so fundamentally different from the terrestrial mind that linguistic communication was
nearly impossible. "Something in us was different, unrelated; I don't doubt
that Tweel thought me just as screwy as I thought him. Our minds simply
looked at the world from different viewpoints."[29] Weinbaum's Mars has the
characteristics of a Dali surrealist painting, poised between prodigal invention
and philosophical glimmers. As with Dali, readers of Weinbaum may never be
entirely sure whether they are being challenged to think differently or are just
being diddled.

A much richer work, and one neglected in many studies of science fiction, is
Planet Plane, published under the name John Beynon, one of the pseudonyms
that John Wyndham invariably used in his works of the 1930s.[30] In *Planet Plane*,
adventurer and inventor Dale Curtance is pursuing the "Keuntz Prize" for the
first roundtrip to another planet (probably inspired by the actual Guzman Prize
established in France to reward the first communication with another planet).
Why he chooses Mars rather than, say, Venus as the goal for his experimental
rocket-plane is explained in Curtance's response to a journalist's question:
"It's always Mars in the stories. Either we go to Mars or Mars comes to us.
What with Wells and Burroughs and a dozen or so others, I feel that I know the
place already" (65). Not the Mars of Lowell and Pickering, or Schiaparelli and
Flammarion (let alone more reputable astronomers), but the Mars of the fictional romancers inspires the voyage. The degree to which literary mythology
has begun to function independently of astronomy is neatly captured in subsequent dialogue. On the outward journey, Froud, the on-board journalist,
expresses his hope that the expedition will find evidence of the creatures who
built the Martian canals. The youngest crew member is incredulous:

> "Canals! Why, everybody knows that that was a misconception from the
> beginning. Schiaparelli just called them *canali* when he discovered them,
> and he meant channels. Then the Italian word was translated literally and it
> was assumed that he meant that they were artificial works. He didn't imply
> that at all."
>
> "I know that," Froud said coldly. "I learnt it at school as you did. But that
> doesn't stop me from considering them to be artificial." (68–69)

Even if the history of Schiaparelli's use of *canali* is oversimplified, here in a
nutshell is the definition of the triumph of journalistic myth over astronomical
truth. Like Froud, many people inside and outside of fiction "learnt" their
science and then simply chose to believe something they found more appealing. Although *Planet Plane* has a conventional Flash Gordon–like protagonist

in Dale Curtance and an unconventional—and interestingly treated—woman stowaway who ends up serving as the expedition's translator, it is the newsman Froud who matters most in Wyndham's conception of a mission to Mars. The biologist on the flight looks forward to a search for some microbial life on Mars—and Froud can't get good copy out of such modest ambitions. "Depressing. Here's the world public, egged on by Burroughs and the rest into thinking that the place is crammed with weird animals, queer men and beautiful princesses, expecting me to go one better; and, according to you, I shall have to make thrilling, passionate romances out of the lives of a few amoebae and such-like" (106).

The tension between romantic expectations and disenchanting reality is a leitmotif in Planet Plane. Although the crew can see the famed criss-cross lines on the pink disc as the rocket-plane nears Mars, once they are on the surface the landscape disappoints them. It is rocky, sandy, hot, barren, inhospitable; when they arrive at a canal, the water is brackish and undrinkable; the vegetation growing near it is in the form of tough, reedy bushes with little variety. Curtance's insistence on the political ritual of planting the Union Jack and declaring Mars "a part of the British Commonwealth of Nations" (117) seems especially ludicrous in context. When at last the crew encounters a group of rogue machines—a Weinbaumian menagerie of spheroidal, cubical, pyramidal, and rectangular forms of various sizes marching in procession across the desert and cannibalizing each other for spare parts—Froud is aghast. Here is more grotesquerie than he bargained for, not the official Martian myth of Burroughs and Wells but the offspring of other, less comfortable literary imaginations: "Damn it all, it can't be real—even here. It's—it's a kind of dream made of Lewis Carroll and Karel Čapek rolled together" (133).

The machines, the terrestrial party comes to find out, were created by the indigenous Martians to supplant themselves once the planet's environment became so degraded that it could no longer sustain intelligent organisms. When one of the last red-fleshed humanoid Martians explains this Martian approach to evolution to Joan Shirning, the stowaway, she takes a decidedly Luddite view, unable to accept the idea of a collection of metal parts replacing human beings. But the Martian, named Vaygan, responds that terrestrial humans fear innovation. He reminds her of various traditions that had to be eradicated for humanity to advance on Earth—human sacrifice, slavery, cannibalism, female infanticide, religious prostitution, among them. And there are still bad traditions to be weeded out: "war, execution, gold fetishism" (154). The idea that life is appropriate to flesh and chemicals but an abomination in machinery is dismissed by Vaygan as irrational: "After all, if a man is equipped with four artificial limbs of metal, if he needs glasses to see with, instruments to hear with and false teeth to eat with, he is still alive. So there is life of a kind in the machines' casings. That their frames are of metal and not of calcium is neither here nor there" (156).

Planet Plane climaxes in scenes of chaotic comedy. A Russian rocket, secretly launched, has landed, and its crew plants the hammer and sickle, dumbfounding Vaygan, who tries to grasp the solemn rivalry over pieces of "coloured cloth" (171). Then an American rocket enters the Martian stratosphere, but crash-lands, and the Russians report that there had also been a German spacecraft that was sabotaged before it ever took off. Suddenly, Mars seems about to be overrun by its planetary neighbors—except that those already on the surface have been put under virtual house arrest inside their vehicles. Froud summarizes the situation with his usual caustic, and relevant, insight:

> We push off with world acclaim, we successfully avoid all perils of space and arrive here safely only to find (a) that the place is overrun with idiotic-looking machines; (b) that two other rockets have also pushed off, but without the acclaim; and (c) that our only safety from the said idiotic machines is to stay bottled up in here. It simply isn't good enough. It's not at all the sort of thing that put Raleigh and Cook in the history books. (183)

To complicate matters still further, Vaygan issues an expulsion order for all the earthly visitors because medical studies, carried out by some of the more sophisticated machines, have indicated that the terrestrials carry bacteria harmful to the surviving humanoid Martians. With what seems a patent echo to the conclusion of Wells's *The War of the Worlds*, the British and Russian expeditions are to carry home a message: "Earth is to leave Mars alone" (187). Again, it is left to Froud to gloss the significance of this unceremonious ouster of the would-be discoverers of Mars. This time he does so by evoking journalism's principles of "who, what, where, when, why, and how":

> We come here, we get chased about by crazy machines and we get told to go home again by slightly less crazy machines. We don't know what makes them work, who made them, how they made them, where they made them, when they made them, nor why they made them. In fact, we don't know a blasted thing, and the whole outing has been too damn' silly for words. . . . If this is interplanetary exploration, give me archaeology. (189)

Wyndham's narrative becomes satiric parable, exposing both the arrogance of the exploring ethos and the impatience of the news media with anything less than scripted or scriptable heroics. The British crew returns to a miserable reception on Earth, with special animosity directed toward Joan Shirning who, as translator, has the job of delivering the message from the Martians ordering hands off their planet. The Americans disbelieve the British reports of the crash of their rocket. The Russians never make it back, and their countrymen suspect that the British disabled the Russian craft and left its crew to die on Mars. Although after five years sentiment restores the cardboard hero Dale Curtance to public favor and grants him status "analogous with that of Christopher Columbus" (192), the discredited Joan Shirning dies in childbirth. Her son survives. An invasion, of sorts, has occurred; she became pregnant on Mars, but not by any member of the terrestrial crews.

Wyndham's goofiness, though not his edge of cynicism, can be found in the finest piece of Martian fiction published in the interwar years, although C. S. Lewis has his own satirical axes to grind in Out of the Silent Planet. Lewis eagerly parodies certain ideologies in his romance (notably, the Darwinism of Wells, the agnosticism of Stapledon, scientific imperialism in the person of his character Weston, and the exploitative capitalism of Weston's sidekick Devine), but all his attacks are in the service of a larger visionary mythmaking project in Out of the Silent Planet. Certainly other romancers before him had toyed with the notion of revealing Mars's "true" name as known to its inhabitants. In Mr. Stranger's Sealed Packet (1889), Mars becomes Glintan; Robert Braine's Messages from Mars (1892) calls it Oron; and Henry Wallace Dowding gives the correct name as Orblar in The Man from Mars (1910). Most famously, Edgar Rice Burroughs renamed the planet Barsoom and elaborated on its geography, inhabitants, and customs throughout his series of Martian stories. But as a coherent fictional entity, Barsoom is a mess, nothing more than a grouping of mismatched furniture from the general storehouse of romance. Among the many reinventions of Mars between Wells in 1898 and Bradbury in 1950, only Lewis's Malacandra carries so much earned authority and achieves the completeness of what his friend Tolkien called a "secondary world" of imagination.

A successful secondary world, as Tolkien explained in his classic essay "On Fairy-Stories," has an internal logic that allows a reader not simply to suspend the inclination to disbelieve but to activate provisional belief. While inside the constructed world, a reader consents to its imaginative existence because the world operates on a set of principles that it consistently applies and obeys.[31] It is left to Lewis's protagonist—a philologist named Ransom—to learn gradually, by trial and sometimes embarrassing error, the imaginative laws that shape Malacandra and its inhabitants. The remarkable thing about Lewis's Malacandra is that most of the principles it uses are based on the discredited Lowellian topographical features of Mars—chiefly, a thin but breathable atmosphere; a chilly but not unbearably cold climate; gravity lighter than Earth's; running water; and a system of artificial channels—as well as the utopian-heroic element of Lowell's theory: a superior civilization that has undergone a crisis threatening its existence. Only the lower gravity had any basis in scientific reality. But Lewis later claimed that he *knew* his fictional Mars was scientifically obsolete. "When I myself put canals on Mars I believe I already knew that better telescopes had dissipated that old optical illusion. The point was that they were part of the Martian myth as it already existed in the common mind."[32] Like Wyndham, Lewis was writing "quite in the best tradition" of the new mythic Mars.

Interestingly, canals are hardly ever mentioned in *Out of the Silent Planet* until the very end. It is a long time into the narrative before a reader begins to grasp that the space vehicle actually landed in one of the *canali* (or in the Malacandrian language "handramits") and that the entire action takes place within the canals. Of canyon-like depth and width, the handramits are the only habitable parts of the planet, and they are of artificial origin. Once the surface of Malacandra (the "harandra") had been inhabited by a flying species, but that civilization has long ended—its images still preserved in rock carvings that Ransom studies. The tutelary spirit who governs Malacandra, the Oyarsa, eventually tells Ransom the full story. Each planet has an archangelic Oyarsa, including the planet known to the Malacandrians as Thulcandra (Earth, the "silent planet" of the title). Earth's Lucifer-like Oyarsa became "bent" and waged war in the solar system, destroying life on Earth's moon and desolating the surface of Mars. In this version of the Christian legend of the angelic war in heaven, God (known to Malacandrians as Maleldil) allows the Oyarsa of Mars to open huge channels and release hot waters from beneath the planet's surface to run through the bottom of them. The surviving Martian species flee into these long, straight handramits as warmth and air vanish from the surface. Lewis achieves a clever variation on the canals of Lowell. They are indeed artificial and geometrical, but the architect is divine. They are many miles wide, as they would have to be to be visible from Earth, although they are not mere conduits but deep shelters, fully landscaped habitats that are linked to one another all across the planet.

It was just this ready inventiveness, oblivious to scientific evidence and probability, that drove the irascible geneticist J. B. S. Haldane to lambaste Lewis in a long, biting review-essay in the 1940s. Like his literary-minded hero Ransom, Lewis had little interest in and no profound understanding of astronomy. Ransom knows so little science, in fact, that while on Malacandra he hasn't the basic information to figure out whether he might be on Venus, Mars, or the Moon. Even more significantly for Lewis's purposes, Ransom rejects the language of science and espouses an older tradition of expression when he has an epiphany on board the spacecraft that carries him—a kidnapping victim—to Malacandra. Wondrous sights glimpsed through the windows of a spacecraft are common representations in interplanetary romances; Ransom's insistence on using religious terminology to describe his visions is more unusual. As Ransom lies naked in a glassed chamber of the spaceship, basking in sunlight and starlight, his meditations disclose much about Lewis' mythopoeic intent in imagining Mars:

> A nightmare, long engendered in the modern mind by the mythology that follows in the wake of science, was falling off him. He had read of "Space": at the back of his thinking for years had lurked the dismal fancy of the black, cold vacuity, the utter deadness, which was supposed to separate the worlds. He had not known how much it affected him till now—now that the very name "Space" seemed a blasphemous libel for this empyrean ocean of radiance in which they swam. He could not call it "dead"; he felt life pouring into him from it every moment. How indeed should it be otherwise, since out of this ocean the worlds and all their life had come? He had thought it barren: he saw now that it was the womb of worlds, whose blazing and innumerable offspring looked down nightly even upon the earth with so many eyes—and here, with how many more! No: Space was the wrong name. Older thinkers had been wiser when they named it simply the heavens.[33]

The process of reimagining and renaming that Ransom undergoes aboard the space vehicle forecasts the theme that matters most to Lewis's narrative: how we see another world, how perceptions are transformed when one surrenders to an experience unfettered by expectations. The moment when Ransom drops from the spacecraft to the surface of Mars he is born again: "head and shoulders through the manhole" (41). Like a newborn, he is unable to focus his vision and can see only blurs of color.[34] "Moreover, he knew nothing yet well enough to see it: you cannot see things till you know roughly what they are" (42). Lewis has often been criticized, with some justice, for propagandizing in *Out of the Silent Planet*, and, even more overtly, in his two other interplanetary romances, *Perelandra* (1943) and *That Hideous Strength* (1945). That Lewis had an anti-scientific bias and was engaging in a form of conservative Christian apologetics is beyond denial, but the power of *Out of the Silent Planet* is proportional to the degree of its pleasure in imagining Mars for its own sake.[35] The poetic evocation of the alien triumphs over the didactic agenda. Repeatedly, Lewis's allegorical tendencies are trumped by a deeper-running commitment to the romance of Malacandra. In fact, at the close of the story, in a postscript supposed to be an extract from a letter from Ransom to Lewis, Ransom laments on the cuts that have been made from his original draft to satisfy Lewis's sense of how fiction works. Such wondrous moments as the "nocturne" (159), when Ransom witnesses during a night-time swim the sight of Jupiter rising in splendor in the Martian sky, are smuggled back into the published book's appendix even though they are irrelevant to the ideological structure of the narrative.

Ransom's effort to learn to see what he does not yet know is mirrored in a distinctive quirk of Lewis's style: the compound simile. When Ransom catches sight of the first of the three intelligent Malacandrian species he encounters, his perception of the "hross" will not resolve into a single image. "It was something like a penguin, something like an otter, something like a seal; the slenderness and flexibility of the body suggested a giant stoat. The great round head, heavily whiskered, was mainly responsible for the suggestion of seal; but it was higher in the forehead than a seal's and the mouth was smaller" (54). The necessity—and ultimate failure—of such multiple analogies to convey a precise picture of the alien being can be found also in Ransom's attempt to describe the distinctive gait of another Malacandrian species, the "sorns." He "was reminded alternately of a cat stalking, a strutting barn-door fowl, and a high-stepping carriage horse; but the movement was not really like that of any terrestrial animal" (98). A medievalist, Lewis was certainly aware of the rhetorical convention that came to be known as the "inexpressibility topos"; the writer simultaneously offers an elaborate description of a person or object and insists on the inability of language to capture the reality. The best instance of Lewis's application of the convention to the imagery of Malacandra comes with Ransom's sense of the failure of his multiple similes to capture the nature of the Oyarsa as it passes in procession:

> He never could say what it was like. The merest whisper of light—no, less than that, the smallest diminution of shadow—was traveling along the uneven surface of the ground-weed; or rather some difference in the look of the ground, too slight to be named in the language of the five senses, moved slowly towards him. Like a silence spreading over a room full of people, like an infinitesimal coolness on a sultry day, like a passing memory of some long-forgotten sound or scent, like all that is stillest and smallest and most hard to seize in nature, Oyarsa passed between his subjects and drew near and came to rest. (119)

One scene that had become commonplace in Martian fictions does not appear in *Out of the Silent Planet*—or, to be more exact, it does not appear in the expected place. As early as the 1890s and as recently as Wyndham's *Planet Plane*, fiction writers had written in a version of the moment in the outward journey to Mars when the spaceship approaches the planet and the network of canals first becomes visible to the crew. Mars immediately becomes the familiar locale of Schiaparelli's and Lowell's maps. Lewis forgoes that scene precisely because he wants a fresh view—Malacandra rather than Mars—and wants his readers to struggle to achieve a perception of a strange and wondrous new place unfamiliar to human eyes. Instead, Lewis saves a glimpse of textbook Mars until the end, when Ransom and his kidnappers have been expelled from Mars, sent back to Earth by the Oyarsa as punishment for Weston and Devine's killing of an innocent Malacandrian. As their ship leaves the Malacandrian stratosphere, Ransom looks back at the planet and sees the geometrical markings of the canyons that he had known as "handramits" coming into view: "long straight lines, some parallel, some intersecting, some building triangles" (144). The farther away the ship moves the more familiar—and the more abstract—the planet becomes. What he had known and cherished as a landscape, a habitat, a world diminishes to a diagram. Ransom sleeps and later wakes to a still more distant view of the whole globe, red-tinged with ice-capped poles, and with two tiny moons orbiting it. "It had ceased to be Malacandra; it was only Mars" (146). The literary imagination had brought the planet to vivid life; for Lewis, the astronomical view is deadening. For very good reasons, the brilliant romancing of *Out of the Silent Planet* has also been understood as a form of antiscience fiction.

In the same year that Lewis published his revisionist myth of Wellsian and Lowellian Mars, Orson Welles broadcast his rewrite of *The War of the Worlds*, forty years after its publication in the last years of Victoria's reign. The world had changed enormously, was on the panicky edge of a second World War, and got its up-to-the-minute news in word-pictures beamed through the atmosphere from transmitter to receiver. The post–World War I era of Martiana that began with efforts to send radio signals to the red planet came to an end in a celebrated event in which radio signals brought Mars to Earth. The script for the Mercury Theatre performance (a regularly scheduled weekly radio program), prepared by Howard Koch, opens with ballroom music, supposedly being broadcast from a New York hotel, being repeatedly interrupted by an announcer reporting the crash of a flaming object in rural New Jersey. With each interruption, the announcer grows more sober and tense. Citing various scientific experts and interviewing a purported professor of astronomy from Princeton, the announcer at last permanently shuts down the music and launches into an extended commentary, punctuated by bulletins with new information, about a destructive invasion from Mars. Logical impediments to belief in the reality of the events being broadcast have been cited often: that the CBS broadcast was introduced with and several times punctuated by announcements that a work of fiction was being presented, that a timeframe that went from the landing of spacecraft in New Jersey to the evacuation of New York City and threatened annihilation of the entire country in less than an hour was impossible, that no other stations on the radio dial had changed their programming. The hysterical reaction to the October 30, 1938, radio-play of The War of the Worlds, which Welles characterized as an act of Hallowe'en mischief, appears so absurd that it seems to defy rational explanation at least as much as the illusion of canals on Mars. "Coming generations," a bemused editorialist in Popular Astronomy wrote two months after the broadcast, "may have difficulty in reconciling such a phenomenon with the level of intelligence characteristic of the present."[36]

Many decades after the event, the still-irreplaceable study of the Welles sensation is a book written within a year of the broadcast. Hadley Cantril's The Invasion from Mars: A Study in the Psychology of Panic was the product of fortuitous circumstances. Princeton just recently had established its Office of Public Opinion Research, under the direction of George Gallup. The Gallup Polls, designed primarily to gauge the sentiments of voters on national issues, were the first systematic samplings of public opinion in the United States. At the same time, Princeton's School of Public and International Affairs had launched a study of the influence of radio on the listening public. The Welles' broadcast was an unexpected gift to the researchers on the project, and an opportunity to make use of Gallup-style questionnaires on the most extraordinary cultural phenomenon in radio's brief history.[37] The imaginary landing spot for the first of the Martian invading ships was just a few miles from Princeton. With modest funds from a grant, Cantril, a Princeton psychologist, put together a team of interviewers to do an immediate canvass of local people using a detailed questionnaire to determine why some people panicked and others didn't. Welles, Wells, Koch, and officials at CBS all gave permission to print a complete text of the adaptation, with full stage directions, so that readers could make their own analysis of what techniques helped trigger belief in the fiction.

Cantril and others have generated a great many plausible interpretations of the panic experienced by an estimated million American radio-listeners on that October evening. As in Wells's original romance, the use of actual place names lent an air of truth even to fantastic reports. By replacing all the names associated with metropolitan London with American equivalents—Princeton, Newark, the Holland Tunnel, Times Square, the East River—the Mercury Theatre enacted the classic strategy of achieving credibility by giving to airy imagination a local habitation and a name. People responded, as well, to what they took to be voices of authority—journalists, scientists, military leaders, and political figures, including at one point in the broadcast the (unnamed) Secretary of the Interior using the conventional rhetorical formulas for rallying people in a crisis ("Citizens of the nation: I shall not try to conceal the gravity of the situation that confronts the country," etc.). A more specific jitteriness also was abroad in October 1938 in the aftermath of the betrayal of Czechoslovakia at the Munich conference between Hitler and Chamberlain. Fear of invasion by Germans easily could have gotten mixed up with fear of attack from another planet. (This too, by the way, could have been granted by H. G. Wells himself, who was unhappy at what he saw as Orson Welles's dumbing down of his novel. A minor character in Wells's original romance, panicked by the invasion, refuses to take refuge in France: "She seemed, poor woman, to imagine that the French and the Martians might prove very similar."[38]) The "live" coverage of news events by on-the-spot reporters, including the interruption of regular programs for special bulletins, was a very recent innovation in broadcasting. The Munich conference and the disastrous crash of the zeppelin *Hindenburg*, both reported with striking immediacy on radio, were fresh in the minds of radio listeners.[39] The degree to which people were willing to put their faith in what they heard on the radio, despite all the contrary evidence of fictional content, alarmed people like journalist Dorothy Thompson. In her *New York Tribune* column, she worried aloud about the facility with which people's anxieties and biases could be manipulated by the political use of the mass media:

> If people can be frightened out of their wits by mythical men from Mars, they can be frightened into fanaticism by the fear of Reds, or convinced that America is in the hands of sixty families, or aroused to revenge against any minority, or terrorized into subservience to leadership because of any imaginable menace.[40]

Of course, a shrewd observer in 1938 would not have to look far for evidence of such manipulation already at work. *Click*, a monthly picture magazine, made "Radio Hypnosis" its cover story for February 1939. A four-page spread juxtaposed pictures of Orson Welles in the studio with Hitler at the lectern, an artist's rendition of people in flight from the Martians with a photo of panic-stricken Chinese running from a Japanese air raid, and accounts of what Americans believed about the radio Martians with analysis of the emotionalism and mass hysteria generated in Germany by Goebbels' radio rants against the Jews.[41] The manic broadcast orations in Germany produced far more worrisome episodes of hysteria and fanaticism than anything generated by Orson Welles's actors. The American correspondent for the *Times* of London seemed to have exactly such a thought at the back of his mind when he opened his dispatch on the Mercury Theatre broadcast with an acid observation on the complacency and isolationism of the United States. Plainly, it was the reporter himself, not the generic "America" of his opening sentence, that couldn't decide whether the panic was more risible or contemptible:

> America today hardly knows whether to laugh or to be angry. Here is a nation which, alone of big nations, has deemed it unnecessary to rehearse for protection against attacks from the air by fellow-beings on this earth and suddenly believes itself, and for little enough reason, faced with a more fearful attack from another world.[42]

As the Hitler menace grew in 1938 and 1939, Mars in its most bellicose associations—the Wellsian images grafted onto the ancient stock of the planet's namesake god of war—kept pace. A new set of fifteen episodes of the popular Flash Gordon movie serial in late 1938 shifted the location from Ming's fictional planet Mongo to the more topical Mars. From Mars, Ming directed a "death ray" at major cities of the Earth. Then, in 1939, there was a major opposition of Mars and Earth—the closest since 1924. In July, stories about the opposition shared news space with stories of rising tension in Europe. *Time* magazine's coverage of the opposition began, "Last week, as the shadow of war hung over Europe, the war planet, baleful red Mars, hung bright and big over the world."[43] A science journalist observed that, seen from Mars, our planet would glow blue—the color of peace. "Which goes to show that the Martian, if he existed, would be just as wrong about the earth as the inhabitants of earth are about Mars."[44] Three days before opposition and six weeks before the German blitzkrieg into Poland, the *New York Times* editorialized on the current state of astronomical knowledge about Mars. The editorial opened with a stately paragraph that simultaneously dismissed and invited superstition:

> If we were living in the tenth instead of the twentieth century we would know definitely that great wars were about to break out on the earth. We would be watching the sign in the heavens with terror. For Mars, planetary symbol of the war god, is blazing with baleful splendor in our southeastern sky. His ruddy glow washes out the pale gold of every wanderer through the lovely spaces into which we gaze.[45]

At the recently opened New York World's Fair, the summer opposition produced a strange mixture of entertainment and civil defense. "Not unmindful of the interest in Mars and Martians that Orson Welles stirred by a radio broadcast last winter," a reporter commented, the Fair's organizers staged a mock-enactment of resistance to a Martian invasion, complete with a flyover of National Guard airplanes, machine-gun fire, and shells fired by the anti-aircraft battery of the Coast Guard.[46] Meanwhile, across the ocean, a German satirist took note of the attempt of a small group of engineers on Long Island to establish—yet once more—radio communication with Mars during the opposition. Recalling the Orson Welles' scare, the Berlin newspaper columnist saw a brooding preoccupation with invasion in America and, in the signaling effort, a hope that "impending doom might be avoided by establishing connection with Mars and convincing the Martians of the United States' democratic good-heartedness." More pointedly, the writer sneered that President Franklin Roosevelt was likely to add Mars to "the list of objects that should be 'protected' from the brutal cupidity of the authoritarian States."[47]

A final piece of Martian fiction from the 1930s emerged from Dublin shortly before the outbreak of the war. James Creed Meredith, a philosopher and playwright, had only the thinnest storyline for *The Rainbow in the Valley*, which operated largely as a beaded string of philosophical dialogues. Meredith's string was an imagined secret scientific gathering in western China that had succeeded in communicating with Mars. In a preface, Meredith admitted that he worked on assumptions "quite regardless of factual probability" about the Martian atmosphere and water supplies.[48] But what is more remarkable than his counterfactual premises, which were increasingly common in fiction about Mars anyway, was his utopian penchant. The Martian story, Meredith said, gave him a convenient literary framework within which to explore a variety of political and philosophical topics. As in Wells's *Star-Begotten*, the Martians themselves in *The Rainbow in the Valley* remain off-stage, a reference point for discussion rather than participants in an action. Concerned about the possible new Great War on Earth, baffled by the colonizing and patronizing behavior of England towards Ireland, eager to instigate a "change of heart" (228) among terrestrials so that they can move beyond internecine conflict to a platonic ideal of benevolent oligarchy, the Martians are didactic abstractions in Meredith's project. But in the joyless year of 1939, his wistful utopianism inevitably feels strained, lacking the innocence, spontaneity, and wit of the many pre–World War I exercises in Martian utopia.

The real coda to Mars in the 1930s is not Meredith's earnest effort to pull humanity out of what his opening chapter called "the valley of shadows" but a news event early in 1941. Astronomers at the Mount Wilson Observatory reported definitive findings that there was simply too little oxygen and too little water on Mars to sustain life in any form that we could recognize. And so, a year and a half into the war, the New York Times again editorialized on the subject of Mars—and found the Wellsian images now irrelevant and obsolete. "Definitely the men on Mars are out. It is only one more coincidence that the warring monsters of H. G. Wells's brilliant imagination should be finally discredited just when they seem to have come to life on earth in gas masks, parachute uniforms and armored tanks."[49] Early in the year that finally would put the United States in the company of the warring nations, the Times writer, anticipating the celebrated insight of Pogo during the Vietnam War, concluded that we had met the Martians, and they were us.

on the
threshold of
the space age

IO

For the first half of the decade, the old god of blood and war, not the romanticized and utopian planet, presided over the 1940s. Perhaps it should not be surprising that the first significant new work of fiction about Mars to appear after the Second World War ended should have borne the title *The Angry Planet*. Written for adolescents, much of John Keir Cross's popular adventure story is derivative of earlier Martian fiction, and on its surface it is remarkably empty of any direct allusion to the world war during which, presumably, the narrative's events occurred. Cross's Mars is a Lowellian dying planet; the mechanics of space travel are treated as casually and incredibly as in C. S. Lewis; there is the customary narrative convenience of a breathable and indeed invigorating Martian atmosphere ("thin and sharp, like a perfect poem of a wine"[1]); the octopus-like monstrosities that threaten the crew from Earth are plainly Wellsian; the battle scenes come straight out of the masculinist tradition of Mars romances; and the three children stowaways are more smart-alecky versions of those from earlier boys' stories of Mars, although Cross includes one girl among the group.

While there is little aside from the device of multiple narrators that is artistically venturesome in *The Angry Planet*, the narrative, for all its effort to evade reference to current events, does bear the marks of the just-concluded global war. A Mars torn between hideously malignant "Terrible Ones" and the kindly "Beautiful People" is taken by one of the book's narrators as an illustration of the polarity of Good and Evil that is a "great principle permeating the entire universe" (156). It is tempting to discern the Axis and the Allies transferred to an extraterrestrial setting, and to find in the climactic eruption of Martian volcanoes whose rivers of lava threaten to engulf all parties in the conflict and put an end to life on Mars an echo of the apocalyptic detonations that closed out World War II. But Cross does not invite an allegorical reading of *The Angry Planet*. Instead, the narrative seems designed as an escape from the Earth, its problems, and its small-mindedness. The epilogue simultaneously celebrates the "detachment" of Mars's Beautiful People from all worldly concerns and suggests flight from terrestrial realities. When the crew returns to Earth, one of its two adult members—a writer straight out of the "best tradition" of the 1930s—is dismayed by the skepticism of scientists and journalists who decry all accounts of the journey to Mars as a hoax. He even grandiloquently likens his experience to Galileo confronting the Inquisition. "I prefer an Angry Planet to a Mean, Envious, Uncharitable Planet," he writes (230). And he then makes plans to return to Mars.

By contrast with Cross's sterilizing of political realities from his narrative, the most widely read American Mars narrative for a young audience from the 1940s broadcasts its ideological commitments from the outset. Robert Heinlein's 1949 *Red Planet: A Colonial Boy on Mars* leaves no doubt about the motives for abandoning Earth for Mars. In the first chapter, a grumpy physician lectures his teenaged patient on the cramping effect of rules and red tape. "Me, I left Earth to get away from all that nonsense. Earth has gotten so musclebound with laws that a man can't breathe. So far, there's still a certain amount of freedom on Mars."[2] Heinlein insists that *Red Planet* be read as an allegory, with Earth as the exemplification of Law and Mars of Freedom; Dr. MacRae's penchant for surly homilies against regulatory bureaucracies, cream puffs, custard heads, pantywaists, and—that bane of libertarianism—gun control supporters marks him out as Heinlein's mouthpiece.

Heinlein celebrates Mars as "a frontier society" where youthful minds, whether embodied in an old rugged individualist like MacRae or the teenagers who model themselves on him, yearn to breathe free, unshackled from "a moribund, age-ridden society like that back on Earth" (158). The young protagonist Jim Marlowe (or James Madison Marlowe, as his tendentious full name goes) takes the actions that lead to a revolt against the effort by corporate headquarters of the Earth-based Mars Company to impose long-distance discipline on the colonials who are establishing the infrastructure for a full-fledged human presence on Mars, but the rhetorical engine for the libertarian vision of Mars belongs to MacRae: "We are the advance guard. When the atmosphere project is finished, millions of others will follow. Are they going to be ruled by a board of absentee overseers on Terra? Is Mars to remain a colony of Earth?" (145). Not surprisingly, the plot culminates in the arrest of the Mars Company stooges and the drafting of a Proclamation of Autonomy, loosely modeled on the American Declaration of Independence.

What is surprising is that the political program of Red Planet is ensconced in a romance narrative that it is one part Percival Lowell, one part C. S. Lewis, and one part a fellow American fantasy writer whom Heinlein made a point later of ridiculing for his failures of scientific imagination—Ray Bradbury. It may be that Heinlein intended a comic glance at Edgar Rice Burroughs when he reveals, late in the story, that the furry, round "bouncer" adopted as a pet by Jim Marlowe and named by him Willis is actually not only female but "sort of a Martian crown princess" (192). But the adoption of earlier fantastic devices is too wholesale to be merely whimsical. Heinlein's Mars for juveniles has towered cities, canals, a subway system beneath the canals, twelve-foot-tall and three-legged inhabitants, vegetation that pulls back into the ground during the cold nights, and nomenclature courtesy of "the immortal Dr. Percival Lowell" (11). The colonial school for boys that Jim Marlowe attends is named Lowell Academy. The Martians are mystics who, like Lewis's Malacandrans, have given up the interplanetary travel they mastered eons ago, and they are governed by a disembodied "old one" who sounds like a first cousin to Lewis's Oyarsa. For all its he-man philosophy, Red Planet is strikingly softheaded in its narrative conventions.

From the moment of its opening sentence, Red Planet announces that it is set in a fairy-tale Mars: "The thin air of Mars was chill but not really cold." Among astronomers, the few remaining adherents to the view that Mars might have a breathable atmosphere had melted away in the 1930s when more sophisticated spectrographic analysis demolished the supposition of an oxygenated atmosphere that might be the equivalent of terrestrial air at the level of the Andes or the Tibetan plateau. Robert Richardson, a writer and astronomer on the staff at the Mount Wilson Observatory, observed that it was too bad that the notion of thin but breathable Martian air had to be relegated to fantasy. "Then science-fiction writers and motion picture producers would not have had to go to the trouble of encasing their characters in space suits as soon as they set foot on Mars. You can have no idea how those confounded space suits slow down a story or a drama." The best guesses around 1950 were that the Martian atmosphere was perhaps 96 percent nitrogen, less than 4 percent argon, with a trace of carbon dioxide. Water vapor and oxygen were not detected by the spectrograph. "Two things one would not need on Mars," Richardson concluded wryly, "are a fire extinguisher and an umbrella."[3] Heinlein has neither umbrella nor fire extinguisher in Red Planet, but he is the same author who scolded Ray Bradbury, whose Martian Chronicles was published the year after Red Planet: "A man who provides Mars with a dense atmosphere and an agreeable climate, a man whose writing shows that he knows nothing of ballistics nor of

Photographic portrait
of Ray Bradbury, 1950,
by Morris Scott
Dollens. Courtesy Ray
Bradbury Collection,
Rare Books and Special
Collections, Bowling
Green State University
Library

astronomy nor of any modern technology would do better not to attempt science fiction."⁴ Not without cause has science-fiction writer and historian Brian Aldiss, commenting on Heinlein's pedantry and the banality of his prose, remarked, "More nonsense has been written about Heinlein than about any other SF writer."⁵ Some of the nonsense came from Heinlein's own typewriter.

The severity of Heinlein's reproaches to Bradbury, whose fantasies about Mars have only a tangential relationship to the genre of science fiction despite the customary use of that term to label them, may reflect a personal irritation. Heinlein had and still continues to have a large and loyal following among science-fiction enthusiasts, but Bradbury reached a broader cross-section of readers and often was reviewed in the mainstream press. Heinlein, eager to discredit his chief American rival for popularity in the 1950s, accused Bradbury of failing at aims that he never embraced and in the process inflated his own commitments to scientific purity. Interestingly, when Heinlein returned to Martian themes in the early 1960s in a pair of novels, the popular *Stranger in a Strange Land* (1961) and *Podkayne of Mars* (1963), the results were closer to fairy tale than to science fiction. *Stranger* opens notoriously with the sentence, "Once upon a time there was a Martian named Valentine Michael Smith."[6]

But there is no doubt that Bradbury's *Martian Chronicles* was the book that dominated the 1950s on the subject of Mars and has in most ways outlasted *Stranger in a Strange Land* as a durable imaginative achievement. It is worth asking what it is about *The Martian Chronicles* that gives it special standing in the twentieth-century literature of Mars, prompting John Noble Wilford's claim, just before the flood of new fiction about Mars in the 1990s, that it is "arguably the best book ever written about Mars."[7] The claim could be argued, but certainly not since Wells's *The War of the Worlds* in 1898 had any work of fiction about Mars attracted so many readers and influenced so many other writers. In some respects, *The Martian Chronicles* is an unlikely icon. The writing is often over the top, although some readers always have been willing to defend as poetic such purpled excesses as a description of "the rich, inky soil, a soil so black and shiny it almost crawled and stirred in your fist, a rank soil from which might sprout gigantic beanstalks from which, with bone-shaking concussion, might drop screaming giants."[8] Scientifically, as this last quotation demonstrates and as Heinlein and others have sometimes loudly complained, the representation of Mars is ludicrous. A loosely amalgamated set of stories rather than a coherent narrative, the *Chronicles*, taken as a whole, is full of inconsistencies and internal contradictions. To say that the characters in the various tales are walking allegorical abstractions is simply to avoid saying that they have no personality or particularizing features of mind or feeling.

And yet, for more than half a century, *The Martian Chronicles* has never been out of print, while a more innovative novel such as Arthur C. Clarke's *The Sands of Mars* has made only intermittent appearances on publishers' lists in the same time span. But *The Martian Chronicles* embodies Americanness at the midpoint of the twentieth century as effectively as *The War of the Worlds* captured the ethos of British imperialism and the last years of Victorianism. With their richness of cultural reference and analysis, Bradbury's stories provide a fascinating glimpse, from the perspective of a fantastically unrealistic Mars, of the desires, anxieties, nightmares, and spiritual aspirations and limitations of the people of the United States at the beginning of the era that brought in atomic weapons, economic prosperity, the Cold War, and the civil rights movement. Bradbury laughed away any notion that his fiction was intended to predict anything about the future exploration and settlement of Mars. In notes he made about the genesis of the *Chronicles*, he wrote that "Mars is a mirror, not a crystal" in which viewers see "the somewhat shopworn image of themselves."[9] Bradbury's aims were satirical, not prophetic; the stories in the *Chronicles* are apocalyptic in the oldest sense of the term: revelations designed to lift the veil from hidden realities. The metaphor of the veil actually is used in "The Million Year Picnic," the final story in the *Chronicles*, just before the climactic vision in the canal waters.

If you look behind the veil of the otherworldly technologies and alien landscapes (and the ornate similes that Bradbury is fond of employing to apprehend their strangeness), the stories in the *Chronicles* are strikingly mundane. The Martian mirror most often reflects ordinary life in the United States of 1950. The Martian couple Mr. and Mrs. K., whose crystal house, singing metal books, and yardful of wine trees occupy the opening paragraph of "Ylla," the first story in the *Chronicles*, are exotic versions of the trapped suburban housewife and her preoccupied, irritable husband whose experiences belie homespun myths about American domesticity. The Investigator of Moral Climates in "Usher II" reflects both the long-standing puritan heritage of American culture and, more immediately, the new censorship both political and aesthetic of the House UnAmerican Activities Committee. The hallucinatory encounter between an ancient Martian and a Latino settler in one of the most delicately managed of the tales, "Night Meeting," speaks to the issue of *difference* (the key, repeated word in the story) in a society in which not all members see the same things or see them in the same way. Bradbury sometimes has been criticized for importing a facile Norman Rockwell sweetness to his Mars, but many of the stories in the *Chronicles* offer devastating critiques of the blandness, the vulgarity, the complacency, the cultural homogenization of mid-century America. "The Off Season," a tragicomic account of one man's peculiar American dream of making a fortune off the Mexican and Chinese laborers shipped off to Mars to work in the new mining industry, centers on the construction of a garish, aluminum hot-dog stand in a despoiled landscape that once contained the now-razed remains of an elegant Martian city. Even in the years before the establishment and metastatic growth of the McDonald's franchise, the story captures something of the blindness of mid-century Americans to environmental blight and of the cynical fleecing by white entrepreneurs of, as the protagonist describes them, "one hundred thousand hungry people" (133).

For an extended sample of Bradbury's critical vision of Americanism, the first set of stories, set in the years 1999 to 2001 and detailing the failures of the first four human expeditions to Mars, are especially revealing. They are tales of would-be conquest, madness, and murder, of American naïveté and arrogance and entitlement. "American" is the key word. A reviewer of the British edition, retitled *The Silver Locusts*, observed acerbically that, at a time when the United

States was in a post-war economic boom while Britons were still on rations, only Americans go to Mars because "other countries cannot afford the equipment."[10] But all the characters who go to Mars in Bradbury's book are American for the same reasons that all the locations of Martian invasion are in England in Wells's *The War of the Worlds*. American history and the American character are the central subjects of *The Martian Chronicles*.

Before "the ugly American" became a catchphrase from the 1958 novel of that title, Bradbury gave the concept a workout. In "The Earth Men," the four crew members of the Second Expedition, expecting to be given "the key of the city" for their achievement in reaching Mars and frustrated at the lack of any interest in their arrival, let alone a welcoming committee, are directed by an impatient Martian to someone who can advise them on what they need to know. "We don't want to know anything," the American captain protests, so comfortable in his know-it-all status that he cannot perceive his arrogance. "We already *know* it" (19). The fullest exposition of ugly Americanism occurs in "—And the Moon Be Still as Bright," the account of the material success and moral failure of the Fourth Expedition. By this time, only a remnant of the indigenous, brown-skinned Martians still survives, most of them having succumbed to the chicken pox virus contracted from crews of the first three expeditions. One of the twenty crew members, the archeologist Jeff Spender, is moved by the elegant artifacts of the Martian culture and what can be deduced from them about the refined minds and sensibilities of those who created them. But all around him are his noisy, drunken, gun-toting fellow Americans with no awareness of or interest in the fact that their presence desecrates an ancient landscape. Spender's sense of shame is triggered by Biggs, one of the most obnoxious members of the crew, who tosses empty wine bottles into the canals, vomits on Martian mosaics, and, in Bradbury's devastating linkage between the violence of imperial conquest and of sexual conquest, brags about his abusiveness:

> "Then there was that time in New York when I got that blonde, what's her name?—Ginnie!" cried Biggs. "*That* was it!"
> Spender tightened in. His hand began to quiver. His eyes moved behind the thin, sparse lids.
> "And Ginnie said to me——" cried Biggs.
> The men roared.
> "So I smacked her!" shouted Biggs with a bottle in his hand. (51)

Conquest and despoliation become Spender's obsessions. "We Earth Men have a talent for ruining big, beautiful things" (54). He likens the fourth expedition to the arrival of Cortez in Mexico and to the white expansionism that drove the Cherokee onto the Trail of Tears. And he foresees that the colonizers of Mars will neither know nor care about the authentic Martian names for the features of the landscape. There will be a wholesale Americanizing of the planet: Rockefeller Canal, Coolidge City, Dupont Sea. After Spender "goes native," calling himself "the last Martian" and beginning a series of sniper attacks on his colleagues, Bradbury has him recount at length the formative experience of ugly Americanism that lies behind his decision to become a Martian terrorist:

> "When I was a kid my folks took me to visit Mexico City. I'll always remember the way my father acted—loud and big. And my mother didn't like the people because they were dark and didn't wash enough. And my sister wouldn't talk to most of them. I was the only one really liked it. And I can see my mother and father coming to Mars and acting the same way here.
>
> "Anything that's strange is no good to the average American. If it doesn't have Chicago plumbing, it's nonsense. The thought of that! Oh God, the thought of that! And then—the war. You heard the congressional speeches before we left. If things work out they hope to establish three atomic research and atom bomb depots on Mars. That means Mars is finished; all this wonderful stuff gone." (64)

The sudden introduction of "the war" into Spender's speech points to one of the major themes being reflected in Bradbury's Martian mirror. As Bradbury drafted and assembled the narratives that make up The Martian Chronicles, newspapers and magazines were full of both scare stories about an impending atomic war and civil defense programs that encouraged Americans to get used to the idea. Late in 1948, a government agency issued a plan, assuming the destruction of many American cities with a minimum of one hundred thousand casualties for each detonation, and a call for the education of the American public "to dispel the current unjustified fear of the radiological hazards involved in such warfare and to develop a wholesome understanding of and respect for the potentials of atomic weapons."[11] Bradbury did not find reassurance in the notion of "wholesome" A-bombs. In "The Taxpayer," an angry American comes to the Ohio launching ground and demands that the guards allow him to board a flight to Mars. "He shook his fists at them and told them that he wanted to get away from Earth. There was going to be a big atomic war on Earth in about two years, and he didn't want to be here when it happened. He and thousands of others like him, if they had any sense, would go to Mars" (31).

The shadow of anticipated atomic war falls over most of the narratives in *The Martian Chronicles*, but there is one major exception. Most of the Americans who emigrate to Mars do so, like the seventeenth-century Pilgrims who are often recalled, to flee from something. At one point we are offered a list of somethings that includes "war and censorship and statism and conscription and government control of this and that" (31). Missing from that inventory is the flight from racism, perhaps because the story that so memorably features that quintessentially American theme is not simply a depiction of an escape *from* an evil but an active seeking after a good. "Way in the Middle of the Air" is the story of an Exodus, and it is told from the point of view of incredulous white men on the front porch of a hardware store who are stunned and angry that the entire African-American population of the Southern region has united to turn its back on the United States and to seek the promised land on another planet. As the Black populace moves in purposeful, stately pace and in enormous numbers through the town on its way to the spaceport, the dominant image is of an unstoppable flood:

> The black warm waters descended and engulfed the town. Between the blazing white banks of the town stores, among the tree silences, a black tide flowed. Like a kind of summer molasses, it poured turgidly forth upon the cinnamon-dusty road. It surged slow, slow, and it was men and women and horses and barking dogs, and it was little boys and girls. And from the mouths of the people partaking of this tide came the sound of a river. A summer-day river going somewhere, murmuring and irrevocable. And in that slow, steady channel of darkness that cut across the white glare of day were touches of alert white, the eyes, the ivory eyes staring ahead, glancing aside, as the river, the long and endless river, took itself from old channels into a new one. From various and uncountable tributaries, in creeks and brooks of color and motion, the parts of this river had joined, become one mother current, and flowed on. (90–91)

In this parable of solidarity, no Black American is to be left behind, as one white boy reports in amazement to his elders. "Them that has helps them that hasn't! And that way they *all* get free!" (95) One of the men on the porch, capturing the cultural moment of the nascent civil rights movement in 1950, whines in exasperation, "I can't figure why they left *now*. With things lookin' up. I mean, every day they got more rights. What they *want*, anyway? Here's the poll tax gone, and more and more states passin' anti-lynchin' bills, and all kinds of equal rights. What *more* they want? They make almost as good money as a white man, but there they go" (96). Bradbury's freedom march to Mars anticipates by four years *Brown vs. Board of Education*; it anticipates the sit-ins and boycotts that began later in the decade, and the great marches of the early 1960s and the rise of Martin Luther King, Jr., as the charismatic leader of the movement. In "Way in the Middle of the Air," Mars is, for once, both mirror and crystal. Speculative fiction rarely had been used so imaginatively to address racial injustice, and not since the beginning of the twentieth century, in Bogdanov's *Red Star*, had a Utopian Mars functioned so effectively as a political statement. But already in "Way in the Middle of the Air"—and especially in the representation of the determination to settle for nothing less than everything—there is a foretaste of what Coretta Scott King many years later would describe as the emerging mood of African Americans in the 1950s: "At first we went for a kinder, gentler form of segregation. Then we went for broke."[12]

"Way in the Middle of the Air" reads best as a detachable story rather than as an integral part of a connected narrative in *The Martian Chronicles*. We never hear again about the African Americans on Mars, the nature of the community they form, or the outcome of their utopian dream of an achieved heaven on Mars. In the closing stories of *The Chronicles*, when nearly all of the immigrants to Mars return to Earth, inevitably one wonders why the African Americans would choose to go back. But when the big atomic war begins in November 2005, nearly everyone responds to the Morse code light messages flashing in the sky: "AUSTRALIAN CONTINENT ATOMIZED IN PREMATURE EXPLOSION OF ATOMIC STOCKPILE. LOS ANGELES, LONDON BOMBED. WAR. COME HOME. COME HOME. COME HOME." (145). Mars is nearly emptied as the homing instinct draws the terrestrials back to the mother planet. By the end of *The Martian Chronicles*, intelligent life on both planets is nearly extinct, and the two most famous images in the narrative address, first, the tragic absurdity of the nuclear holocaust on Earth and then the tentative possibility of a post-holocaust new beginning for a handful of American survivors on Mars.

Probably the most often reprinted story from the *Chronicles* is "There Will Come Soft Rains" in which the one house still standing amid rubble and ash after the atomic destruction of Allendale, California, madly carries on all its automated functions—preparing breakfast, projecting films, filling up bathtubs, warming beds, and reciting the Sara Teasdale poem that gives the story its title. But all the inhabitants, save the family dog, are dead. The presence of their absence is emphasized by a description that Bradbury extrapolated from the common stock of shadow imagery of Hiroshima and of the figures on

Keats's Grecian urn: "The entire west face of the house was black, save for five places. Here, as in a photograph, a woman bent to pick flowers. Still farther over, their images burned on wood in one titanic instant, a small boy, hands flung into the air; higher up, the image of a thrown ball, and opposite him a girl, hands raised to catch a ball which never came down" (167).

In the concluding story in the *Chronicles*, "The Million Year Picnic," we follow a day in the life of a family that used a private rocket to escape the dying cities of Earth for a new life among the dead cities of Mars. It is, in fact, the first full day of what the parents have told their children is a "vacation." Throughout the tale, the father, a former state governor, oscillates back and forth between a reassuring jolliness with his children and a hardly suppressed cynicism about politics and humanistic values. The bitterness climaxes in a bonfire on Mars in which the father puts on the flames his government bonds, a stock report, a variety of philosophical and religious treatises, a map of the world, and other documents he had brought purposefully on the journey in order to destroy them. The speech he makes to his children as he is ceremoniously "burning a way of life" also operates as a dark commentary on the demented automated house of the previous story and its dead inhabitants:

> Life on Earth never settled down to doing anything very good. Science ran too far ahead of us too quickly, and the people got lost in a mechanical wilderness, like children making over pretty things, gadgets, helicopters, rockets; emphasizing the wrong items, emphasizing machines instead of how to run the machines. Wars got bigger and bigger and finally killed Earth. (179–180)

"The Million Year Picnic" does not end with this obituary on terrestrial history, however, but with a glimpse into the genesis of a neo-Martian future. All day long on the family picnic, the younger children have asked if they could see Martians. After the bonfire, the father, knowing that the native Martians are apparently all dead now, tells them nevertheless that he will keep his promise to show them Martians. They walk to the edge of a nearby canal and the father points downward: "The Martians were there—in the canal—reflected in the water. . . . The Martians stared back up at them for a long, long silent time from the rippling water" (181). It is a moment of authentic literary magic, one often alluded to, directly or covertly, in later fiction about Mars. The ambition of "becoming Martian" increasingly displaces earlier fantasies of "discovering Martians." But this image also fully sums up Bradbury's contention that Mars is a mirror in which we see by reflection our own identity, culture, and history. And it operates as a distant but meaningful gloss on the exchange of dialogue

The world's first space suit, Cover of *Collier's Magazine*, 28 February 1953.
Courtesy Boston Public Library

in Wells's *The War of the Worlds* fifty-two years earlier: "What are these Martians? . . . What are we?"

In 1971, as *Mariner 9* began photographing Mars, Bradbury concluded that the "mythology," as he called it, of *The Martian Chronicles* might still keep the book alive even in the face of irrefutable evidence that nothing like his imagined Mars ever was or would be.[13] On that score, Bradbury was right. But its durability finally may have somewhat less to do with its mythic status as the last flowering of a romantic vision of Mars than with its extraordinary acuteness as a work of cultural criticism. For more than half a century, *The Martian Chronicles* has remained one of the half-dozen or so fictions about Mars that are central to the imaginative tradition.

But even as the *Chronicles* were being published, first as separate stories in the late 1940s and then collected in 1950, an alternative way of imagining Mars was being contemplated by the young chairman of the British Interplanetary Society. In both nonfiction and imaginative narrative, Arthur C. Clarke tried to popularize new ways of conceiving the Martian landscape and the voyages that would bring human beings to Mars. In 1951, his *Interplanetary Flight* carefully laid out the practical means and the technical requirements for travel to the Moon and the planets, while introducing readers to a new vocabulary that included the science of "astronautics" and the need to design "what have been christened 'spacesuits.' "[14] The following year, his illustrated history and forecast, *The Exploration of Space*, was a Book-of-the-Month club selection and the subject of the lead review in the *New York Times Book Review*. That year, too, *The Sands of Mars*, one of Clarke's first novels, set out consciously to "abandon the romantic fantasies of Percival Lowell, Edgar Rice Burroughs, C. S. Lewis and Ray Bradbury."[15]

Clarke's books began appearing precisely in the years when a change could be detected in how the press reported on Mars and on the general subject of space flight and exploration. In the United States, *Collier's* published seven articles between March 1952 and March 1954 on space travel and satellites, all of them lavishly decked out with photographs, diagrams, and the paintings of the premier space illustrator of the period, Chesley Bonestell (see color plate 7). The first of these treatments in *Collier's*, under the general heading "Man Will Conquer Space Soon," included twenty-six pages of articles, illustrations, roundtable discussions, and editorial commentaries by Wernher von Braun, Fred Whipple, Willy Ley, and other scientists and academics covering topics from vehicle design to questions of ownership claims to other planets. In 1953, *Collier's* put on its cover the first public photograph of a pressurized space suit, designed and being tested by the U.S. Navy. In 1954, one of the editors at

Collier's observed that the magazine's staff had been teased by some journalistic colleagues for devoting so much space to fantastical notions.

In fact, British reports about astronautics tended more to skepticism than their American counterparts. An editorialist in the summer of 1952, finding a radio program on the coming era of space travel "baffling," resorted to ribald speculations about cash-strapped Britons longing for the day when they could board "the celestial omnibus" for a holiday on Mars rather than in the south of France. "The pundits are divided as to when the first space boat leaves, but there does seem to be a hopeful—or is it an ominous?—unanimity of opinion among them that its E.T.D.—its expected time of departure—is more or less round the corner. E.T.A.—expected time of arrival—remains on the lap of the gods." The unfortunate holidaymakers will learn what every schoolboy ought to know, namely that Mars is "inhabited by sinister octopus-like creatures which are only too intelligent and only too lacking in the moral virtues."[16] While the *Times* of London writer remained stuck in the late Victorian fantasies of Wells, a columnist for the *New York Times* entered enthusiastically into the spirit of Clarke's *Exploration of Space*, "really the outstanding how-to textbook of the year." Celebrating Clarke's vision of fleets of space ships touring the solar system and comparing them with the antique romance of Jason's *Argo*, Charles Poore nevertheless distinguished the realism of *The Exploration of Space* from the cheap thrills of space-opera heroics:

> A spirit of superbly controlled wonder at the possibilities of life on earth and in other parts of the universe animates this book. It is often daring but never preposterous, sometimes fanciful but never foolish. At a moment when science fiction fantasies are as plentiful as zeroes in astronomical calculations, this book stands out for its candor and clarity. It is a challenging link between the lost Atlantis and the unvisited geography of the stars.[17]

Clarke's own venture into a science-fictional narrative about Mars got less attention from the press. *The Sands of Mars* (1952), in the years before the first space-based photographs of the planet, could still suppose substantial vegetation on Mars and even a few marsupial animals, but there are no towered cities, no abandoned docks on the dusty shores of former oceans, no evidence that complex intelligence ever evolved on the planet. Much of the landscape would seem monotonous to terrestrial eyes. The realities of life on Mars, in the first decades of human occupation, Clarke assumed, would be more tedious than exotic. The two small towns, Port Lowell and Port Schiaparelli (their names are nearly the only homage Clarke offers to the old romance of Mars), are cramped, architecturally bland, and disappointing to new arrivals on the planet. Even the

Arthur C. Clarke at
his telescope, c. 1952.
Courtesy Science and
Society Picture Library,
London

spaceship *Ares* that brings the protagonist to Mars departs sharply from the
sleek, cigar-bodied vessels that had become traditional accessories in the literature of outer space. In shape it is a clumsy-looking, asymmetrical dumbbell
whose design is governed by practicality: a large sphere for crew, passengers,
and cargo, and a smaller sphere containing the atomic power plant that fuels
the ship, with a long tube linking the two spheres but keeping the radioactive
materials as far distant from the human voyagers as possible. It was, the
disenchanted protagonist Martin Gibson thinks, the ugliest imaginable solution to an engineering problem.

Once on Mars, Gibson has to adjust his imagination to the actualities of a
new landscape. Like many others, he delights in the Martian place names
"created more than a century ago by astronomers who had certainly never
dreamed that men would one day use them as part of their normal lives. How

poetical those old mapmakers had been when they had ransacked mythology!" But, alluding to Keats's Nightingale ode, Gibson recognizes that the landscape onto which the magical casements of Schiaparelli's poetic nomenclature open is "forlorn" (72). Only after he has been on the planet a while does Gibson begin to appreciate the beauty of its barrenness. Here, Clarke outlines a theme that would be taken up with increasing fervor by later novelists in the 1990s, and most notably by Kim Stanley Robinson: a celebration of the bleak grandeur and theatricality of Martian topography. Clarke's imagination comes most fully into play in two travelogue sections of The Sands of Mars, when Gibson and his companions take a ride across a variety of Martian terrains and when Captain Norden describes his experiences on the first expedition to the moons of Saturn. What might in a different kind of book be described as digressions here become the heart of the narrative—the evocation of the otherness of other worlds in a language that eschews romanticized fantasy in favor of an un-adorned, sometimes clinical, language of physical description. The Sands of Mars has only the slenderest of plots, little dramatic tension, and a forgettably adolescent love interest, but it inaugurates a set of motifs that chart a new direction for the literature of Mars: the challenge of terraforming an environment hostile to human life; the analogy between Martian settlements and the American colonies in the "new world"; the individual process of becoming Martian; the collective struggle for planetary self-sufficiency and for independence from commercial interests on Earth. All these motifs will develop into the new conventions of the post-romantic novel about Mars in the late twentieth century.

Clarke gives special point to his antiromantic Martian odyssey by making the protagonist a novelist whose first, reputation-making novel was called Martian Dust, in an echo of the title of Clarke's own novel. Supposedly written in the 1970s, when space travel was just beginning, Martian Dust became scientifically untenable in the decades following its publication. Some earlier fiction about Mars had taken up the notion of literary obsolescence—notably, the dismissal of Wellsian fantasies in C. S. Lewis's Out of the Silent Planet, a book that Clarke evidently had read closely. But Clarke, in a dialogue between Martin Gibson and the captain of the Ares, offers the earliest extended discussion of the general problem of science fiction in the space age. When Captain Norden pronounces that "Nothing is deader than yesterday's science-fiction," Gibson asks if he believes that science fiction can never have permanent literary value (48). The captain proposes that some science fiction has social value (and he suggests that Gibson's own Martian Dust at least captured the Zeitgeist of the 1970s), but that "to the next generation it must always seem quaint and archaic" (48).

That assertion leads to both men reflecting on the dead genre of voyages to the Moon and on the Mars stories that continued to be written right up to the time of the first human journey to Mars. All that can be written now, the captain insists, are factual accounts of trips within the solar system or "fairy tales" about interstellar travel. The choice appears to be between pure fantasy (acknowledged as such) and journalistic travelogue—the Bradbury model and the model of the very book that Clarke was writing. When Gibson protests that the captain overlooks the fact that "lots of people" are still reading Wells's fiction even though it is a century old, the captain argues that Wells was exceptional:

> "Wells wrote literature," answered Norden, "but even so, I think I can prove my point. Which of his stories are most popular? Why, the straight novels like "Kipps" and "Mr. Polly." When the fantasies are read at all, it's in spite of their hopelessly dated prophecies, not because of them. Only "The Time Machine" is still at all popular, simply because it's set so far in the future that it's not outmoded—and because it contains Wells' best writing." (48–49)

Actually, of course, it is now Wells's "straight" novels that feel dated, while his best science fiction remains vital and provocative. But like all ambitious writers, Clarke was looking back over his shoulder at the author he most wanted to outshine.

In the same year that The Sands of Mars appeared in print, Isaac Asimov published a long story, "The Martian Way," that is the only serious rival in the 1950s to Clarke's effort at a more realistic portrayal of Martian settlement. Asimov's Mars, an iron-mining colony with a single city, is a grittier place than Clarke's. Here the atmosphere is thin but unbreathable. The sights and sounds of construction are constant, and there is nothing beautiful about this strictly utilitarian place being exploited by Earth. Scarce metals—tungsten, magnesium, aluminum—are derived from the cast-off parts of spaceships from Earth. In a bone-dry world, a canteen of water is the most desirable house gift from a visitor. With living space limited, there are few amenities like books or videotapes. The Martian city is populated by third-generation settlers in a cowboy culture where recycling, scavenging, and draconian rules about water use drain the fantasy out of life on another planet. One of the inhabitants compares living on Mars to being stuck permanently on a spaceship:

That's all Mars is—a ship. It's just a big ship forty-five hundred miles across with one tiny room in it occupied by fifty thousand people. It's closed in like a ship. We breathe packaged air and drink packaged water, which we re-purify over and over. We eat the same food rations we eat aboard ship. When we get into a ship, it's the same thing we've known all our lives.[18]

Yet, despite the harshness of existence on Mars, the settlers have come to identify with the planet. The focus of Asimov's tale is water—and the increasing reluctance of Earth to "waste" its resources on a marginally profitable colony. The colonists resent being supplicants, and they chafe at their dependence on terrestrial water for drinking, for hydroponic agriculture, for industry, and for rocket propulsion. As Earth-Mars relations approach a crisis, a few settlers have started a movement for self-sufficiency so that they can do things "the Martian way." The first step is taken when skilled scavengers organize a flotilla of small, patched-together spaceships for a journey to Saturn. They haul back a pure-ice planetoid from the ring system as a first installment of a new freshwater supply for Mars. Not only have they forestalled Earth's plan to close the colony and bring them all back to Earth, not only can they begin to sever "the umbilical cord that ties Mars to Earth" (143), the colonists anticipate that within a few years they will be selling their surplus water to the home planet. In a replay of eighteenth-century American history, the colonists are well on their way to becoming independent Martians.

Few writers in 1952 were willing to follow the lead of Clarke and Asimov in imagining a Mars that fit more credibly into a dawning space age that soon would replace art-deco rocket ships and a fairy-tale Mars with the ugly political, mechanical, and economic realities likely to govern space exploration. Leigh Brackett is a case in point. Her 1953 The Sword of Rhiannon acknowledges that Mars is a desert world and oceanless (though, of course, canaled). She depicts present-day Mars as nothing but "bones" where once there had been "living flesh," a mere shadow of its former glory.[19] And so she has her protagonist time-travel back to a period when Mars had a vigorous if troubled civilization as well as lush vegetation and extensive seas. Although the climactic chain reaction that occurs when ancient Mars frees itself from its weapons of mass destruction clearly echoes the nuclear anxieties of the 1950s, for the most part Brackett avoids the kind of cultural criticism that was at the heart of The Martian Chronicles. Brackett's Mars is nothing more than an exotic setting for tired heroics and bland fantasy.

If the Mars that Bradbury imagined is partly a nostalgic reaching back for the romance possibilities available to Burroughs and Lewis, the antiromantic images in Clarke and Asimov look forward to a new realism that would not fully take hold on authors' imaginations for several more decades. Paradoxically, literary uncertainties about how to treat Mars in the 1950s coincided with a sharp increase in scientific reconsideration of and reawakened public interest in the planet. Close oppositions occurred in 1954 and 1956, the earlier one the closest since the start of World War II and the latter the nearest approach since 1924. The nature of the professional and public discussion had shifted enormously since 1924, with its sideshow about radio signals from Mars and with speculation about Martians still prominent in news accounts, despite the recent death of Lowell and the failing health of Flammarion—the two most prolific champions of Martians and their canals. Within astronomical circles, the obsession with refuting Lowell had come to an end, definitively by 1930 when Eugène Antoniadi (who had once been a protegé and employee of Flammarion, though a prudent dissenter from the Flammarion-Lowell doctrines about Martian life) published his La Planète Mars and pronounced the planet lifeless save for primitive vegetation.[20]

Aside from the retrograde impact of the memory of the Orson Welles broadcast, it was the growth of Nazi power and the war itself that overshadowed the close oppositions of 1939 and 1941. The 1940s were not a fertile period for planetary research, but by the middle of the 1950s, publicity about Mars, particularly in the years of the close oppositions, was framed by the new postwar exhilaration about the imminence of space travel. The most famous of the German rocket scientists to defect to the United States at the war's end, Wernher von Braun, lent weight to that visionary thrill in 1952 when he wrote Das Marsprojekt (translated into English as The Mars Project the following year). An equation-driven argument for how an expedition could be mounted, von Braun's book was designed, as he says in his introduction, to shift public perception from the fictional backyard inventor who blasts off from the field behind his workshop to the contemporary reality of the coordinated teams of scientists, technicians, and bureaucrats that would make extraterrestrial expeditions possible. Proposing exploration of Mars "on the grand scale," von Braun imagined a flotilla of ten ships, assembled in Earth orbit and staffed by trained professionals with a variety of specializations, flying to Mars where "landing boats" would descend to the surface from the mother ships. "I believe it is time to explode once and for all the theory of the solitary space rocket and its little band of bold interplanetary adventurers. No such lonesome, extra-orbital thermos bottle will ever escape earth's gravity and drift toward Mars"[21] (see color plate 7).

Since the 1920s, beginning with the German Society for Space Travel and

including the American Interplanetary Society (1930) and the British Interplanetary Society (1933), a number of organizations of engineers and rocket
enthusiasts had been founded, some publishing their own bulletins and journals, to discuss and promote the practical achievement of space travel. As a
young man in the 1930s, von Braun had been on the board of directors of the
German society, and Arthur C. Clarke became chairman of the British society in
the late 1940s.[22] Before World War II, such organizations usually were thought
to be the province of kooks, but perceptions began to change in the 1950s and
the mainstream press took an interest in conferences organized by the interplanetary societies. In 1954, an international Mars Committee was formed to
revive the study of the planet with the expectation that travel to Mars would
occur in the lifetimes of some of its members. The director of the Fels Planetarium at Philadelphia's Franklin Institute even published *A Space Traveler's Guide
to Mars* (1956) to satisfy public curiosity about the state of the question of
Mars's habitability. His book included specific target dates for the first stages
of space exploration: 1957 or 1958 for the first unmanned satellites, 1968 for a
manned satellite, 1980 for the first space station, 2000 for trips to the Moon
and planets.[23] Altered expectations about space travel are also apparent in the
annual index of the *New York Times*. Until 1955, one could find a modest number
of articles indexed under the heading "Spaceships." But in that year, the *Times*
changed the heading to "Astronautics." There, a researcher can find an eruption of entries, most of them focused on plans for and anticipations of the
launching of the first artificial Earth satellites but a few also concerned with the
practical achievement, perhaps by century's end, of a flight to Mars. The *Times*
editorialized on the subject of Mars, for the first time since 1941, just days
before the nearest approach of Mars in September 1956 and made it clear that
there had been a sea change in Martian studies. Lowell—still to be encountered
in many popular treatments of the subject, especially in both fiction and nonfiction books for children—belonged to the past and to the realm of myth.[24]
"Mars is still an enigma, still a planet that interests astronomers as much as it
does the general public," the editor explained. Controversies over the nature of
the planet's surface and the existence of vegetation remain lively, but "no
astronomer here or in Europe believes that there is intelligent life on Mars, as
Lowell did."[25]

With romantic Mars increasingly untenable and realistic Mars still largely
unpalatable to the literary imagination, writers often turned their Mars narratives in on themselves, reflecting on, paying tribute to, and sometimes bur-
lesquing their genres and the literary history they inherited. Hence Clarke's
inclusion in *The Sands of Mars* of the debate over whether science fiction is

literature and Bradbury's harangue on the American hostility to fantasy in his elaborate homage to Poe, "Usher II," in The Martian Chronicles. Two of the more interesting Mars narratives in the 1950s are not so much stories about Mars as explorations of the nature of fiction and the history of literary imagining. Both these books predict what would perhaps be the dominant mode of imagining Mars until the 1980s: self-consciously artificial and nostalgic evocations of "old Mars" before the big telescopes, spectrographic analyses, and, finally, space probes demolished the myths once and for all. Fiction about the fictions of Mars seems to have been the necessary bridge between the old romance culminating in Bradbury and the new realism being heralded by Clarke and Asimov.

Fredric Brown's occasionally hilarious Martians, Go Home (1955) sends up the tired conventions of Wellsian invasion fiction. The novel opens with a capsule history of Mars in popular culture from Schiaparelli forward. The narrator prefaces his account of a Martian invasion with a rehearsal of the scientific consensus that rejected Lowell's theories of Martian geography and habitation. Playing with the lyrics of a popular Johnny Mercer tune, Brown suggests that the man in the street wasn't buying into that consensus. "But by and large the public, which always tends to accentuate the positive, eliminated the negative and sided with Lowell. Latching onto the affirmative, they demanded and got millions of words of speculation, popular-science and Sunday-supplement style, about the Martians."[26] Part I of Martians, Go Home has the identical subtitle of the first section of Wells's The War of the Worlds: "The Coming of the Martians." And Brown's radio newscast of the invasion of a billion Martians, in which listeners are advised not to panic, evokes the other Welles. One woman tells her newly married husband, "Bill, that's a gag, a fiction program. Like the time my parents told me about—back twenty years ago or so. Get another station" (33).

Brown's Martians are at once comic originals and a pastiche of pulp-fiction motifs. By the 1950s, many of the classic science-fictional themes had been worked out, and Martian fiction, especially, seemed to have come to a dead end. Brown's solution is to embrace banality and fashion his Martians in the most degraded of popular images. "Science fiction had presented them [Martians] in a thousand forms—tall blue shadows, microscopic reptiles, gigantic insects, fireballs, ambulatory flowers, what have you—but science fiction had very carefully avoided the cliché, and the cliché turned out to be the truth. They really were little green men" (4). Grouchy, foul-mouthed, sneering, they have learned everything they know about terrestrial culture by eavesdropping on radio programs and so they call everyone in the United States either Mack or Toots. They enjoy spying voyeuristically on the most intimate human scenes, and a favorite greeting when they materialize suddenly in a room full of human beings is "Fuck you" (printed as "—— you" under the editorial constraints of the 1950s).

The invasion from Mars, for which the narrator insists the public ought to have been well-prepared by a century's worth of imagining, takes place in the political context of the Cold War. Brown's Martians are anarchic clowns who take pleasure in exposing all secrets, whether poker hands or classified documents. A principal effect of the invasion is the termination of East-West hostilities and the neutralizing of repressive agencies on domestic fronts. The United States President, realizing that all secrets are known, gives up on defense spending. In the Soviet Union, leaders discover in the Martians an enemy not susceptible to purging or intimidation. "Concessions *had* to be made; minor variations in opinion had to be permitted. Minor deviations from the party line had to be ignored if not actually winked at" because not everyone could be executed or exiled to Siberia. The invaders fight no wars but they ruin government propaganda in all countries by exposing untruths. "The Martians *loved* it when they found even the slightest misstatement or exaggeration, and told everybody" (91). And Brown includes a sly rebuke of the anti-Communist witch hunts conducted by the United States Congress with an account of how the Chief of the Moparobi tribe in equatorial Africa keeps executing witch doctors who fail to expel the Martians from their midst. The chief's name is M'Carthi.

Brown's protagonist Luke Devereaux, like Clarke's in *The Sands of Mars*, is a science-fiction writer. The ending of *Martians, Go Home* leaves deliberately clouded the mystery of why the invaders suddenly leave the Earth. At least five possible explanations are offered, including the suggestion that the Martians may be nothing more than the invention of the protagonist. The author includes a postscript, supposedly demanded by his publishers, to tell the truth about the Martian invasion. But like his mischief-making Martians, Brown delights in subversion:

> I had wanted to avoid being definitive here, for the truth can be a frightening thing, and in this case it *is* a frightening thing if you believe it. But here it is:
>
> Luke is right; the universe and all therein exists only in his imagination. He invented it, and the Martians.
>
> But then again, I *invented* Luke. So where does that leave him or the Martians?
>
> Or any of the rest of you? (199–200)

Poking fun at the unreality of Martian fiction, at the made-up nature of all speculations about Mars, *Martians, Go Home* uses precisely the opposite strategy from the one Wells had pioneered in 1898 when he invested his account of an invasion with documentary realism. But even though Brown's invasion is represented as an act of pure imagination, three effects persist after the departure of the imaginary Martians: All standing armies on Earth are dismantled; plans for sending rockets to Mars are abandoned; and readers lose their taste for the literary genre that imagines Mars and Martians. "Science fiction's dead. Extraterrestrial stuff is just what people want to escape from right now" (102). Brown's novel manages to dovetail neatly its cultural observations on the Cold War and the space race with a literary obituary notice.

With its occasional allusiveness to other texts outside the tradition of science fiction—"the proper study of Martiankind was man"; "infinite treasures in a little room"; "the way of all edible flesh" (47; 174; 187)—*Martians, Go Home* advertises its literary self-awareness. But the most persistently self-conscious of the Martian fictions of the 1950s is the underappreciated British novel *No Man Friday* by Rex Gordon, the pseudonym of Stanley Bennett Hough. Occupying a middle zone between the Clarke-Asimov new realism (Gordon depicts an unforgiving physical environment) and the traditional fields of Martian romance (he invents a pacifist intelligentsia on the planet), *No Man Friday* is most impressive as a science-fictional revision of and meditation on a classic English novel of survival and dominance. Published in England in 1956 and then retitled *First on Mars* for its United States edition in 1957, the year of Sputnik, Gordon's fantasy imagines a secret project to launch a mission to Mars from Australia with a British crew. With plans only to orbit the planet and bring back photographs with hoped-for evidence of life, the mission is intended to stir worldwide interest in a full-scale Mars program. An accident en route leaves engineer Gordon Holder the only surviving crew member, with virtually no experience in flying and no understanding of the mathematics of plotting courses. Unable to return to Earth and desperate to avoid roasting in the Sun or freezing among the outer planets, he relies on the automatic setting to Mars. He prepares to crash-land the vehicle with the hope of surviving somehow on the surface. "That was the first time I ever consciously thought of Robinson Crusoe in relation to myself."[27]

The Crusoe trope in science fiction extends back to Jules Verne's *The Mysterious Island* (1874) and Robert Braine's *Messages from Mars by the Aid of the Telescope Plant* (1892) and forward to J. G. Ballard's *The Drowned World* (1962) and Terry Sunbord's *Robinson Crusoe 1,000,000 A.D.* (2004), but Rex Gordon's Mars tale is the fullest exploitation of the theme. As Holder struggles to provide breathable air, food, warmth, and transportation for himself by scavenging the ruined spaceship for materials for making Rube Goldberg improvisations, he explicitly reshapes the old story. "I dreamed most horribly during that second night on Mars. I dreamed that I saw myself, a latter-day Crusoe, on some fantastic bicycle I had made from bits and pieces of machinery. Instead of a goatskin coat, a parasol, a gun over my shoulder, and a parrot on my arm I wore an oxygen mask and carried a microscope and a collection box for specimens" (50–51). Overwhelmed by the emptiness of the planet and his loneliness, Holder must repeatedly fight off a sense of spiritual defeat and despair even as he manages to establish the material conditions for survival. "I did not understand Mars," Holder writes as he articulates his anxiety "whether I would perish just because I did not realise enough the strangeness" (108, 109). The narrative of his fifteen-year experience on Mars is in the form of a diary that he begins composing, in the expectation of imminent death, as a message to the future.

Defoe's 1719 novel launched the subgenre of the *robinsonade* that has had a lively history for nearly three centuries. Stories of survival in isolated or hostile environments, by virtue of a combination of ingenuity, technological resources, and true grit, have had a steady appeal to readers, and it is not surprising that in the twentieth century such tales often shifted locale from desert islands to other planets. *No Man Friday*, though, for all its debt to the conventions that Defoe established, is in important respects an anti-*robinsonade*—as its nullifying title implies. Published just as the Space Age was beginning with the effort to launch Earth-orbiting satellites and when books were being issued with titles like *The Conquest of Space* and *A Space Traveler's Guide to Mars*, Gordon's novel repeatedly invokes and challenges the concept of conquest as it has been derived from both historical and literary models. Holder conceives his situation as "like that of the first white men to penetrate into the great plains of North America." But like C. S. Lewis's Ransom, he finds that works of fiction—*robinsonades*—had not prepared him for the harsh realities and the humiliations of the struggle to survive and to understand: "I had read enough books in my time, fanciful stories of how strange Earth-men, strangers on strange planets, had mastered their environment by a few quick moves and ruled triumphantly and all-powerfully" (109). When, again like Ransom, Holder realizes that there are intelligent indigenous Martians, utterly different in appearance from humanity, he feels the urge to demonstrate his superiority. "I needed to prove the dominance of the human species. I needed to prove to myself, as well as for all other men who were to come, that Man, even naked, with no more tools than would fit him for survival, could yet dominate an alien planet" (144). But such triumphalist exercises in terrestrial chauvinism are tempered by realizations of the absurdity of his situation. "All my puny striving on this planet had not been a conquest of Mars but only improvisation, with Earth equipment, to fit me for a strange environment" (88).

Holder's diary in No Man Friday poses questions to 1956 readers, as the realities of space travel were drawing closer: "Why had man ever wished to venture from his world? Why had I come? Why had common people everywhere been interested, passionately interested, in space-flight, as soon as its possibility began tentatively to be established?" (118). Rex Gordon's purpose seems not to be a Luddite rejection of space travel but a philosophical inquiry into the reasons, the assumptions, and the expectations that underlie anticipation of travel to other worlds. Where Fredric Brown stood the Wellsian model of Martian invasion on its head, Gordon used the robinsonade as a route to recover Wellsian insights of modesty and to question colonizing rhetoric. On what he calls his "first morning of knowledge on the planet Mars" (120), just after he has discovered the gigantic, luminescent, biologically inconceivable beings who consume the two-legged humanoid animals on Mars, Holder must acknowledge that "men were not necessarily the Lords of Creation in a biological sense at all" (119). In contemplating the alien dominant Martian species and the sub-human earthly look-alikes, Holder sounds as if he is rehearsing the epigraph to The War of the Worlds ("But who shall dwell in these Worlds if they be inhabited? Are we or they Lords of the World? And how are all things made for man?"). Later, he makes a more pointed critique of anthropocentrism:

> We had been blind. I had been blind. When we had supposed that life could only exist in the form that was adapted to Earth conditions, we had been as self-centered, as egotistical, as when our ancestors had supposed that the Earth was the centre of the universe and that the sun and all the stars and planets revolved around it. (139)

Holder's diary is silent about most of the fifteen years he lives on Mars. Only when he finally is rescued by members of the first American expedition to Mars does it emerge that he spent most of that time as the property of one of the dominant beings, named Eii. Alluding to his narrative's title, Holder comments, "Far from making him my Man Friday in that desert world, it was he who was keeping me as a kind of pet, and it would be I who, if I wished to raise my status, would have to display my value to him" (160). As he explains to the Americans, during his captivity he discussed many features of human culture with Eii, including the history of conquest of other species and races considered "inferior." In this passage, reminiscent of Gulliver's Travels and Wells's First

Men in the Moon, Holder emphasizes that he also withheld some of the most damaging details of human history, details particularly relevant to the Cold War period:

> I didn't tell them about our competing nations. I never mentioned our habit of making wars. I was not a fool. They think of us as a kind of termite as it is. And it's our misfortune to be shaped like the creatures that are their source of food. One word of that will convince them that we belong to a totally lower order. That we should kill not only other species but also one another will be as repugnant to them as the cannibalism of the savages was to Crusoe on his island. (166)

No Man Friday concludes ominously, with Holder returning to Earth with the Americans, whose commander intimates that the pacifist Martians may not survive once multiple terrestrial expeditions arrive on Mars (Russian and British missions are expected soon). Blandly, the American general observes that the Martians would seem to be deficient on the practical side. "This sort of thing has happened before, you know," he says while citing the subjugation of India by British imperialists. "It didn't mean that Indian culture did not have its advantages and value. Just that it didn't stand up to our sort of civilisation" (177). The narrative's last scene is aboard the American spaceship. Holder and the crew's biologist stand watching the receding globe of Mars; the biologist, the only one of the Americans genuinely intrigued by the discovery of intelligence on Mars, tries to hold out hope that scientific exchange between the two cultures rather than extermination will win out. Holder's pessimism and tired resignation, which may represent a grimly revisionist turn on the rhetoric of conquest that concludes H. G. Wells's 1935 film *Things to Come*, casts a shadow on the future:

> "I don't think we'll have the patience," I said. "We won't make contact. People like the General will treat it as a practical problem. They will see it that they have been opposed by power on Mars, and they will seek to overcome it with greater power. I would even go so far as this. In the end, I think we'll win. We'll conquer the strange beasts of Mars just as we conquered the strange beasts of the continents and the oceans. And, in conquering, we'll learn nothing from them. We'll not even treat them as creatures who could see or feel or know. We'll kill them and use them, as I told you, for their bones or blood or oil. Perhaps rightly so. Eii and his kind have no sympathy to spare for their own Martian creatures who are shaped like men. But we will do it, and we will go on. After Mars, it will be Venus,

Jupiter, Saturn, Mercury, and the rest. Then other solar systems in our galaxy, then other galaxies and out beyond space itself. (190–91)

The know-it-all, win-it-all American ethos, which Bradbury had already skewered in *The Martian Chronicles*, gets replayed at the end of Gordon's narrative, but the year after its initial British publication American self-assurance about conquering the universe took a cold bath. The announcement on October 4, 1957, that scientists in the Soviet Union had successfully sent a satellite into orbit was followed shortly thereafter by the ignominious failure of the U.S. Navy's project to duplicate the feat. With Sputnik I, the space age, first broached in 1942 when von Braun made his earliest test-flight of the V-2 rocket later to be used to blitz London, had finally arrived. Within three years, the Russians attempted to launch the first rocket to Mars.

ReTroGraDe VISIONS

From the 1880s on, there always had been writers whose visions of Mars were oblivious to scientific advances in the study of the planet, and even resolutely counterfactual. But perhaps the most conflicted chapter in the literary history of Mars occupies the years between the early space launches of the 1950s and the first automated landing on Mars in 1976. For more than fifteen years, the literary imagination was mostly on hold. Romantic Mars was undoubtedly antiquated, but no new model had formed to put in its place. A portion of the public was reluctant to surrender its fantasies about Mars even as new discoveries about the planet's atmosphere, temperature, and topography accumulated. At the 1956 opposition, the year before the Soviet Union launched Sputnik, astronomers set up shop in various locations around the world—particularly in the southern hemisphere where the viewing conditions would be superior—to try to resolve the still-unsettled question of whether some primitive lichens and mosses survived on the surface of Mars. Larger life-forms, including animals, already had been ruled out by most reputable astronomers. An editorial in a Boston newspaper urged its readers not to get caught up in the scientists' excitement over the opposition: "Put your telescope on Mars and you'll ruin a romantic dream. Watch television these nights instead of the southeast sky and you can continue to think in terms of Buck Rogers, flying saucers and beautiful Martian girls who consider Earthmen the best thing that ever happened along."[1]

The director of Philadelphia's Fels Planetarium noted that the oppositional year of 1956 was also the fiftieth anniversary of the publication of Lowell's *Mars and Its Canals* and that an era was ending. The "simple, unadorned telescope" on which Schiaparelli and Lowell depended was now supplemented by a new arsenal of tools: spectroscopy, radiometry, photoelectric photometry. And, he added, the world was on the verge of the physical exploration of space, which would soon eclipse the findings of the terrestrial telescope.[2] As the infant space programs in both the Soviet Union and the United States worked toward launching cameras to scrutinize Mars in the 1960s, the fissure that had existed between the scientific and the literary imaginations ever since the Lowell controversy appreciably widened. Mars became the cynosure for planetary astronomers once the possibility of sending probes into space was achieved, but it became an onus for the imaginative writer. One significant difference from earlier periods is that by the close of the 1950s the general public had been weaned away from Lowellian fantasies. People no longer formed their impressions of Mars from Sunday supplement articles but rather from the new popular medium of television, which—despite the Boston editorialist's pronouncement—would contribute to the debunking of the Mars of legend. In 1954, ABC began broadcasting *Disneyland*, a television anthology divided into the four segments (corresponding to the layout of the new Walt Disney park in Anaheim) of Adventureland, Frontierland, Fantasyland, and Tomorrowland. One of the highlights of the 1957 season was Disney's "Mars and Beyond," a "science-factual" documentary to which Wernher von Braun had been a consultant. Using animation and simulation techniques, along with talking-heads commentaries, "Mars and Beyond" offered, as one journal of astronautics phrased it, "a sober view of contemporary scientific hypothesis and conjecture." *Time* magazine commended the Disney writers: "They did not confuse the popular with the vulgar, avoided the error of talking down to the viewer."[3] Similarly, a new magazine, *Space Age*, reported early in 1959 that the Air Force (NASA, the National Aeronautics and Space Administration, had only just been authorized by Congress) was developing a program for survey missions to Mars. But the writer cautioned against unfounded expectations of sensational revelations. His article opens with the astringent assertion, "Mars is a graveyard."[4]

In the midst of this new sobriety, fiction about Mars didn't quite die out, but the "Martianity" of the novels moved much more to the periphery. The high romanticism that Frank Herbert aimed for in *Dune* included a parched desert world with a breathable atmosphere and exotic fauna out of the Burroughs menagerie. The planet Arrakis, the glossary of *Dune* informs us, is the third planet of the star Canopus. But, as Oliver Morton has pointed out, when Baron Harkonnen gestures to a miniature globe of Arrakis, with its small polar ice caps, caramel-hued terrain, and absence of any blue areas for rivers, lakes, or seas, the model for Herbert's imagined world is evident.[5] To get away with creating a retrograde Mars, Herbert had to move it out of our solar system. Not every writer in the early space age resorted to Herbert's strategy to smuggle the old Mars into a new dust jacket, but Martian narratives of the 1960s and 1970s became more mythic and reflexive in method, declared themselves artifices, playfully quoted not only from the literature of Mars but from the broader literary tradition, and often veered toward either parable or parody. About the Mars of science they frequently were evasive. Their visions were sometimes hallucinatory, sometimes melancholy, sometimes teasing—and at other times, just perversely retrograde conceptions in defiance of new scientific knowledge.

Back in 1941, the *New York Times* had written the obituary for one of the commonest of post-Schiaparelli Martian fantasies. "He was a useful vehicle, the Man from Mars, and now he is no more."[6] The figure of the lone Martian visitor to Earth (as opposed to the invading expeditions descended from Wells and Lasswitz) was a staple of utopian and satiric texts from the 1880s to the 1920s. By mid-century, the device of an extraterrestrial ambassador to Earth remained common in science fiction but the visitor was more likely to be identified as a denizen of a planet of another star system rather than as a Martian. The tension between the romantic convention of a cautionary "Man from Mars" and the new knowledge that contravened such a possibility can be seen in a novel written in the early years of the space age. Donald Wollheim's *The Martian Missile* (1959) opens with a rocket crashing in the Arizona desert. It is, the narrator assumes, one of the U.S. government's early unmanned Jupiters or Vanguards, but hearing a scraping noise from within the vehicle, he realizes there is a pilot inside. "I'd read a lot of crazy newspaper stories about life on Mars and the Martians. Wells, Burroughs, and that sort of stuff."[7] The dying pilot, the tutored imagination of the narrator tells him, might be a man from Mars. The episodic narrative that follows has little to recommend it, stylistically or psychologically or scientifically, but a long way into the book the narrator must revise his identification of the dead pilot. He is no Martian but a visitor from another solar system—a far safer prospect in an age of doubt.

But if no one could quite believe in Martians any more, two influential works of fiction of the early 1960s resuscitate the Man from Mars as "a useful vehicle" for ironic mythmaking. Valentine Michael Smith, the titular *Stranger in a Strange Land* by Robert Heinlein, and T. J. Newton in Walter Tevis's *The Man Who Fell to Earth* are Martian exiles on Earth, the former a Prometheus-figure and the latter, as the novel's title advertises, a contemporary Icarus. In the tradition of the political and utopian allegorists of the 1890s, Heinlein and Tevis use men from Mars as devices for achieving a subversive vision of American society—a send-up of American sexual Puritanism and fundamentalism in *Stranger in a Strange Land*, and in *The Man Who Fell to Earth* a rather darker and more probing examination of political chicanery and cultural spoilage. Heinlein's Mars, glimpsed only briefly at the beginning of the novel, has the old apparatus of canals, ruins, and an ancient race of wise inhabitants. Smith, the offspring of two members of the first terrestrial expedition to Mars but raised by indigenous Martians, travels back to his parents' world, where he is both an alien and a messianic presence ("a man by ancestry, a Martian by environment").[8] The status of Smith as prophet without honor, man without a planet, and sexual hedonist without inhibition had much to do with the novel's adoption as a countercultural talisman in the later 1960s, but Smith as Martian has more to do with literary tradition than with the science of the 1960s. With its disconcertingly Mormon-like religious figures, the gruff and self-satisfied lawyer Jubal Harshaw, who defends the Martian's legal status, and the bevy of accommodating and shapely women, *Stranger in a Strange Land* is a *jeu d'esprit* for Heinlein, full of his customary libertarian doctrines and cartoon characters masquerading as personalities.

Tevis's *The Man Who Fell to Earth* is better fiction, elegant, well-designed, and moving. Here the utopian Martian visitor who had become a cliché in fiction and drama is given a valedictory and distinctly postmodern treatment. Mars is never specified as the home planet of the alien disguising himself as a Kentuckian and calling himself T. J. Newton, but persistent suggestions indicate that the planet Anthea—located in our solar system, dying of thirst, its minerals and fuels nearly exhausted, its population reduced to a fading remnant of a vibrant and advanced civilization—is clearly the Mars of popular lore. A curious Midwestern scientist spends much of the novel trying to decide whether Newton's strangeness means that he's from Mars or Massachusetts. When he finally has physiological evidence that Newton cannot be *Homo sapiens*, he asks him, "Is it Mars?"[9] But Newton doesn't respond—as neither he nor Tevis ever does to explicit questions about the identity of Anthea.[10] In fact, Tevis uses Newton's career on Earth as an opportunity to depict the Martian going native, the extraterrestrial oddity becoming a terrestrial everyman, the would-be savior of his home world falling to Earth in Icarian humiliation and self-destruction. Near the end of the narrative, Newton acknowledges how closely he has come to identify with the humans who were the subject of his research before he came to Earth. His disguise turns out to be a trap. "I worked very hard to become an artificial human being. . . . And of course I succeeded" (188).

The degeneration of Newton into a lethargic, genteelly drunken, and, finally, blinded imitation of a man points to Tevis's deepest concern in *The Man Who Fell to Earth*: to use his Martian as both an observer of and a participant in the culture of a degenerate America. Newton becomes Tevis's instrument for exposing and assessing corporate greed, academic pretensions, governmental corruption, the lazy-mindedness of American consumers, and the sheer witlessness and incompetence of the large bureaucracies that dictate people's lives. Occasionally, the novel explodes in rage at "this cheap and alien place" inhabited by an "aggregate of clever, itchy, self-absorbed apes," but the predominant tone of the novel is less satiric than elegiac (47). Newton comes from a world whose inhabitants had reduced it to atomic rubble with only a few survivors, and he sees the Earth headed toward the same destiny. His mission is as much to save his adopted world as to ferry his remaining three hundred fellow Antheans to safety. "To tell you the truth," Newton says to a resistant questioner about his motives, "it dismays us greatly to see what you are about to do with such a beautiful, fertile world. We destroyed ours a long time ago, but we had so much less to begin with than you have here" (140).

The novelist has self-consciously identified his protagonist with a variety of literary, historical, and mythic figures to enforce the status of *The Man Who Fell to Earth* as cultural fable: At various points, Newton's career is equated with those of Jesus, Hamlet, Rumpelstiltskin, Ichabod Crane, Orwell's Winston Smith, Cortez, Dante, and Oedipus. But most importantly, with his bird-like physique, large lungs, and hollow bones, he is Icarus, and in evoking the myth of Daedalus and Icarus—one of the earliest examples in Western culture of a parable about the potential for liberation and for disaster in new technologies —Tevis makes his tale of an illegal alien from Mars an examination of the ways in which the products of applied science have saturated, debauched, and imperiled modern humanity. At its most banal, there is the ubiquitous imagery, plotting, and diction of television—from which, intercepting signals on Anthea, Newton has learned everything he knows about American values, behavior, commerce, and politics. Television was his mentor—he even learned the flat, unaccented English of American news anchors from those intercepted broadcasts—but he comes to see what an unreliable tutorial television in the 1960s provided, with its counterfeit America that is largely white, middle-class, conventionally ambitious, and unrelievedly nice.

More dangerously, technological advances have put in terrestrial hands the means for the destruction of the world. *The Man Who Fell to Earth*—first published in the wake of a flood of cautionary anti-nuclear war fiction that included Nevil Shute's *On the Beach*, Walter Miller's *A Canticle for Leibowitz*, and Mordecai Roshwald's *Level 7*—is an example of Mars fiction with a similar impulse to issue warnings and appeals. In certain respects, Tevis's novel is even more despairing than those grim depictions of atomic catastrophe and extinction. T. J. Newton, weeping and drunk on gin and bitters at the novel's end, has decided that the Earth is so corrupt, its civilization so sub-human, that it is not worth saving. Tevis sounds like H. G. Wells in the darkest moods of his old age when, thinking about the technology of air travel that he had so admired and extolled at the beginning of the twentieth century, he observed mordantly that the dilemma for *Homo sapiens* was its fundamental duality: "the superman makes an aeroplane and the ape gets hold of it."[11] In fact, Tevis rediscovered in *The Man Who Fell to Earth* precisely what Wells had figured out sixty-five years earlier in *The War of the Worlds*: that a central value of visitors from Mars as fictional devices is to hold the mirror up to human nature. Wells did it by imagining creatures that were emphatically not *men* from Mars but limbless and soulless monstrosities with mechanical prostheses; Tevis took the opposite route, devising an alien who becomes all too much a man: fragile, vulnerable, self-indulgent, and ruined.

One of the geniuses of American science fiction, Philip K. Dick, produced two novels with Martian locales in 1964, *The Three Stigmata of Palmer Eldritch* and *Martian Time-Slip*. Both depict a near-future Mars, colonized by terrestrials and with the features of a frontier society: "a new place" where people could start "a new life," but also a dreary environment full of "half-abandoned gardens and fully abandoned equipment" and "great heaps of rotting supplies."[12] Dick draws on standard pre-space-age iconography, including canals whose waterflow is managed by "ditch-riders" who ration scarce water to Martian households. The decline of an earlier civilization is suggested by the detail that only about 10 percent of the five thousand-year-old canal system is still functional. The surviving remnant of the indigenous Martians, referred to in *Martian Time-Slip* as "Bleekmen," are nomadic, impoverished, and marginalized by American colonists, except for those that have been "tamed"—that is, turned into servants. The relationship of the Bleekmen to Black Americans is enforced by their dark skin, the repeated reference to them as "niggers," and their deferential addressing of every male colonist as "Mister." Although exploited by the terrestrial settlers, the Bleekmen were already on the brink of Lowellian extinction before their arrival: "Time had run out for the natives of Mars long before the first Soviet ship had appeared in the sky with its television cameras grinding away, back in the '60's. No human group had conspired to exterminate them; it had not been necessary."[13]

If the images of Mars in *Martian Time-Slip* and *Three Stigmata* are retrograde, it is also true that scientific plausibility was no more a priority for Dick than it had been for Bradbury. In fictions that are fundamentally exhibitions of schizophrenia, communal hallucination, and cultural metastasis, the landscapes and conventions of Old Mars serve Dick's purposes well enough as the backdrop to surreal fables about inner space. Dick's Mars is a collection of shopworn delusions—and fits right in with his program. Even Dick, however, could not ignore the unprecedented photographic images of Mars that began to enter the collective consciousness when *Mariner 4* flew by the planet with its camera in 1965 and sent back its pictures of a geologically battered and apparently lifeless world. In his 1966 short story, "We Can Remember It for You Wholesale" (the basis for the 1990 film *Total Recall*), Dick gives up the fantasy of hominid Martians and a breathable atmosphere, and settles for the still-conceivable possibility of worms and cactus-like vegetation. Mars, with its landscape of "profound gaping craters," is now, Dick writes, a "world of dust" where a space traveler from Earth is constantly "checking and rechecking one's portable oxygen source."[14] The uneager transition to a new literary Mars was beginning.

Novelists less famous than Heinlein, Tevis, or Dick can illustrate something of the dilemma of Martian fiction at the historical moment when old mythologies were under threat if not yet fully displaced by the new views of Mars from the first space cameras of the 1960s. Several noir-Mars novels depict grim and hardscrabble colonies struggling for self-sufficiency under harsh conditions and seeking independence from a corrupt and indifferent Earth. In *Outpost Mars* (1952), Cyril Kornbluth and Judith Merril, writing together under the pen name Cyril Judd and under the shadow of the threat of atomic war, imagine Mars as "a second chance" for humanity, although its pollution foretokens the possibility that the small settlement will merely enact "another chance to do exactly as they had done on Earth."[15] While these colonists continue to work to improve their lives and establish a pinched utopia on Mars, the vision of the future is somber and tentative. Lester del Rey's *Police Your Planet* (1956) is still darker, with Mars represented as a toxic slum to which Earth's political dissidents and criminals are exiled: "It wasn't a pretty view that visitors got as they first reached Mars. But nobody except the romantic fools had ever thought frontiers were pretty."[16] Although *Police Your Planet* ends with an attempted revolution designed to cleanse the planet of corruption and sever its ties with an exploitative Earth, the dominant impression left by the novel is of a relentless physical and spiritual dreariness.

The most powerful of the dystopian Martian novels of the 1950s and 1960s is D. G. Compton's *Farewell, Earth's Bliss*. First published in 1966, this novel, like del Rey's, imagines Mars as a dumping ground for Earth's political, sexual, and criminal undesirables, who are given a one-way ticket to the planet. It is an ugly world in every respect, as each new annual shipload of convicts arrives and surveys the empty, arid scene before them, although the newly arrived are advised sardonically by old-timers to think of Mars as a delightfully sunny environment with sweeping views and a thrilling sense of distance. "We believe in the beauties of our landscape," one of them warns some newcomers.

"You're advised to think twice before making derogatory remarks about it."[17] A few rudimentary life forms—lichens, fungi, burrowing rodents referred to euphemistically by the colonists as "rabbits"—provide meager and distasteful sustenance, and those who survive the landings fashion living quarters out of the salvaged spacecraft. All contacts with Earth are severed. Compton's Mars is a cul de sac and the colonists develop their own crude, reactionary, and malignant system of governance. There is a parody of British colonialism in the self-important speech of the settlement's "Governor" who insists he is "not another of those pathetic Englishmen changing for dinner and drinking cold tea out of sherry glasses on some rotting verandah in the Burmese jungle" (133). But the strength of Farewell, Earth's Bliss is not so much in its political parable as in its evocation of an existential despair and brutishness that this inhospitable planet calls forth from its human occupants.

Compton's choice of an aesthetically and morally degraded Mars, drained of all romance, represents one extreme in the struggle in the 1960s to keep Martian fiction alive. Other novelists were more reluctant to give up the faded splendors of Lowellian and Bradburyan Mars. In "Tomorrow's World," a preface to his 1962 novel Marooned on Mars, Lester del Rey reports wistfully that there was a time when scientists were convinced of the presence of intelligence on Mars. Now, faith in a geometrical system of canals has been largely lost and the likelihood of a Martian civilization past or present has dwindled, but "the markings on Mars are real" and the presence of vegetation plain to see through the telescope, del Rey claims (as a very few astronomers still did, such as the elderly E. C. Slipher at the Lowell Observatory).[18] But del Rey hedged his language with uncertainties: "Probably the canals are only some natural phenomena which have nothing to do with intelligent life" (6–7). Certainty would be achieved only when we travel to Mars to see the planet for ourselves, and the fiction that follows this preface imagines the first such voyage. "The technical details are generally accurate," the author announces confidently, "and nothing here is really fantastic" (7).

Like the Disney television show, Marooned on Mars was intended to be "science-factual." Once del Rey's narrative begins, however, the limitations of his realism become humorously evident, with pilot and passengers leaning back in a dining hall over coffee and banana cream pie just a few minutes before they climb up a ladder and flop onto mattresses for the launch. But the story momentarily perks up when a stowaway on board indulges in a last nostalgic reading of Martian pulp fiction on the ship's microfilm machine. Here, with a wry gesture of literary self-consciousness, del Rey glosses the transition from the prehistory of Martian exploration to the new space age:

"He'd missed three issues of *The Outlander*, and it was time he caught up with that 'Martian bandit' and his exploits; once they were actually on Mars, all the stories about the planet were probably going to seem silly. He had to read them while he could still get a kick out of them" (44). On the day before the Martian landing, the stowaway finds that he still wants to believe in the old romance, and so too does Dick Steele, an African-American crew member who first dispels the old illusions and then invokes them as he views the canal-like features close up: "But it's hard to be scientific when you look at that. I keep thinking of strange people coming out to help us. Maybe I should be writing poetry instead of taking up atomic engineering" (66).

Marooned on Mars is full of ambivalence in its effort to reconcile the pleasures of romance with the progress of planetary science. Chapter 12, titled "The Mysterious Canals," is particularly revealing of del Rey's hesitancy as a fiction writer to give up the old Mars. The crew had been charged specifically to solve the mystery of Lowell's canals, and what they discover are rows of pumpkin-like green vegetables linked by tubular filaments that convey from plant to plant the scarce water from the melting polar caps. It remains unclear whether these "canals" are the product of agriculture or of vegetative adaptation to a desiccating environment, of manipulative intelligence or natural selection. The similes used to describe the appearance and function of the filaments—they are like pumps, like laundry lines, like telephone poles—imply intelligent design, although the only Martians the expedition discovers are three-foot-tall bipeds who live underground as a refuge from the cold and who appear never to have reached the threshold of industrialization before their decline into savagery.

Five years later, in 1967, John Brunner published *Born under Mars*. During the space of those five years, a major development affected both the scientific and the popular perception of Mars. Late in 1964, the United States launched a pair of space probes to Mars, part of the series of *Mariner* flyby reconnaissance missions. *Mariner 3* failed shortly after leaving the stratosphere, but *Mariner 4* produced the first successful photographic studies of the Martian surface. In midsummer of 1965, as the small spacecraft sped 6,000 miles above the planet, its single camera slowly started sending back data. Twenty-two pictures were taken before *Mariner 4* passed behind Mars. They were grainy and ill-defined, but these were the first reliable visual record of Martian geological features— and they shocked most astronomers. Scientists expected to put the canal question to rest, expected to see mountains, hoped for the colorful signs of vegetation and other Earth-like topographical features; instead they saw almost nothing but craters. The surface of Mars appeared to be lunar in its emptiness, a blitzed and pulverized wasteland inhospitable either to biological life or to the life of the imagination. The lead engineer assigned to transform the graphic data sent back by Mariner into functional pictures was quoted as saying to his assistant, "You've just seen the death of the planetary program."[19] Just as it seemed that the images of a dead Mars would kill off the scientific investigation of Mars, so too *Mariner 4* threatened literary creativity.

A sour quality is apparent in Brunner's account of Mars that's simply not present in del Rey's novel. Roy Maillin, the first-person narrator of *Born under Mars*, is a twelfth-generation Martian, a descendant of one of the original colonists. The planet has by his time been partially modified for human habitation, but it is nothing like the Mars of earlier romance and myth. Maillin is nevertheless fiercely loyal to his home world and resents the imposition of obsolete and mythological names onto his landscape: the "absurd wet name" of the Grand Canal Apartments and the settlement named Mariner ("How many more of these ridiculous fossilised terms? 'Mariner' on a planet without seas!"). Features of the landscape are described in terminology suitable to Earth rather than Mars. Maillin remarks acerbically (in a novel written before *Mariner 9* revealed that a planet thought to be flat contained the highest mountains in the solar system), "We spoke of a mountain and meant hills a few hundred feet high, rare on Mars."[20] In a foretaste of the new aesthetic for Martian fiction that would start to emerge in the 1980s, Brunner's protagonist struggles to find words to define what he loves about Mars:

> Not even I would call my planet beautiful. Rolling red-brown plains, shifting dunes, the moons petty blinking lights, the native plants majestic rather than handsome—even the famous sandflowers—the winds weak but harsh like much-diluted acid. . . . Yet I would never call it ugly, either. Stark. Plain. What would one call knotted hands scarred by the preference for love over beauty? (26)

Few readers would claim either *Marooned on Mars* or *Born under Mars* as one of the masterpieces of Martian fiction, but to read del Rey's and Brunner's novels now is to sense how much they are regretful swan songs of a certain tradition of Martian novel. A more defiant tone characterizes Leigh Brackett's 1967 collection of five of her stories about Mars, all originally written before *Mariner 4*'s photographs changed the landscape. Her brief foreword acknowledges, grudgingly, the new scientific information of the mid-1960s, but she refuses to retract or modify the Lowellian premises of the stories she composed between 1948 and 1964:

To some of us, Mars has always been the Ultima Thule, the golden Hesperi-des, the ever-beckoning land of compelling fascination. Voyagers, elec-tronic and human, have begun the business of reducing these dreams to cold, hard, ruinous fact. But as we know, in the affairs of men and Martians, mere fact runs a poor second to Truth, which is mighty and shall prevail. Therefore I offer you these legends of Old Mars as true tales, inviting all dreary realities to keep a respectful distance.[21]

The Mars of fantasy remains for Brackett far more enticing to the imagination than the Mars of scientific investigation. She believes in the first half of the great romantic manifesto of Keats that "Beauty is Truth"; its corollary, that Truth also is Beauty, would take most writers about Mars another two decades to grasp and apply to fiction.

Brackett clutches counterfactualism into a raised fist. If she is a radical instance of resistance to the new Mars, she nonetheless dramatizes the imagi-native problems writers faced in the *Mariner* era. The tension between scientific reality and fictional vision, between the virtues of two different modes of truth, was palpable in the Mars fiction written between *Mariner* 4's 1965 photo survey and the arrival on the planet of the *Viking* orbiters and landers in 1976, a period during which scientific interpretation of Mars underwent two revolutions. *The Man Who Loved Mars* by Lin Carter (1973) is an instructive example of what happened when a novelist was pulled toward the Leigh Brackett model of antique heroics and linguistic archaisms on the one hand while trying, on the other, to pay at least token dues to the post-Mariner sensibility. Carter was a one-man mass-production facility for a certain kind of fake-medieval fantasy that was his great passion and that is betrayed in the futuristic *Man Who Loved Mars* by his weakness for locutions like "naught," "mayhap," and "oh, 'tis mad enough."[22] Carter rejects Lowell's canals as waterways but is unable to give them up as a geographical feature; *Mariner* 9's revelation of the gigantic Valles Marineris canyon dictates his depiction of a dusty landscape "cracked apart by gullies the size of the Grand Canyon" (45), but he still retains areas of patchy shrubs and dense mosses; Mars is a "poor, worn-out old corpse of a planet" (59) but Carter cannot resist Burroughsian mumbo-jumbo about an ancient civilization concocted largely out of echoes of Troy, Babylon, and Egypt. Car-ter's twenty-first-century expedition to Mars is full of space-age sophisticates who know better than to search for native Martians: "The very last thing the scientists had expected to find on the desert world was an intelligent indige-nous race: that hoary old dream was a primitive plot concept that even the science fiction writers of the last century had long since abandoned" (76). And yet the author goes ahead and shamelessly uses exactly that retrograde plot device. His nods to current scientific knowledge are merely reactive pieties and the book overflows with every imaginable cliché from juvenile fiction about Mars. While The Man Who Loved Mars explicitly cites Mariner 4 and Mariner 9, it is the tissue of allusions to Wells and Heinlein, to Shakespeare and Robert Frost that define it as a crude literary pastiche rather than a thoughtful or artful response to the state of the Martian question.

In 1971, the editors of a selection of a hundred years' worth of writing about Mars catalogued the visual images and the names of astronomers and fiction writers who had established the tradition of literary Mars. Plaintively titled Mars, We Love You, the anthology takes a more measured approach to its subject than Carter could manage, although the affection for the retrograde vision is apparent in the prominence of "love" in the titles of both books. The editors knew the old imagery no longer could be replicated, but they insisted on the invulnerability of literary history to scientific advancement. Of Wells, Burroughs, Heinlein, Schiaparelli, and Lowell they wrote, "Taken as a whole, they have made of our nearest planetary neighbor a modern myth that will endure even when future interplanetary probes return pictures clearer than those of Mariner 4."[23] That anthology was barely into print when exactly those clearer photographs of Mars, snapped by Mariner 9, started being processed at the Jet Propulsion Laboratory in Pasadena.

In the midst of the various resistant and retrogressive literary responses to the new Mars, one book responded in earnest to the Mariner era. Of all the fiction about Mars published between 1965 and 1976, I know of none that takes the current state of knowledge about the planet more seriously than The Earth Is Near by the Czech writer and painter Ludek Pesek. Originally published in German in 1970—and winner of the German Children's Book Prize in 1971—it was translated into English in 1973. Powerfully influenced by the Mariner 4, 6, and 7 photographs, its view of Mars is probably more drab and desolate than would have been the case if Pesek had seen the more varied landscapes disclosed by Mariner 9. Nevertheless, his book—despite its intended young-adult audience—rests on a deeper literary and scientific commitment to fiction-making about Mars than anything else in the period. Relentlessly anti-nostalgic in its approach, it contrasts starkly with the regressive imagery, style, and concepts of other fiction of the time.

The purpose of Pesek's imagined "Project Alpha" is to settle definitively the question of whether any life, including micro-organic life, exists on Mars. The astrobiological experiments that the novel recounts answer the question roundly in the negative. And in the process, the planet is revealed as a hostile, even nauseating environment for human beings. "God, I feel like death!" says the first crew member to stagger to a porthole and view the rusty sand and purple sky shortly after the landing module reaches the surface.[24] The "monotonous desert" and "shallow craters" (79), the "dead stone" (151), the landscape "reminiscent of the rock formations we knew from the moon" (144)—all derived from the sterile images conveyed by the *Mariner 4* camera—are matched psychologically by a sense of unrewarding tedium and futility in the crew's experience. Cosby, the narrator, observes that the unmanned probes had prepared the crew for an experience that would be neither exotic nor exciting and for the unlikelihood that any complex life forms would be found. "Yet each of us," he admits, "cherished some of that sweet, irrational romanticism that will overstep the bounds of probability" (122). Pesek gratifies none of those cherished desires. "An expedition to Mars is not a dream," Cosby later writes, "but a life and death struggle" (156). The ubiquitous dust causes far more problems than anticipated, fouling filters, blowing into pressure chambers, seeping into clothing, impairing scientific instruments, disabling tractors that keep sinking into powdery sand dunes. Spending so much time in suits and helmets isolates the crew from one another, unable to see another's eyes and expressions, deadening the emotions and any sense of community. The nomenclature of the Schiaparelli maps, which for a century had turned Mars into a fantasyland, loses all its poetry. "Dusty desert stretched as far as the eye could see, a hollow inventory of names that had once sounded so romantic—Aeria and Arabia, and Moab and Edom on the other side. They dried up our throats, they crunched between our teeth like sand" (193). The form of the narrative complements the nondescript landscape and the loss of affect; it is a log of events, deliberately unadorned and dispassionate, with repeated descriptions of failed equipment, repairs, storms, weary treks, unsuccessful experiments.

The climactic episode in this mostly anticlimactic adventure on Mars centers on a biological survey team making a final 150-day "great march" in a last, and fruitless, effort to collect some evidence of life. But the real key to Pesek's purposes is in a lesser episode that interrupts the great march when a geological survey team reports back that they have located the ruins of a city in the desert. Weather conditions prevent them from getting close enough to collect a brick to bring back to the base for study but "staggering pictures" are taken with a telephoto lens—photos that anger the head of the biological survey team for the sheer absurdity of the geologists' claim. Cosby writes on behalf of all the biologists on the expedition, "I don't think any of us were inclined to believe fairy tales of some lost Martian civilization" (157). The fictional episode is an eerie premonition of the brouhaha around a supposed "Face on Mars"—a monumental artifact that some people claimed to be able to discern in some of the *Viking* 1 and 2 orbiters' photographs of Mars from 1976. In Pesek's novel, when the site of the presumed city is finally checked out, it proves to be nothing more than "weathered rocks buried in drifts of sand" (160). Comparison of new photos with the original telephoto lens pictures reveals illusions created by the refraction of light in the dust-laden atmosphere. Reminiscent of the optical illusion of the canals, the Martian city quickly fades into nonsense, as Pesek again eschews the romantic turn from which so many authors of Mars narratives had been unable to abstain.

The Earth Is Near ends in failure and death and unfulfilled obsessions, and Mars itself triumphs over the ambitions of the terrestrial expedition, blowing away the tracks of the explorers, remaining icy, hostile, silent, immutable in the face of the human incursion. Cosby reflects at the end that if space exploration is to have a future, human beings will have to find a way to change themselves—their blood chemistry, their breathing, their body temperature—rather than haul their artifices and their supplies with them. *They* must adapt to new worlds rather than expect those worlds to become tractable to human needs. Later writers would put a name to this kind of human adaptation to Mars: areoformation. Instead of thinking solely in terms of altering the landscape of Mars to make it habitable to Earth-dwellers ("terraforming" Mars), people would adjust their own physiological and psychological makeup to the conditions of the planet named for the old war god Ares.

"A dream come true is a hard thing," Pesek's Cosby writes. "A single real stone is heavier than a whole imaginary mountain" (201). Maybe Pesek would have altered some of the topographical details of his novel had he had the images that *Mariner* 9 collected of Mars, but the visionary center of *The Earth Is Near*—its acknowledgment of the otherness of Mars, its cautions about the seductiveness and perils of romantic dreaming, and its radical revision of the tradition of Martian adventure fiction—is powerful and original. As a portrait of Mars and an account of the nature of exploration, it is the strongest piece of fiction to appear between Bradbury's *Martian Chronicles* in 1950 and Kim Stanley Robinson's *Red Mars* in 1993.

The first space-age revolution in images of Mars was the product of *Mariners* 4 through 7, whose photographs of a cratered and crumpled Mars-scape evoked a monotonous, barren, and nearly featureless world. Pesek's novel is the defining literary reflection of that revolutionary scientific revision of Martian topography. But a second revolution occurred in the 1970s. *Mariners* 8 and 9 were launched in 1971 and were fundamentally different in nature and mission from the earlier probes that had photographed localized portions of Mars as they briefly sped by the planet before passing deeper into the solar system. These two would go into orbit around Mars and were expected to provide months of photographs, collecting images of every region of the planet. An even more comprehensive survey of the planet began in 1975 and 1976 with the dual launch of *Vikings* 1 and 2, each of which would both orbit Mars and dispatch a lander to the surface to provide the first close-up photographic records and to do analyses of the composition of the regolith.

Mariner 8 failed at launch, but *Mariner* 9 was reprogrammed to attempt to cover nearly all the experimental and photographic objectives of both missions. Late in 1971, *Mariner* 9 rendezvoused with Mars. The anticipation that this encounter would result in the most extensive and rewarding haul of Martian data yet prompted a symposium at the California Institute of Technology, home to the Jet Propulsion Laboratory (JPL), where the data from *Mariner* 9 would be received and processed. It was a small gathering but a distinguished one: two scientists, two imaginative writers, and a science journalist. The host was Bruce Murray, astrogeologist on the Cal Tech faculty and JPL's director. The panel he assembled included Cornell astronomer Carl Sagan, writers Ray Bradbury and Arthur C. Clarke, and *New York Times* correspondent Walter Sullivan. They met on the evening before *Mariner* 9 was due to go into orbit around Mars, and their discussion comprised equal parts of speculation about the new knowledge that they would be gaining and homages to the old mythology of Mars. If one were looking for a distinct boundary line in the literary history of Mars between the old traditions and the new scientifically based fictions, it could be drawn through the *Mars and the Mind of Man* symposium at the Jet Propulsion Laboratory on November 12, 1971.

Had Martian topography actually been visible on November 12, perhaps the symposium would have focused on the first new pictures from *Mariner* 9. But Mars was enveloped in an enormous planet-wide dust storm that frustrated the impatient scientific team at Cal Tech. Instead, the panelists mixed pungent and sometimes comic reflections on the follies of past speculations about Mars with fond acknowledgments of the influence on the participants' careers of even the most absurd and discredited theories. Sagan, Bradbury, and Clarke all claimed reading Burroughs' Martian adventure stories as the earliest stimulant to their interest in Mars, despite what Bradbury called his "awful style" and "vulgarian" imagination.[25] Sagan rehearsed the obsessions of the 1890s, including Samuel Phelps Leland's prediction that the University of Chicago's newest telescope soon would disclose views of Martian cities, harbors, navies, and factory smoke.[26] Sullivan, the oldest member of the panel, recalled the 1924 opposition—the closest of the twentieth century—when the Director of the U.S. Army Signal Corps and the Chief of Naval Operations ordered that silence be maintained at their radio stations in order better to track any possible radio signals being sent from Mars to Earth (6). Murray talked about the continuing susceptibility of the scientific mind, not just the popular imagination, to wishful thinking about Mars. The imaginative writings of Lowell, Burroughs, Bradbury, and Clarke, Murray believed, instilled a desire for Mars in the general public that made them willing to pay for missions like *Mariner 9*, but desire itself thwarts the capacity to see "the real Mars." "We *want* Mars to be like Earth," he said in explaining why the propensity to construe data so as to support the hypothesis of Martian life had continued even as recently as the *Mariner 6* and 7 flybys in 1969:

> There was a misinterpretation of the spectral results from one of the instruments on board initially because, I feel, the person really wanted to believe that he discovered something that was a real clue to the existence of life on Mars. In fact, he had found something else that was extremely important, which indicated that parts of the Martian polar caps were not just CO_2 generally but absolutely pure dry CO_2 with no moisture at all upon them. He had made a very important discovery. But he had initially misread it, I feel, because of the expectation of seeing something else. (22–23)

The November 12 symposium was preoccupied with the myth and the romance of Mars, and at this pivotal moment in literary history, Ray Bradbury was its chief spokesman. He asserted that it was fundamental both to human nature and to the process of scientific discovery "to start with romance and build to a reality" (35). But even Bradbury, who jokingly played to the audience with the fantasy that when the current dust storm passed and the cameras got a clear view of the planet they would see Martians carrying signs reading "BRADBURY WAS RIGHT!" (19), admitted that they were entering a new era and that his own Martian stories now were being taught in schools as a form of modern mythology. Once the Martian storm subsided and pictures began flowing back to Earth, it would become apparent that while the old myths were indeed definitively inoperable, the new Mars was not at all what people had been led to suspect from the earlier Mariner probes.

Only the first third of *Mars and the Mind of Man* is taken up with the transcript of the November 12 symposium. The remainder of the book is composed of reflective essays by each of the participants more than a year later, after *Mariner 9*'s seventy-five hundred stunning photos had been received and assimilated into a revolutionary revision of the scientific understanding of Mars. In his retrospective piece, Sagan emphasized that the vegetation theory that had so long been appealed to as an explanation for the seasonal darkenings of the surface observed through terrestrial telescopes was conclusively dead. With the new understanding of gigantic storms that rearrange the sandy fines on the planet and cause variations in reflected light on the surface, meteorology and geology began to seem more crucial than the life sciences for unlocking the secrets of Mars. When the Viking landers reached Mars in 1976, Sagan predicted, organic chemistry experiments would not necessarily be more important than analyses of mineralogy, atmospheric gases, volcanic and seismic activity, and wind speeds and patterns. In his essay, Clarke described the transcript of the 1971 panel discussion as a relic of "the prehistory of Martian studies" (79). Envying the science-fiction writers whose careers would be founded on the post–Mariner 9 Mars, he was confident that science would enhance rather than diminish the "magic" of Mars and result in fiction "far more strange and wonderful than the wildest fantasy" (85). Sullivan echoed Clarke, pronouncing the obituary for the "dreamworld" of old Mars but insisting that "no myth or legend could be as rich in beauty, wonder, and awe as the full reality of the universe that is our home" (117, 127). The "real Mars" to which Murray and the Cal Tech scientists aspired turned out to be so geologically dramatic that it was capable of engendering a new romance with the planet.

The findings from Mariner 9 were collected and analyzed in The Geology of Mars, a magisterial illustrated volume by a prominent group of scientists led by the Brown University geologist Thomas A. Mutch. All the data from the early Mariners were, Mutch wrote, "fragmentary, misleading, and totally eclipsed" by the results of the 1971–1972 mission.[27] What Mariner 9 revealed was a planet that was not only startlingly and even mysteriously varied topographically but constituted on a gigantic scale. One assured fact that had become a truism about Mars over the decades was that it must be largely flat; Mariner 9 upended that assumption when it revealed four huge extinct volcanoes that dwarfed the largest volcanoes on Earth. The area that had been known as "Nix Olympica" (the snowfields of Olympus) since Schiaparelli introduced his new nomenclature for Martian topography in the 1870s, now was re-perceived as "Olympus Mons," a titanic volcanic mountain nearly triple the height of Mount Everest— so high that its top poked out above the atmosphere of Mars.

Arthur C. Clarke noted ruefully that he had incorporated that mistake in his novel The Sands of Mars and had even had it printed in italics: "There are no mountains on Mars."[28] Even more amazing than the fifteen-mile-high Olympus Mons, however, was Mariner 9's revelation of a complex canyon system that slashed through the equatorial regions. The largest canyon of all was Valles Marineris, named for the Mariner mission that had revealed it, and it spanned nearly 3,000 miles, was 200 miles wide in places, and had depths of up to 4 miles. The northern and southern hemispheres of Mars had strikingly different topographical features, and it happened that the relatively few photographs sent back by the earlier *Mariner* flybys were mostly of the heavily cratered southern hemisphere. Craters had been mistaken as the *defining* topographical feature of the planet, but *Mariner* 9 uncovered an intriguing variety of land formations, including channel systems cut into rock that suggested an earlier period when water flooded the Martian surface and carved its landscape. Thus, Schiaparelli's (though not Lowell's) *canali* got a new lease on the imagination. A startling new planet was revealed, and by the 1980s and 1990s, fiction writers began to see what they could do with it.

But even after the breakthrough visions of *Mariner* 9 and of the double *Viking* mission of 1976, with its two photographic orbiters circling the planet and its two landers conducting experiments on the surface, not all imaginative responses to Mars fully embraced the new scientific understandings. John Varley's 1977 story "In the Hall of the Martian Kings" exemplifies the contrary pulls of the new and the old Mars. Sharply written and richly inventive, Varley's narrative details the transformation of a failed Martian scientific exploration, in which fifteen of the twenty Americans on the surface die when their pressurized dome blows open, into a successful settlement (with children) in the course of twelve years. "Instead of an expedition, we are now a colony," the crew historian asserts when he urges his four surviving comrades to inventory what they will need to make a life on an inhospitable and dangerous world.[29] The struggles of the survivors to fend off despair and secure a cramped environment that will provide them with sufficient air, warmth, water, and food take a sudden turn into old-fashioned Martian romance with the appearance of living plastic gewgaws of various colors, sizes, and shapes as well as hard-shelled, wheeled bugs that begin sprouting up near their habitat and near the burial ground of the dead astronauts. Readers cognizant of Martian literary history might momentarily feel that they have passed through a time warp and found themselves in the world of Stanley Weinbaum's 1934 "Martian Odyssey." As the plot grows more extravagant (with a plastic model of the Earth and its moon rising out of the ground as a calling card), we are left with the theory that an advanced species of intelligent Martians, in hibernation during Mars's current cold and dry spell, has anticipated the arrival of adventurers from the third planet. These indigenous inhabitants will materialize again when Mars moves back into a warmer period, and the settlers decline the offer to return to Earth when a very startled international expedition visits what they expect to be the site of the total extermination of the first mission to Mars. By then, the settlers have come to think of Mars as home. The very retrograde notion of a lost (but not really extinct) Martian civilization of a higher order co-exists in Varley's tale with the more distinctively late-twentieth-century motif of settlers from Earth becoming Martian.

The most notorious post-1976 retrograde visions have emerged from a popularizer working largely on the fringes of science, Richard Hoagland. Blowing up photographs taken by the Viking orbiters, Hoagland claims to have seen a number of artifacts on the Martian surface in the region known as Cydonia Mensae, including a gigantic, sphinx-like sculpted face, a trapezoidal pyramid, a fortress, and the remains of a city. His numbingly detailed, obsessively repetitive The Monuments of Mars was first published in 1987 and, at this writing, has gone through five editions, with ever-increasing apparatus intended to bolster his case for the one-time presence of an eventually abandoned society of extraterrestrial visitors to Mars.[30] Novelists have found the Hoagland face, pyramid, and city useful gimmicks for reviving narratives about alien life on Mars, and the preference has been for fictions that are premised on long-ago visitors from other star systems who left these artifacts behind on Mars. That premise creates what little suspense can be found in Ian Douglas's valentine to the Marine Corps, Semper Mars (1998), centered on the discovery of five hundred thousand-year-old mummified human beings by archeologists excavating the Cydonian artifacts. Douglas offers no explanation of the mystery of the identity of the artifacts' builders, their reason for leaving Mars, their destination or purpose, or the precise relationship of the Martian Homo sapiens to terrestrial Homo sapiens. The "Face" and its meaning end up being a narrative red herring and an excuse for drawing out a flag-waving, United Nations–bashing compendium of Marine lore and libertarian sentiment.[31] Other novels that batten off Hoagland's notions about alien artifacts on Mars include Terry Bisson's whimsical shaggy-dog story about a Hollywood-financed expedition, Voyage to the Red Planet (1990) and Allen Steele's Labyrinth of Night (1992), which the author, an agnostic on the question of the reality of "the Face," used as a springboard for the invention of an alien civilization and its technologies.[32] The so-called "face on Mars" has replaced Lowell's "canals" as the reigning image of retrograde visions, although it should be said in fairness to Lowell that Hoagland's single-mindedness about his propositions lacks both Lowell's effort at scientific rigor and the charm and eloquence of his literary style.

Other, more strictly literary instances of retrograde fictions after 1976 include Robert Forward's The Martian Rainbow, which tries to have it both ways. It makes constant reference to the Viking missions, to the scientific work of Carl Sagan and Thomas Mutch, and to the "Case for Mars" symposia of the 1980s that tried to build grassroots support for manned expeditions to Mars. Forward boasted that his novel drew on "sources of factual information" and he even provided a bibliography.[33] But his plot is a throwback to Heinlein, Clarke, and Weinbaum, with a conventional discovery-of-life scene at the north pole of Mars and critters like giant, six-segmented caterpillars who are harnessed by the terrestrial settlers to do the work of terraforming the planet. Another novel that has a foot in two imaginative universes is Christopher Pike's *The Season of Passage* (1992). Pike pays due attention to *Viking*'s evidence that Mars had once had surface water and that large reservoirs of water might yet be locked below the regolith, but he uses that information to revive the old imagery of canals. When the first American expedition discovers an underground passage filled with water, the explorers immediately dub it a "canal" and they find that "Lowell's drawings were coming back to haunt them."[34] "Haunt" turns out to be the operative word for this novel—a fantastic hybrid of Stephen King and Ray Bradbury; there is a running allusion to *The Martian Chronicles*, which one of the characters is re-reading, and Pike's Mars turns out to be populated by vampires.

One of the most unclassifiable Martian narratives of the late twentieth century, Paul J. McAuley's *Red Dust*, is set in the far future on a Mars settled initially and unsuccessfully by North Americans and then taken over by a vast influx of Chinese and Tibetans. The capital city of Mars, formerly called Lowell, has become Xin Beijing—and indeed all the nomenclature for regions and features of the planet that had been derived from European mythology has been altered, so that Olympus Mons, for instance, is known in this book as Tiger Mountain. The terraforming initiated by the Chinese scientist Cho Jinfeng, however, was never completed and Mars has begun sliding back into its previous dry and dusty condition. The first sentence of the novel evokes the old Lowellian planetary condition: "Mars was dying."[35] McAuley's plot hinges on efforts of a "People's Scientific Liberation Movement" to reestablish the terraforming project and prevent Mars from dying for a second time, but the issue of terraforming is overshadowed by the old-fashioned but well-executed space-opera exploits of its central character, Wei Lee, who rides with yak-herding Martian cowboys, sails both the Grand Canal and the Dust Seas on the vast plains of the northern hemisphere, harpoons a giant dust ray, fights off swarms of feral children, and revels in martial arts combat with a superwoman warrior. *Red Dust* has some of the 1980s ambience of cyberpunk fiction—virtual reality, nanotechnology, and sensory enhancements—overlaying the retrograde action-adventures reminiscent of Flash Gordon or Burroughs' John Carter. And in the background is the mythology of the "King of the Cats"—the deified Elvis Presley, reconstructed out of his songs and surviving fragments of his films, "who was born in a stable and became a planet-wide media star" and "was crucified upon a burning cross, and returned as a thousand acolytes who surgically altered themselves to look exactly like him" (7). The result of this splendid hodge-podge is one of the most surreal Marses of recent fiction, in many ways scientifically knowledgeable but magical-realist in execution.

Finally, an ingenious example of retrograde visions is Colin Greenland's *Harm's Way*, which finesses the disruptive impact of the new knowledge about Mars from the *Mariner* and *Viking* missions by premising an alternate history in which space travel first occurs during the Victorian era. The novel's science therefore can be premised on nineteenth-century concepts, including the notion of the "aether flux" as the sailing medium through space and Lowellian images of Mars, where several chapters of the novel are set.[36] From the clipper-like ship that sails the protagonist to Mars, the canals look like "a ragged green net stretched around the globe" (150) and the capital city has a Grand Canal; there are indigenous Martians (winged) who are persecuted by the French colonizers and the capital city is reminiscent of the industrial cities of Victorian-era Europe—sleazy, dirty, crowded, confused. Greenland's Mars is not a glamorous place—and perhaps here the author does betray the influence of late-twentieth-century knowledge. In fact, Mars is represented as a back-water in the solar system, "like a ball of orange brick that someone had carved and hung in space to lampoon the poor old Earth" (149). Those who arrive from Earth find the place depressing rather than exotic and are eager to get out as soon as they can. "Life on Mars wears you down," the protagonist says. "After a while the heavy red sand that creeps into the folds of your clothes and the creases of your body finds its way into your brain, into your very sleep, rubbing you away and making you its own" (167). This is a retrograde vision, we may be reminded at this point, that precedes Barsoomian romance as well as twentieth-century astronomy, and yet the Mars of *Harm's Way* is as grim and unlovely a planet as Philip K. Dick or Ludek Pesek made it. Greenland's device for detouring his Martian fiction around the discoveries of the 1960s and 1970s does not completely exclude the Mars of the *Mariner* and *Viking* era. Efforts to recover the old Mars had a way of participating in the larger literary project of remaking the image of Mars in the late twentieth century.

Mars Remade 12

Mariner 9 and the two *Viking* missions of 1976 cleared the air of many misconceptions and obsolete fantasies about Mars. The possibilities of low-level, perhaps underground, micro-organisms or at least relics of earlier and now-extinct simple life forms continued to engage scientific curiosity and speculation, but the experiments on dirt samples carried out by the two *Viking* landers indicated that the surface was sterile. By the second half of the 1970s, the baton had been passed from the biologists to the geologists, who were now the most active scientists studying the planet. What was clear beyond any doubt was that Mars, with its varied and dramatic topographies, provides a rich laboratory for geological research, and tantalizing evidence suggesting that a substantial amount of frozen water might still be locked up beneath the regolith meant that hydrogeologists also would be kept busy working out the possibilities. Biological interest in Mars did not vanish, but it was redirected from the present to the future; in fact, exobiology—or astrobiology—emerged in the late twentieth century as a field of active inquiry, with Mars as the most notable research site. How might life, including human life, be introduced to Mars once the planet began to be explored not by remote-controlled machinery like the *Vikings* but by people? In what ways and by what means could Mars, already so terrestrial in its familiar—if outsized—geological features, be re-made to accommodate an imported human civilization? How long would it take to "terraform" Mars and what would the consequences be both for the planet itself and for its settlers? Such questions began in the mid-1970s to loom large in the imaginative constructs of a new phase in the literary history of Mars, for while manned expeditions to other worlds actually ceased after the Apollo missions to the Moon as NASA focused on robotic exploration, the prospect of human exploration and settlement stimulated new fiction and poetry.

Ian Watson's *The Martian Inca* (1977) provides an interesting early illustration of new directions for literary Mars. The narrative alternates between a Martian and a terrestrial plot; as the first U.S. expedition to Mars sets out, a Russian capsule containing mechanically collected Martian soil samples crashes in the Bolivian Andes. The novel's geopolitical context is the competition between the United States and the Soviet Union, in the aftermath of the 1969 Moon landing, for prestigious firsts in space exploration. The Americans intend to begin the terraforming process, the first stage of what is, we can now understand, a highly unrealistic master plan to make Mars habitable by the middle of the twenty-first century. The expedition is more ideological than scientific in orientation, but the narrator's observation on the voyage out predicts the fundamental imaginative premise that would underlie much of the post-*Viking* fiction about Mars: "It wasn't the real alien world of Mars they were heading towards any more, but a vision of Mars remade as Second Earth."[1] Writing after *Mariner* 9 and making final corrections just as the *Vikings* were beginning their work on the Martian surface, Watson is cautious about what he says about Mars, aware that knowledge about the planet was in flux. Details of the landscape are sparse and localized to a few passages, such as this textbook-like description of the planet from the perspective of the descending landing module named, with a nod to Percival Lowell, the *Flagstaff*: "The great volcano Olympus swelled from the surrounding lava plain, soaring up from two-kilometre-high perimeter cliffs in feathery waves to a summit pocked with collapsed caldera vent holes, which even from this distance was more than Himalayan. In afternoon sunlight the volcano glared brilliantly, sweating light. Then the vastest hillside in the Solar System fell away as they soared eastwards across volcanic plains towards gently rolling hills with ripple dunes, channels, and levees, sure sign of drainage northwards from the equatorial highlands" (126–27). It has been reported that Watson was so concerned that he get topographical details like these as correct as possible that he was still tweaking his descriptions when the text was in page proofs to accommodate the latest data from the *Viking* orbiters.[2]

The Martian Inca introduces the notion of a debate among the American scientists about whether the terraforming project is ethically and ecologically justifiable—a foretaste of the more detailed and extensive debates central to many later imaginative treatments of the subject. It invokes, only to dismiss, Lowell's canals. It limits the search-for-life motif that was a staple of pre-1960 fiction to the new orthodoxy of viruses and microbes only. And Watson uses his double plot cleverly to link the mountain highlands of the Bolivian Altiplano to the desire for a terraformed Mars: "It's almost like Mars will be," one character says about Bolivia, "after we've switched the climate. When the icecap and the permafrost melt and the flashfloods flow. Same dry, thin, freezing air. . . . Those Indians in the high Andes are the best adapted humans to colonize Mars" (29).

The *Martian Inca* offers one of a number of multicultural Marses that began appearing as the Martian literary image was being remade in the post-*Viking* era. Philip José Farmer imagined a planet of orthodox Jews who speak New Testament Greek in *Jesus on Mars*. In Tim Sullivan's hallucinogenic, time-tripping *The Martian Viking*, NASA's *Viking* meets some medieval Vikings as the terraforming of Mars is undertaken by Geats led by King Hygelac. Muslims settle Mars in Donald Moffitt's *Crescent in the Sky* and plan to establish an "Islamic civilization as Islam should be." The Chinese dominate Mars in Paul J. McAuley's *Red Dust* and Native American landscapes and cultures are emphasized in Ben Bova's *Mars*.[3] These novels vary wildly in their degree of scientific plausibility but all of them seek a greater sociological realism and pluralism than was common in earlier Martian romances. While Russians and white Americans continued to be the preponderant terrestrial colonizers in fiction, the idea of an empty and unpopulated Mars has given authors license to imagine a Mars made in the image of any number of cultural, religious, and ethnic models.

With the scientific reconfiguration of Mars thoroughly underway by 1976, as Watson was finishing *The Martian Inca*, its imaginary past became a dilemma. For the scientific community, the old Schiaparelli-Lowell Mars was an irrelevance, even an embarrassment, a musty relic of obsolete thinking. Science looks forward, with little sentiment for earlier outworn and disproven hypotheses, and mention of canals vanished from scientific discourse throughout the period of the dissemination of the *Mariner 9* and *Viking* data. As planetary geologist Thomas Mutch put it, "modern scientists want to steer clear of the whole subject. It is a controversy without attraction for 'objective' people unwilling to indulge in flights of fancy." The old Mars was "purged from public discussion," at least to the degree that astronomers and geologists could dictate the discussion.[4] Many science-fiction writers of the mid-1970s also felt constrained by the new information; Mars was not a favored setting for narratives, and when writers did choose that locale, they continued, like their predecessors in the 1960s, to bounce back and forth schizophrenically between nostalgia for a Mars that never was and grim resignation to a Mars that would be less than the heart's desire. Robert Young evaded some difficulties by setting his 1979 juvenile fantasy "The First Mars Mission" back in 1957 "before *Mariner 4* pulled the plug on Giovanni Schiaparelli's *canali*, Percival Lowell's canals, and Edgar Rice Burroughs's 'waterways.'"[5] On the other hand, Gordon Eklund and Gregory Benford in "Hellas is Florida" constructed a brutalist account of an expedition to a Mars that mocks terrestrial norms and is "ugly, ugly, ugly."[6] A resolutely antiheroic, even nihilistic, Martian story by Harry Harrison opens with a description of an utterly lifeless world. "This landscape was dead. It had never lived. It had been born dead when the planets first formed, a planetary stillbirth of boulders, coarse sand, jagged rock."[7] The genre of science fiction, which for nearly a century had worked every variation on the theme of "life on Mars," seemed largely to have fallen into a state of imaginative paralysis on the subject of Mars.

One writer, however, who reveled in the possibilities of a low-end vision of Mars was Lewis Shiner. Associated with the cyberpunk movement that linked high technology with grungy physical settings and fostered an anti-aesthetic for science fiction, Shiner situated his 1984 *Frontera* in a tired-looking Mars of rust, collapse, and despair. It is not just that the planet itself is lifeless; the colonists bring desolation with them, along with the habits of their terrestrial throwaway culture. A scene on the Martian moon Deimos, where American space transports dock and deposit travelers and supplies to be ferried down to the planet, is the antithesis of the shiny futuristic spaceport of Kubrick's *2001: A Space Odyssey*. Instead, it mirrors the imagery of Ridley Scott's popular 1982 *Blade Runner*, the iconic cyberpunk film, with its titanic and soulless skyscrapers looming over dark, filthy, trash-strewn, congested streets:

> Kane was reminded of the garbage dumps on the outskirts of Houston. With the exception of a melted patch near the domes and tunnels of the base, the entire visible surface was littered with cast-off technology. Propellant tanks, some empty, some fully charged, lay around like oversized soup cans. Abandoned shelter halves were scattered randomly among plastic bags, tripods, and scraps of crumpled foil. The conical outline of one complete lander and the ruins of a second were visible from the ship, the exposed metal sparkling cleanly in the faint sunlight.[8]

Not only is Shiner's Mars inhospitable to human life, but most human beings appear to have little appetite or capacity for beauty, order, or joy. His protagonist Kane flees the decay of Earth to the Mars colony of Frontera and finds only a place "without promise," "a desolation that went on endlessly," "the underbelly of Utopia" (147, 148). The old romance of televised landings and flag-raising beamed back to an enraptured terrestrial audience is long past in this novel, and the anemic new fantasies of terraforming do little to reconcile Kane to a life on this world of desert and debris. What possible appeal could a terraformed Mars have if the "terra" being reproduced is no better than a slum?

Such resolutely anti-romantic visions became a commonplace in Mars fiction in the years after *Viking* 1 and 2. Even Jack Williamson, the writer who first invented the word "terraforming" in a 1942 short story, in his own post-*Viking* Martian narrative emphasized the deadness of the planet, "a globe of old iron splotched with the bright hue of new rust and the dark of old rust, scarred everywhere by the wounds of unthinkable time."[9] For the astronauts in Williamson's Beachhead (1992), domed cities on Mars belong to old fiction or barely imaginable distant futures rather than present realities. The only terraforming visions in Beachhead are a slick marketing ploy by a scamming Texas industrialist and a hallucination suffered by one of the first explorers as she nearly freezes to death on Olympus Mons. As in Shiner's novel, the operative adjectives for Williamson's Mars are "desolate," "forlorn," "disheartened."

Into this suddenly chastened and shrunken literary universe came a most unlikely figure who took a quite different, and prescient, approach not only to the uses of Mars past in constructing visions of Mars future but also to the aesthetics of the post-Mariner Martian landscape. The polymath critic, poet, translator, environmentalist, and editor of The Kenyon Review Frederick Turner first directed his attention to the subject of Mars in the 1970s. Not primarily identified with the science-fiction writing community, and trained as a Shakespeare scholar, Turner was nevertheless so catholic in his intellectual tastes that he learned a great deal from science-fiction writers. And he got a jump on most of them in recognizing the imaginative possibilities of the post-Mariner, post-Viking Mars. Over the course of two decades, he wrote fiction, poetry, and essays focused on the transformation of Mars in the imagination. Writers, he argued, could decide to work with current scientific understandings of the planet and at the same time to conserve the imagery of romantic Mars for fictional use. Clearly Mars never had any canals or civilizations, but an outpost of terrestrial civilization on Mars in the coming centuries would be a likely aim and accomplishment of the Space Age. The imaginary past might be prologue to the actual future. "No doubt we will build canals on Mars, and turn it into exactly the place of Edgar Rice Burroughs' poetic visions, if we so choose."[10] In his prose romance A Double Shadow (1978) and his later epic poem Genesis (1988), Turner celebrates the Martian landscape, transforms the history of Martian astronomical study and fiction into a new mythology of Mars, and gives the dream of terraforming the planet and creating a new Martian civilization its first detailed treatment and its first philosophically grounded rationale. In both fiction and poetry, Turner used his visionary Mars of the future to articulate the ecopoetics and neo-Arcadianism that he was pursuing elsewhere in his cultural, political, and scientific writing.

The putative author of A Double Shadow, a twenty-fourth-century settler from New Zealand who lives underground and observes on television Mars's surface and atmosphere being remade for human use, sets his narrative still further in the future: in the thirty-third century when the terraforming has been

Frederick Turner,
watercolor pastel by
Michael Osbaldeston,
1994. Courtesy of the
artist and Frederick
Turner.

completed. The ambition of this sibylline narrator is to create "a charter-myth of Martian civilization" and in so doing he moves dramatically away from Eklund and Benford's characterization of Mars as "ugly, ugly, ugly."[11] Nearly all his nomenclature is correctly post-*Mariner*: the Tharsis ridge, Hellas Basin, Nix Olympica, but he finds in these landscape features, even in the dawn of the planet's terraformed state which he witnesses, a subject in need of a poet.[12] "There is a dangerous beauty about Mars in the throes of its metamorphosis. Everything is raw and livid. Bolts of lightning burn patterns in your eyes. There is a steady fall of volcanic ash. I played Beethoven's *Spring* sonata and turned off the outside audio, so as to move in a light cocoon of music in the center of the silent violence of the new world" (3). Venturing from his cavern to make an expedition to Coprates Canyon where he does research for the novel that will be called *A Double Shadow*, the narrator revels in hurricanes and austere vistas that other writers might have described as infernal. When an avalanche nearly buries him alive, the narrator is self-conscious enough to belittle his terrifying experience as "a horrible and banal adventure, out of a thousand space thrillers" (5).

Both the supposed and the actual author of *A Double Shadow* want to do more with the Martian landscape than simply use it as a backdrop for melodrama. An early incident in the novel, once the prologue about its writing has ended, takes a husband and wife on a ritual weeks-long climb of Olympus Mons. They experience this climb as a kind of backwards time travel; as they move higher up the volcano they are also moving "back through the Terraforming to the old Mars" (40). As a Martian painter tells them on the eve of the beginning of their climb, "So you might say the journey upward is also a journey inward, into the secrets of the past . . . as the bulk of the mountain diminishes, you pass through the concentric layers of the planet's history" (40). A key passage in the novel that illustrates the precise nature of the novel's fascination with the past and the aesthetic that Turner practices describes the frescoes adorning a Martian house in the thirty-third century. They depict

> in dry ochres and terra-cottas and sky-blue the imaginary lives of the prehistoric indigenous Martians (who never existed) from the works of Burroughs and Bradbury. Further on there are heroic, perspectiveless renderings of the terraforming of Mars; of the cannibalizing of the rings of Saturn for ice and frozen air; of the nuclear kindling of Phobos; of the terrifying eruptions of the Martian volcanoes, including the one that rises so peacefully above the tiles, that were triggered by human geologists to help create a biosphere; of the blooming of the Martian deserts. (20–21)

The mingling of literary fantasies with the technological processes of remaking the planet acknowledges that Mars has an imaginary past as well as a scientific history and that human beings inevitably will bring that imagined Mars with them when they settle the planet and will cherish it as well as the technology that reshapes Mars.

Throughout *A Double Shadow*, Turner is persistently conscious of the space probes of the 1970s, in one passage even explicitly citing the *Mariner 9* photographs that first revealed Coprates Canyon. He uses an extended excerpt from a fictional textbook, Gunther's *Introduction to Martian Morphology*, to open the final section of the novel, and the imaginary textbook reads something like an *actual* scholarly study, Thomas Mutch's 1976 *Geology of Mars*. What makes Turner's work distinctive is his refusal to polarize literary and scientific understandings of Mars. Nowhere is this commitment more evident than in his handling of the canal motif, to which he devotes an entire chapter. The scientific discrediting of *canali* does not undermine the literary history of the canals. In *A Double Shadow*, both science and fiction are valid sources of inspiration, and for Turner's Martians there is an aesthetic demand for canals. Future history mimics the astronomical fancies of Lowell, and the terraformers work from blueprints that bear the mark of scientific romancers as well as engineers: "Mars is covered with a network of canals, constructed about six hundred years ago [i.e., in the twenty-seventh century] partly for irrigation, partly for pleasure-craft, but mainly because the sheer poetry of Schiaparelli's optical illusions has appealed as much to the builders of Mars as to its early fictioneers. So fiction tends to become truth" (53).

A *Double Shadow* is not entirely successful as a novel. It is a fascinating experiment, an allegorical planetary fiction generated out of admixtures of 1970s astronomy, syncretic myth, a narrative style flavored by John Barth (another 1970s phenomenon), and characterization and ambience reminiscent of Mervyn Peake. If parts of it read like a manifesto for Turner's antimodernist pastoralism, in form it is a pastiche whose artistic provenance seems uncannily like the camp scientism and scholastic theology of the novel's thirty-third-century cognoscenti: "a sort of aesthetic-philosophical slumming in the mythical regions of 'fact' " (115).[13] Late in A *Double Shadow*, a Miltonic allusion can be read in the description of the fall of the protagonist who is defeated in an aerial duel over the abyss of Coprates Canyon: "he drops from the zenith like a shooting star" (204).[14] This evocation of *Paradise Lost* and the Fall of the Angels points the way to Turner's second—and more extraordinary—effort to write a future history of Mars: his ten thousand-line epic poem *Genesis*, published in 1988.

In the preface to *Genesis*, Turner lays out his ambition to offer a poetic account of the transformation of Mars from a red wilderness to a green garden. The central event—and central conflict—of the poem is the terraforming project, which draws on sophisticated and detailed biochemical experimentation and arouses the passionate and murderous opposition of the "ecotheists" on Earth who are hostile to tampering with nature. Turner likens the process of creating the epic poem to the task of bringing a dead planet to life: "the unwritten poem is the barren planet, and the composition of the poem is its cultivation by living organisms."[15] It is a daring poetic experiment, perhaps the first poem in English to take up fully and exuberantly, if belatedly, Wordsworth's declaration about the poetry of the future in the 1800 Preface to *Lyrical Ballads*: "The remotest discoveries of the Chemist, the Botanist, or Mineralogist, will be as proper objects of the Poet's art as any upon which it can be employed, if the time should ever come when these things shall be familiar to us, and the relations under which they are contemplated by the followers of these respective Sciences shall be manifestly and palpably material to us as enjoying and suffering beings."[16] Turner took up the challenge of writing his terraforming poem as a rarity among contemporary writers—an *experienced* epic poet who in 1985 had already published *The New World*, a path-breaking heroic poem of love and war set in the post-apocalyptic former United States of the twenty-fourth century. Like *The New World*, *Genesis* is written in iambic pentameter, pays frequent homage to the tradition of Homer, Virgil, Dante, and Milton, and brims with self-conscious literary references. But *Genesis* is even more tightly constrained in form than Turner's first epic; he divides the poem into five "acts," each with five "scenes" of exactly four hundred lines. Within those boundaries, Turner also distills and incorporates the latest chemical, biological, ecological, and cybernetic reports in *Scientific American* and draws with explicit acknowledgment on the scenario for terraformation in *The Greening of Mars*, the 1984 conflation of popular science and fiction by James Lovelock and Michael Allaby. The result is a poem whose diction often startles and disorients (and then thrills) a reader, with antique lines lifted from Milton's *Lycidas* or Spenser's *Faerie Queene* cohabiting with allusions to twentieth-century popular film. Scientific and demotic language frequently play off each other, as in this account of the effort to raise the temperature and the atmospheric pressure on Mars:

> So how
> To get the heat we needed for the pressure
> Needed for the heat? We used albedo.
> The first bacteria just darkened up
> The surface—and especially the caps—
> To stop enough reradiation out
> Of the planet to get the cycle going.
> We helped it all along with little strikes
> From comets, ringstuff—what we could lay hands on.
> Planetmaking's not a precise art.
> Then we got oxygen-excreting algae
> And sowed them in the mulch the first bugs made
> By dying of the heat they generated.
> They used the carbon in the CO_2
> To make their bodies, and just shat the ox—
> If you'll excuse me, ladies—into the air. (III.iii.262–77)

Turner is a poet not at all unfriendly to the science-fiction tradition, which he already had both exploited and augmented in *A Double Shadow* and *The New World*. *Genesis* includes an often-cited panegyric that begins, "Poor science-fiction. Last muse of the gods, / The late child, stepchild, of our legendry"

(II.ii.63–64). He refers approvingly in his preface to "the matter of Mars" (by analogy with the "matter of Britain," by which the complex of Arthurian legends is known to scholars) to encompass the body of science fiction centered on other worlds—and Mars, in particular—as the backdrop to his poem. The pioneer of Turner's terraforming operation on Mars, the assassinated hero Chance Van Riebeck, is apostrophized as an apotheosis of Edgar Rice Burroughs' emblematic space-opera hero, "my John Carter of Mars" (II.i.146); when the landscape of Mars is being designed by Chance's daughter Beatrice Van Riebeck, she deliberately includes the construction of canals, "in honor of the ancient fiction" (IV.v.294); and one of the most extensive narrative actions in the poem is a *Star Wars*–like outer-space battle in which the great ark-ship *Kalevala* is blown up in the midst of the carnage brought on by the ecotheists who want to subvert the transformation of Mars. These salutes to science-fictional convention dramatize Turner's interest in examining the implications of a future built environment on Mars—what the poet of *Genesis* calls "this / Wildest and most intentional of worlds" (I.ii.14–15). The voice that chronicles the terraformation belongs, we are told, to a twenty-second-century poet who somehow has insinuated his verses into the head of Frederick Turner, who styles himself the poem's "redactor and editor" (1). Late in the epic, in the midst of the narration of the process of cultivating the Martian garden, that poetic voice asserts the central duty and dilemma of *Genesis*. "The poets of Mars must make the myths from scratch" (IV.v.167). Like other writers who have understood science fiction as a modern form of mythmaking, Turner sees Mars as a site for a new mythology that will illuminate the great cultural, ethical, and spiritual questions of our day. And those questions are centered largely and inescapably on the human relationship to the natural world. Writing a year after the publication of *Genesis*, Turner made it clear that his poem about the gardening of Mars had large stakes. He urged the importance of lifting our sights and hitching our minds to "a grand collective project—a project such as bringing life to Mars. This will be for us what the cathedrals were for medieval European culture. . . . The transformation of Mars would be a necessary education for the human species, not only a scientific and technological exercise but also an alchemical one. Its deepest meaning would be the spiritual metamorphosis of the alchemist, of us."[17]

It is not quite true, of course, that Turner is making myths from scratch. *Genesis* scavenges earlier myths and texts from both elite and popular cultures to fashion its own mythology whose originality resides largely in the unanticipated combinations of images, allusions, quotations, and evocations that make up the texture of the epic. "Since all material is but arrangement / Each new arrangement's new material," as the poetic voice observes (IV.v.396–97). A simple and straightforward instance of how this syncretic technique works appears in the description of the architecture, public transport, and vacation spots of the newly transformed Mars, where the science-fictional novelty of the vista is approached through images drawn from Gershwin's music and L. Frank Baum's fairy tale, from the one-time luxuries of the Union Pacific Railroad and the colorful styles of twentieth-century Miami and New York:

> And then there are the rhapsodies in blue,
> The landscapes of the jazz age, the new world.
> The Martian airports, with their lettering
> Of flanged silver like the Emerald City
> Look out from lounges, where you sip a cocktail,
> On sunlit hills with round trees in their clefts.
> You take a streamlined monorail as neat
> As was the California Zephyr in its prime
> Through a dramatic evening scene of cloud
> And silver-shine suspension bridge to towns
> Whose transit stations and whose trocaderos
> Are lit and pink with parabolic neon.
> Seaside resorts are smart with small hotels,
> Striped canopies, and staircases and pools
> In a Miami Art Deco pastiche,
> With bronze door-lintels like the Empire State,
> And ocean-scenes of palms and pink flamingos
> And blues as frail and pale as frosted glass,
> Dimmed lamps and the sound of saxophones. (IV.v.372–90)

Turner's epic is most impressive in its evocation of Paradise Attained, the condition of terraformed Mars achieved through heroic struggle against both a hostile physical environment and hostile minds. With its persistent allusions to and echoes of Milton, it stands *Paradise Lost* on its head, cataloguing any number of individual falls but culminating in the collective Rise of Humanity in the creation of a new world. And that act of creation—the terraforming and seeding of Mars—is also Turner's central homage to Milton, especially to the magnificent Book 7 of *Paradise Lost* in which the Angel Raphael describes to Adam and Eve the seven days of creation and the transformation of their own Earth into a living ecological system. Turner's poem responds with imagination and subtlety to what we have seen as the despairing cry of "ugly, ugly, ugly" that characterized some of the fictional representations of Mars in the first years after *Mariner 9*. This is an epic account of the process by which a wasteland became a thing of beauty and a joy forever (for Keats is also never far from Turner's thoughts).[18]

For the "speechless astronauts" (IV.v.59) who first step onto the Martian surface in the early twenty-first century, the planet is breathtakingly repulsive: "bleached to tired red with ultraviolet," "a waste of cold," and "sucked dry" (IV.v.61, 63, 64). It is a world with "a stunted and abortive chemistry, / A backward travesty of life" (IV.v.72–73). To these earliest arrivals, Mars seems "a poor old cretin / Worth but a handful of Earth's golden summers" (IV.v.86–87). And yet—and here Turner ushers in the great debate over the respective beauties of "red" versus "green" Mars that would be at the center of fictional visions of the planet in the last decade of the twentieth century—many of those first explorers discover that the barrenness of Mars has an aesthetic of its own:

> Those who first walked there
> Said it was fresh as the true feel of death,
> As Kyoto earthen teaware, as the Outback;
> As clear as is geometry, as bones. (IV.v.88–91)

To justify the transformation of this pristine, lifeless Mars into a habitat accommodating to terrestrial humanity (for what is known as the Ares Project is under assault from the start by the ecotheists who want the planet to be maintained in its "red" state), the seeding of Mars must produce a green world, a paradise, that is still more beautiful than the original. The earliest stages of terraformation seem to do just the opposite. The opening "vision" of the poem shows Chance Van Riebeck and his daughter Freya being pursued across the plains of Mars by forces of the United Nations that, at the instigation of Chance's estranged ecotheist wife Gaea, are seeking to arrest them for the blasphemous crime of altering the natural environment of the planet. The landscape the poet first sees in mind's eye is, indeed, horrific:

> What is this foul place, where the sun is shrunk
> To a pinhead over the close horizon?
> —This plain of inky slush, black as the sludge
> Oozing like ordure from a well of oil? (I.i.68–71)

What the poet observes is the product of Chance and Freya's dispersal of black algae around the Martian south pole, a first step in raising the temperature of the planet before other life forms can be introduced. But the poet's language suggests that far from a paradise, in this stage of ecogenesis, Mars has the features of a hell ("this malebolge," "this desolation, these cocytean swales," "tartaruses" [I.i.73, 88, 91]). When the bodies of Chance and Freya later are brought back to Mars after their trial before the World Court on Earth, the landscape has grown more colorful. We are offered a rhapsodic description of

> a magic carpet
> Of golden furs and powdery crimsons,
> Spore-yellows, saturated browns and blues,
> Purples shot with greens, and fleshy pinks,
> Open mild glitterings of slimes and foams:
> The saprophytes that feed on defunct germs,
> Funguses, orchidoids, mycetozoa,
> Slime molds with delicate sporangia
> Like little lampshades, phalluses, or combs,
> Formed from the mobile eggwhite of that mass
> Of naked zygotes called plasmodium;
> Yeasts in their glorious and rancid forms;
> The air softened with spores and protoplasts. (II.v.6–18)

The ancient epic device of the catalogue here has been adapted to create a poetry of anaerobic organisms.

Those passages of *Genesis* that narrate the details of the terraforming are often reminiscent of Milton's descriptions of the third day of creation when the bare Earth suddenly bursts into vegetative life "whose verdure clad / Her universal face with pleasant green" (*Paradise Lost*, VII.315–16). Turner's Mars becomes a new Arcadia and a new Eden, the product of advanced scientific techniques and ancient human fantasies. The necessary prelude to the seeding of Mars with larger and more complex life-forms is the moisturizing of this exceedingly dry world, and Turner borrows from Lovelock and Allaby's *Greening of Mars* the notion of directing an ice-comet to crash into the planet in an apocalyptic unleashing of water:

> No garden
> Ever in the history of the world
> (Unless old Terra in the fiery days
> Of coalescence when the stars were young
> Might be called garden without gardener)
> Stood to receive such watering as this,
> Such fiery fertilizer, ash or sulphur,
> Scattered by the careful human hand. (II.v.206–13)[19]

The comet approaches Mars, "its volatiles / Like the aurora, fluorescing wildly" (II.v.277–78), and causes a planetary shock wave and a global firestorm as the gases of the shattered comet ignite. And at last "out of skies as black as Noah's Flood / Falls the first rain that Mars has ever known" (II.v.314–15). When, finally, the epic voice celebrates the later introduction of fauna to Mars—from an Ark that is both a computer disk of genetic codes and the spaceship that transported it—we are given a vigorous and lengthy catalogue that convinces us not only of the beauty but the peaceableness of this extraterrestrial animal kingdom. Among the vertebrates are "*Bufo* the toad, who bloats his moony toot, / The bustly cassowary, with slim toes, / The teleosts, their scaled eyes set in bone" (V.ii.18–20). Here Turner is at his most Miltonic. The inventiveness, linguistic energy, and onomatopoetic wit in the language recalls especially the ways in which animals are described in *Paradise Lost*: the elephant who "wreathed / His lithe proboscis" to amuse Adam and Eve (IV.346–47) or "the swan with archèd neck / Between her white wings mantling proudly" (VII.438–39).

In its depiction of a Martian paradise, *Genesis* (despite Turner's general dislike of postmodernist hijinks) also makes room for ironies that undercut or qualify the aesthetic of terraformed Mars. There is a striking instance of dual vision in the arrival on Mars of Chance's assassin Tripitaka, who is taken into a lush, artificially lit underground habitat in Syrtis, with walls that portray major events in the history of the planet's settlement, painted in "brilliant oxides, cupreous / And ferrous, ocher, lampblack, limestone white" (III.iii.169–70). Tripitaka gazes on the cave-walls in stunned silence "as once / Aeneas did in Virgil's grand romance, / In Carthage, where the frescoes told of Troy" (III.iii.164–66). But this epic gesture towards the *Aeneid* as the forebear of *Genesis* is juxtaposed with a mock-epic wink to the twentieth-century reader. The bio-engineer Charlie Lorenz looks not at the frescoes but at the underground landscape of groves of trees surrounding hummocks of green grass and poses an anti-pastoral question: " 'Now why,' / Asks Charlie, 'Must our paradises all / Resemble golf-courses?' " (III.iii.159–61).

Even Beatrice herself, the presiding "gardener" of Mars, is capable of divided responses to her own work, suffering occasional moments of revulsion at the outcome of the Ares Project: deploring her "plastic life on a defiled planet" and reconsidering a technological feat that has "Massaged the rich sweet land into a message" (IV.iv.47, 52). While Turner in both this poem and his essays makes a forceful case in defense of terraformation, he also opens the door to the green-red debate that his successors, notably Kim Stanley Robinson, will put at the center of their imagined Marses.

In one other important respect, Turner's *Genesis* is also an inaugurator of themes that dominate the remade Mars of late-twentieth-century fiction. He envisions Mars as an opportunity for establishing a just and enlightened society—and thus brings back into play the notion, which had its first heyday in the 1890s, of Mars as a site for Utopia. Tripitaka, the "frenzied Galahad" (III.v.193), virginal, mystical and psychically damaged, has an epiphany on the battlefield in Australia in which he sees "the star of gold" as a world being birthed (III.ii.364), as a second chance for humanity, "the new / Republic of the breath of humankind" (III.ii.377–78). Less reverently, the poet speaks of Mars as "this cloudcuckooland" whose constitution has been consciously modeled on *The Federalist Papers* and de Tocqueville (V.ii.241). In imagining Mars as the birthplace for Utopia, Turner sees this locale as different from all others in humanity's efforts to start afresh on a new frontier. So he insists in his *Harper's* essay on "Life on Mars": "And no native tribes would have been displaced or murdered; no living species would have paid by extinction for human progress."[20]

Not nearly enough readers have discovered the pleasures of *Genesis*, although science-fiction writers such as Brian Aldiss and Kim Stanley Robinson have recognized the powerful originality of Turner's imagination and themselves have been moved to pursue some of the leads he has taken in inventing the Mars of the future. The classicist Judith de Luce admires his "skilled manipulation of tradition" in adopting the epic as the most appropriate literary form, in scale and in stature, for registering so sublime and heroic a task as the terraformation of another world. She observes, shrewdly, that in all other epics it is human beings who are creatures standing in relationship to their creator, but in *Genesis* men and women have become as gods and must determine their relationship to the world they have created.[21] Peter Kemp, reviewing the poem in *Nature*, viewed it less generously, finding only the Martian landscapes worth praising. Apart from those descriptive passages, *Genesis* is full of "comic-strip adventures" and barbarities that he sees only as throwbacks to the outmoded violence of an outmoded literary genre. And neither Turner's skill with pentameter nor his mixing of linguistic styles meets with Kemp's approval.[22] Turner, who already had met with a number of hostile responses to his first epic, *The New World*, was prepared for the skepticism of critics the second time around. One of the more delightful passages of *Genesis*, when the unrhymed pentameter briefly slips into mocking rhymed couplets, itemizes the talents and qualifications of a book reviewer:

First, a becoming modesty of style;
The aspirations of a crocodile;
A Shiite mullah's open-mindedness,

A moral backbone of boiled watercress;
All the prophetic vision of a sheep
(But not so witty, and not quite as deep);
A diction as unblemished by a thought
As is a baby's bottom by a wart;
You stand in the traditions of our art
As a blocked artery in a dying heart. (I.v.361–70)

Turner's *Genesis* is the most original literary treatment of Mars produced in the 1980s, and it was noticed by Kim Stanley Robinson, who had begun to experiment with Mars as a setting in a novel, a short story, and a novella that began to lay the groundwork for the masterwork he would produce in the 1990s: *Red Mars*, *Green Mars*, and *Blue Mars*. Robinson's first effort at a novel focused on the remaking of Mars is the 1984 *Icehenge*. Relying on a twenty-third-century journal by Emma Weil, a participant in an unsuccessful rebellion against an Earth-controlled "development committee" governing Mars, and a twenty-sixth-century memoir by the archeologist who found the spiral notebook containing Emma's journal, *Icehenge* provides a foretaste of the visionary politics, unfolding against a backdrop of terraformation, that distinguishes Robinson's two decades of work constructing an epic account of a future Mars. *Icehenge* includes a five hundred-year terraforming project, gerontological treatments that extend the human life-span, and perhaps most centrally, a conception of Mars as the site of a fresh political start and as the impetus for a renewal of utopian aspiration. "We didn't come to the red planet to repeat all the miserable mistakes of history, we didn't," Emma Weil insists at the end of her journal.[23] And the archeologist Hjalmar Nederland, his own utopian longings fired by the journal that he has discovered, reinforces Emma's passion by referring to the mutiny of 2248 as "an attempt to enact ideals that never were realized on Earth"—including the ideals that underlay the American and Bolshevik revolutions (87). Robinson has insisted that *Icehenge*'s Martian narrative cannot be made consistent retrospectively with the details of his later Mars novels, but represented a stage in the evolution of his imagination.[24] While this early novel can stand on its own legs, it is remarkable to see how, ten years later, Robinson fully developed the possibilities in *Icehenge* into the much more politically subtle and more psychologically textured narratives of *Red Mars*, *Green Mars*, and *Blue Mars*.

Robinson's most interesting Martian storytelling in the 1980s, though, is not to be found in *Icehenge* but in shorter forms: his 1982 story "Exploring Fossil Canyon" and a novella that staked his claim to a title he would recycle later,

"Green Mars." In "Exploring Fossil Canyon," Robinson's viewpoint character, Eileen Monday, undergoes a transformative experience while on a group hike through a canyon system near Olympus Mons. Mars here has been partly remade, with domed settlements and some domed natural parks, but most of the landscape has remained unhumanized. Having spent nearly all her life under the domes, Eileen ventures into the canyon wilderness as part of a tour group led by Roger Clayborne (whose surname Robinson later would appropriate for one of the most haunting and complex characters in his three Mars novels). The terrain is not conventionally beautiful (the convention here being the aesthetic of terrestrially landscaped nature) but even in this very early work Robinson's evocation of the Martian regolith suggests the poetry of rock and mineral that he later practices so skillfully: "it was composed of dirt of every consistency and hue, so that it resembled an immense layered cake slowly melting, made of ingredients that looked like baking soda, sulfur, brick dust, curry powder, coal slag, fertilizing mulch, and alum."[25] As the party makes its way through a canyon, one of the hikers imagines how beautiful it would look with creeks running down it, alpine flowers, toads, finches, tundra grass on its banks. But Clayborne, identifying himself with what would become in Robinson's fictions of Mars a "Red" ideology, disagrees. A domed canyon would constitute merely "an imitation Earth. That's not what Mars is for. Since we're on Mars, we should adjust to what it is, and enjoy it for that" (32). The critical event on the hike is the discovery of what are at first taken to be fossils in the canyon, but Clayborne punctures that hoary staple of Martian fiction and demonstrates that the shell-shapes are simply lava pellets from an ancient eruption of Olympus Mons. The news depresses Eileen, who has made a literary study of all the old terrestrial stories about Mars and who desperately wanted there to be life, even if only extinct life, on the planet, without which "this landscape's awful barrenness" remains meaningless (43).

The expedition appears to have cast Eileen only deeper into a sulky disillusionment. In a brilliant passage that sums up the end of one tradition of romantic Mars, Eileen contemplates red and dead Mars as nothing but a void, a catalogue of absences and deficits that extends from the most outlandish and famous literary fantasies to the most modest of mid-twentieth-century scientific hopes for living micro-organisms:

All the so-called discoveries, all the Martians in her books—they were part of a simple case of projection, nothing more. Humans wanted Martians, that was all there was to it. But there were not, and never had been, any canal-builders; no lamppost creatures with heat-beam eyes; no brilliant lizards or grasshoppers; no manta ray intelligences; no angels and no devils; there were no four-armed races battling in blue jungles; no big-headed skinny thirsty folk; no sloe-eyed, dusky beauties dying for Terran sperm; no wise little Bleekmen wandering stunned in the desert; no golden-eyed, golden-skinned telepaths; no doppelganger race, human in every way—not a fun-house mirror-image of any kind; there weren't any ruined adobe palaces; no dried oasis castles; no mysterious cliff dwellings packed like a museum; no hologrammatic towers that would drive humans mad; no intricate canal systems, locks all filled up with sand; no, not a single canal; there were not even mosses creeping down from the polar caps every summer; nor any rabbitlike animals living far underground; no plastic windmill-creatures, no lichen capable of casting dangerous electrical fields, no lichen of any kind; no algae in the hot springs; no microbes in the soil ... no primeval soup. (44)

Here Robinson, in the aftermath of the Viking experiments that found no hint of life, firmly slams the door on a tradition of Martian fiction. But the story does not end here with merely negative vision. "Exploring Fossil Canyon" takes a final turn, a turn that links Robinson to Turner rather than to Shiner and the "ugly" school of post-Mariner Martian fiction. Eileen has a moment of epiphany when she glimpses the tall, graceful figure of Roger Clayborne moving efficiently, comfortably, beautifully through the canyon "in a sort of boulder ballet" that lifts her heart. And there is the almost inevitable literary allusion as Robinson allows the full significance of the character's name to sink in. As "Roger" chimes with "rouge" we come to see that this man born of red clay is the authentic Martian: "Now there, she thought, is a man reconciled to the absolute deadness of Mars. It seemed his home, his landscape. An old line occurred to her: 'We have met the enemy, and they is us.' And then something from Bradbury: 'We are the Martians' " (44).

In a 1985 novella, Robinson revisited the characters of Roger Clayborne and Eileen Monday, but nearly three centuries later, when the former lovers re-encounter one another on a wilderness experience that involves a weeks-long climb up the extinct volcano Olympus Mons. (Scaling Olympus Mons, the highest mountain in the solar system, has become something of a recurrent motif in post-Viking Martian fiction, beginning with Turner's "A Double Shadow," setting up the climactic adventures in Paul McAuley's 1993 space opera Red Dust, lending the title to Kevin J. Anderson's 1994 Climbing Olympus, and dominating Dan Simmons' wildly inventive melding of the Olympos of Greek myth with the Martian volcano in his Ilium of 2003.) On its surface, "Green Mars" is a mountaineering adventure, but at its richest level the story is a parable about Clayborne's spiritual metamorphosis. Gerontological treatments have given most Martian settlers extended life spans but limited memories of their earlier lives. Clayborne is the exception who can remember all the details of his youth (including his fling with Eileen Monday which she has long forgotten). Most powerfully, Clayborne can remember what Mars was like before terraforming altered its climate and atmosphere and allowed for the introduction of fauna and flora that could tolerate its arctic conditions. As a holdout against terraformation and leader of the "Red" faction of the Martian populace, Clayborne has had to accept political defeat. He explains to his fellow climbers why, as a Martian environmental activist, he had fought unsuccessfully against the terraformers:

> Because I liked the planet the way it was when we found it! A lot of us did, back then. It was so beautiful . . . or not just that. It was more overwhelming than beautiful. The size of things, their shapes—the whole planet had been evolving, the landforms themselves, I mean, for five billion years, and traces of *all* that time were still on the surface to be seen and read, if you knew how to look.[26]

The experience of climbing Olympus and making a close observation of the juxtaposition of the beauty of the new Mars with its varied life forms and the sublimity of the still-unspoiled upper reaches of Olympus draws Clayborne into a mystical reconciliation with the greener Mars that is the product of terraformation. Robinson makes even more pointed use of the suggestive name of his protagonist than he did in "Exploring Fossil Canyon," for Clayborne becomes both a lover of rock and an Adamic steward of the animals being introduced into the Martian landscape. Most of those animals are modified but recognizable versions of species native to the colder regions of Earth. But near the end of "Green Mars," Clayborne sees something utterly novel to him hatching from a quivering, ovoid sphere of yellow ice:

> A beak stabs out of the globe, breaks it open. Busy little head there. Blue feathers, long crooked black beak, beady little black eyes. . . . The bird (though its legs and breast seemed to be furred, and its wings stubby, and its beak sort of fanged) staggers out of the white bubble, and shakes itself like a dog throwing off water. . . . Roger has never heard of such a thing, and he watches open-mouthed as the bird-thing takes a few running steps and glides away. A new creature steps on the face of green Mars. (103–104)

Clayborne observes this strange nativity in fascination and wonder—a response that signals a departure from his earlier distaste for genetically engineered animals as symbols of the degradation of the authentic Mars. Then, as he reaches the summit of Olympus Mons, his own psychological transformation becomes complete in an echo of the birth of the "bird-thing." The novella's last sentence works a tiny variation on the words Robinson had used earlier: "A new creature steps on the peak of green Mars" (113). This time the new creature is the reborn Roger Clayborne himself, at last adapted to a changed Mars. The new creature he becomes is a Martian.

Newness, celebrated in Turner's *Genesis* and in Robinson's early forays into the "Matter of Mars," is the predominant feature of the Martian narratives of the 1990s and beyond. Many of the earlier conventions are shed as authors aim for a new realism in their accounts of the processes of getting to Mars, settling on Mars, transforming Mars and its immigrants from Earth, and becoming Martian. The last chapters will explore some key texts in which the fictional conceptions of Mars get transformed, while still often paying homage, by allusion, nomenclature, or the raised eyebrow of parody, to the earlier, foundational traditions.

Being There

In a preface offered for Jack Williamson's *Beachhead* (1992), Arthur C. Clarke, writing forty years after the publication of his then-revolutionary anti-romantic *The Sands of Mars*, pointed to the renewed taste for Martian narrative. "The first flight to the Moon was a major theme in science fiction right up to the 1960s. Now the first expedition to Mars is the topic for the closing decade of this century—and the opening one of the next."[1] Clarke's prediction has proved to be accurate. Politics, science, and popular culture (the three of them often inextricably entangled in events) all encouraged writers at the *fin de siècle* to imagine journeys to Mars in the near future and to use fiction to create the vicarious experience of getting to and inhabiting another world. On the occasion of the twentieth anniversary of the first human landing on the Moon, President George H. W. Bush spoke at the National Air and Space Museum on July 20, 1989, and sketched a vision of a series of space endeavors that would culminate in a manned expedition to Mars. The following spring, in his commencement address at Texas A&M University, Bush named 2019 as the target year for the arrival of American astronauts on Mars.[2] Although Bush's ceremonial announcements caused a revival of planning activity at NASA (where plans for human-based Mars expeditions had lain dormant from the early 1970s until a NASA conference on Mars was held in July of 1986), no money was ever forthcoming that would pay the huge price tag of $450 billion that NASA estimated would be needed.[3] The depth of Bush's understanding of and commitment to a mission to Mars was undercut from the start by Vice President Dan Quayle, who served as chair of the National Space Council and who blithely pronounced in a television interview: "Mars is essentially in the same orbit [as Earth]. Mars is somewhat the same distance from the sun, which is very important. We have seen pictures where there are canals, we believe, and water. If there is water, there is oxygen. If oxygen, that means we can breathe."[4]

If the political vision of a mission to Mars in the early twenty-first century was largely an off-the-cuff fantasy, it nevertheless provided fresh impetus to a group of aerospace enthusiasts, calling themselves "Mars Underground," who had been holding occasional conferences since 1981 to make the "Case for Mars." The driving force behind the Mars Underground and its early conferences was Christopher McKay, in 1981 a graduate student at the University of Colorado and eventually a NASA astrogeologist. But one of the new names to emerge from the "Case for Mars" conferences at the end of the 1980s was Robert Zubrin, a high school teacher turned aerospace engineer turned populist Mars advocate. Zubrin became the leading voice in the 1990s for Mars exploration, even in the face of the disinclination of the Clinton administration and the Newt Gingrich–led Republican Congress to carry forward Bush's agenda for Mars. Developing a "Mars Direct" plan that would accomplish a streamlined mission at a cut-rate $40 billion, Zubrin turned increasingly to the possibilities of private funding to replace or augment governmental sponsorship. In 1998, he established the Mars Society—a more visible and vocal incarnation of the Mars Underground—that unites scientific experts, businessmen, students, and space enthusiasts from the public at large and that works to generate interest in, planning for, and funding of Mars exploration.[5]

A third phenomenon that kindled the public imagination of Martian ventures was the construction in the late 1980s of the enclosed ecological environment called Biosphere 2, near Tucson. Biosphere 2 had a number of scientific objectives, including what could be learned about Biosphere 1 (the planet Earth) from the ecological experiments conducted within the artificial environment. But it was the notion that Biosphere 2 could serve as an experimental prototype for a self-sustaining habitat on Mars that became the dominant public perception, even though some scientists complained that this was largely false advertising designed to muster support for the project.[6] People flocked to tour Biosphere 2 during its construction and until it was sealed in 1991 for an ultimately failed two-year experiment in which eight people tried to demonstrate that they could survive for that period on internal resources alone. Jack Williamson claimed that it was a visit to Biosphere 2 that inspired his novel *Beachhead*, and Ben Bova included Biosphere 2 as a stop on his book-signing tour when he published *Mars* in 1992.[7]

The fourth development that kept Mars in the public eye as well as in the eyes of science-fiction writers was the launch of the *Pathfinder* mission to Mars in 1996, with its famous, miniature robotic rover, *Sojourner*. The first successful mechanical mission to Mars since the *Vikings* of 1976, *Pathfinder* did more than anything else to revitalize the public romance with Mars and to reestablish belief in the value of exploring it. The cameras on the lander and on *Sojourner* sent seventeen thousand images back to Earth, accessible by the Internet to a global audience of many millions more than saw the *Viking* photographs in the 1970s. The leader of NASA's camera team memorably and accurately captured the effect of *Pathfinder*'s small but potent imaging devices: "These are our eyes. . . . We are all on Mars."[8]

The Bush agenda for a grand mission to Mars by 2020 was already collapsing by the end of 1989 and the likelihood of its failure, in the light of NASA's cost-estimate, may have been one of the stimuli to Terry Bisson's *Voyage to the Red Planet*. Bisson's journey to Mars does indeed take place in the early 2020s, in line with Bush's announced goal, but neither the United States nor the Russian space programs has survived a global depression in the early years of the new century and the gigantic, never-flown interplanetary space vessel constructed by the two superpowers has been mothballed in Earth orbit for twenty years. Instead, a Beverly Hills production company bankrolls the Mars project in order to make a film to be titled *Voyage to the Red Planet*. That the spacecraft is not named the *Ares*—as in so many science-fiction narratives about Mars—but the *Mary Poppins* gives away from the start the mischief Bisson intends, which is directed at the U.S. space agency as well as at Hollywood. In fact, this spoof opens with a joke about the price tag for a painting on the hull of the ship's namesake, "a woman with high-button shoes and an umbrella." "In the manner of the NASA projects of the time, the painting had cost $114,750.36 even though it was only standard Chevy van-grade airbrush work."[9]

The *Mary Poppins* is no stripped-down Mars Direct workhorse but a deluxe Stanley Kubrick model, a mile long, nuclear-powered, and fitted with wood paneling, carpets, paintings, a library, and accommodations for sixty-six. The narrative is every bit as extravagant as the spacecraft, full of ebulliently deployed clichés: there are *two* stowaways aboard the *Mary Poppins* (a girl and a cat); a mysterious stairway is found inside Candor Chasma leading to an artifact from an ancient civilization; a desperate struggle ensues to get enough fuel to power the Martian lander back to the mother ship before it crashes into the moon Phobos; and there is a reprise of the hoary old problem of which crew member to leave behind on Mars so that the lander's weight limit is not exceeded. With those familiar plot elements alternating with the goofy goings-on of the film shoot, a reader does not expect to discover *Voyage to the Red Planet* breaking new ground in the literature of Mars. But Bisson is actually quite successful at working with the knowledge and the imagery generated by the *Viking* missions of the 1970s to create a plausible and often beautiful rendition of the Martian landscape in the midst of the Hollywood silliness. And he is smart enough to know when to topple a cliché rather than simply make fun of it. A splendid paragraph eschews the banality of describing the landing on Mars and chooses instead to celebrate the altered consciousness of one of the crew who meditates on the marvel of living on another world:

> There is something about waking up on a new planet. The first sighting, the long approach from space, the fiery descent through the atmosphere, the historic first footstep—all are so melodramatic, so shaped and colored by the entire history of discovery and exploration, so written about and cele-brated as to lack both subtlety and surprise. But waking up, that's some-thing else. A new light taps at the eyelids. A new gravity pulls at the blood. When the night's dreams fly away in the daylight, where do they go on a world undreamed-in before, where there are no drifts of old dreams filling the gutters like dry leaves? A new world. And the consciousness, which the ancients used to think was newly created every day, almost seems truly to be so here on Mars, as the realization steals over you that you are no longer on the world whose turning awakened your fathers and their fathers for a half a million years, but on another. (160)

Here Bisson captures what would turn out to be the central accomplishment of Martian fiction in the last decade of the century: imagining the human experi-ence of being on Mars.

That experience of being there, as imagined by the novelists of the 1990s, includes several recurring themes with many variants: the rethinking of Mars as home rather than as outpost or colony; an alternately respectful and ironic consciousness of the old Mars of literary tradition; a new human adjustment to the actual rather than to a romanticized Mars; a heightened attention to the Martian landscape and the redefinition of standards of planetary beauty; a restoration of the nineteenth-century belief in the utopian promise of Mars, but focused on building a new utopia rather than discovering a pre-existing one; the emergence of an independent, self-sufficient Martian society under threat from political and commercial interests on Earth. Perhaps an overarching, though often implicit, premise of much of the Martian fiction of this period is a revision of William Herschel's often-cited eighteenth-century observation, "The analogy between Mars and the earth is, perhaps, by far the greatest in the whole solar system."[10] The newest novelists have found thinking about the planet analogically both inadequate and inimical to an appreciation of Mars on its own terms. While the triple-decker novel of Kim Stanley Robinson (to be considered in the next chapter) is the most visible and acclaimed instance of the emphasis on experiencing Mars, many works of the 1990s exhibit this set of themes and preoccupations and revisions of the literary tradition, with varying degrees of imaginative power and artistic success.

In Sondra Sykes's *Red Genesis*, the first station on Mars is established ahead of Bush's schedule in 2015, with a full base by 2028 where people are rotated in and out every two years. Not a widely read novel even by science-fiction enthusiasts, *Red Genesis* focuses interestingly not on the technical challenges of inhabiting Mars (and terraforming isn't even brought up) but on the economic, political, and organizational challenges of making a society on Mars work. The first civilian settlements are devastated by disease, and by the mid-twenty-first century, in which the narrative of *Red Genesis* is set, there are five fragile communities, each specialized in its work and distinctive in its ideology, with only a minimum of cooperation among them. Settlers have difficulty adjusting, physically and psychologically, to conditions on Mars—with pink-sky intolerance the most common ailment, along with claustrophobia from the confining habitats and frequent dust storms and the "just plain alienness" of the place.[11] The central figure in Sykes's novel, the wealthy Chinese-American business executive Graham Kuan Sinclair, is sentenced to permanent banishment to Mars when he is scapegoated and convicted of responsibility for the deaths of more than three million people in an environmental disaster. Killing clouds of poisonous gas on Earth, released from the ocean depths by dumped pesticides and war chemicals whose containers have burst, lead to Sinclair's being reviled as "the Cloud Man" and his exile to Mars; the judicial sentence, it is gradually revealed, was deliberately intended to exploit his managerial skills to rescue the foundering Martian colony. "It did not look inviting, this world, with its pockmarked face and deep scars," Sinclair thinks when he has his first close-up view from low Mars orbit (90). He spends much of the novel longing to find a way to reverse his conviction so that he may return to Earth, without fully realizing how deeply drawn in to Mars he is becoming. The doctor to whom he is apprenticed on Mars first announces the utopian possibilities that a few of the most committed settlers embrace: "We adapt and create from *nothing* a world moving toward Eden" (135).

But the Martian outposts are a losing proposition economically for Earth and it is unclear how much longer Mars will be subsidized as "a curiosity and an exotic adventure" (194). With his background in managing complex financial organizations, Sinclair gradually begins to lead the five settlements to greater coordination for mutual benefit and to make the entire consortium more self-sufficient by starting the export of hand-crafted glass objects, using the superior sand of Valles Marineris, which will become a coveted commodity on Earth:

"Equivalent to Venetian glass during its peak in the Middle Ages" (212). His successes as an outlaw in getting the colonies to transcend religious, cultural, and economic disagreements, to resist the surveillance that shadows their every move, to begin work on an underground monorail system that will prevent paralysis each time a dust storm occurs, and to adopt a new planetary governance system becomes the stuff of legend on both Mars and Earth. Masterminding negotiations between striking and rioting miners on Mars and their terrestrial bosses, the semi-mythical "Cloud Man" accomplishes the apparently miraculous feat of improving living conditions for the miners, increasing the productivity of the operations, and further uniting the separate Martian colonies. By the time the order of exile is lifted at novel's end, Sinclair—in a gesture characteristic of the new Martian novel of the 1980s and 1990s—finds that his identity and his sense of home have changed permanently. He declines the offer to return to Earth: "I already have a home" (332). Colonial Mars has begun its metamorphosis into an independent entity.

Because Jack Williamson invented the word "terraforming" in a 1942 short story, his Mars novel, published fifty years later, might be expected to have a place of honor in the literary history of the planet.[12] Unhappily, *Beachhead* is not a coherent or plausible narrative—and the only terraforming portrayed is an hallucination experienced by one of the dying astronauts. Williamson's protagonist, Sam Houston Kelligan, shares some of the recurrent attributes of main characters in other Martian fiction of the 1990s: a longstanding romance with Mars since his youth, a literary inspiration for his career in space (in Kelligan's case, Heinlein's 1949 children's book *Red Planet*), a name that evokes the American western frontier, and a visionary commitment not just to explore but to live on Mars. At the same time, Kelligan is a distinctly old-fashioned space-opera hero, a throwback to the Flash Gordon model of a rich, fair-haired boy, a daredevil, and a doer of the impossible, including most emphatically in *Beachhead* his engineering of a rescue mission for the stranded first settlers on Mars by flying solo from Mars to Earth in a tiny lander vehicle.

Writing in the shadow of NASA's twenty-year dependence on remote-control, mechanical planetary exploration after the last *Apollo* mission to the Moon, Williamson imagines that only a multinational authority or a profit-seeking private enterprise would support sending a staff of scientists to Mars. But *Beachhead* does not follow the Zubrin recipe for an economical Mars Direct approach; the *Ares* that carries a crew of eight is a behemoth of the old school of space travel. "We're living an epic," the crew members believe, and Williamson does everything on a grandiose scale, but without the saving ironies of the sort that Terry Bisson manages.[13] *Beachhead* comes most fully alive in its descriptions of the landscape of Mars, where the opulently romantic language is grounded in precisely formulated topographical detail. Like many of his contemporaries who feasted on the visual images of the *Mariner* and *Viking* expeditions, Williamson is drawn to a new aesthetic that defines Mars as austerely beautiful and that strives to create a poetry of rock and dust and redness. Kelligan in his rover rejoices in the grandeur of Coprates Chasma at sunrise:

> East and west, it fell forever. Abrupt cliffs of iron-red stone towered over yellow shelves above bottomless gorges of old black basalt. A flood of red fire poured down it out of the west, a fog-laden hurricane flowing around buttes and towers of wind-carved rock on its rush to meet the rising sun. Far mountains loomed out of gold-red haze beyond it. (178–79)

The other achievement of *Beachhead*, paradoxically, is that it captures the deadliness of Mars. To imagine domed cities and a terraformed climate in the future challenges each of the eight first astronauts in different ways as they face the frigid emptiness, grand though it may be, of the Martian wasteland. Williamson allows the beauty and the horror of Mars to co-exist without fully developing and certainly without resolving the tension. Kelligan, grinning through every catastrophe, has moments when he feels Mars as hopelessly forlorn but always shoves his doubts aside and bucks up the flagging spirits of his comrades. The flattening of issues and the lack of a critical perspective are evident throughout *Beachhead*—in the superficial deployment of "new frontier" language (302), in the too-innocent designation of Kelligan as "the Columbus of Mars" (285), and even in the allusion to colonialism in the expressed hope that the discovery of precious metals near the north pole could motivate terrestrial financiers to mount a rescue expedition for the struggling astronauts: "Bring rescue here the way Inca gold brought the Spanish to the old New World?" (272) A sobering question. Experiencing Mars, in both its geographical wonders and the physical and psychological hardships it inflicts on would-be human inhabitants, is central to Williamson's narrative, but other writers in the 1990s have made the experience of being on Mars more complex and nuanced.

Greg Bear's *Moving Mars* opens with the puzzling declaration that the "old Mars" of rusty regolith, unbreathable atmosphere, and required pressure suits is gone. "Mars is young again."[14] Constructed as a posthumously published memoir by Casseia Majumdar, the second president of the Republic of Mars, *Moving Mars* does not disclose the meaning of its opening paragraph until the novel's conclusion. In fact, for most of its length, Bear's narrative is very deeply rooted in the imagery of domed habitats in a wilderness of dust and sand.

There are no terraforming projects and approximately three million Martians in the late twenty-second century are still living mostly underground, referring to themselves self-deprecatingly as "red rabbits." To venture out onto the surface, in pressurized suits, is a rarity. Typically, Casseia writes, Martians go "Up" perhaps nine or ten times during their lives and they behave like "tourists on their own planet" (59). Those who spend the most time on the surface are paleontologists, searching for fossils from the distant past when Mars was a living world. (One of the curiosities of *Moving Mars* is its old-fashioned plot device of a search for some still-living organisms—a search that implausibly succeeds.)

With its persistent homages to *The Martian Chronicles*, including its dedication to Ray Bradbury, Bear's novel has a foot in older, and even retrograde, Martian romances. Throughout *Moving Mars*, there are allusions to the Tharks of Burroughs' Barsoom, the Russian silent film *Aelita, Queen of Mars*, the Clay People of the 1930s movie serial *Flash Gordon's Trip to Mars*, Isaac Asimov's 1950s story "The Martian Way," and—no surprise here—canals. The justification for this tissue of allusions is offered by the narrator who says that "no Martian can escape the past; we are told tales in our infant beds" (60). The persistence of Earth-created Martian mythology, whether in the form of the literary classics of the twentieth century or the computer-generated images that Bear foresees for the centuries following, shapes the experience of his underground settlers: "We live on three Marses, don't we?" the protagonist asks. "The Mars they made up back on Earth centuries ago. LitVid Mars. And this" (73).

But *Moving Mars* also reflects the new Martian ethos of the fiction of the 1980s and 1990s. Even though their environment is harsh and unforgiving of carelessness, Bear's Martians are fiercely loyal to their "heart-achingly beautiful" world (60). Like other Martian fictions written in the postcolonial era, this one also rejects terminology about Mars as a colony of Earth, whose rulers nastily accent the second syllable of "colonists" when talking about Martians. "It was," Casseia writes, "one word never heard on Mars even in its correct pronunciation. Settlers, settlements; never colonies, colonists" (166). The political tension between Mars and its parent planet, the desire for independence, a spirit of rebellion, the drafting of a Martian constitution, the economic double-dealing of Martian quislings, the threat of being swallowed up or massacred by the superior terrestrial forces—these are all staples of many other Martian novels of the period. What is startling and disquieting about *Moving Mars* is the way in which Bear disposes of the political conflict—and here, once again, *Moving Mars* demonstrates its allegiance to romantic plotting, to fantasy rather than scientific realism. The fantasy is cloaked in technojargon about "descriptor theory," "tweaking," "particle redescription," "boson world-lines," and "orthonormal bases"—but this is a trick as old as H. G. Wells's "ingenious use of scientific patter" to bolster an act of pure imagination.[15] When Mars is on the point of being destroyed by Earth's military assault, its leading physicist, who has discovered a means of instantaneous travel through space, moves the planet out of the solar system and relocates Mars in an orbit around another sun, ten thousand light years distant. This is the Mars that has become young again, warmer in temperature with its closer proximity to the new sun, its frozen subterranean aquifers now melted, and its dead volcanoes coming back to life. All of this is as unbelievable as the instant terraforming that climaxes Paul Verhoeven's 1990 film *Total Recall*. In fact, we never get a resolution of the political dilemma the novel dramatizes; the dilemma simply, and literally, goes away. At the conclusion of her memoir, written, we learn, while she is in prison, Casseia Majumdar foresees a utopian future for the new Mars under its new sun: "Children will be born who remember nothing of the Old Sun. The new bright-flowered skies will be home for them—for you. . . . I see you playing in the shadow of the bridges of Old Mars, your skin revealed to the air, a hundred, a thousand years from now. For you there will be no time, no distance, no limits; nothing but what you will" (444).

Bear does not ignore then-current information about Mars. Indeed, the epigraph to the novel is a catalogue of data about length of day and year, gravity, diameter, temperature, and atmosphere. But novelists had been doing that kind of thing for many decades to establish the scientific *bona fides* of their fiction. Science provides a backdrop, not the intellectual scaffolding, for Bear's plot, which sacrifices credibility to the fantasy of his grand inventions. If *Moving Mars* doesn't entirely succeed as a science-fiction novel, it nevertheless does exhibit important features of the new Martian novel that developed in the late twentieth century: an emphasis on the difficult beauty of a wilderness planet, a topographically correct representation of the physical details of Mars, a redefinition of Martian identity, a persistent allusiveness to earlier literary traditions about the planet, and a new conceptual framework in which dead Mars is supplanted by a revivified planet that is the site for building a new, human, progressive community.

The first and second expeditions to Mars are the subjects of Ben Bova's *Mars* and its sequel *Return to Mars*. In both books, the central figure is Jamie Waterman, a geologist and a Navaho who takes the exploration of the planet more seriously than the governments of the industrial nations funding the missions. The politicians are focused narrowly on a "flags and footprints" showcase, and both missions, reflecting NASA's controversial mantra of the 1990s, "faster, better, cheaper," are to follow a premeditated script and to be carried out as quickly as possible.[16] Bova's two imagined Mars Projects, in technical terms, are plausible incarnations of that NASA ethos, and the claustrophobic space-craft, the cumbersome extravehicular suits, and the boring adherence to repeti-tive procedures reflect the anti–Star Wars naturalism characteristic of the 1990s mood of imaginative writing about planetary adventure. The physical descrip-tion of various space vehicles and habitats is deliberately drained of glamour:

> They all looked alike from the inside. The space stations in Earth orbit, the shuttles that carried the Mars explorers to them, the Mars-bound craft themselves—their interiors were all almost identical. Cramped compart-ments, narrow passageways, the constant hum of electrical equipment, the glare-free, shadowless, flat lighting, the same smell of cold metal and canned stale air. The packed-in feeling that someone was waiting in line behind you, even in the toilet. (Mars, 160)

In Return to Mars, published seven years later, Bova gets on the Zubrin bandwagon in his acknowledgments: "The mission plan for the Second Mars Expedition was adapted from the Mars Direct concept originated by Robert Zubrin, as detailed in his book, The Case for Mars."[17] Specifically, the second mission is funded by private enterprise at 10 percent of the cost of the first mission, which had been supported by an international consortium of govern-ments. And when Return appeared in 1999, the global romance with the Path-finder mission was in full bloom and Bova includes in the narrative an effort to salvage the lander and the Sojourner rover and return them to Earth. When the astronauts arrive at the Pathfinder site and see the familiar rocks and peaks, future fiction amusingly validates history: "They're all here. They're really here. After all the years of looking at the pictures and watching the videos, it's all real! It really all happened. They landed the spacecraft here back when they could barely fly a ton of payload to Mars" (Return, 262).

The effort at realism in the hardware, the routines, and the (very few) creature comforts that would be part and parcel of the first journeys to Mars clashes uneasily with the sentimentality of Bova's plotting and the flatfooted characterization more typical of the romance tradition of literary Mars. But Bova is heavily indebted to that tradition, too. Like many other protagonists of late-century Martian fiction, Jamie Waterman brings literary history with him: "beautiful fantasies of cities built like chess pieces and houses that turned to follow the sun" as well as "tales of creatures made of silicon and green-skinned Martians with six limbs" (Mars, 25, 70). Waterman's memories of his childhood reading of Edgar Rice Burroughs, Stanley Weinbaum, and Ray Bradbury reproduce exactly the homage that Bova pays to those same authors in his acknowledgments. Both Bova and Waterman enact one significant element of those older Martian fantasies in both *Mars* and *Return to Mars*: They are pre-occupied with the search for evidence of life, present as well as past, and particularly for evidence of an extinct earlier civilization. This latter is a fantasy that refuses to die an easy death in some fiction of the past two decades, although Bova is aware enough of the old-fashionedness of this part of his plot that he has other crew members perceive Waterman's search as quixotic. When he observes what he takes to be a building, an artifact in a cliffside cave in Tithonium Chasma, the Russian commander of the mission asks if this isn't just a Lowellian "optical illusion" (*Mars*, 232). Waterman's effort to defend his thesis as unbiased is discounted immediately by the Indian and the Egyptian astronauts, who refuse to let him depart from the mission schedule to investigate more closely, and the crew physician later makes his own diagnosis. " 'It's a projection on Jamie's part, a well-known psychological problem,' he said. 'We see what we want to see' " (*Mars*, 312).

This balancing act in which the conflict between realism and fantasy is left in suspension is abandoned, unaccountably, in the sequel. Jamie Waterman is vindicated by conclusive evidence that the object in Tithonium Chasma is a building, with writing on its walls, including what appears to be the depiction of the destruction of intelligent life by a meteor collision contemporaneous with a major collision on Earth sixty-five million years ago in which three-quarters of the living beings on Earth, including the dinosaurs, were extinguished. The conclusion that Waterman draws is that there were indeed Martians who were all "killed off" in this cosmic catastrophe (*Return*, 343). Here, as elsewhere, *Return to Mars* is a cruder book than Bova's earlier novel. *Mars* self-consciously incorporated a great deal of data about Mars as it had been observed and studied up to 1992, but the sequel is more heavy-handed in its didacticism. Waterman has a doctorate in geology and is thoroughly versed in Martian topography, so that his reminder to himself here is clearly only an authorial excuse for the technical education of the reader: "He pulled on the rod, extending it out to its full two meters, then planted it firmly in the red, dusty soil. Not soil, he reminded himself. Regolith. Soil is honeycombed with living things: worms, bugs, bacteria. This rusty iron sand of Mars was devoid of any trace of life" (*Return*, 53). If an occasional science lesson were the only narrative flaw in *Return to Mars*, it would be no different from many other Martian novels of the period. But the book is full of button-pushing. The anticolonialism of Jamie Waterman's perspectives from the first novel becomes insistent, shrill, and repetitive in the second. Here is a fairly typical exchange between Waterman and another crew member over the question of terraforming (which Kim Stanley Robinson had made a hot one in his three *Mars* novels, all published in the years between Bova's two):

> "You want to change the entire planet, make it just like Earth."
> "That's the basic idea. Then it'll be a lot safer for visitors. Then we can build permanent settlements on Mars. Build cities, colonies."
> "Just like the Europeans did to the Americas," Jamie said.
> Trumbull laughed out loud. "I knew it'd torque you. Cultural bias and all that."
> "And you'll put the lichen on a reservation, where the visitors can come and stare at them." (*Return*, 69–70)

Bova's two *Mars* novels are richly responsive to the times in which they were written and exemplify some of the most interesting features of the new Martian fiction of the 1990s, including above all the effort to get scientific romance into line with scientific fact. And he is capable of sometimes delightful and inventive similes that domesticate the exotic features of space travel. Detailing the clumsiness of getting into the hard suits required for venturing outside on Mars, Bova depicts the astronauts "struggling into their suits like a short-handed football team getting into its padding and uniforms. Or like knights putting on their armor. Jamie wondered if King Arthur's men grumbled and swore while they suited up for battle" (*Mars*, 110). When his novels focus on Waterman's experience of being on Mars, Bova is skilled at summoning up the novelty of the first day inside a transparent plastic igloo that insulates the astronauts from the frigid and lethal Martian atmosphere, the look of the color lines of sediment in a canyon wall and the feathery morning clouds flowing through the canyon, the graceful bobbing of hydrogen-filled balloons carrying sensing instruments to survey the landscape from pole to pole. Like all the memorable new fictions about Mars, Bova's two books strive to capture the desolate beauty and alienness of the place, as well as the thrill of living extraterrestrially.

Between Bova's first and second Mars novels, William K. Hartmann published *Mars Underground*, among other things a worthy contribution to the "alien artifact" tradition in science fiction—most memorably visualized in the mysterious black monolith that recurs in the Arthur Clarke/Stanley Kubrick *2001: A Space Odyssey*. Hartmann's work deserves a place among the more thoughtful and subtle representations of the encounters between the human mind and alien intelligence, including Stanislaw Lem's *Solaris* (which depicts a sentient planet) and Clarke's own enigmatic giant spaceship that dominates his underrated, nearly plotless meditation on the unknowable, *Rendezvous with Rama*. In *Mars Underground*, alien intelligence is embodied in a titanic construction whose existence is shrouded in secrecy and deceptions contrived by U.S. security officials. A machine—if that is what it is—of vast proportions is found buried beneath ice and dust at the Martian south pole by scientists drilling for water (see color plate 8). Slowly they uncover an elaborate network of tubing that spirals around the magnetic pole "like a giant burner on an old-fashioned electric stove."[18] At one end of the tubing, workers excavate "a huge, organ-pipe mass of vertical cylinders" extending deep into the ground (359). The discovery of this artifact, for which the terrestrial analysts have no workable paradigms that enable them to interpret its nature or purpose, is an occasion for Hartmann to inquire into the political, cultural, aesthetic, and philosophical consequences of the human encounter, however indirect, with intelligence outside its own sphere and outside its ken. As the journalist in the narrative comes to realize, one of the most powerful of the consequences of the evidence that humanity is neither unique nor at the center of all things is "disillusionment" (367)—that resonant Wellsian word that climaxes the narrator's reflections on "intelligences greater than man's" in the magnificent opening paragraph of *The War of the Worlds*.

But *Mars Underground* plays for larger stakes than a sensationalist account of the alien encounter. Ultimately, the author is more interested in Mars itself and the fresh and iconoclastic start that it offers human beings and their institutions than he is in the pot-boiling possibilities of Ian Douglas' *Semper Mars*, which battens on popular fantasies about the so-called "Face" on Mars. Elsewhere, Hartmann, a serious and accomplished planetary scientist, has described the "Face" controversy as a "time-wasting, deliberately orchestrated, and pseudoscientific frenzy."[19] The more moving event in *Mars Underground* is the discovery not of the 3.2-billion-year-old extra-Solar artifact but the more homely "historic relic" (131) of the human exploration of Mars, the battered Soviet probe *Mars 2*, the first humanly created object to arrive on Mars when it crash-landed in 1971. Here, Hartmann's interest in the history of the human encounter with Mars dovetails with his affection for the literary history of the planet. That dual interest is centered in Carter Jahns, whose name is a genuflection to Edgar Rice Burroughs' hero John Carter. An environmental engineer devoted to the building of a humanly viable new Mars, Jahns is as much artist as scientist, drawn to the ambition of "sculpting Mars City out of steel, soil, and people" (270). Jahns' mentor is a pioneering exobiologist, the aging, eccentric, but shrewd Alwyn Stafford, "a biologist of the dead world" (12), whose mysterious disappearance is linked to the alien artifact and to the political effort by U.S. authorities to conceal the artifact from public view. Stafford inspires in Carter Jahns a distaste for seeing Mars as "a streamlined suburb of Earth" (9) and an appreciation for the distinctiveness of Martian topography, since earthly analogues are always inadequate. One of the finest passages of writing in Mars Underground is Jahns's meditation on the differences between rock on Earth and rock on Mars. Rocky terrestrial landscapes, for him, suggest "protruding bare bones that should have been clothed with flesh" and strip mining and other "wounds" and "sores" on the planet (184). But on Mars, rocks have "as many textures as trees and flowers." There are "dark rocks with gleaming crystals and bubbly rocks like sponges on the sea floor"; there is "dense basalt sculpted with conchoidal fractures like the sides of elephants' skulls"; and, he reminds himself, not all rocks are red when he luxuriates in "a meadowlike patch of faintly greenish olivine cinders, a striking color contrast with the rusty vistas" (184). Observing a plain full of scattered black basalt boulders, Jahns becomes even more rhapsodic: "Flat-lit by the high sun, the plain looked like a giant's sheet of music, with rocks scattered like notes that would play some strange music if only you knew how to read it" (185).

While Stafford tutors Jahns's political and scientific imagination, his closest friend is not another scientist but Philippe Brache, who holds a fellowship as artist-in-residence on Mars and who is constructing large-scale installations that celebrate the Martian landscape and the arrival of humanity into that landscape. Brache's major project, an immense tree of aluminum and crystal, with each leaf inscribed with the name of one of the first six thousand inhabitants of Mars, is set in a "Zen garden" of boulders and it strikes Jahns as an emblem of the future of Mars and the marriage of tradition and innovation. "To a thousand travelers of this future, this would be an introduction to the new culture that was growing on Mars, the twig, the new offshoot from Earth's ancient ways, budding now on a new world" (265). The other major character, the Hawaiian journalist Annie Pohaku, also extends the novel's concern with the relationship between history and the future on Mars. Trying to develop a newsworthy angle on what interest remains in Mars two decades after the first human presence, she wants to find more to Mars than a dead and dry planet where people constantly struggle simply to maintain things. She wants to emphasize—what in fact had become a cliché by the time the novel appeared in 1997—Mars as a new frontier and, more provocatively, as "an empty slate" and a place "where no history had accumulated" (31). In defying and outwitting the security chief who tries to prevent her from broadcasting back to Earth the discovery of the alien artifact, Annie makes her own contribution to history. Insisting on the freedom of the press to report news without governmental restriction, she appeals to the reader's desire to see Mars as an opportunity to reinvent freedom. "We're supposed to have an open world," she tells Jahns. "History doesn't just hand it down to us, we have to keep re-creating it" (379). Even the somewhat tired figure of the pushy journalist is put to interesting work in *Mars Underground*. It is left to Annie Pohaku to find a way to phrase the historical watershed represented not only in the discovery of the alien artifact but in the effort to build a new Martian society. It is "like the Renaissance, when the discoveries of Copernicus and Columbus had forced everyone from poets to popes to recognize that the real world was much wider than they had thought" (366).

The Renaissance was also on the mind of Gregory Benford, who opens his tale of the first missions to Mars with an epigraph taken from the fifteenth-century Portuguese Prince Henrique, known as Henry the Navigator, sponsor of numerous colonizing and trading expeditions to Africa. The Prince's assertion that contemporary merchants and mariners would not "trouble themselves to sail to a place where there is not a sure and certain hope of profit" epitomizes the commercial motives that govern the race to reach Mars in the years 2016 to 2018.[20] To a considerable extent, Benford's *The Martian Race* is a fully fleshed scenario of the Robert Zubrin Mars Direct proposal, including the $30 billion prize that Zubrin suggested as bait to lure private entrepreneurs to invest in a (relatively) cheap mission to Mars. A grey-haired Zubrin himself appears briefly in the novel, and the first astronauts to reach Mars establish Zubrin Base, "their unofficial name, in honor of the hot-eyed founder of the Mars Society" (137). Benford imagines a consortium of Western businessmen—led by John Axelrod, a multibillionaire CEO of a biotechnology firm (the novel's modern Henry the Navigator)—who hope to make a profit by spending $20 billion to send a four-person team to Mars for an eighteen-month stay. The financial backers can net the prize if their astronauts return to Earth with the data and the achievements required to claim it: "geologic mapping, seismic testing, studying atmospheric phenomena, taking core samples, looking for water and, of course, fossils or life" (16). During the course of the nearly three years of the round-trip mission, the investors sell virtually every aspect of the expedition to the mass media to ensure continuing profits. The rampant commercialism includes not only television and newspaper rights to the ongoing story but the marketing of consumer goods ranging from sweatshirts to Mars Bars. The scientific work to be carried out on Mars is often curtailed or compromised by the amount of time the astronauts are required to spend on "retailing" their work, their daily lives, and their discoveries through regular interviews and broadcasts. Even more disturbingly, the astronauts discover after they have arrived on Mars that the investors quietly deep-sixed a key part of the Mars Direct plan—sending a back-up Earth-return vehicle to Mars in case the one that has been sitting on the Martian surface for several years proves unflyable—because they were unwilling to spend the extra money. The crew learns that for all NASA's faults, there is a crucial difference between private enterprise and the government space agency for whom "astronaut safety was not just the first rule, it was the only rule" (117).

This cheap and risky venture by Axelrod's consortium, dependent on salvaging used NASA equipment and jerry-built improvisations by the crew's mechanic, suddenly turns into a race when a rival Asian consortium, led by China, emerges out of secrecy, using cutting-edge nuclear technology and new equipment. When this rival group of three astronauts arrives on Mars, intending to make a quick stay in which they make a grab of the data that the first team of astronauts has gathered painstakingly over a year and a half and then bolt away in their fast ship to beat them back to Earth, Benford's novel begins to take an intriguing departure from the Zubrin recipe. The disturbing possibilities of Martian exploration beholden to prize money and economically driven competition—already suggested by the commercialization of Axelrod's consortium—are now fully exposed. The tension between the two teams of astronauts, already high when it becomes clear that the newcomers have no plans to do any new scientific research but simply intend to steal the work that already has been done, is exacerbated when the Westerners' Earth-return vehicle turns out to be damaged beyond repair. Lacking the means now to win the race, the Western astronauts also may be condemned to death, since the only available vehicle for the flight back belongs to the Chinese consortium, and it was built to accommodate only three astronauts. Reluctantly, they will squeeze in one extra from Axelrod's group—but only at the price of the surrender of the most important biological discoveries they have made.

What Benford does with the old truism of discovering life on Mars is a surprise. While it at first seems a facile gesture to traditional Martian romances, the plot turn in which Julia Barth, an Australian biologist, finds living, bioluminescent, anaerobic organisms in warm, moist caverns beneath the surface gives Benford an opportunity to use biology as a way of critiquing capitalist economics and the ethics of individualism. The anaerobes grow in large, light-sensitive mats resembling clumps of wet algae—and the mats are mobile and capable of shifting their shapes. Two of the astronauts from the second expedition die on their descent into the caves, smothered by the "Marsmats" whose biological behavior they do not understand, after the Australian refuses to turn over her biological samples in return for a seat on the ship home. As Julia continues to analyze the specimens, she becomes convinced that they represent "life unlike any analogy with Earthly biology" (311). A Marsmat, she concludes, "is not a single organism at all. It's a cooperative community of different kinds of single-celled organisms" (326). Just as the Martian anaerobes work together to ensure their survival, she realizes, so too must the remaining five astronauts disentangle themselves from the competing consortia in order to survive. Instead of continuing the race against each other, they must collaborate; that is, they need to adopt a Martian spirit, an alternative ethos to the social-Darwinist application of the principle of the survival of the fittest. They are still stuck with a space vehicle that can take only three—or, with increased risk—four astronauts back to Earth. Julia volunteers to stay on Mars and continue her scientific research until she can be rescued a couple of years later. Once she makes that decision, her identity dramatically shifts. "I suddenly felt like a resident in a frontier settlement, not an astronaut on a space junket" (325–26). The move is sudden but it is also subtle and powerful; it is the difference between exploring Mars and experiencing Mars.

Julia's Russian husband (they are the only couple on either team of astronauts) chooses to stay with her. The decision enrages the two terrestrial consortia, because now the return will be made by a composite group of three astronauts from two different teams and no one consortium will be entitled to all the prize money. The defiance of the astronauts and the Martian ethic that is entailed in their decision to cooperate for their own survival is crystallized in their rechristening of the Earth-return vehicle. It had been called by its manufacturers *The Valkyrie*, with all its associations with battle and apocalypse; they rename it *The Spirit of Ares*. Julia Barth's final sentence in the novel, italicized, is a greeting utterly unlike the scripted words spoken for the television cameras when the astronauts first arrived on Mars. "*Hello, Mars. From a member of the Martian race*" (337). The clever variation on the original connotation of the novel's title connects Benford's narrative to one of the prominent motifs of recent Martian fiction (to be explored fully in the next chapter): the process by which terrestrial human beings become Martian.

The plotting of Geoffrey Landis' *Mars Crossing*, published at the turn of the new century, itself enforces a focus on "being there," on experiencing Mars.[21] The six astronauts on an international third expedition to Mars spend the early chapters detailing their arrival on the planet in exclamatory mode, each of them providing variations on "I can't believe I'm really here" as they romp in the sand and dust. Bu the novel quickly takes a more serious turn on the expedition's second day on the planet, when a Thai crew member is killed by a burst fuel tank on the mission's return spacecraft. With the vehicle beyond repair, the remaining five astronauts embark on a four-thousand-mile journey to the north pole to reach an ice-bound Brazilian return vehicle left behind years earlier by the failed first expedition. The journey north is shadowed by the sobering reality that the small ship they seek can accommodate only two passengers. This plot turn, dictating a trek from the southern hemisphere to the extreme north, including a descent into Valles Marineris, calls up time-worn storytelling dilemmas about who will be saved and who might plot against whom for a seat on the escape vessel, but above all it is an excuse for a narrative of the extended experience of being on Mars. *Mars Crossing* is in essence a travelogue—"constantly new vistas, every mile a new planet, fresh and exciting" (92)—punctuated by the backstories of each of the astronauts' earlier experiences on Earth.

If Landis were a stronger novelist, this narrative strategy might have worked with some effectiveness. While those backstories add texture to the narrative on Mars, the characters are not psychologically interesting enough to warrant such expansive attention. What really ignites Landis's passions as a writer is his designer's approach to imagining space stations, Mars-walking suits, rovers and rockhoppers, and airplanes that would work in the Martian atmosphere. There is vigor and solidity in Landis' catalogue of space-station garbage that highlights the comparative lifelessness of his portraits of the astronauts:

> Garbage accumulates. Food containers and byproducts, used and re-used pieces of paper, human waste, broken equipment, worn-out underwear, used chemicals, filled barf-bags, shaving bags, and vacuum-cleaner bags, sanitary napkins, used-up sponges, biological sample containers, dead petri dish cultures, used personal hygiene supplies, wastewater too contaminated to recycle—garbage accumulates. With every docking of a logistics transfer vehicle, more material is brought up to the space station, and all of it, eventually, becomes garbage. (149–50)

Even though the human dimension of *Mars Crossing* does not match up to the technical know-how, the frequent and lovingly particularized descriptions of how space-age technologies work do give some concrete sense of what living on Mars might entail.

Most valuably, *Mars Crossing* demonstrates some of the ways in which recent novelists have tried to recombine romance and science in constructing Martian narratives. The young astronaut Brandon Weber is influenced in his training program on Earth by a biologist who is convinced that fossils, and possibly even some surviving organic forms, will be found on Mars, despite the pessimism of most other scientists: "I guess I'm just a heretic, an old-fashioned Percival Lowell who just refuses to see the evidence" (77). And, not surprisingly, Landis does allow Brandon to discover a small fossil in Valles Marineris and, at the moment of his death, a huge trove of tentacular fossils "of every size from tiny ones to one three feet long. There were other fossils, too, smaller ones in different shapes, a bewildering variety" (275). This throwback to an old motif in Martian fiction of discovering life or its remains is accompanied by a scene that often appears in newer Martian narratives: a scene in which the fiction intersects with history. In this case, that scene occurs when one of the three surviving astronauts on the journey north crosses through Ares Vallis and feels that the landscape looks oddly familiar:

> Suddenly it all came back to him in vivid detail: the Twin Peaks, the oddly named rocks: Yogi, Flat-top, Barnacle Bill, Moe. As a kid, he'd spent whole days downloading the pictures of this place from the Internet; it was when he'd first become interested in Mars. More than anything else, this place was the whole reason he was here. It was the landscape of his dreams. (287)

The site of the *Pathfinder* mission from 1997, whose camera transmissions enabled it to be the first of the actual Mars missions to gain an immediate world-wide audience, prompts Landis' imaginary explorers to see themselves as "walking on history" (287).[22] Almost certainly, the astronaut Ryan Martin's recollection of his long-standing desire to experience Mars stands in for the author's ambitions as a writer: "Mars was his obsession. He thought about Mars, made calculations, read every book, science or science fiction, that had ever been written about Mars, published papers suggesting possible solutions to the finicky engineering details of a Mars mission" (305–6). With varying talents and conceptual frameworks, writers enact their obsessions with Mars, but a mix of scientific and literary research and the ability to imagine the experience of being on Mars came to be prerequisites for Martian fiction as the twentieth century drew to a close.

As a footnote to this body of Martian fictions of the 1990s, Robert Zubrin's 2001 novel *First Landing* is worth some brief attention. Not a novelist by vocation, Zubrin takes the "Mars Direct" proposals that he had been developing in various fora and media throughout the previous decade and decks them out in a fantasy about the first five-person expedition to Mars, plagued by sabotage at Mission Control in Houston and by internal rancor within the crew. Not unexpectedly, *First Landing* adopts the lecturing tone of the true believer, and Zubrin isn't loath to self-praise, having one of his characters invoke his 1996 *The Case for Mars* as one of the "classics" of Martiana.[23] And because Zubrin so often has claimed the search for life as one of the central rationales for exploring Mars, his novel dutifully supplies both fossilized organisms and still-extant "pre-cellular" life forms, with DNA, proteins, amino acids, and sugars in "a simpler and less efficient arrangement than we see in terrestrial life, but much more robust against radiation damage during long periods of dormancy" (75). When an abundance of these primitive life forms is observed at the bottom of Valles Marineris, the find prompts a Zubrinesque I-told-you-so outburst: "There's more life here than we thought. *There is much here that is left to discover*" (189).

The central figure in *First Landing* is the expedition's historian, Kevin McGee, derided as "the Professor" by the rest of the crew and early on perceived as useless to a scientific mission. But McGee clearly is useful to Zubrin as a surrogate for the author. When the spacecraft *Beagle* is approaching Mars, McGee begins to reflect on his task of recording the landing with the requisite eloquence. "The pen of an epic poet like Homer or Milton, or a great historian like Herodotus or Thucydides, should be here to record the experience for future generations" (21). But McGee (and Zubrin), unable to find suitably Miltonic or Thucydidean language, resort to an alternative literary history to capture the moment. Evoking Burroughs and the end of the canal myths in the 1960s, McGee intones, "Ah, Barsoom, you were destroyed by the Mariner probes, which banished you into mere fiction. But now we are here to make amends. Once again, there are people on Mars, and before long there will be cities" (24).

Zubrin brings to the writing of fiction the same passionate commitment of his manifestoes about Mars Direct, and the result, perhaps inevitably, is a propaganda novel. Throughout *First Landing*, the fiction works largely as window-dressing for Zubrin's favored positions. When McGee, insisting on his status as professional historian, asserts that "we came here to conquer a frontier" (222), he is echoing the essays that Zubrin had published applying Frederick Jackson Turner's 1893 American frontier thesis to the challenge of Martian exploration.[24] A terraforming debate also underpins the rationale for this account of the journey to Mars. Zubrin pits an "ecogoth" who believes that "all human actions that affect the environment are intrinsically harmful" against a terraforming enthusiast who sees the alteration of Mars into a new Earth as "the most ethical thing humanity could possibly do" (56). Zubrin had made the latter argument himself in *The Case for Mars* when he foresaw the creation of a humanly viable Martian biosphere as "the most profound vindication of the divine nature of the human spirit, exercised in its highest form to bring a dead world to life" (*Case for Mars*, 249). *First Landing*, more transparently than any other end-of-century Martian fiction, keeps its author's agenda in full view. If it lacks the novelistic graces of the major works of fiction that celebrate being on Mars, in its bluntness, Zubrin's polemical fiction outlines the terms of the great debate over whether Mars should be left in its untransformed "red" state or should be turned "green" by human intervention. That controversy, approached with critical detachment and tact, generated several major literary texts in the last quarter of the twentieth century, including the masterworks on the subject of terraforming Mars by Kim Stanley Robinson.

Becoming Martian

By the early 1990s, terraforming was no longer a novelty in the literature of Mars. As scientists and scientific popularizers gave increasingly visible practical attention to the challenges of mounting a twenty-first-century expedition to Mars and of establishing a settlement on the planet, the techniques by which Mars might be metamorphosed into a more temperate locale with a breathable atmosphere and liquid surface water became part of the public discussion. Robert Zubrin and Christopher McKay, both associated with the "Mars Direct" proposal to establish a human base on Mars in the twenty-first century, couched the project of remaking Mars as a human habitat in the anxieties of overpopulation and the risks of a mass extinction on Earth. "The task facing our generation—that of exploring Mars and learning enough about the planet and the methods of utilizing its resources to begin to transform it into a habitable planet—could not be more urgent or more noble."[1] Zubrin, the most passionate of polemicists on the subject of Mars exploration and terraformation, argued elsewhere that a "land grab" of the planet and the creation of a humanly viable Martian biosphere would be "the most profound vindication of the divine nature of the human spirit, exercised in its highest form to bring a dead world to life." In Zubrin's view, *not* to attempt the transformation of Mars would be a confession of human failure, of the absence of the will to dominate our surroundings. He asked tendentiously, "Are we first-class citizens of the cosmos, or are we beings of lesser order?"[2]

Interestingly, the concept, the justification, and the outcome of terraforming projects have been scrutinized more closely and warily in much of the late twentieth-century fiction about Mars than in the pronouncements of the Mars Direct advocates. The linking of issues of human survival with spiritual cheerleading in Zubrin's writings closes down debate on the subject of terraforming at precisely the points where fiction has sought to complicate the practical, aesthetic, ethical, political, and spiritual consequences of an effort to remake another world in the image of Earth. Declining the binary reductiveness of the are-we-men-or-mice questioning that Zubrin enjoys, the shrewdest novelists have tended to look at terraforming Mars as something more than a technical challenge. Even more tellingly, fiction writers have wanted to ask not only how we might change Mars but how Mars, and the experience of living on it, might change us.

"Exploring Fossil Canyon" and "Green Mars"—the stories from the early 1980s that serve as overtures to Kim Stanley Robinson's 1990s sequence, Red Mars, Green Mars, and Blue Mars—had introduced a key concept in late twentieth-century fiction about Mars, a concept that both parallels and modifies the concept of terraformation. The visions at the end of both of those stories of Roger Clayborne remade as a new Martian epitomize the concept that Robinson will name "areoformation" in the later novels. While terraformers work to alter Mars into a replica of Terra, modifying its climate, atmospheric pressure and composition, and topographical features to make it a tolerable habitat for Homo sapiens, areoformation is the process of altering the human species to accept Martian conditions. Becoming Martian, becoming a subspecies that can be appropriately designated Homo martial, conceivably could be accomplished artificially by re-engineering the human body, but it also may involve an inevitable psychological adjustment as ideological fixities soften in response to life on a new world. In this chapter, we will see some examples of the ways in which novelists have begun to explore how human beings might be shaped for life on Mars and might be shaped by living on Mars. Above all, we will see how Robinson, the most accomplished of the new Martian novelists, has turned the relationship between terraforming and areoforming, between the urge for a green Mars and the commitment to a red Mars, between utopian progress and arcadian preservation into the central dramatic and spiritual tension underlying his masterpiece, the sequence of three Mars novels that began appearing in 1993. By juxtaposing terraforming experiments with the reshaping of humanity to Martian standards, writers have made the human settlement of Mars a philosophical rather than a merely technological problem. What would it mean to become Martian? Some of the most provocative Martian fiction of the later twentieth century raises fundamental questions about nature and human nature, about the obligations of science, about the uses of the past in the shaping of the future, and about anthropocentric fixations on human survival.

Although he never uses the term "areoformation," Frederik Pohl anticipates that concept in the 1976 Man Plus as he makes an extended foray into the subject of the remaking of humanity to fit the conditions of Mars. The remaking here is literal and physical. The prototypes of Martian settlers undergo complex, multiple surgeries to turn them into mechanical beings, more metal, glass, and plastic than flesh, able to negotiate the extremes of temperature and the absence of a breathable atmosphere. The astronauts become monstrosities with red crystalline eyes, copper nails, bat wings, synthetic skin, filtering systems in place of lungs, and blank crotches. The scientific team that performs these alterations aims to create on the operating table an artificial Martian. As the narrator says of one man who undergoes this metamorphosis, "In the sense that form follows function, Martian he was. He was shaped for Mars."[3] Later writers would make much more of the idea of shaping human beings into Martians—emphasizing the psychological adaptations more than the physical ones on which Pohl concentrates—but *Man Plus*, as its suggestive title promises, goes against the grain of imagining Mars as a world to be renovated for *Homo sapiens*.

In its move away from terraformation and its tentative adoption of the principle of areoformation, Pohl's novel is worth extended attention. In many other respects, it is a conventional novel of its period, with its Cold War context, its NASA-era unglamorous picture of the routines of space travel, its crass American president interested in Mars as "the only piece of real estate around that's worth having" (16), and its cheap trick of revealing only at the end that the first-person-plural narrator is a computer network attempting to preserve itself by saving humanity from nuclear self-destruction and establishing its colony of cyborgs on Mars. *Man Plus* also is burdened with the cliché of the Jesuit scientist trying to reconcile his religious and scientific impulses (a figure to be found earlier in Arthur Clarke's "The Star" [1955] and James Blish's *A Case of Conscience* [1958]). It is the Jesuit who also enacts the obligatory discovery of a surviving life-form on Mars (in this case a crystalline plant with a root system and ultraviolet protection) and who is the spokesperson for the litany of references to earlier Martian fiction and speculation that has been a staple of the literary history of Mars at least since Elwin Ransom in C. S. Lewis' *Out of the Silent Planet*. For Father Kayman, the works of Lowell and Burroughs are the imaginative baggage he carries with him to Mars:

He knew all about Mars. He always had.

As a child he had grown up on the Edgar Rice Burroughs Mars, the colorful Barsoom of the ocher dead sea bottoms and hurtling tiny moons. As he grew older he distinguished fact from fiction. There was no reality in the four-armed green warriors and the red-skinned, egg-laying, beautiful Martian princesses, to the extent that science was in touch with "reality." But he knew that scientists' estimates of "reality" changed from year to year.

Burroughs had not invented Barsoom out of airy imaginings. He had taken it almost verbatim from the most authoritative scientific "reality" of his day. It was Percival Lowell's Mars, not Burroughs's, that was finally denied by bigger telescopes and by space probes. In the "reality" of scientific opinion, life on Mars had been born and died a dozen times. (211)

Despite both the conventionality of the references and the considerable overstatement in the claim that Burroughs' invented Barsoom came "almost verbatim" from Lowell, Pohl's Jesuit explorer does articulate the importance to late twentieth-century writers of getting their Martian fictions "in touch with" the state of the scientific question. But Pohl's most significant achievement may have been to anticipate the state of the *fictional* question on the sufficiency of terraforming as the central imaginative conception for the colonization of Mars. *Man Plus* was reprinted—as much ephemeral science fiction never is—in 1994, at the height of a new interest among writers in areoformation, when the originality of Pohl's premise could be appreciated more fully than it had been in 1976.

A much stronger narrative about areoformed human beings, and one that explicitly acknowledges the influence of *Man Plus*, is the undervalued *Climbing Olympus* by Kevin J. Anderson.[4] Anderson has been most visible as a frequent "novelizer" of the *Star Wars* films, and that line of work for hire may have deflected serious attention from *Climbing Olympus*. But the subject of Mars stoked Anderson's creativity, and in this book he also drew on his long-standing interest in Russian history. The cultural context of *Climbing Olympus*, published in 1994, is the collapse of the Soviet Union and the revolt in Chechnya against the Russian rulers. In Anderson's imagined aftermath of the breakup, the newly independent "Sovereign Republics," composed of many of the former subsidiary states in the old U.S.S.R., experience a resurgence both of nationalism and of intolerance for their ethnic minorities. The exploration of Mars in the twenty-first century offers the disaffected, the persecuted, the undesirable, and the impoverished in the Sovereign Republics a symbol of hope and a possible escape route. Despite its inimical physical environment, Mars is a locale without ethnic pasts and it holds out the promise of a fresh start. So understood, Mars is not merely a colony or an extension of Empire (although the terrestrial governments and organizations that fund the exploration certainly view Mars through imperialist lenses); it is a place without a history and thus a site for utopian beginnings.

The conception of a Martian utopia is made explicit by Dr. Pchanskii, a surgically altered human being from Uzbekistan known as a *dva*—"an English bastardization of the Russian word for 'two' " (4)—since the *dvas* are the second generation of artificially augmented men and women dispatched to Mars with enough "man plus" adaptations to carry out the early stages of the terraforming process relatively unencumbered. The first generation of enhanced humans—known as *adins*—are much more grotesquely deformed by their adaptive surgeries than the *dvas*. The *adins* were drawn largely from life-prisoners in Siberian camps for whom Mars was (barely) preferable to the brutal Earthly environment where they were condemned to work until they died. But the *dvas* were mostly volunteers from the intelligentsia—research scientists and doctors—who went willingly to Mars for the purposes both of scientific and of political experimentation. Pchanskii's group of *dvas* vanished not long after they arrived to join the terraforming work and were presumed dead in an avalanche, but in fact they had established a secret and experimental utopian community in tunnels and caves in the Noctis Labyrinthus region. As Pchanskii explains when the lost group of *dvas* is discovered:

> You see, no place on Earth is actually safe. Every square meter of the planet could be construed as having belonged to someone else at some time in the past. The Native Americans could demand the United States back, the Saxons could demand England back from the Normans. Siberia goes back to the Mongols. Kiev goes back to the Varangian Vikings. . . . But not on Mars! Here, there is no such precedent. No such precedent. We would be the first. The cornerstone, the foundation of a new society. (209)

Mars has had a fruitful affiliation with utopia in literary history—one that had lapsed by the 1950s but was being revived by Frederick Turner in the 1980s. What is distinctive in Anderson's narrative design is what was already being carried out on a far grander scale and with exquisite political nuance in the utopian Mars novels published by Robinson between 1993 and 1996: the interweaving of terraformed landscape and areoformed human beings to produce a debate on the philosophical standing of the planet itself and the ethical and ecological questions raised by its human occupation. In that respect, while the utopian project of the *dvas* is an interesting feature of *Climbing Olympus*, it is the first generation of modified humans, the *adins*, that engage Anderson's imagination most fully. Above all, the figure of Boris Tiban—a career criminal on Earth, a murderous rebel on Mars, and an obsessed and crazed partisan of a "red" and unterraformed Mars—dominates the book. Because the *adins* underwent more extensive surgical adaptations than the later *dvas*, they looked more ghastly and less human than the *dvas*, but they also were better able to endure and even thrive in the harsh Martian environment without special equipment. "The *adins* had been the first true Martians, feeling the soil with their bare feet, breathing the razor-thin air directly into their enhanced lungs" (85). The physiological and psychological price the *adins* paid for their adaptability to Mars, however, is nearly unbearable: their hunchbacked appearance from the two auxiliary lungs built under their shoulder blades, the lizard-like hood protecting their deep-set eyes, the plasticized skin that deprives them of most of their sense of touch. As Boris complains to Cora Marisovna, the *adin* woman who is his mate, "I can barely feel you against me. . . . I'm like a man in a rubber monster suit from one of those ridiculous American films about Martians" (80).

"Monster" is the key word here. Rachel Dycek, the scientist who designed both the *adins* and the *dvas*, is pilloried as the "Frankenstein Doctor" by the prosecutor at her trial after the secret project of the creation of the *adins* is exposed (26). Anderson repeatedly evokes Mary Shelley's novel throughout *Climbing Olympus*. When Rachel confronts Boris at the top of Pavonis Mons, we can recall Victor Frankenstein meeting his creature on Mont Blanc; Anderson even has Rachel paraphrase Milton, just as Shelley uses *Paradise Lost* to suggest the Satanic heroism of Frankenstein's creature.[5] Like Frankenstein's artificial man, Rachel's is astoundingly strong and consumed with the desire for revenge against his maker and everyone associated with her. When Boris leaps on top of Rachel's Martian rover, there is a particularly striking redaction of *Frankenstein*: "Then a face and shoulders appeared from above like a gunshot in the stillness, hands thrusting down from the roof of the rover, brushing the dust aside. The upside-down face pressed against the glass, peering inside at them and grinning" (200). The motif of the grinning monster at a window occurs four times in Shelley's novel—a powerful emblem of the creature's status as both alienated outsider and confident superior. And Anderson ends his narrative with Boris ascending Olympus Mons (296). The highest place on Mars functions as the equivalent of the North Pole at the end of *Frankenstein*: the most remote, cold, extreme, inaccessible, inhuman place on the planet. Boris, like Shelley's creature, is given the last words of the novel as he journeys onward seeking his own extinction—and in this case the last words are also a condemnation of terraforming:

> The humans would continue terraforming Mars. He could never stop that. The red planet would stir with spreading signs of life, while at the same time, for him it would be dying. In a few centuries Mars would be a green world, warm and wet and bursting with new species.
>
> Boris Tiban had no desire to live to see that day. He would reign here by himself on Mars. He would always be the king of the mountain.

For a long time, he surveyed his planet from the height, then he turned, gripped his bent staff, and climbed higher. (296–97)

In modeling the key figure who critiques the terraforming process on Mary Shelley's complex artificial human being—both a murderer and an outcast of considerable sympathy, both a monster and a man plus—Anderson ensures that Boris cannot be dismissed simply as a fiend and madman. The controversy over a red versus a green Mars is left unresolved.

Climbing Olympus makes some advances over its parent text, *Man Plus*, with its richer psychological exploration of the effects of the physical areoformation of human bodies and with its nascent, if inchoate, utopian politics. For the deepest and fullest inquiry into the interplay between human development and extraplanetary habitation, as well as one of the great American imaginings of the building of utopia, the work of Kim Stanley Robinson is indispensable. The nearly seventeen hundred pages of *Red Mars*, *Green Mars*, and *Blue Mars*—which Robinson conceived as a single triple-decker novel although it was marketed as a trilogy—represent, in both scale and depth, the most ambitious effort to imagine Mars in fiction to date. Although Robinson's Mars novels often are described loosely as the best fiction about the terraforming of another world, what they are "about," actually, is a persistent dialectical exploration of the creative and destructive tensions between terraformation and areoformation. Within that dialectical framework, Robinson generates ongoing arguments about civilization and wilderness, colonialism and self-rule, independence and interdependence, ideological principle and pragmatic calculation. The novels chart the evolution of a society—tentative and risky, frequently painful, without historical parallel—into "*something new and strange, something Martian.*"[6]

One indicator of the amplitude of Robinson's design is the sheer number of characters readers must track—literally a cast of hundreds. The settling of Mars begun in 2027 by "the First Hundred" (in actuality the first 101, including a stowaway) is carried forward into the early twenty-third century, and while most of the First Hundred die during the course of the narrative, some—thanks to longevity treatments that allow gene repair and the prolongation of life—are still central to the events unfolding at the end of *Blue Mars*. And the constant influx of immigrants over the course of two centuries as well as the births of new generations descended from the original settlers mean that the key figures in the novel remain a large critical mass.

All of the first settlers (except for Desmond, the Trinidadian stowaway who goes by the name "Coyote") were scientists, chosen after training in Antarctica for their perceived psychological stability under stress and with the expectation that they would be apolitical. Neither assumption turns out to be very accurate. Each of the original crew members, as the psychologist Michel Duval grasps very early on, has some element of craziness and alienation (skillfully disguised during the Antarctic test period) or they wouldn't be willing to leave Earth forever. The scientists (engineers, biologists, geologists, medical specialists principally) were selected so that there was an even proportion of thirty-five Russians and thirty-five Americans, reflecting the dominant pools of technical expertise and experienced astronauts as well as the major financial backers of the Mars mission; the remainder represent an international cross-section to buttress the image of a venture operating under United Nations authority. While some of the First Hundred try to cling to the belief that their mission is strictly scientific and therefore sequestered from politics, even during the flight to Mars it becomes clear that commercial interests on Earth are dictating the mission, to which a few of the Americans—alone among the international crew—are deferential. One of the Russians, the anarchist Arkady Bogdanov (whose name is Robinson's homage to Alexander Bogdanov, the author of the 1908 Martian utopian novel *Red Star*), becomes the spiritual battery of a movement for declaring independence from the plans of Mission Control and making the Martian settlement their own—in everything from the design of their habitats to the governance of their community. Arkady's tirades annoy the more conservative of the First Hundred and polarize discussions, but they have the effect of defining the uniqueness of the opportunity of settling Mars and of introducing some of the most important and thorny issues that Robinson's novels will explore. When some of his opponents ridicule Arkady's defiance of regulations as nothing more than crisis-mongering and revolutionary sentimentality, he replies:

"We have come to Mars for good. We are going to make not only our homes and our food, but also our water and the very air we breathe—all on a planet that has none of these things. We can do this because we have technology to manipulate matter right down to the molecular level. This is an extraordinary ability, think of it! And yet some of us here can accept transforming the entire physical reality of this planet, without doing a single thing to change ourselves or the way we live. To be twenty-first century scientists on Mars, in fact, but at the same time living within nineteenth-century social systems, based on seventeenth-century ideologies. It's absurd, it's crazy, it's—it's—" he seized his head in his hands, tugged at his hair, roared "It's *unscientific!* And so I say that among all the many things we transform on Mars, ourselves and our social reality should be among them. We must terraform not only Mars, but ourselves." (RM 81)

The moody and passionate Maya Toitovna, co-commander of the expedition, says of the relationship of the emerging Martian society to its parent planet: "We exist for Earth as a model or experiment. A thought experiment for humanity to learn from" (GM, 323). Here and elsewhere, Robinson picks up a venerable motif in Martian fiction: the notion of Mars as a reflector of terrestrial concerns. Much later, the charismatic third-generation Martian, Nirgal, uses it explicitly: "Mars is a mirror . . . in which Terra sees its own essence" (BM, 141). But Robinson pushes the figure of Mars as model and mirror in a new direction. His reflective Mars is neither a recapitulation of Earth's past nor, solely, a simulacrum of the present; it is designed to be a harbinger of things to come. The distinctive mirroring effects of the *Mars* novels can be grasped most clearly by comparison with Robert Zubrin's vision of the Martian frontier.

Zubrin's notions of Mars as a necessary—and thoroughly American—new frontier and as a refuge from terrestrial problems are inimical to Robinson's imagination. The *Mars* novels persistently repudiate the concept of the fourth planet as a "bolt-hole" for the desperate inhabitants of the third. At the same time, Robinson's thought experiment resists crude analogical thinking about Mars and Earth based on the cliché of a new frontier. "Mars is to the new age of exploration what North America was to the last," Zubrin insists, and he refurbishes Frederick Jackson Turner's famous 1893 paper that argued for the frontier mentality as essential to the American character and relocates that frontier to Mars: "The creation of a new frontier thus presents itself as America's and humanity's greatest social need. Nothing is more important."[7] As Robinson's characters become more and more Martian in culture and conceptual thinking and, to some degree, in physiology, they assert the inadequacy of analogies drawn from terrestrial history. During the disastrous first revolution that is the climax of *Red Mars*, Frank Chalmers loses patience with one of the hot-headed rioters who try to defy the United Nations police force on Mars without a rational plan. "You and all your friends are trying to live out a fantasy rebellion, some kind of sci-fi 1776, frontiersmen throwing off the yoke of tyranny, but it isn't like that here! The analogies are all wrong." When his interlocutor insists that the analogy is correct and that the rebels will produce their own Washington and Paine and Lincoln, Frank's reproach is that "historical analogy is the last refuge of people who can't grasp the current situation" (RM, 422).

This kind of claim and counter-claim is ingrained in the rhythm of the *Mars* novels. In Robinson's ongoing dialectic, the two most crucial members of the

101 founding settlers are the allegorically named Saxifrage Russell and Ann Clayborne: the rock breaker and the daughter of the land. Sax, a plant geneticist and the inventive moving force behind the major terraformation projects on Mars, and Ann, a geologist who becomes the iconic leader of those who want to preserve Mars in as "red" and undeveloped a condition as possible, are among only a small handful of the First Hundred characters still alive at the end of Blue Mars. The running argument between Sax and Ann, to which all three volumes continually return, is essential to Robinson's design and it is therefore important that they both survive the entire narrative; only when their argument is resolved can the Mars novels reach provisional closure. Near the end of Blue Mars, Sax makes a telling observation. "All his reflections on what happened to Mars, he thought, were framed as an internal conversation with Ann" (BM, 545). Here, Robinson indirectly states one of his own aesthetic principles—the narrative and didactic organizational strategy for Red Mars, Green Mars, and Blue Mars is an internal conversation between red and green ways of thinking, into which the attentive reader inevitably is drawn.[8]

Over the course of the three volumes, Sax goes through a series of metamorphoses—physical, psychological, political, intellectual, spiritual—that we come to understand as his gradual areoformation, his evolution into a new being. Cosmetic surgery allows him to work undercover in the aftermath of the failed first revolution when the First Hundred are on Earth's Most Wanted list. But when Sax is unmasked and tortured, he suffers brain trauma that impairs his memory and speech. As he slowly recovers, he turns increasingly political, even sabotaging some of the large terraforming devices that had begun to raise the average temperature on Mars. Relearning language, Sax also starts to relearn how to see the planet and to gauge the risks and losses that have been incurred by its fast-paced greening. The character whom Martian children, tellingly, used to call "Dr. Robot" (GM, 5) grows in imagination and in emotional vulnerability. By the last volume, now looking at Mars through Ann's eyes and more and more urgently seeking her out despite repeated rejections, Sax has significantly moderated his approach to and his work on behalf of terraformation. His trajectory through the three volumes illustrates the most vivid and poignant instance of the areoformation of a new Martian.

Ann's change happens in a very different way. Her espousal of the planet itself—the rock, the sand, the cold, the stillness of red Mars—leaves her distrustful of talk about areoforming. ("That's just a word. We took this planet and plowed it under" [BM, 204]). Unlike the phlegmatic Sax, Ann is blunt, outspoken, and rude in nearly all her exchanges with others. Often, when she is communicating by wrist-phone with someone (including her own son Peter), she will end the conversation without warning and "cut the connection." That repeated act of impatient contempt points to Ann's persistent cutting of human connections in her life, her sense of spiritual isolation, even her periods of suicidal longing. For most of the duration of the three books, Ann is an absolutist who believes that "red" versus "green" ideologies can never really be reconciled; they are two utterly opposed visions. The mere blending of red and green, as Sax and Maya figure out during a long discussion of color, would be reductive, producing some indeterminate shade of brown that swallowed up both the red and the green. In political terms, to try to synthesize red and green visions would lead only to false, temporary, and dangerous compromises—a "spiraling down," as Maya describes it, into chaos and war (BM, 524). Instead, Robinson seeks not to erase the dialectic of red and green but to transcend it with a third term: "blue." The emergence of the new paradigm of a blue Mars is the breakthrough for Ann, who through nearly all of her two centuries on the changing planet had lived in splendid but self-punishing denial, preferring "the Mars in her mind, red Mars" (BM, 603). That mental enclosure left Ann almost completely isolated from her peers and friends among the First Hundred—and it drove her into a deep depression most often manifested in unrelenting anger, directed even and especially toward those she loves. When she first observed the creation in the northern hemisphere of the great planet-girdling ocean freed by the terraformers from vast subterranean reservoirs, Ann dreamed of others among the First Hundred each itemizing the "net gains" as Mars became wetter and greener. Her dream closes with all the others turning their eyes on Ann: "And she stood up, quivering with rage and fear, understanding that she alone among them did not believe in the possibility of the net gain of anything at all, that she was some kind of crazy reactionary; and all she could do was point a shaking finger at them and say, 'Mars, Mars, Mars' " (GM, 116).

Only late in life does what she names a "Counter-Ann" start to emerge: "A kind of opposite. My shadow, or the shadow of my shadow. Seeded, and growing inside me" (BM, 555). The seed is planted by Sax, who arranged for her to visit Miranda, one of the moons of Uranus, where the "red" ideals have been put totally in place, preserving an unspoiled and nonhuman world. Later, Sax visits her unexpectedly at Olympus Mons and hikes with her into the giant caldera, the landscape that most fully embodies Ann's red Mars. The crucial breakthrough occurs when Sax tells her that he is going to sail around Chryse Gulf—the rugged southern inlet of the Northern Ocean whose flooding had triggered her anger and her nightmare in Green Mars. But now Ann asks if she can join him on this sailing trip. More than a sightseeing jaunt, it is a dangerous, a life-threatening journey that brings Sax and Ann into intimate contact with the planet—and with each other. It is Ann who takes the initiative in defining the new Mars that she is seeing with open eyes for the first time. "Many times they came back to what it might mean to be brown. 'Perhaps the combination should be called blue,' Ann said one evening, looking over the side at the water. 'Brown isn't very attractive, and it reeks of compromise. Maybe we should be thinking of something entirely new' " (BM, 584).

The blue Mars that Ann experiences on this journey with Sax finally dislodges the red Mars that had monopolized her mind—and fully reconciles her with Sax. While she never abandons the beauty of that Mars of her imagining (and while Sax finally has come to appreciate the beauty of the pristine red Mars that has been diminished by the terraforming), in the final episodes of *Blue Mars*, Ann is herself areoformed by Mars as it has come to be. A "fully Martian Ann at last" emerges. "On a brown Mars of some new kind, red, green, blue, all swirled together" (BM, 604). The last paragraph of the last volume is given entirely to Ann's interior monologue on the new Mars—a world at peace, a world with a rich utopian social promise, and a world that is undeniably beautiful. The ultimate setting—a classic one for many science-fiction narratives that explore beginnings and endings—is on a beach, and this beach is on the huge northern sea, the sight of which had once reduced Ann to helpless fury. The final sentence—ending with a perfect iambic pentameter—echoes and recasts the angry staccato voice of Ann's nightmare in *Green Mars*. She is alive and *there* on this brave new world: "Waves broke in swift lines on the beach, and she walked over the sand toward her friends, in the wind, on Mars, on Mars, on Mars, on Mars, on Mars" (BM, 609).

The struggle between Ann and Sax, their effort to reach a state of blueness that transcends exclusively red and green perspectives, limns in miniature the larger social movement towards a Martian utopia. Robinson's distinctive way of imagining the building of a utopian society is signaled by one of the early Bedouin settlers on Mars who speaks of "the hadj to utopia"(RM, 380). An ongoing pilgrimage, a process rather than a destination, a provisional not an ultimate achievement, more a demeanor and a state of being than a social recipe or a fixed system, utopia on Mars is as delicate and as contentious a political ideal as the ecological ideal sought by the competing Reds and Greens.[9] There are nearly as many utopian models in the *Mars* novels as there are characters, and Robinson makes it clear that "utopia" is a personal as well as a political ideal. The shape of his Martian utopia will arise out of sometimes complementary and sometimes competing visions. We get a very broad spectrum of such ideals, from Arkady's anti-authoritarian anarchism at one end to the dystopian, big-business police state of Phyllis Boyle at the other. The radical Reds and the moderate Reds have differing perceptions of how much terraforming should occur and how visible a human footprint should be planted in the Mars of their desires. The Green terraformers who style themselves as "Saxaclones" are focused on the technical processes of reshaping the landscape of their ideal planet, whereas Hiroko Ai's more mystical Greens emphasize what she calls the "areophany"—a spiritual communion between the planet and its inhabitants. Michel Duval's nostalgic utopia would emerge from "reconciling the centrifugal antinomy of Provence and Mars" (GM, 212), while Nirgal, a native-born Martian who is the biracial child of Hiroko and Desmond the "Coyote," charts the route to utopia through ecopoetic farming. Chinese immigrants to Mars want to live in ethnically identified towns and settlements, but the nomadic Bedouins aspire to be un-settlers in a Mars without borders. And so on.

Robinson dramatizes the challenges of building a utopian society out of such a variety of personal and cultural priorities in the great weeks-long conference at Dorsa Brevia in *Green Mars*. He gives this chapter the title "What Is to Be Done?"—and in doing so brings his novel into dialogue with Lenin's famous polemical pamphlet on revolutionary strategy. In the workshops of the Dorsa Brevia Congress, the difficulties of reaching consensus are always palpable. Ann argues that they must not abjure violence in setting up a free society and that a bloodless revolution against the metanational corporations on Earth then running Mars is a fantasy. Hiroko immediately resists, championing a "silk revolution. An aerogel revolution. An integral part of the areophany" (GM, 312). The Swiss want every detail about the legal code and economic system of the Martian society to be parsed out; the Bogdanovist anarchists are disgusted: "Do we *really* have to go through all this?" (GM, 318). The "Mars First" faction of the Reds wants nothing to do with Earth and advocates armed revolt and sabotage, while Maya and Nirgal argue that they must not only deal with Earth but also must try to help Earth solve its population problem. One of the most contentious workshops is the one on drafting a bill of rights. Here the parties clash repeatedly, and an extended excerpt of the debate reveals just how deeply the divisions run:

> Nadia quickly saw that this topic tapped into a huge well of cultural concerns. Many obviously considered the topic an opportunity for one culture to dominate the rest. "I've said it ever since Boone," Zeyk exclaimed. "An attempt to impose one set of values on all of us is nothing but Ataturkism. Everyone must be allowed their own way."

"But this can only be true up to a point," said Ariadne. "What if one group here asserts its right to own slaves?"

Zeyk shrugged. "That would be beyond the pale."

"So you agree there should be some basic bill of human rights?"

"This is obvious," Zeyk replied coldly.

Mikhail spoke for the Bogdanovists: "All social hierarchy is a kind of slavery," he said. "Everyone should be completely equal under the law."

"Hierarchy is a natural fact," Zeyk said. "It cannot be avoided."

"Spoken like an Arab man," Ariadne said. "But we are not natural here, we are Martian. And where hierarchy leads to oppression, it must be abolished."

"The hierarchy of the right-minded," Zedyk said.

"Or the primacy of equality and freedom."

"Enforced if necessary."

"Yes!"

"Enforced freedom, then." Zeyk waved a hand, disgusted. (GM, 317)

The debate over nature and culture, including Ariadne's assertion that to be Martian is to be unnatural, raises a question that Robinson repeatedly addresses: How possible is it to make a complete break with the past, to alter what has been taken to be immutable in human nature? If in this particular thought experiment Homo martial is, in fact, an artificial species, a mutation of Homo sapiens, all bets are off on what constitutes a "natural fact."

The Dorsa Brevia Declaration that finally emerges from the conference consists of seven points on which the participants have reached consensus:

1. The value of cultural diversity;
2. Universal rights to the material needs of life, health care, education, and legal equality;
3. No private ownership of land, air, or water which are in the stewardship of all Martians;
4. The right of individuals to keep the fruits of their labor but all labor understood as part of a communal enterprise that is directed to the common good;
5. Rejection of metanational governance as hostile to ecological principles;
6. Minimalist environmental alterations to the planet, with higher elevations (30 percent of the planet) kept in a wilderness state;
7. A spirit of reverence for the planet and an acknowledgment of the special historical role of Mars as the first site of extraterrestrial human habitation.

The generality of the principles and the absence of any statement on how the principles will be made operational disappoints most of the attendees. Coyote is dismissive: "Anyone can agree things should be fair and the world just. The way to get there is *always* the real problem" (GM, 334). But the coalition is far too fragile to get beyond principles to tactics and specifics. It is Hiroko who saves the occasion with a choreographed spectacle, "reaching directly into some paleolithic part of their minds" (GM, 337), as she arrives on the evening of the last day of the congress, naked, painted green, and staging a procession with Sufi chants, dancing, and communal bathing. The experience is "a shock to the senses, a challenge to their notion of what a political congress was, or could be" (GM, 337). The entire ritual is a reminder that, at levels other than ideological discourse and beneath language itself, there are powerful bonds that bridge differences and unite the Martians. It is what Hiroko—and Robinson—mean by the areophany.

For all its bare simplicity, the Dorsa Brevia Declaration is a step forward on the hadj to utopia. Over the course of the rest of *Green Mars* and all of *Blue Mars*, its seven principles stand as serviceable reference points for all the major decisions in the construction of an independent Mars. The Declaration is the single most utopian document in the Mars novels precisely because it looks forward to a Mars that doesn't yet exist except in the imagination, the Mars of the inhabitants' desires. Interestingly, Robinson does not choose to print the much more detailed text of the Martian Constitution in *Blue Mars*. The debates over the contents of the Constitution at a conference held in 2128 on Pavonis Mons are recorded fully and the results of the global referendum on the Constitution are also reported, but Robinson provides a text only in the miscellany that he published three years after the appearance of *Blue Mars*.[10] For the purposes of his utopian fiction, the more specific and fixed the social compact and system become the less utopian they are. It is the talk, not the text, that is the most utopian, or as Sax puts it, a conference itself can be a "little utopia enacted" (BM, 64). In the final section of *Blue Mars*, with only a small handful of the original First Hundred still alive, Ann and Sax anticipate a golden age "which will only come to pass when our generation has died"; they will have the experience of Moses glimpsing but not passing the threshold of Israel (BM, 582). They have become Martian but they have not yet completed the hadj. Utopia is still on the horizon as *Blue Mars* ends, and that is probably where it belongs. Robinson's Martian utopia fits exactly Carl Freedman's definition, derived from Ernst Bloch: "Utopia is the homeland where no one has ever been but where alone we are authentically at home."[11]

Although Ann and Sax establish the dialectical opposition that governs the intellectual structure and political dynamic of the three Mars novels, in one important respect they are really very much alike. Each is devoted to what Sax calls the "haecceity" of their experience of another world. The term has been appropriated by Robinson from the late medieval philosopher Duns Scotus to describe an intense engagement with the here and now, with the "thisness" of Mars. Haecceity is as important to Robinson's aesthetic as dialectic, and it grounds the novels' arguments in a dense texture of observed detail. The dialectic generates a great deal of talk, often eloquent and just as often abstract, but haecceity is all about seeing what is in front of you. It is this feature of Robinson's writing that moves his *Mars* novels well beyond the ideological screed of Zubrin's *First Landing* and the dry didacticism of Brian Aldiss' utopian *White Mars* (2000). While Robinson's fiction is persistently engaged with political and philosophical ideals and problems, he never loses sight of the romance of Mars. His novels are focused on the *creation* of a world from a dead planet, the emergence of a utopia from within an alien environment, and so his narrative is always alive to sensation, to spectacle, to the cleansing of perception. The First Hundred's psychologist, Michel Duval, constantly struggling with his nostalgia for the green world of his native Provence in the middle of the rusty rocks of Mars, meditates on the ways in which a living world begins to take form when human minds encounter the Martian wasteland. "It was as if the planet itself had felt something missing, and at the tap of mind against rock, noosphere against lithosphere, the absent biosphere had sprung into the gap with the startling suddenness of a magician's paper flower" (GM, 212).

The magic of Mars, the splendor of the environment in both its terraformed and unterraformed states, is essential to the visionary power of Robinson's narrative. His development of the concept of the scientist as hero and the number of episodes devoted to scientific experiment and talk may obscure the degree to which the scientific realism of the Mars novels is leavened by romance and fantasy. (Consider, for instance, the multiple allusions throughout the novels to Tolkien and to *The Wizard of Oz*.) While so-called "hard" science fiction tends to focus on getting things done, fantasy, especially in the Tolkienian line, has emphasized perception, and in particular the "recovery" of lost or forgotten ways of seeing.[12] Repeatedly in Robinson's volumes, characters are drawn willingly or reluctantly into an experience of the beauty, the thrilling uniqueness, of the landscape to which they have committed their lives. One of the most impressive instances of how haecceity can educate the senses and the imagination, subverting the traps of analogical complacency, comes early in the history of the settlement of Mars. Nadia Cherneshevsky, the brilliantly pragmatic engineer who designs the living and working quarters for the First Hundred, is so obsessed with the problems of survival in a harsh environment, so absorbed in nuts and bolts and washers and wrenches, that she has taken no time to look at or to savor the peculiarities of her new world until Ann, in one of her gentlest moments, entices Nadia at the end of a long and exhausting day of labor to come out of the sealed habitat and watch a Martian sunset:

> Stars were popping out everywhere, and the maroon sky shifted to a vivid dark violet, an electric color that was picked up by the dune crests, so that it seemed crescents of liquid twilight lay across the black plain. Suddenly Nadia felt a breeze swirl through her nervous system, running up her spine and out into her skin; her cheeks tingled, and she could feel her spinal chord thrum. Beauty could make you shiver! It was a shock to feel such a physical response to beauty, a thrill like some kind of sex. And this beauty was so strange, so *alien*. Nadia had never seen it properly before, or never really felt it, she realized that now; she had been enjoying her life as if it were a Siberia made right, so that really she had been living in a huge analogy, understanding everything in terms of her past. But now she stood under a tall violet sky on the surface of a petrified black ocean, all new, all strange; it was absolutely impossible to compare it to anything she had seen before; and all of a sudden the past sheered away in her head and she turned in circles like a little girl trying to make herself dizzy, without a thought in her head. Weight seeped inward from her skin, and she didn't feel hollow anymore; on the contrary she felt extremely solid, compact, balanced. A little thinking boulder, set spinning like a top. (RM, 128)

In both language and conception, this gorgeous scene recalls the transformative "spots of time" that Wordsworth recorded in his autobiographical epic poem *The Prelude*, particularly his famous recollection of boyhood ice-skating when he spun himself round and round until he was absorbed into the rotation of the Earth, feeling himself intensely alive and intimately connected to the cosmos.

Robinson's passion for the haecceity of Mars—his love of place and specificity—shows itself, for instance, in the litany of rock that peppers the narrative: alases, splosh craters, taliks, creep features, polynyas, ventifacts, siderome-lane, lemniscate, lobate, rutile. The words are technical enough that non-specialist readers will frequently be scurrying to a large dictionary for help, but the effect is not so much of technical jargon as of an epic inventory of mineral and geological details that define a Martian reality against which the fictional imagination plays itself out. As Mars metamorphoses over the course of two centuries into a more complex environment—gradually becoming more temperate, with a more tolerable atmosphere and alternating land masses and water bodies, and with an increasing variety of fauna and flora—Robinson invites the reader to pay careful attention too. In *Blue Mars* especially, when the terraforming has made substantial alterations to the planet, there are long sections of travelogue in which characters make a close reading of the world that Mars is coming to be: there are Ann's walkabout, Nirgal's global runabout, Sax's sailabout, Zo's flyabout, not to mention Maya and Michel's twelve-hundred-mile barge trip down the Grand Canal that links the great northern ocean to the Hellas Sea in the southern hemisphere. And then there is the four-person embassy to Earth that also operates as a window onto Mars, as the wonder-struck Nirgal realizes: "Earth was so vast that in its variety it had regions that even out-Marsed Mars itself" (BM, 159). All these travels are occasions for Robinson to give us richly specific and felt observations of the Martian landscape. One long section of *Green Mars* is famously titled "The Scientist as Hero," but in *Blue Mars*, it is the planet itself that acquires heroic and epic status, and as Robinson persistently, even compulsively, names and characterizes and charts and visualizes every site across which the plot moves, we can see how supremely the author understands the power of nomenclature to create reality. Like Giovanni Schiaparelli and Percival Lowell a hundred years earlier, Robinson is able to give a distant planet a feeling of intimacy and familiarity through the alchemy of naming and mapping.

In an interview, Robinson recognized that he was going against the grain of expectations about how a science-fiction novel works. The "density of information" and the "expository lumps" in his Mars novels belong more to the tradition of nineteenth-century realism, he admitted, than to the conventions of science fiction, which most often have involved the use of "novums"—new and usually unexplained givens in the narrative whose meanings the reader is expected to infer from context.[13] But it would be a mistake to conclude from Robinson's remarks that his Mars novels are artless or untransmuted gobbets of data and referentiality. The iambic pentameter that concludes *Blue Mars* is no anomaly. All the volumes are in fact as carefully shaped and designed as an epic poem. *Red Mars* opens *in medias res*, in the middle of the twenty-first century on the night of the assassination of John Boone, the iconic American leader of the First Hundred who had been the first man on Mars in 2017. After the assassination, the novel backtracks to 2027 and the voyage out to Mars by the First Hundred. It takes Robinson 350 pages to bring *Red Mars* back to the time of the assassination. In constructing the novel, he begins, in Miltonic fashion, with an ending just as he will end *Red Mars* with a beginning: the arrival of the surviving members of the First Hundred at a refuge at Mars's south pole where they will hide from the United Nations police force that is trying to hunt them down after the failed revolution. "This is home," Hiroko Ai tells her friends. "This is where we start again" (RM, 519).

Like an epic poet, Robinson delights in the sound of the words on the tongue. John Boone, encountering a group of Sufi immigrants to Mars, joins in a whirling dance with them and starts a rhythmic multilingual recitation of the words for Mars: "Al-Qahira, Ares, Auqakuh, Bahram. Harmakhis, Hrad, Huo Hsing, Kasei. Ma'adim, Maja, Mamers, Mangala. Nirgal, Shalbatanu, Simud, and Tiu." Soon the Sufis pick up the chant. "He shouted the planet's names and they repeated them after him, in call and response style. They chanted the names, Arabic, Sanskrit, Inca, all the names for Mars, mixed together in a soup of syllables, creating a polyphonic music that was beautiful and shivery-strange, for the names for Mars came from times when words sounded odd, and names had power" (RM, 283). While Robinson's expansive, playful variations of words and sound effects often bring delight for its own sake, he also can deploy these strategies in ways that open up a character's psychology. Recuperating from the aphasia that he suffered after his brain was damaged, Sax, with the aid of the psychologist Michel Duval, slowly begins to recover his ability to use language. But as he relearns speech, Sax starts to take a poetic liberty with words that is a striking departure from the clinical and disembodied style of speaking that had characterized him before the injury. Standing on the Martian moon Deimos, he reflects on the collisions that produced the planet's two oddly contoured satellites; in his interior monologue, with its alternating technical and lyrical language and complete sentences interspersed with shimmering verbal fragments, Robinson reveals a new Sax emerging from his old habits of scientific curiosity:

> It was so obvious that the moonlet was shaped like some paleolithic hand tool, with facets knapped off by ancient strikes. Triaxial ellipsoid. Curious that it had such a circular orbit, one of the most circular in all the solar system. Not what you would expect of a captured asteroid, nor of ejecta flung up from Mars in one of the big impacts. Leaving what? Very old capture. With other bodies in other orbits, to regularize it. Knapp, knapp. Spall. Spallation. Language was so beautiful. Rocks striking rocks, in the ocean of space. Knocking bits off and flying away. Until they all either fell into the planet or skittered off. All but two. Two out of billions. Moon bomb. Gun stand. Rotating just faster than Mars above, so that any point on the Martian surface had it in the sky for sixty hours at a time. Convenient.

The known was more dangerous than the unknown. No matter what Michel said. Clomp, clomp, on the virgin rock, of a virgin moon, with a virgin mind. The Little Prince. The planes rising over the horizon looked absurd, like insects from a dream, chitinous, articulated, colorful, tiny in the starry black, on the dust-blanketed rock. (GM, 359–60)

In various large and small ways, Robinson crafts the shape of his epic. Each volume ends with a revolution: In *Red Mars*, it is a global catastrophe, resulting in many deaths among the Mars settlers and the imposition of martial law by the United Nations Authority; the revolution in *Green Mars*, though marred by the destructive and self-destructive activities of a faction of Red extremists, results in a fragile independence from the transnational corporations on Earth that had been exploiting the planet; and *Blue Mars* concludes with a velvet revolution "so complex and nonviolent that it was hard to see it as a revolution at all, at the time" (BM, 595). Such large structural effects are characteristic of the epic imagination, as in Dante's ending each of the three parts of his *Comedy* with the word "stars." But Robinson also incorporates some of the characteristic micro-effects of epic. Recalling the Homeric catalogue of the ships that came to Troy in *The Iliad* and Spenser's evocative catalogue of the trees in the forest where the Red Crosse Knight loses his way at the opening of *The Faerie Queene*, Robinson's prose is studded with catalogues of Martiana that contribute to the rich texture of his novels. Using a color chart, Sax and Maya study the Martian sunsets and try to determine as precisely as they can the profusion of purplish hues that appear in the sky each night:

But in that stretch between red and blue, English had surprisingly little to offer; the language just was not equipped for Mars. One evening in the dusk, just after a mauvish sunset, they went through the chart methodically, just to see: purple, magenta, lilac, amaranth, aubergine, mauve, amethyst, plum, violaceous, violet, heliotrope, clematis, lavender, indigo, hyacinth, ultramarine—and then they were into the many words for the blues. There were many, many blues. But for the red-blue span that was it, except for the many modulations of the list, royal violet, lavender gray, and so on. (BM, 523)

The rich coloring of the Martian sky, in fact the intense color-consciousness that imbues the details and textures as well as the titles of Robinson's sequence of novels, appears to have been contagious. In the years immediately following the publication of *Blue Mars*, a small epidemic of chromatic Marses broke out. Lance Parkin and Mark Clapham produced *Beige Planet Mars*, Larry Niven came up with *Rainbow Mars*, and even Robinson himself got into the act with a short autobiographical essay titled "Purple Mars."[14] But the serious entrant in the colors sweepstakes was Brian Aldiss. *White Mars, Or, The Mind Set Free: A 21st-Century Utopia*, written in collaboration with Roger Penrose, reads like a rejoinder to Robinson. More prescriptive and homiletic than Robinson's Martian utopia, *White Mars* foregoes Robinsonian dialectic for a committed message. The allusions to H. G. Wells's *The World Set Free* and *A Modern Utopia* in Aldiss's alternative title and subtitle suggest plainly enough that *White Mars* is situated in the tradition of the utopian *argument* rather than in the form of the utopian novel Robinson favors both in the *Mars* book and in his earlier *Pacific Edge* (1988). And although Aldiss and his collaborator pay their literary respects by including a K. S. Robinson Avenue in their domed Martian city, there can be little doubt that they are looking to construct an alternative to Robinson's vision of the planet.

The difference is partly ideological. *White Mars* relentlessly pursues the anti-terraforming, preservationist convictions of Tom Jefferies, the intellectual force behind the concept of a "white" Mars modeled on the terrestrial Antarctic wilderness: "We should not alter this planet. We must try to alter ourselves."[15] While other colonists put up some resistance to Jefferies' single-minded pursuit of an areoformed Martian society, *White Mars* has nothing like the alternating current of dialogue that is integral to the structure of Robinson's *Mars* novels. But to terraform or not to terraform is not the only question that Aldiss would answer differently than Robinson. The two writers have competing sensibilities about the nature of life in Utopia. The delight in food, drink, drugs, travel, architectural flamboyance, and sensual vitality that permeates Robinson's fiction is almost entirely absent from *White Mars*. The nascent utopia of Aldiss's Mars is spartan and severe—and as monochromatic as the book's title, almost as if to stand as a reprimand to Robinson's Californianized ideal of the good life. Robinson and Aldiss share an interest in some of the same problems that might beset a Martian community trying to achieve its own identity: the predatory behavior of multinational corporate interests on Earth; the danger to Mars from ecological and political collapse on the home planet; the struggle for independence and self-sufficiency; the debates over social arrangements and cultural priorities as prerequisites to the drafting of a Martian constitution. Aldiss is thoroughly Wellsian—and in agreement with Robinson —in his view of utopia as a process rather than a fixed state: "a condition of becoming, a glow in the distance, a journey for which human limitations precluded an end" (260). His work certainly joins the chorus of late twentieth-century fiction centered, not on conquest or colonization and not even on anthropocentric terraformation, but on the question of what it means to become Martian. The reason *White Mars* does not make the impact of Robinson's books is, finally, literary, not ideological. Although Aldiss has a long career as a gifted, inventive storyteller, in *White Mars*, story has become too attenuated to make its ideas compelling.

Red Mars, Green Mars, and *Blue Mars* have a reputation as "discussion novels" that are hard work for the reader. But no other Martian fiction has ever been so profuse, so prodigal in its spending of words to conjure up a world at once alien and alluring. The exuberant romance of Mars in Robinson's imagination gives his Martian utopia the one quality that readers so often miss in traditional utopian literature: a soul. Its soul is rooted in Robinson's cultivation of story and storytelling. As he says at the opening of *Red Mars,* Mars has always been a site for storytelling, no matter how much or how little we have known about the planet. "And all of these tales are told in an attempt to give Mars life, or to bring it to life" (RM, 3). Robinson's own narrative is interspersed with episodes of his invented legends of "Big Man" and of the "little red people"— competing mythologies that give Mars an imaginative history that predates the arrival of human beings. Authors, imagining the future of Mars, now instinctively and reflexively invoke and fold into their narratives past imaginings of Mars and Martians. The old and discredited stories about canals and oceans, indigenous flora and fauna, exotic princesses and monsters, and lost civilizations that belong to the literary history of Mars are reshaped and echoed and acknowledged in many recent fictions, but nowhere as subtly as in Robinson. By building new stories upon old ones, in much the same way that Renaissance buildings in Rome were raised on the foundations of older structures from imperial and medieval Rome, writers give imaginative depth and heft to the new Martian fiction.

Robinson does this repeatedly in his *Mars* novels—and nowhere so cleverly as in the account in *Blue Mars* of Maya and Michel's journey down the Grand Canal, a construction that Maya regards as "a kind of giant joke" in its homage to Percival Lowell's delusion (BM, 457). All the towns along the more than thousand-mile length of the Canal even bear the names of the canals that appeared on Lowell's maps and globes designed between 1895 and 1916. The entire region becomes the center of the Martian tourist industry, "a kind of dream Mars, a canal cliché from the ancient dreamscape, but nonetheless beautiful for that" (BM, 465). As in his other conjurings of the literary and cultural history of Mars, here Robinson's purposes are complex; he is not merely facetious or parodic or nostalgic but rather is intent on integrating into his imagined future the visions of the past and on leavening the utopian agenda of his novels with the romantic spell of those past imaginings. The Grand

Canal, we are reminded, is a rarity among the engineering feats of the Martian terraformers; they wanted to evoke the memory of Lowell's Mars and its literary heritage, not reproduce Lowell's Mars:

> [I]t was hard to remember that this was the only one, that such canals were not webbed everywhere, as on the maps of the ancient dream. Oh there was one other big canal, at Boone's Neck, but it was short and very wide, and getting wider every year, as draglines and the eastward current tore at it; no longer a canal, really, but rather an artificial strait. No, the dream of the canals had been enacted only once here, in all the world; and while here, cruising tranquilly over the water, one's view of everything else cut off by the high banks, there was a sense of romance in the air, a sense that their political and personal squabbles had a kind of Barsoomian grandeur. (BM, 466)

Making an utterly new Mars and new Martians out of the materials of both contemporary science and literary tradition, Robinson has brought the history of imagined Mars to a new plateau.

afterword
mars under
construction

Literary histories rarely are good at predicting the literary future. Could anyone in January 1897, surveying the output of Martian fiction since 1880, have imagined what Wells would produce in *The War of the Worlds*? Does anything in the history of Martian narratives in the first half of the twentieth century really lead logically and inevitably to the publication of *The Martian Chronicles* in 1950? Who could have foreseen the emergence in the 1980s of Frederick Turner's *Genesis* from what seemed the exhausted subject of Mars and the moribund genre of the epic poem? The improbable, the original, and the masterful have a way of disrupting any neat, linear unfolding of a literary history. The patterns in the history of a literary subject may be glimpsed, fitfully and uncertainly, in the moment; only retrospectively do they achieve full definition.

Therefore, we should be wary of succumbing to the temptation to judge Kim Stanley Robinson's *Mars* novels as the omega-point toward which the literary history of Mars has been tending. Capping, as they do, the late twentieth-century movement toward a new realism in fiction about Mars, Robinson's works do not close the book of Mars but simply complete one of its chapters. When Milton published *Paradise Lost*, his ideological enemy and aspiring epic poet John Dryden read it with mixed admiration and chagrin. "This man cuts us all out," he is reputed to have said. But not exactly. The long poem in English moved on and took wonderful new shape in Alexander Pope's translations of the Homeric epics, in Wordsworth's poetic autobiography *The Prelude*, in Tennyson's Victorianized account of the Arthurian legend in *Idylls of the King*, in Pound's *Cantos*, eventually, if unexpectedly, in Turner's *Genesis*. Perhaps no one else for quite some time will want to try to outdo Robinson on the subject of Martian terraformation. Nevertheless, Mars narratives refuse to wither and dissolve in the winds of time's passage. Where imagined Mars will go as the twenty-first century unfolds cannot be prophesied, because—undoubtedly— improbable, original, and masterful talents will work new variations on the matter of Mars. The conventional wisdom would suggest that the next great phase of Martian writing will coincide with the actual arrival of human beings on the planet. Many writers, both inside and outside the literary community, have said so. But suppose, for the sake of argument, that it turns out otherwise— as future history has a way of doing.

Let me end by considering an early twenty-first-century novella that exhibits such a defiance of expectations. It appeared in 2002 in a volume of new stories edited by Peter Crowther titled Mars Probes. The anthology includes many homages to and pastiches of previous fictions, including Paul Di Filippo's "A Martian Theodicy," which plays in a jokey way with the characters from Weinbaum's "Martian Odyssey" of 1934; "Flower Children of Mars," Mike Resnick and M. Shayne Bell's variation on Burroughs' A Princess of Mars; and James Morrow's Wellsian parody, "The War of the Worldviews." The volume also offers a return to the world of The Martian Chronicles with the first U.S. publication of an old Bradbury story, and we find a tribute to Leigh Brackett in Michael Moorcock's "The Lost Sorceress of the Silent Citadel." The inescapable implication of so many backward-looking gestures in Mars Probes is that early twenty-first-century fiction about Mars feeds on the literary history of the planet. Imagining Mars in the new century requires writers to know both their science and their fiction, both the data amassed by cameras, scientific instruments, and computer imaging and the body of story that has constructed our cultural memories of Mars.

The best story in Mars Probes skillfully captures the paradoxical nature of imagined Mars in the post-Robinson era. Here, the writer imagines that humanity never gets to Mars at all—and yet the desire to imagine Mars does not die with the death of space programs. In "The Old Cosmonaut and the Construction Worker Dream of Mars," Ian McDonald imagines a twenty-first century in which the space age has come to an end without human beings ever having made an expedition to Mars. But while no people from the third planet have gone physically to the fourth, their dreams and fantasies about Mars persist. Mars is always under construction in the imagination. "Deep down," one character says, "everything is a story. We're all tales. Tell me. Tell me your stories. We've got a world to build."[1] The embittered, elderly cosmonaut of the title, an Estonian who had been part of the four-man crew designated for the aborted first and only Russian mission to Mars, is haunted for the rest of his life by his unfulfilled dream of going to Mars. The Russians never got off the launch pad. The Americans never even tried. Without the competition between the old U.S.S.R. and the United States, with the unwillingness of nations to pay the price tag for interplanetary adventures, and with the supplanting of the lure of outer space by the cheaper attractions of cyberspace, the cosmonaut spends four decades obsessed with his fantasies of what might have been. But in a parallel universe inhabited by a young construction worker in India, Mars is reached by virtual travel; advanced computer technology and brain chemistry allow workers to "commute" to Mars, leaving their terrestrial bodies behind and acquiring mechanical bodies that they inhabit while employed on a project to roof over the Valles Marineris. Using the techniques of magical realism, McDonald creates a scene in which the old Estonian and the young Indian— each with his dreams of Mars—meet in quantum space, a kind of twilight zone in which the parallel universes converge. There they find themselves surrounded by a mass of people, all of them "telling their tales and dreams of that little red light in the night" (148).

In this wonderful fable, McDonald registers the special power of the literary history of Mars to bring our neighboring planet, visited or unvisited, to richly creative life. "People make it a world," the old cosmonaut comes to understand. "Their stories, their words, their never-ceasing definition of its reality. Without them, it is just a planet. Dead" (152). The difference between a planet and a world is imagination. Throughout much of the twentieth century, the emphasis in the literature of Mars was on anticipating the physical human presence on another planet: human beings settling Mars, terraforming it to terrestrial standards, becoming Martians. McDonald—who has said that narratives of terraformed Mars are "just so last century"—may be the harbinger of a new phase of the history of imagined Mars that is yet continuous with what has gone before.[2] His Mars is primarily a verbal construct, a world inhabited by the human imagination before—and whether—it is ever inhabited in the flesh. As it has always been so far.

NOTES

1. The Meaning of Mars

The first epigraph is from Updike's "Mars as Bright as Venus," *New York Times Book Review*, September 28, 2003, 24; the second from Robinson's *Red Mars* (New York: Bantam, 1993), 3; and the third from Chaucer's "The Wife of Bath's Prologue," line 610, *Canterbury Tales*, in *The Riverside Chaucer*, 3rd ed., ed. Larry Benson (Boston: Houghton Mifflin, 1987).

1. Camille Flammarion, *Popular Astronomy: A General Description of the Heavens*, trans. J. Ellard Gore (New York: D. Appleton, 1894), 373.

2. Quoted in Flammarion, *Popular Astronomy*, 25.

3. All quotations from Homer's *Iliad* are in the translation by Stanley Lombardo (Indianapolis: Hackett, 1997).

4. *The Homeric Hymns*, trans. Charles Boer (Chicago: Swallow Press, 1970), 63.

5. John Lydgate, *Troy Book*, ed. Henry Bergen (London: Oxford University Press, 1935), lines 1–7.

6. Marjorie Hope Nicolson, *Voyages to the Moon* (New York: Macmillan, 1948), 256.

7. Among Patrick Moore's many books, see his recent *Patrick Moore on Mars* (London: Cassell, 1998). See also Mark Washburn, *Mars At Last!* (New York: Putnam's, 1977); Eric Burgess, *Return to the Red Planet* (New York: Columbia University Press, 1990); John Noble Wilford, *Mars Beckons* (New York: Knopf, 1990); Jay Barbree and Martin Caidin with Susan Wright, *Destination Mars in Art, Myth, and Science* (New York: Penguin, 1997); Michael Hanlon, *The Real Mars* (New York: Carroll and Graf, 2004); Oliver Morton, *Mapping Mars: Science, Imagination, and the Birth of a World* (New York: Picador, 2002); Robert Markley, *Dying Planet: Mars in Science and the Imagination* (Durham: Duke University Press, 2005).

8. William Sheehan, *Planets and Perception: Telescopic Views and Interpretations, 1609–1909* (Tucson: University of Arizona Press, 1988), 9–10.

9. Rudolf Thiel, *And There Was Light: The Discovery of the Universe*, trans. Richard and Clara Winston (New York: Knopf, 1957), 262.

10. Robert Zubrin with Richard Wagner, *The Case for Mars: The Plan to Settle the Red Planet and Why We Must* (New York: Simon and Schuster, 1996); Kerry Mark Joels, *The Mars One Crew Manual* (New York: Ballantine, 1985); James Lovelock and Michael Allaby,

The Greening of Mars (New York: St. Martin's, 1984); Donald Goldsmith, The Hunt for Life on Mars (New York: Penguin, 1998); Richard C. Hoagland, The Monuments of Mars: A City on the Edge of Forever, 5th ed. (Berkeley: Frog, Ltd., 2002); Hugh H. Kieffer, Bruce M. Jakowsky, Conway W. Snyder, and Mildred Matthews, eds., Mars (Tucson: University of Arizona Press, 1992).

11. Edgar Rice Burroughs, A Princess of Mars (1912; reprint, New York: Penguin, 2007), 103.

12. Lucretius, On the Nature of the Universe, book II, trans. R. E. Latham (Baltimore: Penguin, 1951), 91.

13. Frederick Turner, Genesis: An Epic Poem (Dallas: Saybrook, 1988), 7.

14. E. L. Trouvelot, The Trouvelot Astronomical Drawings Manual (New York: Scribner's, 1882), 71. According to a note in the journal The Observatory (1884), Trouvelot produced "no fewer than 415 careful drawings" based on his observations of Mars (p. 177). His unpublished sketches are in the Wolbach Library at the Harvard-Smithsonian Astrophysical Center.

15. Morton, Mapping Mars, 116.

16. Poster for "Robinson Crusoe on Mars," directed by Byron Haskin, Paramount Pictures, 1964 (Popular Culture Library, Bowling Green State University).

17. Markley, Dying Planet, 289.

18. Walt Whitman, "When I Heard the Learn'd Astronomer," in Leaves of Grass and Other Writings, ed. Michael Moon (New York: Norton, 2002), 227. The poem was first published in 1865.

19. Robert Frost, "The Star-Splitter," lines 18–19; 33–37, in New Hampshire: A Poem with Notes and Grace Notes (New York: Henry Holt, 1923).

20. Agnes M. Clerke, A Popular History of Astronomy during the Nineteenth Century, 2nd ed. (New York: Macmillan, 1887), vii. The quotation comes from her preface to the first edition of 1885.

21. "The planet Mars, during the few years past, has received considerable attention from journalists and writers, who have discussed it with that tendency towards the sensational which is so characteristic of these days." Focused largely on the question of the canals, John Ritchie's "Our Knowledge of Mars" was reprinted from its original appearance in The Boston Commonwealth (18 October 1890) in The Sidereal Messenger 9 (1890): 450–54.

22. Mary Proctor, "Making Astronomy Popular," Popular Astronomy 2 (1895): 419. Her father, Richard Proctor, was the author of such often-reprinted books as Half-Hours with the Telescope (1868) and Other Worlds Than Ours (1870).

23. "Science Seeks to Get Into Communication with Mars," New York Times, 2 May 1909, VI, 7:1.

24. Garrett P. Serviss, "If We Could Move to Mars," Harpers Round Table, 25 February 1896, 408.

25. "The Planet Mars," *Popular Astronomy* 15 (1907): 449–50.

26. Edward S. Holden, "What We Know About Mars," *McClure's Magazine* 16 (March 1901): 440.

27. Olaf Stapledon to Agnes Miller, 1 March 1914, published in *Talking Across the World: The Love Letters of Olaf Stapledon and Agnes Miller, 1913–1919*, ed. Robert Crossley (Hanover, N.H.: University Press of New England, 1987), 32.

28. Patrick McGuinness, *The Canals of Mars* (Manchester, U.K.: Carcanet, 2004), 29.

29. Kim Stanley Robinson, *The Martians* (New York: Bantam, 1999), 320.

30. Turner, *Genesis*, 1.

31. Robinson, *Red Mars* (New York: Bantam, 1993), 2.

32. Kim Stanley Robinson, *Pacific Edge* (1988; reprint, New York: Tom Doherty, 1995), 156.

33. Robinson, *Red Mars*, 349.

34. C. S. Lewis, *Out of the Silent Planet* (1938; reprint, New York: Scribner, 2003), 143–44.

35. Clarke's recollections came a year after a symposium of writers and scientists gathered to mark the historic occasion of the arrival of Mariner 9 at its destination. See Ray Bradbury, Arthur C. Clarke, Bruce Murray, Carl Sagan, and Walter Sullivan, *Mars and the Mind of Man* (New York: Harper and Rowe, 1973), 83.

36. Lewis, *Out of the Silent Planet*, 43.

37. Ben Bova, *Mars* (New York: Bantam, 1992), 70.

2. Dreamworlds of the Telescope

1. Quoted from Camille Flammarion, *La Planète Mars et ses Conditions D'Habitabilité* (Paris: Gauthier-Villars, 1892), 6. My translation.

2. Karl S. Guthke, *The Last Frontier: Imagining Other Worlds from the Copernican Revolution to Modern Science Fiction*, trans. Helen Atkins (Ithaca, N.Y.: Cornell University Press, 1990), 58, 98–99.

3. John Milton, "Areopagitica," in *The Prose of John Milton*, ed. J. Max Patrick (1644; reprint, New York: Doubleday Anchor, 1967), 306.

4. John Milton, *Paradise Lost*, ed. Gordon Teskey (New York: Norton, 2005). All extracts from *Paradise Lost*, originally published in 1667, are from this edition.

5. See Roger Shattuck's discussion of "knowledge within bounds" in *Paradise Lost* in his *Forbidden Knowledge: From Prometheus to Pornography* (1996; reprint, New York: Harvest, 1997), 62–67.

6. Bernard le Bovier de Fontenelle, *Conversations on the Plurality of Worlds*, trans. H. A. Hargreaves, intro. Nina Rattner Gelbart (Berkeley: University of California Press, 1990), 5–6. Originally published as *Entretiens sur la pluralité des mondes* in 1686, the last edition supervised by Fontenelle appeared in 1742, when he was 85.

7. See Rev. W[ladislaw] S[omerville] Lach-Szyrma, *Aleriel, or A Voyage to Other Worlds*

(London: Wyman and Sons, 1883), xi. Strangely, in the translator's preface to the California edition of Fontenelle's *Conversations*, H. A. Hargreaves tries to distance Fontenelle from the origins of science fiction. While grudgingly acknowledging an influence on Jules Verne, he grants only a possible indirect influence on Poe and Wells while insisting "there is no clear evidence that the science/speculative fiction of anyone else in the nineteenth or twentieth century was influenced more than vaguely by the writings of Fontenelle and his contemporaries" (xliii).

8. Christiaan Huygens, *The Celestial Worlds Discover'd*, translated from Latin (reprint, London: Timothy Childe at the White Hart at the West-end of St. Paul's Church-yard, 1698; facsimile reprint, London: Frank Cass, 1968), 1–2; the publisher's preface is not paginated. Originally published in Latin as *Cosmotheoros* (The Hague: Adriaan Moetjens, 1698).

9. Blaise Pascal, *Pensées and Other Writings*, trans. Honor Levi (New York: Oxford University Press, 1995), 73.

10. Huygens, *Celestial Worlds Discover'd*, 9.

11. John Milton, *Paradise Lost*, V.498.

12. Huygens appears to suggest that Kircher's *Itinerarium Exstaticum* [*Ecstatic Journey*], (Rome: typis Vitalis Mascardi, 1656), was compromised by the same constraints on liberty of thought that had been imposed on Galileo. See *Celestial Worlds Discover'd*, 15, 105.

13. William Herschel, "On the Remarkable Appearances at the Polar Regions of the Planet Mars, the Inclination of its Axis, the Position of its Poles, and its Spheroidical Figure, with a few Hints relating to its real Diameter and Atmosphere," *Philosophical Transactions of the Royal Society of London* 74, part 2 (1784): 260. Herschel's earlier paper, "Astronomical Observations on the Rotation of the Planets," appeared in *Philosophical Transactions* 71, part 1 (1781).

14. Herschel, "On the Remarkable Appearances at the Polar Regions," 245, 273. The other allusion to "inhabitants of Mars" occurs at 259.

15. Emanuel Swedenborg, *Concerning the Earths in Our Solar System, Which Are Called Planets*, translated from Latin by John Clowes (London: Hindmarsh, 1787), vi. Originally published as *De Telluribus In Mundo nostro Solari, Quæ vocantur Planetæ: Et De Telluribus In Cœlo Astrifero: Deque illarum Incolis; tum de Spiritibus & Angelis ibi; Ex Auditis & Visis* (London: John Lewis, 1758).

16. William Blake, *The Marriage of Heaven and Hell*, in *The Poetry and Prose of William Blake*, ed. David V. Erdman (1794; New York: Doubleday, 1970), 40.

17. *A Fantastical Excursion into the Planets* (London: Saunders and Otley, 1839), vi.

18. Camille Flammarion, *Popular Astronomy: A General Description of the Heavens*, trans. J. Ellard Gore (New York: D. Appleton and Co., 1894), 373.

19. K. Maria D. Lane, "Geographers of Mars: Cartographic Inscription and Exploration Narrative in Late Victorian Representations of the Red Planet," *Isis* 96 (2005): 478.

20. Percival Lowell, *Mars* (Boston: Houghton Mifflin, 1895), 141.

21. "The Newton-Herschel Canal," *New York Times*, April 27, 1882, 8-5. The report on Schiaparelli's recent observations, "Canals on the Planet Mars," appeared in the *Times* on 24 April 1882, 3-2.

22. "The Newton-Herschel Canal," 8-5.

3. Inventing a New Mars

1. "Is Mars Inhabited?" *New York Times*, 12 August 1877, 4; Oliver Wendell Holmes, "Wind-Clouds and Star-Drifts," part III, "Sympathies," in *The Complete Poetical Works of Oliver Wendell Holmes*, ed. Horace E. Scudder (Boston: Houghton Mifflin, 1908), 174.

2. Samuel Phelps Leland, *World Making* (Chicago: Women's Temperance Publishing Association, 1895), cited by Carl Sagan in Ray Bradbury, Arthur C. Clarke, Bruce Murray, Carl Sagan, and Walter Sullivan, *Mars and the Mind of Man* (New York: Harper and Rowe, 1973), 14.

3. Isobel Gill, *Six Months in Ascension: An Unscientific Account of a Scientific Expedition* (London: J. Murray, 1878), 132.

4. Nathaniel E. Green, "Observations of Mars, at Madeira, in August and September 1877," *Memoirs of the Royal Astronomical Society* 44 (1877–1879): 124, 134.

5. The *Spectator* article was reprinted, with no author specified, as "A Miniature World," *New York Times*, 18 November 1877, 10-4. In a similar vein, see also Richard Proctor, "How the Possible Inhabitants of the Martian Moon Manage," *New York Times*, 13 January 1878, 3-6.

6. For a detailed account of why Schiaparelli's maps ended up achieving more authority than Green's (or that of any other nineteenth-century observer), see K. Maria D. Lane's fascinating "Geographers of Mars: Cartographic Inscription and Exploration Narrative in Late Victorian Representations of the Red Planet," *Isis* 96 (2005): 477–506.

7. Green quotes from Schiaparelli's letter to him in a brief report, "Mars and the Schiaparelli Canals" in *Observatory* 3 (December 1879): 252.

8. "Canals on the Planet Mars," *New York Times*, 24 April 1882, 3.

9. "Proctor on the Canals of Mars," *New York Times*, 2 May 1882, 3. The article is a reprinting of a letter written by Richard Proctor to the *Times* of London.

10. Mark R. Hillegas, "Martians and Mythmakers: 1877–1938," in *Challenges in American Culture*, ed. Ray B. Browne et al. (Bowling Green, Ohio: Bowling Green University Popular Press, 1970), 150–77. See also Hillegas, "Victorian 'Extraterrestrials'" in *The Worlds of Victorian Fiction*, ed. Jerome H. Buckley (Cambridge: Harvard University Press, 1975), 391–414.

11. In *Exposition du Système du Monde* (Paris: Cercle-Social, 1796), Perre Simon Laplace proposed that planets were an inevitable byproduct of the collapse of a nebular cloud which had triggered the development of our sun. Since the planets all had a common origin, Laplace reasoned that they were all likely to be habitable.

12. Hillegas, "Martians and Mythmakers," 156.

13. Percy Greg, *Across the Zodiac: The Story of a Wrecked Record*, ed. Sam Moskowitz (1880; reprint, Westport, Conn.: Hyperion Press, 1974), vol. 1, 26. The original two volumes are contained in a single volume in the Hyperion reprint, but the pagination retains the two-volume structure.

14. On the predilection for anti-gravity devices in nineteenth-century space fiction, see Adam Roberts, *The History of Science Fiction* (New York: Palgrave Macmillan, 2006), 108–10.

15. For further discussion of Greg's utilitarianism, and the relation of *Across the Zodiac* to his earlier survey of contemporary issues in social philosophy *The Devil's Advocate* (1878), see Brian Stableford's helpful entry on *Across the Zodiac* in *Survey of Science Fiction Literature*, vol. 1, ed. Frank N. Magill (Englewood Cliffs, N.J.: Salem Press, 1979), 11–15.

16. Rev. W[ladislaw] S[omerville] Lach-Szyrma, *Aleriel, or A Voyage to Other Worlds* (London: Wyman and Sons, 1883), v, xii.

17. An alternative derivation of *Aleriel* has been suggested by my colleague Kenneth Rothwell, who sees in the name Aleriel a combination of the Latin *ala* (wing) and Shakespeare's Ariel, the sprite from *The Tempest*.

18. Hudor Genone [pseudonym of William J. Roe], *Bellona's Bridegroom: A Romance* (Philadelphia: Lippincott, 1887), 330.

19. Hugh MacColl, *Mr. Stranger's Sealed Packet* (London: Chatto and Windus, 1889), 28.

20. William Herschel, "On the Remarkable Appearances at the Polar Regions of the Planet Mars, the Inclination of its Axis, the Position of its Poles, and its Spheroidal Figure, with a few Hints relating to its real Diameter and Atmosphere," *Philosophical Transactions of the Royal Society of London* 74, part 2 (1784): 260, 273.

21. Robert Cromie, *A Plunge into Space*, 2nd ed., with preface by Jules Verne (1891; reprint, Westport, Conn.: Hyperion Press, 1976), 11, 46, 51. The first edition, without Verne's prefatory note, appeared in 1890.

22. H. G. Wells, *A Critical Edition of The War of the Worlds*, ed. David Y. Hughes and Harry M. Geduld (Bloomington: Indiana University Press, 1993), 149.

23. Robert D. Braine, *Messages from Mars, By the Aid of the Telescope Plant* (New York: J. S. Ogilvie, 1892), 12. This is the complete title as it appears on the title page. An alternate subtitle—perhaps another indication of lack of copy-editing—appears at the beginning of the narrative on page 9: *or The Strange Revelation of the Telescope Plant.*

24. Quoted in "Watching All Over the Globe," *New York Times*, 5 August 1892, 6.

25. Camille Flammarion, *La Planète Mars et ses conditions d'habitabilité* (Paris: Gauthier-Villars, 1892), viii, 50, my translations.

4. *Percival Lowell's Mars*

1. Quoted in David Strauss, *Percival Lowell: The Culture and Science of a Boston Brahmin* (Cambridge, Mass.: Harvard University Press, 2001), 183. I owe a general debt to Strauss's magisterial biography.

2. Edward Pickering, *Annual Report of the Director of the Astronomical Observatory of Harvard College for 1894*, 12; copy in the Wolbach Library, Harvard-Smithsonian Center for Astrophysics.

3. A. Lawrence Lowell, *Biography of Percival Lowell* (New York: Macmillan, 1935), vi.

4. Percival Lowell, typescript of "Astronomy Today: Address before the Harvard Union, Dec. 13, 1910," 3–4. Lowell Observatory Archives.

5. In retelling this story, which goes back to the early biography by Abbot Lawrence Lowell and a collective biography of the Lowell family, Ferris Greenslett's *The Lowells and Their Seven Worlds* (Boston: Houghton Mifflin, 1946), William Graves Hoyt points out that Percival Lowell himself never documented his decision to take up planetary astronomy (*Lowell and Mars* [Tucson: University of Arizona Press, 1976], 26). William Sheehan also casts doubt on the authenticity of the story, or at least its sufficiency as an explanation of Lowell's decision, by noting that Schiaparelli was still using his telescope to observe Mars in 1894 and may not yet have known that his sight was starting to fail; see *Planets and Perception: Telescopic Views and Interpretations, 1609–1909* (Tucson: University of Arizona Press, 1988), 165–67.

6. Strauss, *Percival Lowell*, 176–77.

7. This latter detail is mentioned in a flattering article, obviously written with Lowell's cooperation, in the *Boston Herald's* Sunday Magazine for 29 October 1905, "How a Boyish Fad Made Percival Lowell Famous," 8.

8. Copies of both these dated presentation volumes are in the Percival Lowell archives at the Lowell Observatory. The annotations to Flammarion were entered at various times over the course of at least fifteen years.

9. Camille Flammarion, *Popular Astronomy: A General Description of the Heavens*, trans. J. Ellard Gore (New York: Appleton, 1894), 397.

10. Edward S. Holden, "The Lowell Observatory, in Arizona," *Publications of the Astronomical Society of the Pacific* 6 (June 1894): 165. Edward Pickering deplored his brother's "colossal newspaper reputation" and scolded him, "I should have restricted myself more distinctly to the facts in this as in other cases." Bessie Z. Jones and Lyle G. Boyd, *The Harvard College Observatory: The First Four Directorships, 1830–1919* (Cambridge, Mass.: Harvard University Press, 1971), 307.

11. Pickering's response to Holden, "The Arequipa Observations of Mars and Jupiter," appeared in the next issue of *Publications of the Astronomical Society of the Pacific* 6 (August 1894): 221–25, followed immediately by Holden's "Addendum" (225–27), in which he forcefully restated his criticism of Pickering's press releases.

12. See William Sheehan, *The Planet Mars: A History of Observation and Discovery* (Tucson: University of Arizona Press, 1996), 146 and 251n1.

13. Michael J. Crowe, *The Extraterrestrial Life Debate, 1750–1900* (1986; reprint, New York: Dover, 1999), 545–46.

14. Percival Lowell, *Mars* (Boston: Houghton Mifflin, 1895), 35, 49, 186, 212.

15. Ibid., 84–85.

16. Except for one that resides at the Smithsonian's National Air and Space Museum, all Lowell's Martian globes remain in the Archives at the Lowell Observatory in Flagstaff.

17. A heavily revised notebook manuscript of "Mars"—clearly a work-in-progress that eventually was abandoned—is in the Lowell Observatory Archives. Because of references to Martian seas in the poem, Sheehan, in *Planets and Perception* (181), has dated it to a period before July 1894, when Lowell abandoned Schiaparelli's assumption that Mars had oceans.

18. Sheehan, *Planets and Perception*, 214.

19. The slab containing this inscription on the mausoleum is reproduced in William Lowell Putnam, *The Explorers of Mars Hill: A Centennial History of Lowell Observatory* (West Kennebunk, Me.: Phoenix Publishing, 1994), 258.

20. Edward S. Holden, "Mistakes about Mars," *San Francisco Weekly Post*, 13 March 1895. As with other newspaper citations without page numbers in this chapter, my source is Percival Lowell's scrapbooks of newspaper cuttings in the Lowell Observatory Archives.

21. Quoted in Sheehan, *The Planet Mars*, 132.

22. Alfred Russel Wallace, *Is Mars Habitable? A Critical Examination of Professor Percival Lowell's Book "Mars and Its Canals," with an Alternative Explanation* (London: Macmillan, 1907).

23. Mark Wicks, *To Mars Via the Moon: An Astronomical Story* (Philadelphia: Lippincott, 1911). A presentation copy of the book, which includes in its preface (xi) thanks to Lowell for several years' worth of advice and information, is in the Lowell Observatory Archives. Wicks addresses his dedicatee as "professor," a term his academic rivals declined to apply to Lowell. See Strauss, *Percival Lowell*, on Lowell's effort to achieve academic respectability by negotiating with MIT for the honorary title of "Non-Resident Professor of Astronomy" (56–57).

24. James Keeler to George Ellery Hale, 27 December 1894. Quoted in Sheehan, *The Planet Mars*, 110.

25. Percival Lowell, *Mars as the Abode of Life* (New York: Macmillan, 1908), 73–74.

26. "The Man Who Explored Mars," *New York City Literary Digest*, 2 December 1916.

27. Louise Leonard, *Percival Lowell: An Afterglow* (Boston: Richard G. Badger, 1921), 25. Early biographical accounts of Lowell are silent about Leonard, but William Lowell

Putnam, in *The Explorers of Mars Hill*, leaves little doubt that his great-uncle's relationship with her was intimate (69–86). See also Strauss, *Percival Lowell*, 41–43.

28. *Boston Post*, 16 October 1906; *Boston Evening Transcript*, 9 November 1906. The unsigned author of all the *Transcript* reviews is identified in Percival Lowell's scrapbooks as the science journalist John Ritchie (Lowell Observatory Archives).

29. Lowell, *Mars*, 128.

30. Lowell, "Mars," Lowell Observatory Archives.

31. Percival Lowell, *Mars and Its Canals* (New York: Macmillan, 1906), p. 382.

32. Edward S. Morse, "My 34 Nights on Mars," *The World Magazine*, 7 October 1906, 9. In the article, Morse indicates that he came to Flagstaff with a bias against the canals. He wrote more expansively of the experience in *Mars and Its Mystery* (Boston: Little, Brown, 1906). See Strauss, *Percival Lowell* on Lowell's deployment of his Boston Brahmin friends in the campaign to defend his views of Mars (203–19); as Lowell's "bulldog" (215), Morse played a role, Strauss suggests, analogous to that of T. H. Huxley as a defender of Darwin.

33. "What He Saw on Mars," *New York World*, Sunday, 24 February 1895.

34. Camille Flammarion, *Uranie*, trans. Mary J. Serrano (New York: Cassell, 1890), 190.

35. Louis Pope Gratacap, *The Certainty of a Future Life in Mars* (New York: Brentano, 1903), 183.

36. Lowell, *Mars and Its Canals*, 93.

37. Ibid., 193.

38. Percival Lowell, "Is Mars Inhabited?" *The Outlook* 85 (13 April 1907): 848.

39. Percival Lowell, "Other Worlds Than Ours," corrected typescript, dated c. 1894, 14. Lowell Observatory Archives.

40. Percival Lowell, Outline of a talk on "Education" to Miss Hersey's Students Association, Somerset, 27 May 1902. Lowell Observatory Archives.

41. "Flagstaff, Arizona, Photographs Showing the Canals of Mars, On Exhibition," *Boston Post*, 2 February 1906.

42. E. M. Antoniadi to Percival Lowell, 9 October 1909, Lowell Observatory Archives; Antoniadi, *La Planète Mars* (Paris: Librairie Scientifique Hermann, 1930), 29–30, my translation. See Sheehan, *Planets and Perception*, 95–99.

43. Quoted in A. L. Lowell, *Biography of Percival Lowell*, 66.

44. "Flagstaff, Arizona, Photographs," *Boston Post*, 2 February 1906.

45. *London Daily News*, 6 July 1907; Lilian Whiting, "There Is Life on the Planet Mars," *New York Times*, 9 December 1909.

46. *New York Herald Sunday Magazine*, 30 December 1906.

47. *Chicago Evening American*, 14 February 1910, 1.

48. E. M. Antoniadi, "Report of the Section for the Observation of Mars, 1909,"

Memoirs of the British Astronomical Association 20 (London: Eyre and Spottiswoode, 1916): 353–420.

49. Eliot Blackwelder, "Mars as the Abode of Life," *Science* n.s. 29 (23 April 1909); I quote from a monograph containing all the letters in the controversy assembled by the editors of *Science* under the title, *Our Friends, the Enemy: A Discussion Bearing on Scientific Ethics, with Concrete Illustrations* (1910), 3.

50. "How a Boyish Fad Made Percival Lowell Famous," *Boston Sunday Herald*, Magazine Section (29 October 1905), 8.

51. Lowell, *Mars as the Abode of Life*, 153–54, 185, 189.

52. Riso Levi to Percival Lowell, 27 October 1909. Lowell Observatory Archives.

53. J. F. Earhart to Percival Lowell, 30 July 1907. Lowell Observatory Archives.

54. Mrs. J. L. Washburn to Percival Lowell, undated. Lowell Observatory Archives.

55. C. G. Lagerlof to Percival Lowell, 10 February and 27 February 1905. Lowell Observatory Archives.

56. E. B. Braemer to Percival Lowell, 5 September 1909, Lowell Observatory Archives.

57. Charles Rupert to Percival Lowell, 23 August 1910. Lowell Observatory Archives.

58. H. Jacob to Percival Lowell, 21 February 1916. Lowell Observatory Archives.

59. Presentation copy of Sara Weiss, *Journeys to the Planet Mars, or Our Mission to Ento* (Rochester, N.Y.: Austin Publishing, 1905); E. B. Ringland to Percival Lowell, 29 September 1909. Both in Lowell Observatory Archives.

60. Quoted in Leonard, *Percival Lowell: An Afterglow*, 156.

61. Percival Lowell, "Mars: Forecasts and Fulfillments" (Lowell Observatory Archives). The quoted sentence also supplied the headline title for a lavish illustrated tribute to Lowell in the *Philadelphia Public Ledger*, 10 December 1916.

62. "Percival Lowell's Martians," *Kansas City Star*, 3 December 1916; "The Man Who Explored Mars," *New York City Literary Digest*, 2 December 1916.

63. "The Mars Man," Paterson, New Jersey, *Guardian*, 1 December 1916.

5. Mars and Utopia

1. L. Frank Baum, *The Emerald City of Oz* (Chicago: Reilly and Britton, 1910), 293.

2. Anonymous, *Politics and Life in Mars: A Story of a Neighbouring Planet* (London: Sampson Low, Marston, Searle, & Rivington, 1883), iii.

3. Most often, the suggestion has been that the author of *Politics and Life in Mars* was the early science fiction writer L. Edgar Welch, but John Clute and Peter Nicholls challenge that attribution in their entry for Welch in *The Encyclopedia of Science Fiction* (New York: St. Martin's, 1995), 1311.

4. Mark Wicks, *To Mars via the Moon: An Astronomical Story* (Philadelphia: Lippincott, 1911), x.

5. See Alfred Russel Wallace, *Is Mars Habitable? A Critical Examination of Professor Percival Lowell's Book "Mars and Its Canals," With an Alternative Explanation* (London: Macmillan, 1907), 20.

6. Alice Ilgenfritz Jones and Ella Merchant, *Unveiling a Parallel: A Romance*, introduction by Carol Kolmerten (Syracuse: Syracuse University Press, 1991), 1. Originally published in 1893 as by "Two Women of the West," without the authors' names.

7. Henry Olerich, *A Cityless and Countryless World* (1893; reprint, New York: Arno Press, 1971), 6, 20.

8. William Simpson, a California state senator, first published *The Man from Mars: His Morals, Politics, and Religion* in 1891. It was reprinted several times with altered pagination, and I quote from the revised third edition (San Francisco: E. D. Beattie, 1900) which includes an extensive preface and a new chapter on woman suffrage. On the Martian's mode of travel, see 86.

9. Richard Ganthony, *A Message from Mars: A Fantastic Comedy in Three Acts* (New York: Samuel French, 1924), 27. A note to the text indicates that Ganthony made some revisions to his original script in 1923. I have been unable to locate a copy of the original 1899 script.

10. See "Talking with the Stars: Prof. Davidson's Views of Interplanetary Signals," *New York Times*, 26 July 1891, 15:3; "Earth May Signal Mars," *New York Times*, 5 August 1892, 1:6.

11. Pickering's campaign is reported by Mary Proctor, daughter of the nineteenth-century astronomer and writer Richard Proctor, in her column, *Gossip of Starland*. I have been unable to trace this column to its source or date it precisely, but a clipping in a scrapbook at Wellesley College's Whitin Observatory gives a date of 1909. Raymond Taylor, *A Signal from Mars: March and Two Step*, arranged by E. T. Paull (New York: E. T. Paull Music Co., 1901).

12. Henry Wallace Dowding, *The Man from Mars, or Service for Service's Sake* (New York: Cochrane, 1910), 62.

13. The first of E. M. Antoniadi's "Interim Reports for 1909" appeared in the *Journal of the British Astronomical Association* 19, no. 10 (1909): 427–33, and they continued over the next year.

14. Kurd Lasswitz, *Two Planets*, abridged by Erich Lasswitz, trans. Hans Rudnick, with afterword by Mark R. Hillegas (New York: Popular Library, 1971), 41.

15. Alexander Bogdanov, *Red Star: The First Bolshevik Utopia*, ed. Loren R. Graham and Richard Stites, trans. Charles Rougle (Bloomington: Indiana University Press, 1984), 34, 29.

16. The nebular hypothesis was the subject of Lowell's undergraduate commencement address at Harvard in 1876, underpinned much of his writing about Mars as a dying planet, and was most fully articulated in his *The Evolution of Worlds* (New York: Macmillan, 1909).

17. Alexander Bogdanov, "The Engineer Menni," in *Red Star: The First Bolshevik Utopia*, 204.

6. H. G. Wells and the Great Disillusionment

1. The classic study of the tradition is Marjorie Hope Nicolson's *Voyages to the Moon* (New York: Macmillan, 1948).

2. David Y. Hughes and Harry M. Geduld, eds., *A Critical Edition of The War of the Worlds: H. G. Wells's Scientific Romance* (Bloomington: Indiana University Press, 1993), 51. All my citations from *The War of the Worlds* are taken from this indispensable annotated edition.

3. "Earth May Signal Mars," *New York Times*, 7 August 1892, 5:2.

4. "Shining Specks on Mars," *New York Times*, 5 August 1894, 1:3.

5. "Name of God on Mars' Canals," *New York Herald*, 19 May 1895, 4, 4:6.

6. "A Strange Light on Mars," *Nature*, 2 August 1894, 319.

7. H. G. Wells, "The Star," in *The Door in the Wall and Other Stories* (1911; reprint, Boston: David Godine, 1980), 39. Both "The Crystal Egg" and "The Star," originally published in magazines in 1897 shortly before *The War of the Worlds* appeared, were collected by Wells in *Tales of Space and Time* (London and New York: Harper and Brothers, 1899).

8. On Wells's early thinking about Mars, see the definitive biography by David Smith. *H. G. Wells: Desperately Mortal* (New Haven: Yale University Press, 1986), 64–65, and the introduction to Hughes and Geduld's *Critical Edition*, 1. Wells's "Intelligence on Mars" originally appeared in *Saturday Review* 81 (4 April 1896): 345–46; my quotations are from the reprinted text of the article in Hughes and Geduld, *Critical Edition*, 296, 297.

9. A letter to Wells from Richard Gregory, dated 22 June 1899, urges him to read Lowell's *Mars*—advice that suggests Wells had no first-hand acquaintance with Lowell's work before he completed *The War of the Worlds* (David C. Smith, ed., *The Correspondence of H. G. Wells* [London: Pickering and Chatto, 1998], I, 342). No letters to or from Lowell and no other mention of Lowell's name appear in the four volumes of Wells's collected correspondence. Lowell's *Mars* was reviewed favorably by William Lockyer, the son of *Nature* editor Norman Lockyer, in *Nature* 54 (29 October 1896): 625–27.

10. Percival Lowell, *Mars* (Boston: Houghton Mifflin, 1895), 211.

11. For other examples of scientific and fictional portrayals of red Martian vegetation, see Hughes and Geduld, *Critical Edition*, 218n12.

12. Anonymous review, *Academy*, 29 January 1898; reprinted in Patrick Parrinder, ed., *H. G. Wells: The Critical Heritage* (London: Routledge and Kegan Paul, 1972), 72. In his magisterial survey *The Biological Universe: The Twentieth-Century Extraterrestrial Life Debate and the Limits of Science* (Cambridge: Cambridge University Press, 1996), 232, 236, Steven J. Dick suggests, incorrectly I believe, that Lowell's *Mars* influenced *The War of the*

Worlds. Dick may have overestimated the significance of Wells's casual reference in "The Things That Live on Mars" (*Cosmopolitan* [March 1908], 335–43) to "my friend, Percival Lowell." If there was a friendship it is likely in 1908 to have been of recent origin; no correspondence between the two men and no other documentation of any connection between them survives. They may have met on either one of Lowell's lecture tours in England or one of Wells's in the United States.

13. Hadley Cantril, *The Invasion from Mars: A Study in the Psychology of Panic* (1940; reprint, Princeton: Princeton University Press, 1982), 42. Cantril's invaluable study of the Mercury Theatre broadcast prints the radio script in its entirety, 4–44.

14. See Smith, *H. G. Wells, Desperately Mortal,* 76; Patrick Parrinder, *Shadows of the Future: H. G. Wells, Science Fiction and Prophecy* (Liverpool: Liverpool University Press, 1995), 87. A full discussion of the Welles and Haskin adaptations appears in Hughes and Geduld, *Critical Edition,* 237–48.

15. David Y. Hughes, "*The War of the Worlds* in the Yellow Press," *Journalism Quarterly* 43 (Winter 1966): 639–46; reprinted in Hughes and Geduld, *Critical Edition,* appendix II, 281–89.

16. Mary Shelley, *Frankenstein, or The Modern Prometheus: The 1818 Text,* ed. Marilyn Butler (New York: Oxford University Press, 1993), 104; vol. I, ch. 7.

17. Preface to a 1933 edition of Wells's *Scientific Romances,* reprinted in *H. G. Wells's Literary Criticism,* ed. Patrick Parrinder and Robert Philmus (Sussex: Harvester, 1980), 243.

18. For an important consideration of the discourse of colonialism in *The War of the Worlds* in the context of other early works of science fiction, see John Rieder, *Colonialism and the Emergence of Science Fiction* (Middletown, Conn.: Wesleyan University Press, 2008), 3–10; 125–35.

19. In an interview two decades after the initial publication of *The War of the Worlds,* Wells traced the romance back to a casual remark made by his brother Frank when the two of them were discussing the Tasmanian genocide: "Suppose some beings from another planet were to drop out of the sky suddenly . . . and begin laying about them here!" H. G. Wells, interview, *Strand Magazine* 109 (1920): 154.

20. Parrinder analyzes the relationship of the provincial to the universal, effectively answering skeptics about *The War of the Worlds,* in *Shadows of the Future,* especially 80–95.

21. Eden Phillpotts to H. G. Wells, 26 November 1904, H. G. Wells Archive, University of Illinois.

22. H. G. Wells, "From an Observatory" in *Certain Personal Matters* (London: T. Fisher Unwin, 1901), 176.

23. Garrett Serviss, *Edison's Conquest of Mars,* intro. A. Langley Searles (Los Angeles: Carcosa House, 1947), 6.

24. Garrett Serviss, "If We Could Move to Mars," *Harpers Round Table,* 25 February 1896, 408–10.

25. H. Bruce Franklin, *War Stars: The Superweapon and the American Imagination* (New York: Oxford University Press, 1988), 67. See also Rieder, *Colonialism and the Emergence of Science Fiction*, 136–38.

26. H. G. Wells, "The Things That Live on Mars," *Cosmopolitan* 44 (March 1908): 335–42. Not collected in any of Wells's books, the article has been reprinted as an appendix in Hughes and Geduld's *Critical Edition of The War of the Worlds*, 298–305.

27. C. S. Lewis, *Out of the Silent Planet* (1938; reprint, New York: Scribner, 2003), 37.

7. Mars and the Paranormal

1. David Strauss, *Percival Lowell: The Culture and Science of a Boston Brahmin* (Cambridge: Harvard University Press, 2001), 138; Janet Oppenheim, *The Other World: Spiritualism and Psychical Research in England, 1850–1914* (Cambridge: Cambridge University Press, 1985), 137.

2. Strauss, *Percival Lowell*, 133; see his entire discussion of Lowell's research into occult phenomena, 133–50.

3. See chapter 4, p. 88, for Lowell's reaction to a medium who attempted to draw him into her Martian "discoveries."

4. Reprinted by Flammarion as the introduction to his *Haunted Houses*, trans. E. E. Fournier (New York: Appleton, 1924), 13; emphasis in original.

5. Quoted in Renée Haynes, *The Society for Psychical Research 1882–1982: A History* (London: Macdonald, 1982), 202. Among other prominent literary, scientific, and philosophical figures who served as president in the early decades of the international SPR's existence were Oliver Lodge, Andrew Lang, Henri Bergson, and Gilbert Murray.

6. Roger Luckhurst, *The Invention of Telepathy, 1870–1901* (Oxford: Oxford University Press, 2002), 10.

7. See Strauss's important discussion of the essentially multidisciplinary character of Lowell's notion of "planetology" as the appropriate term for his kind of scientific study of Mars (*Percival Lowell*, 197–219). Lowell devoted his *Mars as the Abode of Life* to an extensive illustration of how planetology, the "science of the making of worlds," extends the reach of astronomy (New York: Macmillan, 1908), 2.

8. The *Oxford English Dictionary* records the first occurrences of "parapsychology" in the 1920s.

9. Eliot Blackwelder, "Mars as the Abode of Life," in *Our Friends, the Enemy: A Discussion Bearing on Scientific Ethics, with Concrete Illustrations* (New York: American Association for the Advancement of Science, 1910), 3.

10. This cartoon and others by Gordon Ross illustrate an article by F[inlay] P[eter] Dunne, "Mr. Dooley Reviews the Year 1906," *New York Times Magazine*, 30 December 1906, 19. The cartoon, unattributed, is pasted into one of Lowell's scrapbooks, held at the Lowell Observatory, Flagstaff.

11. Gauri Viswanathan, "The Ordinary Business of Occultism," *Critical Inquiry* 27 (Autumn 2000): 6.

12. The 1994 edition of Théodore Flournoy's *From India to the Planet Mars: A Case of Multiple Personality and Imaginary Languages*, trans. Daniel Vermilye (Princeton, N.J.: Princeton University Press, 1994), has extensive scholarly apparatus, including a brief essay on the Hélène Smith case by Carl Jung and a long and superb introduction by the editor, Sonu Shamdasani, to which I owe a general debt. This reprint alters the subtitle of the original 1899 text in its 1901 English translation, which was *A Study of a Case of Somnambulism with Glossolalia.* Vermilye's 1901 translation was also an abridgement, and Shamdasani has restored the excised passages, in his own translations, as an appendix.

13. Wells's review appeared in *Nature* 51 (6 December 1894): 121–22.

14. Edgar Rice Burroughs, *A Princess of Mars* (1912; reprint, New York: Penguin, 2007), 12.

15. Henry A. Gaston, *Mars Revealed, or Seven Days in the Spirit World* (San Francisco: A. L. Bancroft, 1880), 28.

16. Mark Wicks, *To Mars via the Moon: An Astronomical Story* (Philadelphia: Lippincott, 1911), 204.

17. George DuMaurier, *The Martian*, 1897; reprinted in *Novels of George DuMaurier*, intro. John Masefield and Daphne DuMaurier (London: Pilot Press, 1947), 695.

18. "Romance of fact" was Lowell's hopeful term for his own writings about Mars—and much preferable, he thought, to the "romance of fiction." See *Mars and Its Canals* (New York: Macmillan, 1906), 382.

19. Camille Flammarion, *Uranie*, trans. Mary J. Serrano (New York: Cassell, 1890), 161.

20. Louis Pope Gratacap, *The Certainty of a Future Life in Mars* (New York: Brentano, 1903), 61.

21. Olaf Stapledon to Agnes Miller, 28 October 1913; privately held. This letter was not printed in *Talking across the World: The Love Letters of Olaf Stapledon and Agnes Miller, 1913–1919*, ed. Robert Crossley (Hanover: University Press of New England, 1987); however, it was cited in the introduction, xxxvii.

22. My text is the second edition of Sara Weiss, *Journeys to Mars* (Rochester, N.Y.: Austin Publishing Co., 1905).

23. Robert Markley, *Dying Planet: Mars in Science and the Imagination* (Durham: Duke University Press, 2005), 117–18.

24. An autographed copy is held in the library of the Percival Lowell Archives at Lowell Observatory, Flagstaff, Arizona.

25. Sara Weiss, *Decimon Huydas: A Romance of Mars* (Rochester, N.Y.: Austin Publishing Co., 1906), 154.

26. J. L. Kennon, "ed." *The Planet Mars and Its Inhabitants: A Psychic Revelation by Iros*

Urides (A Martian). Privately printed by Mabel J. Kean, 1922. The quotations are from an unnumbered page in the editorial foreword.

27. J. W. Gilbert, *The Marsian* (New York: Fortuny's, 1940), 12.

28. W. Olaf Stapledon, *Last and First Men: A Story of the Near and Far Future* (London: Methuen, 1930), 177.

29. Ray Bradbury, *The Martian Chronicles* (1950; reprint, New York: Bantam, 1979), 21.

30. Translated and quoted by Sonu Shamdasani in his introduction to Flournoy, *From India to the Planet Mars*, xxix.

31. "Mars Is Heaven" was the original title of the story (published in 1948) that became the chapter "The Third Expedition" in *The Martian Chronicles*.

8. Masculinist Fantasies

1. Among C. S. Lewis's essays on this subject, see especially "On Stories" and "On Science Fiction," in the posthumous collection *Of Other Worlds*, ed. Walter Hooper (New York: Harcourt Brace, 1966).

2. See, for example, Charlotte Perkins Gilman's extensive essay in definition, "Feminism," intended for the 1908 *New Encyclopedia of Social Reform*. The essay in fact was never published until it appeared in *Charlotte Perkins Gilman: A Nonfiction Reader*, ed. Larry Ceplair (New York: Columbia University Press, 1991), 183–87.

3. Ellsworth Douglass, *Pharaoh's Broker: Being the Very Remarkable Experiences in Another World of Isidor Werner* (1899; reprint, Boston: Gregg Press, 1976), 202. The identity of Ellsworth Douglass is a mystery and his career largely a blank; the authors of *The Encyclopedia of Science Fiction* speculate that the name may be a pseudonym for Elmer Dwiggins—an equally obscure figure.

4. George Griffith, *A Honeymoon in Space* (1901; reprint, New York: Arno, 1974), 275. George Griffith was the pen name of the magazine journalist George Chetwynd Griffith-Jones. A useful overview of Griffith-Jones' career is in Brian Stableford, *Scientific Romance in Britain, 1890–1950* (London: Fourth Estate, 1985), 44–55.

5. Walter Stetson's words are cited in Ann J. Lane, *To Herland and Beyond: The Life and Work of Charlotte Perkins Gilman* (New York: Pantheon, 1990), 82.

6. Douglass, *Pharaoh's Broker*, 239.

7. Edgar Rice Burroughs, *A Princess of Mars* (1917; reprint, New York: Penguin, 2007), 103. The earliest version of *Princess*, titled "Under the Moons of Mars," was published under the pseudonym of Norman Bean in magazine form in 1912.

8. Q[ueenie] D[orothy] Leavis, *Fiction and the Reading Public* (London: Chatto and Windus, 1932), 50, 54, 58. Burrough's jab at scholars and literati occurs in a letter to Leavis, quoted on 41.

9. Brian W. Aldiss with David Wingrove, *Trillion Year Spree: The History of Science Fiction* (New York: Atheneum, 1986), 163.

10. For the classic reading of Burroughs' imaginative deficiencies, see Richard D.

Mullen, "The Undisciplined Imagination: Edgar Rice Burroughs and Lowellian Mars," in *SF: The Other Side of Realism*, ed. Thomas D. Clareson (Bowling Green, Ohio: Bowling Green University Popular Press, 1971), 229–47.

11. Edwin L. Arnold, *Lieut. Gullivar Jones: His Vacation* (1905; reprint [as *Gulliver of Mars*], New York: Ace, 1964), 134, 70. The American reprint, in altering the title and changing the spelling of Gullivar, makes an unconvincing attempt to attach Arnold's escapist narrative to the tradition of Swiftian satire.

12. Gustavus Pope, *Journey to Mars: The Wonderful World: Its Beauty and Splendor; Its Mighty Races and Kingdoms; Its Final Doom* (1894; reprint, Westport: Hyperion Press, 1974), 185.

13. Marcianus F. Rossi, *A Trip to Mars* (San Jose: Smith, McKay, 1920), 88.

14. Pope, *Journey to Mars*, 230.

15. Frederick Jackson Turner, *The Significance of the Frontier in American History*, ed. Harold Simonson (New York: Ungar, 1963), 28.

16. Quoted in Richard White, "Frederick Jackson Turner and Buffalo Bill," in *The Frontier in American Culture*, ed. James R. Grossman (Berkeley: University of California Press, 1994), 50. I owe a general debt both to White and to Patricia Nelson Limerick's essay in the same volume, "The Adventures of the Frontier in the Twentieth Century." See also Robert M. Zubrin, "The Significance of the Martian Frontier," *Ad Astra: The Magazine of the National Space Society* 6 (September/October 1994): 30–37.

17. Burroughs, *Princess of Mars*, 20.

18. Rossi, *Trip to Mars*, 36.

19. Burroughs, *Princess of Mars*, 17.

20. Griffith, *Honeymoon in Space*, 162.

21. Arnold, *Lieut. Gullivar Jones*, 174–75.

22. H. Rider Haggard, *King Solomon's Mines* (1895; reprint, Harmondsworth: Penguin, 1958), 39, 160.

23. Ibid., 95.

24. Douglass, *Pharaoh's Broker*, 191.

25. Griffith, *Honeymoon in Space*, 151.

26. Pope, *Journey to Mars*, 102.

27. Arnold, *Lieut. Gullivar Jones*, 92.

28. Ibid., 121; Haggard, *King Solomon's Mines*, 10.

29. Pope, *Journey to Mars*, 216.

30. Ibid., 59.

31. Arnold, *Lieut. Gullivar Jones*, 137.

32. Pope, *Journey to Mars*, 207.

33. Ibid., 202.

34. Griffith, *Honeymoon in Space*, 161.

35. Ibid., 144.

36. Pope, Journey to Mars, 195, 384; Burroughs, Princess of Mars, 99.

37. Griffith, Honeymoon in Space, 147.

38. Ibid., 148.

39. Burroughs, Princess of Mars, 11–12.

40. Ibid., 99.

41. Arnold, Lieut. Gullivar Jones, 140.

42. Burroughs, Princess of Mars, 110.

43. Ibid., 171.

44. Ibid., 97.

45. Ibid.

46. Griffith, Honeymoon in Space, 275; Douglass, Pharaoh's Broker, 173.

47. Pope, Journey to Mars, 260.

48. Wendy R. Katz, Rider Haggard and the Fiction of Empire: A Critical Study of British Imperial Fiction (Cambridge: Cambridge University Press, 1987), 140, 141.

49. Pope, Journey to Mars, vi.

50. Ibid., 522.

51. Ibid., 523.

52. Ibid., 279n1.

53. Griffith, Honeymoon in Space, 72.

54. Rossi, Trip to Mars, 26.

55. Burroughs, Princess of Mars, 62.

56. Ibid., xxxiii.

57. In The Encyclopedia of Science Fiction, John Clute and Peter Nicholls speculate that Wicks's book "was probably intended as a fictionalization of popular science for younger readers" (New York: St. Martin's, 1995), 1323. But most of the themes of To Mars via the Moon derive from the familiar (and rarely exciting) repertoire of conventional utopianism, with no hint of the adventures and fantasies that are typical of boys' books of the period.

58. Fenton Ash, A Trip to Mars (1909; reprint, New York: Arno, 1974), n.p. "Fenton Ash" was one of the pseudonyms of the British popular novelist Francis Henry Atkins. The adventures in Trip to Mars were first produced in 1907 and 1908 as installments in a magazine for boys.

59. Ibid., 3.

60. "Roy Rockwood," Through Space to Mars, Or The Longest Journey on Record (New York: Cupples and Leon, 1910), 21.

61. David I. Macleod, Building Character in the American Boy: The Boy Scouts, YMCA, and Their Forerunners, 1870–1920 (Madison: University of Wisconsin Press, 1983), 32.

62. Sir Robert S. S. Baden-Powell, Scouting for Boys: A Handbook for Instruction in Good Citizenship (London: C. Arthur Pearson, 1910), 208. The Arthurian references are frequent, and all of chapter 7 is given over to "Chivalry of the Knights." For a thoughtful

investigation of the conservative and "defensive" ideology of *Scouting for Boys* with its "aggressively masculine" orientation, see Robert H. MacDonald, *Sons of Empire: The Frontier and the Boy Scout Movement, 1890–1918* (Toronto: University of Toronto Press, 1993), 8 and *passim*.

63. Ash, *Trip to Mars*, n.p.

64. Rockwood, *Through Space to Mars*, 218.

65. Carl H. Claudy, *The Mystery Men of Mars* (New York: Grosset and Dunlap, 1933), 47. The parallels with Wells's *First Men in the Moon* (1901) are extensive: Claudy's Mars adventure takes place mostly underground, in blue-lit tunnels and chambers presided over by a ruler reminiscent of Wells's Grand Lunar and referred to by the boys as the "Lord High King Bug" (70).

66. Baden-Powell, *Scouting for Boys*, 272. The patriotic motif also looms large in Baden-Powell's advice to Scout instructors, and he includes a chapter on "How the Empire Must Be Held."

67. Claudy, *Mystery Men of Mars*, 44.

68. Rockwood, *Through Space to Mars*, 236.

69. Ibid., 239.

70. Ibid., 242.

9. *Quite in the Best Tradition*

1. "Listening for Mars; Heard Anything?" *New York Times*, 22 August 1924, 13:1.

2. "Beyond Earth," *Time*, 31 July 1939, 24.

3. William H. Pickering, *Mars* (Boston: Richard Badger, 1921).

4. Camille Flammarion, *Dreams of an Astronomer*, trans. E. E. Fournier D'Albe (London: T. Fisher Unwin, 1923), 112. He repeated the claim in his feature article, "Science Again Tries to Read Mars Riddle," *New York Times*, 2 March 1924, IX, 3:1.

5. "Flammarion Predicts Talking with Mars," *New York Times*, 12 December 1923, 3:2; "An Astronomer Out of His Element," *New York Times*, 13 December 1923, 20:5.

6. Flammarion, "Science Again."

7. Garrett Serviss, "Mars a Fascinating Study," a newspaper article dated May 1907, appears in one of Percival Lowell's scrapbooks at the Lowell Observatory Archives, Flagstaff. I have been unable to locate the newspaper from which the clipping was taken.

8. Louise Hathaway, "Mars Meets Earth," in her *The Enchanted Hour* (San Francisco: John J. Newbegin, 1940), 91.

9. C. S. Lewis, "A Reply to Professor Haldane," in *Of Other Worlds: Essays and Stories*, ed. Walter Hooper (New York: Harcourt Brace, 1966), 76. J. B. S. Haldane, biologist and former editor of the *Daily Worker*, had written a scathing review of Lewis's three scientific romances, *Out of the Silent Planet* (1938), *Perelandra* (1943), and *That Hideous Strength* (1946); Lewis's response was never published until after his death.

10. Lester Lurgan (pseud. Mabel Winfred Knowles), *A Message from Mars* (London: Greening and Co., 1912), 196–97.

11. See, for instance, "Talking with the Stars," *New York Times*, 26 July 1891, 15:3; "What Mars May Be," *New York Times*, 25 September 1892, 20:1; "Planetary Intercommunication," *New York Times*, 18 December 1892, 4:4. For a discussion of "the signal question," applied to the Moon as well as to Mars from the 1860s to 1920, see Michael J. Crowe, *The Extraterrestrial Life Debate, 1750–1900* (1986; reprint, New York: Dover, 1999), 393–400.

12. See "Messages from Mars," *The Observatory* 24 (1901): 102.

13. "Plans Messages to Mars," *New York Times*, 19 April 1909, 1:2; "Pickering's Idea for Signaling Mars," *New York Times*, *Sunday Magazine*, V, 1; "Science Seeks to Get into Communication with Mars," *New York Times*, 2 May 1909, VI, 7:1; "Proposes a Costly Experiment," *New York Times*, 20 April 1909, 8:4.

14. "East Side, Not Mars, Needs Attention," *New York Times*, 13 May 1909, 6:6.

15. "First Mars Message Would Cost Billion," *New York Times*, 30 January 1920, 18:1.

16. "Opposing Views of Mars Signals," *New York Times*, 31 January 1920, 24:3; "Offers a $20,000 Prize for Sign to a Planet," *New York Times*, 2 February 1920, 24:2.

17. "Asks Air Silence When Mars Is Near," *New York Times*, 21 August 1924, 11:3; "Radio Goes On Here," *New York Times*, 22 August 1924, 13:1; "Calls Attempt Nonsense," *New York Times*, 23 August 1924, 9:2; "Mars Nearest at 7 P.M.," *New York Times*, 23 August 1924, 9:3.

18. Flammarion, *Dreams of an Astronomer*, 118–19.

19. See "Radio to Stars, Marconi's Hope," *New York Times*, 20 January 1919, 1:5; "Marconi Sure Mars Flashes Messages," *New York Times*, 2 September 1921, 1:4; "Marconi Not Interested," *New York Times*, 23 August 1924, 9:1; "Messages Would Be Different," *New York Times*, 25 August 1924, 12:6. An excellent discussion of the signaling craze and Marconi's place in it appears in Steven J. Dick, *The Biological Universe: The Twentieth-Century Extraterrestrial Life Debate and the Limits of Science* (Cambridge: Cambridge University Press, 1996), 401–14; Dick seems to be unaware, however, of Marconi's 1924 disclaimers.

20. George Babcock, *Yezad: A Romance of the Unknown* (Bridgeport, Conn.: Co-Operative Publishing Co., 1922), 25. Babcock's elaborate glossary at the conclusion of the 448-page romance explains the exotic names and concepts used in the narrative, including the sources he consulted and the terms he simply made up.

21. Alexei Tolstoi, *Aelita, or The Decline of Mars*, trans. Leland Fetzer (Ann Arbor, Mich.: Ardis, 1985), 30. Fetzer's is the only English translation of the original version of *Aelita*, first published in *Red Virgin Soil* 10 (November–December 1922) and 11 (January–February and March–April 1923). Tolstoi later revised the work several times to keep it current with both scientific knowledge and Stalinist expectations.

22. Yury Tynanov's criticism, originally appearing in *Russkii Sovremennik* 1 (1924): 297, is quoted by Fetzer in his translator's introduction to *Aelita*, 12.

23. H. G. Wells, *Star-Begotten: A Biological Fantasia*, ed. John Huntington (Middletown: Wesleyan University Press, 2006), 62.

24. Olaf Stapledon to H. G. Wells, 16 October 1931; quoted in full in Robert Crossley, *Olaf Stapledon: Speaking for the Future* (Syracuse: Syracuse University Press, 1994), 197–98.

25. John Wyndham, *Stowaway to Mars* (Greenwich, Conn.: Fawcett, 1972), 49. Originally published in 1936 under the pseudonym John Beynon and with the title *Planet Plane*.

26. Hugo Gernsback to H. G. Wells, 18 July 1927 and 1 November 1927. H. G. Wells Archive, University of Illinois Champaign-Urbana Library. The archive contains many of Gernsback's letters to Wells between 1926 and 1936, a number of them annotated in Wells's hand. For a fuller discussion of this prickly literary relationship, see Gary Westfahl, "The Jules Verne, H. G. Wells, and Edgar Allan Poe Type of Story: Hugo Gernsback's History of Science Fiction," *Science-Fiction Studies* 19 (November 1992): 340–53.

27. C. S. Lewis, *Out of the Silent Planet* (1938; reprint, New York: Macmillan, 1965), 35.

28. W. Olaf Stapledon, *Last and First Men: A Story of the Near and Far Future* (London: Methuen, 1930), 174.

29. Stanley G. Weinbaum, *A Martian Odyssey*, ed. Sam Moskowitz (New York: Lancer, 1966), 20. Weinbaum's story has been anthologized frequently. The best critical commentary is by John Huntington in *Rationalizing Genius: Ideological Strategies in the Classic American Science Fiction Short Story* (New Brunswick: Rutgers University Press, 1989), 119–25.

30. *Planet Plane* gets only a passing mention in two of the standard surveys of science fiction: Brian W. Aldiss with David Wingrove, *Trillion Year Spree: The History of Science Fiction* (New York: Atheneum, 1986), 253; and Brian Stableford, *Scientific Romance in Britain, 1890–1950* (London: Fourth Estate, 1985), 152.

31. See J. R. R. Tolkien, "On Fairy-Stories," in *Tree and Leaf* (Boston: Houghton Mifflin, 1965), 37. Originally given as a lecture in 1938—the same year that Lewis published *Out of the Silent Planet*—"On Fairy-Stories" has been reprinted frequently.

32. C. S. Lewis, "On Science Fiction," in *Of Other Worlds: Essays and Stories*, ed. Walter Hooper (1966; reprint, New York: Harcourt Brace, 1975), 69.

33. Lewis, *Out of the Silent Planet*, 32.

34. Chad Walsh has an extended discussion of such images of birth in *Out of the Silent Planet* in *The Literary Legacy of C. S. Lewis* (New York: Harcourt Brace, 1979), 86–90.

35. In a letter of 9 July 1939 to an unnamed correspondent, Lewis observed that almost no reviewers of *Out of the Silent Planet* realized that his fiction of the "Bent"

Oyarsa was a variation on the story of Satan's fall. "Any amount of theology can now be smuggled into people's minds under cover of romance without their knowing it." *Letters of C. S. Lewis*, ed. W. H. Lewis (New York: Harcourt Brace, 1966), 167.

36. "Astronomical Fiction," *Popular Astronomy* 47 (1939): 1.

37. " 'War' Broadcast Studied," *New York Times*, 20 December 1938, 29:1.

38. H. G. Wells, *A Critical Edition of The War of the Worlds*, ed. David Y. Hughes and Harry M. Geduld (Bloomington: Indiana University Press, 1993), 134.

39. For a provocative assessment of the panic as a product of new applications of broadcasting technology, including footage of the near-hysterical live reporting of the *Hindenburg* crashing and burning, see the television documentary "Invasion from Mars" (British Broadcasting Company: Open University production, 1988); videocassette distributed in the United States by San Diego: Media Guild.

40. Dorothy Thompson's *Herald Tribune* column, "Mr. Welles and Mass Delusion," 2 November 1938, was reprinted in Howard Koch's *The Panic Broadcast: Portrait of an Event* (1967; reprint, New York: Avon, 1970), 92–93.

41. "Radio Hypnosis," *Click* 2 (February 1939): 8–11.

42. "Panic Caused by Broadcast," *London Times*, 1 November 1938, 14g.

43. "Beyond Earth," *Time*, 31 July 1939, 24.

44. William L. Laurence, "Science in the News," *New York Times*, 23 July 1939, II, 4:6.

45. "Topics of the Times," *New York Times*, 24 July 1939, 12:4.

46. "Fair 'Arms' Against Mars," *New York Times*, 27 July 1939, 13:6.

47. "Wireless Signals to Mars," *London Times*, 29 July 1939, 14a; "Nazi Satirist Sees Mars Courted by 'Encirclers,' " *New York Times*, 30 July 1939, 23:2.

48. James Creed Meredith, *The Rainbow in the Valley* (Dublin: Browne and Nolan, 1938), v.

49. "Topics of the Times," *New York Times*, 30 January 1941, 20:4.

10. On the Threshold of the Space Age

1. John Keir Cross, *The Angry Planet* (New York: Coward-McCann, 1946), 66. It had been published first in England in 1945.

2. Robert A. Heinlein, *Red Planet: A Colonial Boy on Mars* (1949; reprint, New York: Ballantine, 1976), 6.

3. Robert S. Richardson, *Exploring Mars* (New York: McGraw-Hill, 1954), 103, 109. Later in the century, the ratios of nitrogen and carbon dioxide would be reversed. Measurements at the *Viking* landing sites showed an atmosphere composed of 95.32 percent carbon dioxide, 2.7 percent nitrogen, 1.6 percent argon, 0.13 percent oxygen, and tiny percentages of other gases. Hugh H. Kieffer, Bruce M. Jakowsky, Conway W. Snyder, and Mildred Matthews, *Mars* (Tucson: University of Arizona Press, 1992), 30.

4. Robert A. Heinlein, "Science Fiction: Its Nature, Faults, and Virtues," in *Turning*

Points: Essays on the Art of Science Fiction, ed. Damon Knight (New York: Harper and Row, 1977), 15.

5. Brian W. Aldiss with David Wingrove, *Trillion Year Spree: The History of Science Fiction* (New York: Atheneum, 1986), 268.

6. Robert A. Heinlein, *Stranger in a Strange Land* (1961; reprint, New York: Berkley, 1969), 9.

7. John Noble Wilford, *Mars Beckons: The Mysteries, the Challenges, the Expectations of Our Next Great Adventure in Space* (New York: Knopf, 1990), 48.

8. Ray Bradbury, "The Green Morning," *The Martian Chronicles* (1950; reprint, New York: Bantam, 1979), 76.

9. Ray Bradbury, "A Few Notes on 'The Martian Chronicles,'" *Rhodomagnetic Digest* (May 1950): 21.

10. Review of *The Silver Locusts*, *Times Literary Supplement*, 19 October 1951, 657.

11. "Use of Atom Bomb by a Foe Assumed," *New York Times*, 14 November 1948, 40:1.

12. Coretta King quoted from *Eyes on the Prize*, Vol. 1. Alexandria, Va.: PBS Video, 2006; originally broadcast in 1986.

13. See Ray Bradbury, Arthur C. Clarke, Bruce Murray, Carl Sagan, and Walter Sullivan, *Mars and the Mind of Man* (New York: Harper and Row, 1973), 19.

14. Arthur C. Clarke, *Interplanetary Flight: An Introduction to Astronautics* (New York: Harper and Brothers, 1951), 119.

15. Willy Ley's review of *The Exploration of Space* (New York: Harper and Brothers, 1952) appeared as "Out of This World by Spaceship," *New York Times*, 22 June 1952, VII: 1. Clarke stated his aims in a preface to a reprint of the original 1952 edition of *The Sands of Mars* (New York: Signet, 1974), v.

16. "Going Spaces," *London Times*, 30 July 1952, 7d.

17. Charles Poore, "Books of the Times," *New York Times*, 21 June 1952, 13:6.

18. "The Martian Way," in Isaac Asimov, *The Complete Stories*, vol. 2 (New York: Doubleday, 1992), 145. It originally appeared in *Galaxy Science Fiction*, November 1952.

19. Leigh Brackett, *The Sword of Rhiannon* (New York: Ace, 1953), 128.

20. E[ugène] M[ichel] Antoniadi, *The Planet Mars*, trans. Patrick Moore (Devon: Keith Reid, 1975). Acknowledging that he knew Lowell "personally" and that he was "sincere" (80), Antoniadi nonetheless insists that the observations of canals by Lowell and his disciples was "completely illusory" (40).

21. Wernher von Braun, *The Mars Project* (1953; reprint with foreword by Thomas O. Paine, Urbana: University of Illinois Press, 1991), 1, 2.

22. For more details, see P[hilip] E[llaby] Cleator, "History," in *Space Research and Exploration*, ed. David R. Bates (New York: William Sloane, 1958), 29–41.

23. Dr. I[srael] M[onroe] Levitt, *A Space Traveler's Guide to Mars* (New York: Henry Holt, 1956), 147.

24. For instances in this period of books designed for child readers that offer uncritical accounts of Lowell's canals, see Roy A. Gallant, *Exploring Mars* (New York: Garden City Books, 1956); and Robert Silverberg, *Lost Race of Mars* (New York: Scholastic Book Services, 1960).

25. "A Closer Look at Mars," *New York Times*, 2 September 1956, IV, 8:2.

26. Fredric Brown, *Martians, Go Home* (1955; reprint, New York: Baen, 1992), 2.

27. Rex Gordon, *First On Mars* (1957, as *No Man Friday*; reprint, New York: Avon, 1976), 26.

11. Retrograde Visions

1. "Mars on Trial," *Boston Herald*, 7 September 1956, 20:1.

2. Dr. I[srael] M[onroe] *A Space Traveler's Guide to Mars* (New York: Henry Holt, 1956), vii–viii.

3. "Space Preview: Mars and Beyond," *Space Journal* 1 (Spring 1958): 29; "Review," *Time* (9 December 1957), 82.

4. Martin Caidin, "The Mars Probe," *Space Age* 1 (February 1959): 9.

5. Frank Herbert, *Dune* (New York: Ace, 1965), 20–21, 523. See Oliver Morton, *Mapping Mars: Science, Imagination, and the Birth of a World* (New York: Picador, 2002), 178.

6. "Topics of the Times," *New York Times*, 20 January 1941, 20:4.

7. David Grinnell [pseudonym of Donald Wollheim], *The Martian Missile* (New York: Ace, 1959), 10.

8. Robert A. Heinlein, *Stranger in a Strange Land* (1961; reprint, New York: Berkley, 1968), 12; the explicit allusion to Prometheus is on p. 369.

9. Walter Tevis, *The Man Who Fell to Earth* (1963; reprint, New York: Avon, 1976), 129.

10. Tevis, more interested in mythical resonances than astronomical science, has not troubled to provide reliable clues about the identity of Anthea. A reference to thirty-five Anthean years being the equivalent of forty-five terrestrial years, for instance, leads the reader on a wild goose chase, since no planet in the solar system fits that equivalency.

11. H. G. Wells, *Star Begotten: A Biological Fantasia*, ed. John Huntington (Middletown, Conn.: Wesleyan University Press, 2006), 110.

12. Philip K. Dick, *Martian Time-Slip* (New York: Ballantine, 1964), 24; Dick, *The Three Stigmata of Palmer Eldritch* (1964; reprint, New York: DAW, 1983), 121.

13. Dick, *Martian Time-Slip*, 27.

14. Philip K. Dick, "We Can Remember It for You Wholesale" (1966), in *Fourth Planet from the Sun: Tales of Mars from the Magazine of Fantasy and Science Fiction*, ed. Gordon Van Gelder (New York: Thunder's Mouth, 2005), 110–11.

15. Cyril Judd [pseudonym of Cyril Kornbluth and Judith Merril], *Outpost Mars* (New York: Dell, 1952), 12, 13.

16. Erik van Lihn [pseudonym of Lester del Rey], *Police Your Planet* (1956; reprint, New York: Ballantine, 1975), 3.

17. D[avid] G. Compton, *Farewell, Earth's Bliss* (1966; reprint, San Bernardino, Calif.: Borgo, 1979), 60.

18. Lester del Rey, *Marooned on Mars* (1962; reprint, New York: Paperback Library, 1967), 6. In his *The Photographic Story of Mars* (Cambridge, Mass.: Sky Publishers, 1962), published in the same year as del Rey's novel and three years before *Mariner 4*'s first close-up pictures of a barren and canal-less Mars, Earl C. Slipher insisted that photography continued to document the reality of the network of canals and oases.

19. Quoted in Michael Hanlon, *The Real Mars* (New York: Carroll and Graf, 2004), 110. For other valuable accounts of the *Mariner* missions and their impact on perceptions of Mars, see also William Sheehan and Stephen James O'Meara, *Mars: The Lure of the Red Planet* (Amherst, N.Y.: Prometheus Books, 2001); Paul Raeburn, *Uncovering the Secrets of Mars* (Washington, D.C.: National Geographic Society, 1998); John Noble Wilford, *Mars Beckons* (New York: Knopf, 1990).

20. John Brunner, *Born under Mars* (New York: Ace, 1967), 27, 30, 124.

21. Leigh Brackett, *The Coming of the Terrans* (New York: Ace, 1967), p. 5.

22. Lin Carter, *The Man Who Loved Mars* (New York: Fawcett, 1973), 109–10.

23. Jane Hipolito and Willis McNelly, Foreword, *Mars, We Love You: Tales of Mars, Men and Martians* (1971; reprint, New York: Pyramid, 1973), ix.

24. Ludek Pesek, *The Earth Is Near*, trans. Anthea Bell (Scarsdale, N.Y.: Bradbury Press, 1973), 73.

25. Ray Bradbury, Arthur C. Clarke, Bruce Murray, Carl Sagan, and Walter Sullivan, *Mars and the Mind of Man* (New York: Harper and Row, 1973), 18.

26. Ibid., 14. Sagan quotes from Leland's *World Making: A Scientific Explanation of the Birth, Growth and Death of Worlds.* First published in Chicago by the Woman's Temperance Publishing Association in 1896, it had gone into its seventeenth edition by 1906.

27. Thomas A. Mutch, Raymond E. Arvidson, James W. Head, Kenneth L. Jones, and R. Stephen Saunders, *The Geology of Mars* (Princeton: Princeton University Press, 1976), 34.

28. Clarke, in *Mars and the Mind of Man*, 85. He slightly misquotes from his novel: "*There were no mountains on Mars.*" *The Sands of Mars* (1952; reprint, New York: Signet, 1974), 128.

29. John Varley, "In the Hall of the Martian Kings" (1977), reprinted in Gordon van Gelder, ed., *Fourth Planet from the Sun* (New York: Thunder's Mouth Press, 2005), 160.

30. Richard C. Hoagland, *The Monuments of Mars: A City on the Edge of Forever*, 5th ed. (Berkeley: Frog, Ltd., 2002).

31. Ian Douglas, *Semper Mars* (New York: Eos, 1998). Robert Markley, in an astute commentary on *Semper Mars* as a "fable of techno-militarism," suggests that, using Hoagland's speculations about "the Face" as a convenient vehicle, "Douglas remascu-

linizes the high frontier" of Mars. See Markley, *Dying Planet: Mars in Science and the Imagination* (Durham, N.C.: Duke University Press, 2005), 292–93.

32. Terry Bisson, *Voyage to the Red Planet* (1990; reprint, New York: Avon, 1991); Allen Steele, *Labyrinth of Night* (New York: Ace, 1992), vii–viii. Steele came to regret using Hoagland's notions as a fictional premise once he was besieged by "UFO buffs and pseudo-scientific types" who assumed that he was a true believer. See his interview with Steven Silver at SF Site, www.sfsite.comm/12b/as47.htm.

33. Robert L. Forward, *The Martian Rainbow* (New York: Ballantine, 1991), vii.

34. Christopher Pike, *The Season of Passage* (New York: Tor, 1992), 178.

35. Paul J. McAuley, *Red Dust* (New York: William Morrow, 1993), 1.

36. Colin Greenland, *Harm's Way* (New York: Avon, 1993), 140.

12. *Mars Remade*

1. Ian Watson, *The Martian Inca* (1977; reprint, London: Gollancz, 1993), 26.

2. Oliver Morton, *Mapping Mars: Science, Imagination, and the Birth of a World* (New York: Picador, 2002), 174.

3. Donald Moffitt, *Crescent in the Sky* (New York: Ballantine, 1989), 280; Philip José Farmer, *Jesus on Mars* (Los Angeles: Pinnacle, 1979); Tim Sullivan, *The Martian Viking* (New York: Avon, 1991); Paul J. McAuley, *Red Dust* (New York: William Morrow, 1993); Ben Bova, *Mars* (New York: Bantam, 1992).

4. Thomas A. Mutch, Raymond E. Arvidson, James W. Head, Kenneth L. Jones, and R. Stephen Saunders, *The Geology of Mars* (Princeton: Princeton University Press, 1976), 25.

5. Robert Young, "The First Mars Mission" (1979), reprinted in *Fourth Planet from the Sun: Tales of Mars from The Magazine of Fantasy & Science Fiction*, ed. Gordon Van Gelder (New York: Thunder's Mouth, 2005), 201.

6. Gordon Eklund and Gregory Benford, "Hellas is Florida" (1977), reprinted in *Fourth Planet from the Sun*, 130.

7. Harry Harrison, "One Step from Earth" (1970), reprinted in *Mars, We Love You: Tales of Mars, Men and Martians*, ed. Jane Hipolito and Willis E. McNelly (New York: Pyramid, 1973), 295.

8. Lewis Shiner, *Frontera* (New York: Baen, 1984), 18–19.

9. Jack Williamson, *Beachhead* (New York: Tom Dohery, 1992), 130. The *Oxford English Dictionary* credits Williamson for the first use of "terraform" in his story "Collision Orbit," published under the name of Will Stewart in *Astounding Science Fiction*, July 1942.

10. Frederick Turner, "Such Stuff as Dreams: Technology and the Future of the Imagination," in *Natural Classicism: Essays on Literature and Science* (1985; reprint, Charlottesville: University Press of Virginia, 1992), 234.

11. Frederick Turner, *A Double Shadow* (1978; reprint, New York: Berkley, 1979), 1.

12. Schiaparelli's "Nix Olympica"—the Snows of Olympus—was renamed Olympus

Mons in the 1970s, but Turner, while sometimes using the older term, clearly understands that the feature is a volcano, not a snowfield.

13. See Gerry O'Sullivan and Carl Pletsch, "Inventing Arcadia: An Interview with Frederick Turner," *The Humanist* 53 (November/December 1993): 9–18. There, as elsewhere, Turner takes the position that anti-representational modernist literature, music, and visual arts were a twentieth-century aberration and he anticipates a restoration of the idea and the practice of beauty in the arts.

14. See the account of the fall from Heaven of the rebel angel-architect Mulciber, who "Dropped from the zenith like a falling star" (*Paradise Lost*, I, 745).

15. Frederick Turner, *Genesis: An Epic Poem* (Dallas: Saybrook, 1988), 7. Citations from the poem in the text will be by act, scene, and line numbers.

16. William Wordsworth, Preface to *Lyrical Ballads*, 2nd ed. (1800) in *Lyrical Ballads*, ed. R. L. Brett and A. R. Jones (London: Methuen, 1963), 254.

17. Frederick Turner, "Life on Mars: Cultivating a Planet—and Ourselves," *Harper's Magazine* 278 (August 1989): 37.

18. The poem includes phrases appropriated from Keats's "Ode to a Nightingale" at III.iv.293 and V.ii.105.

19. See James Lovelock and Michael Allaby, *The Greening of Mars* (New York: St. Martin's, 1984), 111.

20. Turner, "Life on Mars," 40.

21. Judith de Luce, "Genesis: An Epic Poem: Inventionist Ecology in Iambic Pentameter," *The Humanist* 53 (November/December 1993), 19–22.

22. Peter Kemp, "Life and Loves of a Martian Pioneer," *Nature* 337 (19 January 1989): 221.

23. Kim Stanley Robinson, *Icehenge* (1984: reprint, New York: Tor, 1990), 62–63.

24. Bud Foote, "A Conversation with Kim Stanley Robinson," *Science-Fiction Studies* 21 (March 1994): 51.

25. Kim Stanley Robinson, "Exploring Fossil Canyon," in *Universe* 12, ed. Terry Carr (New York: Doubleday, 1982), 27.

26. Kim Stanley Robinson, "Green Mars" (1985; reprinted with Arthur C. Clarke, "Meeting with Medusa" as a Tor Double (New York: Tom Doherty, 1988), 36.

13. Being There

1. Arthur C. Clarke, Introduction to Jack Williamson, *Beachhead* (New York: Tom Doherty, 1992), 10.

2. "Martian Dawn," *New Scientist* (19 May 1990), 27.

3. See Greg Klerkx, *Lost in Space: The Fall of NASA and the Dream of a New Space Age* (2004; reprint, New York: Vintage, 2005), esp. 270–300. The proceedings of the 1986 NASA gathering on Mars—dominated by presentations on robotic exploration and concluding with papers outlining the rationales for manned missions and lamenting

the problems of financial resources—were published as *The NASA Mars Conference*, ed. Duke B. Reiber (San Diego: Univelt, 1988).

4. Dan Quayle's interview on Cable News Network, 11 August 1989, was reported widely in the media, as in Kathy Sawyer's article, "A Quayle Vision of Mars," *Washington Post*, 1 September 1989, A25. Allen Steele made satiric use of Quayle's interview in his novel *Labyrinth of Night* (New York: Ace, 1992), 22.

5. Between 1984 and 2000, the San Diego publisher Univelt has issued six volumes of proceedings of the various Case for Mars conferences. Robert Zubrin, writing with Richard Wagner, adopted the name for his book, *The Case for Mars: The Plan to Settle the Red Planet and Why We Must* (New York: Touchstone, 1997). On Zubrin's career, see Klerkx, *Lost in Space*, 270–73, 283–300, 311–15.

6. See Tim Appenzeller, "Biosphere 2 Makes a New Bid for Scientific Credibility," *Science* 263 (11 March 1994): 1368–69.

7. Williamson, *Beachhead*, 7. On Bova's meeting with fans at Biosphere see www .detailguys.com/nw33.shtml.

8. As reported by NASA's manager of the Pathfinder mission, Donna Shirley, in her memoir, written with Danelle Morton, *Managing Martians* (New York: Broadway Books, 1998), 27.

9. Terry Bisson, *Voyage to the Red Planet* (1990; reprint, New York: Avon, 1991), 13.

10. William Herschel, "On the Remarkable Appearances at the Polar Regions of the Planet Mars, the Inclination of its Axis, the Position of its Poles, and its Spheroidical Figure, with a few Hints relating to its real Diameter and Atmosphere," *Philosophical Transactions of the Royal Society of London* 74, part 2 (1784): 260.

11. S[ondra] C[atherine] Sykes, *Red Genesis* (New York: Bantam, 1991), 89.

12. Williamson published "Collision Orbit" under the pseudonym Will Stewart in the July 1942 issue of *Astounding Science Fiction*.

13. Williamson, *Beachhead*, 122.

14. Greg Bear, *Moving Mars* (New York: Tor, 1993), 11.

15. H. G. Wells, "Preface to *The Scientific Romances*," in *H. G. Wells's Literary Criticism*, ed. Patrick Parrinder and Robert Philmus (Totowa, N.J.: Barnes and Noble, 1980), 241–42.

16. Ben Bova, *Mars* (New York: Bantam, 1992), 16; hereafter, identified as *Mars*.

17. Ben Bova, *Return to Mars* (New York: Avon, 1999), no page; hereafter, cited as *Return*.

18. William K. Hartmann, *Mars Underground* (1997; reprint, New York: Tor, 1999), 354.

19. William K. Hartmann, *A Traveler's Guide to Mars: The Mysterious Landscapes of the Red Planet* (New York: Workman, 2003), 337.

20. Gregory Benford, *The Martian Race* (New York: Warner Books, 1999), 1.

21. "Experiencing Mars" is the title of Part 5, chapter 4, of Geoffrey Landis, *Mars Crossing* (New York: Tor, 2000), 238.

22. A similar scene, in which astronauts arrive at the *Pathfinder* site and recall the names assigned to its topographical features occurs in Ben Bova's *Return to Mars* (New York: Avon, 1999), 262. At least as popular an encounter between fiction and fact is the scene of the *Viking I* lander in Chryse Planitia, which can be found in Bova's *Mars* (New York: Bantam, 1992), 265; and Robert Forward's *Martian Rainbow* (1991; reprint, New York: Ballantine, 1992), 156. In a further interweaving of invention and history, both Bova and Forward imagine a memorial to the NASA astrogeologist Thomas Mutch at the *Viking* site, as does Lewis Shiner in the map that serves as frontispiece to *Frontera* (New York: Baen, 1984).

23. Robert Zubrin, *First Landing* (New York: Ace, 2001), 69.

24. Frederick Jackson Turner, *The Significance of the Frontier in American History*, ed. Harold Simonson (New York: Ungar, 1963). See also Robert Zubrin, "The Significance of the Martian Frontier: Mars as the Final Hope for Earth," *Ad Astra* (September/October 1994): 30–37, slightly revised and reprinted as the epilogue to *The Case for Mars: The Plan to Settle the Red Planet and Why We Must* (1996; reprint, New York: Touchstone, 1997), 295–306.

14. Becoming Martian

1. Robert M. Zubrin and Christopher P. McKay, "Terraforming Mars," in *Islands in the Sky: Bold New Ideas for Colonizing Space*, ed. Stanley Schmidt and Robert Zubrin (New York: John Wiley & Sons, 1996), 145.

2. Robert Zubrin with Richard Wagner, *The Case for Mars: The Plan to Settle the Red Planet and Why We Must* (1996; reprint, New York: Touchstone, 1997), 248–49, 270.

3. Frederik Pohl, *Man Plus* (1976; reprint, New York: Baen, 1994), 19.

4. Kevin J. Anderson, *Climbing Olympus* (New York: Warner, 1994). In addition to a reference in the text to a " 'man plus' project" (99), Anderson pays tribute to Pohl's *Man Plus* in his acknowledgments.

5. On Pavonis Mons, Rachel justifies herself to Boris: "We gave you a world to tame and the freedom to do it. Better to rule in hell than to serve in heaven, is that not correct?" (135).

6. Kim Stanley Robinson, *Green Mars* (New York: Bantam, 1994), 2. Hereafter in the text GM. Quotations from *Red Mars* (New York: Bantam, 1993) and *Blue Mars* (New York: Bantam, 1996) will be identified parenthetically as RM and BM, respectively.

7. Zubrin, *The Case for Mars*, 239, 297. See also Frederick Jackson Turner, *The Significance of the Frontier in American History*, ed. Harold Simonson (New York: Ungar, 1963).

8. In " 'If I Can Find One Good City, I Will Spare the Man': Realism and Utopia in Kim Stanley Robinson's *Mars Trilogy*," Fredric Jameson makes a similar observation

about the debate between red and green perspectives furnishing "the principal structural allegory" of the books. However, he takes the central figures in this debate not to
be Ann and Sax but Ann and Hiroko Ai. See his *Archaeologies of the Future: The Desire Called
Utopia and Other Science Fictions* (London: Verso, 2005), 403–4.

9. Carol Franko argues that by making debate integral to the structure of the *Mars*
novels, Robinson succeeds in "making Utopia seem plausible and desirable: attrac-
tively dynamic, humane, joyful, open-ended, and 'open-sided'—culturally diverse." See
her "Kim Stanley Robinson: Mars Trilogy," in *A Companion to Science Fiction*, ed. David
Seed (Oxford: Blackwell, 2005), 545.

10. See Kim Stanley Robinson, *The Martians* (New York: Bantam, 1999), 192–204,
for a full text of the Constitution as well as notes and commentary on various articles of
the document.

11. Carl Freedman, *Critical Theory and Science Fiction* (Hanover and London: Wesleyan
University Press, 2000), 65.

12. Tolkien's essay "On Fairy Stories" is the classic discussion of the values of
"escape," "recovery," and "consolation" in fantastic literature. The essay is most
readily available in *The Tolkien Reader* (New York: Del Rey, 1986).

13. Kim Stanley Robinson with David Seed, "The Mars Trilogy: An Interview,"
Foundation 68 (Autumn 1996): 79. For the best introduction to "novums" and the
navigation of the conventions of science fiction, see Tom Shippey, "Hard Reading: The
Challenges of Science Fiction," in Seed, ed., *A Companion to Science Fiction*, 11–26.

14. Lance Parkin and Mark Clapham, *Beige Planet Mars* (London: Virgin Books,
1998); Larry Niven, *Rainbow Mars* (New York: Tor, 1999); Kim Stanley Robinson, "Purple Mars," in *The Martians*, 332–36.

15. Brian Aldiss in collaboration with Roger Penrose, *White Mars, Or, The Mind Set
Free: A 21st-Century Utopia* (New York: St. Martin's, 2000), 16.

Afterword: Mars under Construction

1. Ian McDonald, "The Old Cosmonaut and the Construction Worker Dream of
Mars," in *Mars Probes*, ed. Peter Crowther (New York: Daw, 2002), 147.

2. Nick Gevers, "Future Remix: An Interview with Ian McDonald," www.infinity
plus.co.uk/nonfiction/intimcd/htm. The interview was conducted in October 2001.

index

Blaine, James, 36

Blake, William, *Marriage of Heaven and Hell*, 32

Blish, James, *A Case of Conscience*, 286

Bloch, Ernst, 298

Blue Mars (Robinson), 6, 258, 285, 290–306

Bogdanov, Alexander, *Engineer Menni*, 109; *Red Star*, 97, 103, 105–9, 168, 175, 204, 291

Bonestell, Chesley, 207, pl. 7

Born under Mars (Brunner), 230–31

Bova, Ben, *Mars*, 19, 245, 264, 271–74; *Return to Mars*, 271–74

Boy Scouts, 164, 166; *see also* Baden-Powell, Robert S. S.

Brackett, Leigh, 231–32, 308; *Sword of Rhiannon*, 212

Bradbury, Ray, 97, 147, 185, 198, 211–12, 227, 229, 235–37, 249, 272; *Martian Chronicles*, 7, 58, 144–45, 197–207, 215, 221, 241, 260, 270, 307–8

Bradley, Mary, 150

Brahe, Tycho, 35–36

Braine, Robert D., *Messages from Mars, By Aid of the Telescope Plant*, 43, 59–66, 110, 153, 185, 217

Brera Observatory, 38

British Interplanetary Society, 207, 214

Brown, Fredric, *Martians, Go Home*, 51, 215–17, 219

Brunner, John, *Born under Mars*, 230–31

Bruno, Giordano, 141

Buck Rogers, 4, 222

Bulwer-Lytton, Edward, 141

Bunyan, John, 49, 99

Burgess, Eric, 4

Burroughs, Edgar Rice, 126, 150, 168, 182–83, 185, 197, 207, 212, 223–24, 232–33, 236–37, 241, 245, 247, 249, 252, 270, 272, 275, 282, 286–87; *A Princess of Mars*, 7, 131, 133, 151–55, 159–63, 176, 308, 326n7

Burton, Robert, *Anatomy of Melancholy*, 117

Bush, George H. W., 263, 265, 267

Byron, George Gordon, 157

Caidin, Martin, 4

California Institute of Technology, 236, 238

Campbell, William Wallace, 76, 103

Cantril, Hadley, 190

Čapek, Karel, 183

Carroll, Lewis, 183; *Alice in Wonderland*, 51, 118

Carter, Lin, *The Man Who Loved Mars*, 232–33

Cassini, Giovanni, 26–27, 30

Castelli, Benedetto, 20

Certainty of a Future Life in Mars (Gratacap), 81, 91, 135, 138–40, 147

Chaucer, Geoffrey, 3, 19

Cityless and Countryless World, A (Olerich), 97–98

Clapham, Mark. See Parkin, Lance.

Clarke, Arthur C., 18, 207–17, 236–38, 241, 274; *The Exploration of Space*, 207–8; *Interplanetary Flight*, 207; *Rendezvous with Rama*, 275; *The Sands of Mars*, 199, 207–11, 216, 238, 263; "The Star," 286. *See also* Kubrick, Stanley

Claudy, Carl H., *The Mystery Men of Mars*, 166, 329n65

Clerke, Agnes, 10, 34

Climbing Olympus (Anderson), 260, 287–90

Close Encounters of the Third Kind (film), 93

Collier's Magazine, 206–8

Columbus, Christopher, 13, 32–33, 44,

Wellington, Arthur Wellesley, 34

Wells, Frank, 323n19

Wells, H. G., 12, 33, 95, 105, 113, 133, 159, 168, 194–95, 210–11, 217, 224, 233, 271; "The Crystal Egg," 94, 112; *The First Men in the Moon*, 166, 219–20, 329n65; "From an Observatory," 123; *The History of Mr. Polly*, 211; "Intelligence on Mars," 112–14, 117; *Kipps*, 211; *A Modern Utopia*, 304; *Outline of History*, 179; "The Star," 112; *Star-Begotten*,127, 177–78, 193, 226–27; "The Things That Live on Mars," 126–27; *Things to Come* (film), 220; *The Time Machine*, 58, 211; *The War of the Worlds*, 8, 13, 51, 57, 110–28, 131, 141, 152, 159, 171, 176–92, 199, 201, 207–8, 215, 227, 275, 307–8, 322n9, 322n12, pl. 6; *The World Set Free*, 304

Whipple, Fred, 207

White Mars (Aldiss), 304–5

Whitin Observatory, Wellesley College, 1

Whitman, Walt, 9–10, 14

Wicks, Mark, *To Mars via the Moon*, 77, 91–94, 134, 141, 162

Wilford, John Noble, 199

Williamson, Jack, 246, 263–64, 268–69, 336n9; *Beachhead*, 247, 268–69

Wollheim, Donald, *The Martian Missile*, 224

Wordsworth, William, 14, 300, 307; "Preface" to *Lyrical Ballads*, 250

World Set Free, The (Wells), 304

Wyndham, John, 170, 186; *Planet Plane*, 178, 182–85, 189

Yezad (Babcock), 173–74

Young, Robert, "The First Mars Mission," 245

Zubrin, Robert, 264, 268, 272, 277, 281–85, 292, 299, 327n16; *First Landing*, 281–82, 299

THE WESLEYAN EARLY CLASSICS
OF SCIENCE FICTION SERIES

General Editor ● Arthur B. Evans

ABOUT THE AUTHOR

Robert Crossley is professor emeritus of English at the
University of Massachusetts Boston. He is the author of *Talking
Across the World* (1987) and *Olaf Stapledon: Speaking for the Future*
(1994), and editor of *An Olaf Stapledon Reader* (1997).